Colley Cibber

The Dramatic Works of Colley Cibber

Volume 3

Colley Cibber

The Dramatic Works of Colley Cibber
Volume 3

ISBN/EAN: 9783337332280

Printed in Europe, USA, Canada, Australia, Japan

Cover: Foto ©Andreas Hilbeck / pixelio.de

More available books at **www.hansebooks.com**

THE DRAMATIC

WORKS

COLLEY CIBBER, Esq.

In FIVE VOLUMES.

VOLUME the THIRD.

CONTAINING

The Double Gallant.
Ximena.
The Comical Lovers.
The Non-Juror.

LONDON:

Printed for J. Rivington and Sons, T. Longman, T. Lowndes, T. Caslon, S. Bladon, and W. Nicoll.

M.DCC.LXXVII.

THE

DOUBLE GALLANT:

OR, THE

SICK LADY's CURE.

A

COMEDY.

PROLOGUE.

COU'D those, who never try'd, conceive the sweat,
The toil requir'd to make a play compleat ;
They'd pardon, or encourage all that cou'd,
Pretend to be but tolerably good.
Plot, wit, and humour's hard to meet in one,
And yet without 'em all—all's lamely done :
One wit perhaps, another humour paints ;
A third designs you well, but genius wants ;
A fourth begins with fire—but, ah! to weak too hold
it, faints.
A modern bard, who late adorn'd the bays,
Whose muse advanc'd his fame to envy'd praise,
Was still observ'd to want his judgment most in plays.
Those, he too often found, requir'd the pain,
And stronger forces of a vig'rous brain :
Nay, even alter'd plays, like old houses mended,
Cost little less than new, before they're ended ;
At least, our author finds the experience true,
For equal pains had made this wholly new :
And tho' the name seems old, the scenes will show
That 'tis, in fact, no more the same, than now
Fam'd Chatsworth is, what 'twas some years ago.
Pardon the boldness, that a play shou'd dare,
With works of so much wonder to compare :
But as that fabrick's antient walls or wood
Were little worth, to make this new one good ;
So of this Play, we hope, 'tis understood.
For tho' from former scenes some hints he draws,
The ground-plot's wholly chang'd from what it was :
Not but he hopes you'll find enough that's new,
In plot, in persons, wit, and humour too :
Yet what's not his, he owns in other's right,
Nor toils he now for fame, but your delight.
If that's attain'd, what's matter whose the play's ;
Applaud the scenes, and strip him of the praise.

Dramatis Perſonæ.

M E N.

Sir *Solomon Sadlife,*	Mr. *Johnſon.*
Clerimont,	Mr. *Booth.*
Careleſs,	Mr. *Wilks.*
Atall,	Mr. *Cibber.*
Captain *Strut,*	Mr. *Bowen.*
Sir *Squabble Splitbair,*	Mr. *Norris.*
Saunter,	Mr. *Pack.*
Old Mr. *Wilfull,*	Mr. *Bullock.*
Sir *Harry Atall,*	Mr. *Croſs.*
Supple,	Mr. *Fairbank.*
Dr. *Bliſter,*	
Rhubarb,	
Finder.	

W O M E N.

Lady *Dainty,*	Mrs. *Oldfield.*
Lady *Sadlife,*	Mrs. *Croſs.*
Clarinda,	Mrs *Rogers.*
Sylvia,	Mrs. *Bradſhaw.*
Wiſhwell,	Mrs. *Saunders.*
Situp,	Mrs. *Brown.*

THE

DOUBLE GALLANT:

OR, THE

SICK LADY'S CURE.

ACT I. SCENE I.

The PARK.

Enter Clerimont *and* Atall.

CLERIMONT.

MR. *Atall*, your very humble fervant.

At. O *Clerimont*, fuch an adventure, (I was juft go-ing to your lodgings) fuch a tranfporting accident! in fhort, I am now pofitively fix'd in love for altogether.

Cler. All the fex together, I believe.

At. Nay, if thou doft not believe me, and ftand my friend, I am ruin'd paft redemption.

Cler. Dear Sir, if I ftand your friend without be-lieving you, won't that do as well? But why fhou'd you think I don't believe you? I have feen you twice in love within this fortnight; and it wou'd be hard indeed to fuppofe a heart of fo much mettle could not hold out a third engagement.

At. Then to be ferious in one word, I am honourably in love; and if fhe proves the woman I am fure fhe muft, will pofitively marry her.

Cler. Marry! O degenerate virtue!

At. Now will you help me?

Cler. Sir, you may depend upon me: But that I may be the better able to ferve you——all things in order ———pray give me leave firft to afk a queftion or two: What is this honourable lady's Name?

At. Faith, I don't know.

Cler. What are her parents?

At. I can't tell.

Cler. What fortune has she?

At. I don't know.

Cler. Where does she live?

At. I can't tell.

Cler. A very concise account of the person you design to marry. Pray, Sir, what is't you do know of her?

At. That I'll tell you! Coming yesterday from *Greenwich* by water, I overtook a pair of oars, whose lovely freight was one single lady, and a fellow in a handsome livery in the stern. When I came up, I had at first resolv'd to use the privilege of the element, and bait her with waterman's wit, till I came to the Bridge: But as soon as she saw me, instead of turning her head aside, or cramming her hoods in her mouth to raise my curiosity, she very prudently prevented my design; and as I pass'd, bow'd to me with an humble blush, that spoke at once such sense, so just a fear, and modesty, as put the loosest of my thoughts to rout. And when she found her fears had mov'd into me manners, the cautious gloom that sat upon her beauties, disappear'd; her sparkling eyes resum'd their native fire; she look'd, she smil'd, she talk'd, while diffusive charms new fir'd my heart, and gave my soul a softness it never felt before——— To be brief, her conversation was as charming as her person, both easy, unconstrain'd, and sprightly: But then her limbs! O rapturous thought! The snowy down upon the wings of unfledg'd love, had never half that softness.

Cler. Raptures indeed. Pray, Sir, how came you so well acquainted with her limbs?

At. By the most fortunate misfortune sure that ever was: For as we were shooting the bridge, her boat, by the negligence of the waterman, running against the piles, was over-set; out jumps the footman to take care of a single rogue, and down went the poor lady to the bottom. My boat being before her, the stream drove her, by the help of her clothes, towards me; at sight of her I plung'd in, caught her in my arms, and with much ado supported

her till my waterman pull'd in to fave us. But the charming difficulty of her getting into the boat, gave me a
tranfport that all the wide water in the *Thames* had not
power to cool: for, Sir, while I was giving her a lift
into the boat, I found the floating of her clothes had
left her lovely limbs beneath as bare as new-born *Venus*
rifing from the fea.

Cler. What an impudent happinefs art thou capable
of!

At. When fhe was a little recover'd from her fright,
fhe began to enquire my name, abode, and circumftances,
that fhe might know to whom fhe ow'd her life and
prefervation. Now, to tell you the truth, I durft not
truft her with my real name, left fhe fhould from
thence have difcover'd that my father was now actually
under bonds to marry me to another woman; fo faith
I ev'n told her my name was *Freeman,* a *Gloucefterfhire*
gentleman, of a good eftate, juft come to town about
a *Chancery* fuit. Befides, I was unwilling any accident fhould let my father know of my being yet in
England, left he fhould find me out, and force me to
marry the woman I never faw (for which, you know
he commanded me home) before I have time to prevent it.

Cler. Well, but cou'd not you learn the lady's name
all this while?

At. No 'faith, fhe was inexorable to all intreaties:
only told me in general terms, that if what I vow'd to
her was fincere, fhe wou'd give me a proof in a few days
what hazards fhe would run to requite my fervices; fo,
after having told her where fhe might hear of me, I faw
her into a chair, prefs'd her by the cold rofy fingers,
kifs'd 'em warm, and parted.

Cler. What! Then you are quite off of the lady, I
fuppofe, that you made an acquaintance with in the
Park laft week.

At. No, no; not fo neither: one's my *Juno,* all
pride and beauty: but this my *Venus,* all life, love,
and foftnefs. Now, what I beg of thee, dear *Clerimont,* is this: Mrs. *Juno,* as I told you, having done me
the honour of a civil vifit or two at my own lodgings, I

muſt needs borrow thine to entertain Mrs. *Venus* in ;
for if the rival goddeſſes ſhould meet, and claſh, you
know there wou'd be the devil to do between them.

Cler. Well, Sir, my lodgings are at your ſervice? But
you muſt be very private and ſober, I can tell you ; for
my landlady's a *Preſbyterian* ; if ſhe ſuſpects your deſign,
you're blown up, depend upon't.

At. Don't fear, I'll be as careful as a guilty conſcience :
But I want immediate poſſeſſion ; for I expect to hear
from her every moment, and have already directed her
to ſend thither.   Prythee come with me.

Cler. 'Faith, you muſt excuſe me ; I expect ſome ladies in the *Park* that I would not miſs of for an empire :
But yonder's my ſervant, he ſhall conduct you.

At. Very good ! that will do as well then : I'll ſend
my man along with him to expect her commands, and
call me if ſhe ſends : And in the mean time I'll e'en go
home to my own lodgings : for to tell you the truth,
I expect a ſmall meſſage there from my goddeſs imperial.
And I am not ſo much in love with my new bird in the
buſh, as to let t'other fly out of my hand for her.

Cler. And pray, Sir, what name does your goddeſs
imperial, as you call her, know you by ?

At. O, Sir, with her I paſs for a man of arms, and
am call'd Col. *Standfaſt* ; with my new face, *John Freeman*, of *Flatland Hall*, Eſq ; but time flies ; I muſt leave
you.

Cler. Well, dear *Atall*, I'm yours——Good luck to
you, [*Exit* At.] What a happy fellow is this, that owes
his ſucceſs with the women purely to his inconſtancy ?
What a blockhead am I, to taint my inclinations with
virtue, when I have ſo many daily examples before my
eyes, of people's being ill us'd for their ſincerity ? Here
comes another too almoſt as happy as he, a fellow that's
wiſe enough to be but half in love, and make his whole
life a ſtudied idleneſs.

Enter Careleſs.

Cler. So, *Careleſs !* you're conſtant, I ſee, to your
morning's ſaunter.   Well ! how ſtand matters ?   I hear
ſtrange things of thee ; that after having rail'd at mar-

riage all thy life, thou haft refolv'd to fall into the noofe at laft.

Care. I don't fee any great terror in the noofe, (as you call it) when a man's weary of liberty : The liberty of playing the fool, when one's turn'd of thirty, is not of much value.

Cler. Hey-day ! Then you begin to have nothing in your head now, but fettlements, children, and the main chance ?

Care. Ev'n fo faith ; but in hopes to come at 'em too, I am forc'd very often to make my way thro' pills, elixirs, bolus's, ptizans, and gallipots.

Cler. What, is your miftrefs an apothecary's widow ?

Care. No, but fhe is an apothecary's fhop, and keeps as many drugs in her bed-chamber ; fhe has her phyfic for every hour of the day and night—for 'tis vulgar, fhe fays to be a moment in rude and perfect health. Her bed lin'd with poppies ; the black boys at the feet, that the healthy employ to bear flowers in their arms, fhe loads with *diafcordium,* and other fleepy potions ; her fweet-bags, inftead of the common and offenfive fmells of mufk and amber, breathe nothing but the more modifh and falubrious fcents of hart's horn, rue, and affafœtida.

Cler. Why, at this rate, fhe's only fit to be the confort of *Hippocrates.* But pray what other charms has this extraordinary Lady ?

Care. She has one, *Tom,* that a man may relifh without being fo deep a phyfician.

Cler. What's that ?

Care. Why, two thoufand pound a year.

Cler. No vulgar beauty, I confefs, Sir ; but can'ft thou for any confideration throw thyfelf into this hofpital, this box of phyfick, and lie all night like leaf-gold upon a pill.

Care. O, dear Sir, this is not half the evil ; her humour is as fantaftic as her diet ; nothing that is *Englifh* muft come near her ; all her delight is in foreign impertinences : Her rooms are all of *Japan* or *Perfia,* her drefs *Indian,* and her equipage are all monfters : The coachman came over with his horfes, both from *Ruffia,*

(*Flanders* are too common) the reſt of her trim are a motly crowd of blacks, tawny, olives, feulamots, and pale blues: In ſhort, ſhe's for any thing that comes from beyond ſea; her greateſt monſters are thoſe of her own country; and ſhe's in love with nothing o'this ſide the line, but the apothecaries.

Cler. Apothecaries quotha! why your fine Lady, for aught I ſee, is a perfect doſe of folly and phyſick; in a month's time ſhe'll grow like an antimonial cup, and a kiſs will be able to work with you.

Care. But to prevent that, *Tom*, I deſign upon the wedding-day to break all her gallipots, kick the doctor down ſtairs, and force her, inſtead of phyſic, to take a hearty meal of a ſwinging rump of boil'd beef and carrots, and ſo 'faith I have told her.

Cler. That's ſomething familiar: Are you ſo near man and wife?

Care. O nearer, for I ſometimes plague her till ſhe hates the very ſight of me.

Cler. Ha! ha! very good! So being a very troubleſome lover, you pretend to cure her of her phyſick by a counter poiſon.

Care. Right; I intend to fee a doctor to preſcribe her an hour of my converſation to be taken every night and morning; and this to be continued till her fever of averſion's over.

Cler. An admirable recipe!

Care. Well, *Tom*, but how ſtand thy own affairs? Is *Clarinda* kind yet?

Cler. Faith I can't ſay ſhe's abſolutely kind, but ſhe's pretty near it; for ſhe's grown ſo ridiculouſly ill-humour'd to me of late, that if ſhe keeps the ſame airs a week longer, I am in hopes to find as much eaſe from her folly, as my conſtancy would from her good-nature —but to be plain, I'm afraid I have ſome ſecret rival in the caſe; for women's vanity ſeldom gives them courage enough to uſe an old lover heartily ill, till they are firſt ſure of a new one, that they intend to uſe better.

Care. What ſays Sir *Solomon?* He is your friend I preſume.

Cler. Yes, at leaſt I can make him ſo when I pleaſe:

There is an odd five hundred pound in her fortune, that he has a great mind fhou'd ftick to his fingers, when he pays in the reft on't; which I am afraid I muft comply with, for fhe can't eafily marry without his confent. And yet fhe's fo alter'd in her behaviour of late, that I fcarce know what to do—Pr'ythee take a turn and advife me.

Care. With all my heart.   [*Exeunt.*

The S C E N E *changes to Sir* Solomon Sadlife's *Houfe.*

Enter Sir Solomon, *and* Supple *his man.*

Sir *Sol.* *Supple,* doft not thou perceive I put a great confidence in thee ? I truft thee with my bofom fecrets.

Sup. Yes, Sir.

Sir *Sol.* Ah, *Supple !* I begin to hate my wife—but be fecret.

Sup. I'll never tell while I live, Sir.

Sir *Sol.* Nay then I'll truft thee further: Between thee and I, *Supple,* I have reafon to believe my wife hates me too.

Sup. Ah! Dear Sir, I doubt that's no fecret; for to fay the truth, my Lady's bitter young and gamefome.

Sir *Sol.* But can fhe have the impudence, think'ft thou, to make a cuckold of a knight, one that was dubb'd by the royal fword ?

Sup. Alas! Sir, I warrant fhe'as the courage of a countefs, if fhe's once provok'd, fhe cares not what fhe does in her paffion; if you were ten times a knight, fhe'd give you dub for dub, Sir.

Sir *Sol.* Ah! *Supple,* when her blood's up, I confefs fhe's the Devil; and I queftion if the whole conclave of cardinals could lay her. But fuppofe fhe fhou'd refolve to give me a fample of her fex, and make me a cuckold in cool blood ?

Sup. Why if fhe fhou'd, Sir, don't take it fo to heart, cuckolds are no fuch monfters now-a-days: In the city you know, Sir, it's fo many honeft men's fortune, that no body minds it there; and at this end of the town a cuckold has as much refpect as his wife, for aught I fee; for gentlemen don't know but it may be their own cafe another day, and fo people are willing to do as they would be done by.

Sir *Sol.* And yet I do not think but my fpoufe is honeſt —and think ſhe is not—would I were fatisfy'd !

Sup. Troth, Sir, I don't know what to think, but in my confcience I believe good looking after her can do her no harm.

Sir *Sol.* Right, *Supple* ; and in order to it, I'll firſt demoliſh her vifiting days: For how do I know but they may be fo many private clubs for cuckoldom.

Sup. Ah ! Sir, your worſhip knows I was always againſt your coming to this end of the town.

Sir *Sol.* Thou wert indeed, my honeſt *Supple :* But woman ! fair and faithlefs woman, warm'd and work'd me to her wiſhes ; like fond *Mark Anthony*, I let my em- pire moulder from my hands, and give up all for love. O fool, to truſt thy honour with a woman ! a race of vipers ! They were deceivers, *Supple*, from the begin- ning. I'll have no vifitors, that's determined.

Sir *Sol.* Truly, Sir, I begin to think there's nothing fav'd by them in the year's end.

Sir *Sol.* O *Supple*, I run mad when I think on't ; every powder'd wig I meet is a piece of ordnance planted againſt my honour ; the rattling of a fine chariot gives me the fpleen, and my very foul's fet on edge at the fqueak of a fiddle.

Sup. And what's more provoking, Sir, the abominable rogues always pitch upon this fide the park for their mufic and intrigues.

Sir *Sol.* Dogs ! villains ! monſters ! Zbud ! I've been in a fweat ever fince I liv'd here——twice or thrice a week all the cuckold-makers in town rendezvous under my window. Infupportable—I muſt have a young wife with a murrain to me—I hate her too—and yet the devil on't is, I'm ſtill jealous of her—Stay, let me reckon up all the faſhionable virtues ſhe has that can make a man happy. In the firſt place—I think her very ugly—

Sup. Ah ! that's becaufe you are marry'd to her, Sir.

Sir *Sol.* As for her expences, no arithmetic can reach 'em ; ſhe's always longing for fomething dear and ufe- lefs ; ſhe will certainly ruin me in china, filks, ribbands, fans, laces, perfumes, waſhes, powder, patches, jeſſa- mine-gloves, and ratifia.

Sup. Ah, Sir, that's a cruel liquor with 'em.

Sir *Sol.* To fum up all wou'd run me mad——The only way to put a ftop to her career, muft be to put off my coach, turn away her chairmen, lock out her Swifs porter, bar up the doors, keep out all vifitors, and then fhe'll be lefs expenfive.

Sup. Ay, Sir, for few women think it worth their while to drefs for their hufbands.

Sir *Sol.* Then we fha'n't be plagu'd with my old Lady *Tittle Tattle*'s howd'ye's in a morning, nor my Lady *Dainty*'s fpleen, or the fudden indifpofitions of that grim beaft her horrible *Dutch* maftiff.

Sup. No, Sir, nor the impertinence of that great fat creature, my Lady *Swill-Tea.*

Sir *Sol.* And her fquinting daughter. No, no: Let the tide run fomewhere elfe ; I am refolv'd to know the happinefs of living in filence, without the din of a vifiting-day, fpent in a continual jargon of impertinence, of this pretty lace, and that pretty ribband ; this news of the ring, and that of the circle ; this party for *plays*, and t'other for *eunuchs* and *operas*; one laughs in *gamut*, another fneezes in *elami alt* ; and hey ! all their clacks go together with a *babel* of founds, till their fcandal and fafhions are all run over; and then to the peace of the neighbourhood, they part with the fame impertinence they enter'd——No, *Supple*, after this night, nothing in petticoats fhall come within ten yards of my doors.

Sup. Nor in breeches neither ?

Sir *Sol.* Only Mr. *Clerimont* ; for I expect him to fign articles with me for the five hundred pound he is to give me, for that ungovernable jade my niece *Clarinda.* [*Afide*] Ha ! fee, who's that ?   [*Knocking.*

Sup. O, Sir, 'tis the three ftrange fuitors that wou'd marry Madam *Clarinda.*

Sir *Sol.* Let 'em come in : I'll divert myfelf by laughing at them a little, and then fend them about their bufinefs like fools as they came.

Re-enter Supple, *with Capt.* Strut, *Sir* Squabble
Splithair, *and* Saunter.

Sir *Sol.* Well, gentlemen, your bufinefs with me, I underftand is much the fame ; my confent to your marrying my kinfwoman; I fhould be glad if any of you bring pretences that I like; and fo if you pleafe, gentlemen,———one after another; and when I have heard you all, I'll give you my anfwer:———And in the firft place, what are you, Sir?

Capt. I, Sir, am———a man of honour.

Sir *Sol.* Pray, Sir, what's that, a Lord?

Capt. No, Sir, one that fcorns to take the lye, or pay debts.

Sir *Sol.* Humh! that's pretty near the matter——— an extraordinary perfon. Where do you live, Sir?

Capt. Why, here,———and there, Sir: I'm a man of a frank nature, and am always at home.

Sir *Sol.* Where do you fleep a-nights?

Capt. No where! I fit up every night at the tavern: and in the morning,—lie rough in the *round-houfe.*

Sir *Sol.* Pray, Sir, how do you fpend your time when you are out of a tavern?

Capt. I play at *crimp*, matches at *tennis*, *bowls* and *picquet*; and get in defperate debts for young fellows, that dare not fight for themfelves.

Sir *Sol.* Are you never run through the body?

Capt. Often, Sir; yet I fear nothing but a *bailiff*, or a *court-martial.*—Sir, I kifs every woman that fmiles, and kick every man that frowns upon me: for I take both to myfelf, whether they meant me, or not.

Sir *Sol.* How, Sir! ftrike before you know whether you are affronted, or not? I thought you were a man of honour.

Capt. So I am Sir, and would not have it ftain'd——— in quarrelling. Delays look fcurvily: Firft blows are beft. When a man looks angry upon me, and fays any thing I don't underftand, I knock him down; and then 'tis no matter whether I underftand him or no—Shall a rafcal, becaufe he has read books, talk pertly to me?

Sir *Sol.* Why, Sir, are not your men of honour given to learning?

Capt. Thofe that think it worth their while, are; but we generally leave that to the chaplain, and the chaplain fometimes leaves it to the agent—Our difputes need but little reading; blows, blood, and wounds, are foldiers arguments, Sir.

Sir Sol. Nay, Sir, I shan't difpute with you—But pray, Sir, what can you fettle upon my kinfwoman ?

Capt. My glory, and my fword.

Sir Sol. A jointure of vaft honour, I muft confefs ; pray, Sir, where may your glory lie ?

Capt. In the *Gazette.*

Sir Sol. And your fword——the filver-hilted one I mean.

Capt. At the *pawn-broker's.*

Sir Sol. And pray, Sir, why would you marry ?

Capt. Sir, I owe about fifteen hundred pound ; befide I have a mind to leave off whoring, and keep a frefh girl to myfelf.

Sir Sol. Hah ! a very fober principle, truly. Well, Sir, fince I know your pretences, will you give me leave to talk with the other gentlemen————Pray, Sir, what are you ?

Sir Squab. I, Sir, am none of your fkip-jacks, no fpend-thrift courtier, nor beggarly foldier, but a folid fubftantial man, with a thinking head, and a prudent confcience ; that have liv'd thefe twenty years in St. *Magnus* parifh, have lent my money to the government, and owe none of my neighbours a fhilling.

Sir Sol. Pray, Sir, what may be your name ?

Sir Squab. My name, Sir, is Sir *Squabble Splithair,* Knt. and Citizen of *London.*

Sir Sol. And what may be your profeffion, Sir ?

Sir Squab. Sir; I profefs :—Troth I can hardly tell you what I profefs ; but turning of money is my chief bufinefs. Sir, I'll make a bargain with any man in the city, and defy him to out-wit me.—I have been too fharp for every body I have dealt with, and have got a plentiful eftate by other people's folly and my own in-duftry. Befide, I am a member of the Old *Eaft-India* Company, and no man alive will ever be able to tell what I'm worth.

Sir Sol. Very likely, Sir.

Sir Squab. Sir, I live foberly, and mind the main chance : I never fpend an idle penny out of *Robin*'s or *Garraway's* coffee-houfe : I dine for a groat at the Chop-houfe : I fell by a fhort yard, and bring in a long bill.

Sir Sol. Hah! you are rich, no doubt, Sir.

Sir Squab. Then, Sir, I am a fevere perfecutor of ill women, and never let any of them 'fcape the beadle's correction, without a valuable confideration.

Sir Sol. Ay, ay, you're much in the right, Sir; make 'em pay for their wickednefs.

Sir Squab. Then I difcountenance the enemies of the government, by encouraging them firft to run prohibited goods, and then I difcover 'em to fhew my loyalty.

Sir Sol. You'll be a great man, Sir.

Sir Squab. Then, Sir, I am guardian to my only fifter; and tho' fhe is fix years above age, I ftill keep her fortune carefully in my own hands, for fear fhe fhou'd idly throw it away upon fome beggarly young fellow: Not but I give her a good gentlewomanly education; for I have taught her feveral tunes myfelf upon the *Dulcimer*; and to fave the charge of a finging-mafter, I let her go once a week with her maid in the gallery, to learn the fongs out of the *Opera.*

Sir Sol. Good again, Sir; why this will certainly carry my niece: Thefe are qualities not to be refifted. But now, Sir, what are you willing to fettle upon her?

Sir Squab. Settle, Sir! why I'll—look you, Sir, I don't underftand your law-terms, and hard words:—— But I'll make her a happy woman. She fhall want for nothing: I'll fettle a good hufband upon her; fhe fhall have money in her pocket, and good clothes upon her back; fhe fhall have her youngeft 'Prentice in a *Blue Livery*, carry her *Gilt Bible* before her to church every *Sunday*; fhe fhall wear a gold chain upon her neck, and fit in the great pew next the pulpit.

Sir Sol. Ay!

Sir Squab. Nay, Sir, if fhe pleafes my humour, fhe fhall wear her funday clothes every day; go abroad once a month in a fedan; go to a goffipping once a quarter: and once a year fhe fhall conftantly lie in.

Sir Sol. Hold! hold! Sir, that I'm afraid is more than you can promife.

Sir Squab. Sir, what I fay I'll ftand to; and if you doubt my word, I'll give you city-fecurity for the performance of it.

Sir Sol. Nay, Sir, what you can't perform, there's no doubt but your fecurity will.————Well, Sir! now

I have heard what you can do.——I have but a word
or two with this gentleman, and then——

Sir *Squab.* Sir, with all my heart; if you can get a
better bargain, take it.

Sir *Sol.* Well, Sir! now, pray what are you?

Saun. I, Sir!—ha, hah! I'm nothing at all, Sir.

Sir *Sol.* Ha! that is not much indeed, Sir.——But
pray, Sir, have you no employment?

Saun. Employment! what do you mean, old gentleman, joiner's work?——Sir, I'm a gentleman.

Sir *Sol.* Very good, Sir:—And pray, what eftate have
you.

Saun. I can't tell, Sir:——I never mind accounts; I
don't underftand 'em.

Sir *Sol.* Pray, Sir, what is't you do underftand?

Saun. Bite, bam, and the beft of the lay, old boy.

Sir *Sol.* Hah; that's every word more than I underftand, I muft confefs. Do you know nothing of the law,
Sir?

Saun. Um!—juft as much as I got from being often
arrefted.

Sir *Sol.* Do you follow no bufinefs, Sir?

Saun. No, Sir, I hate it—I avoid it.—I'll make
bufinefs follow me; a gentleman's above it.

Sir *Sol.* Hah! you feem to lead a pleafant life, Sir.

Saun. Yes, Sir, Pleafure's my principle, and I'll ftick
to it as long as I live.

Sir *Sol.* Pray, what's your chief diverfions?

Saun. Sauntering!——As thus, Sir, from my lodging
to the *Smyrna,* thence to *White's,* then to the *Smyrna* again,
then to *White's* again; and all the while my chair follows me empty. Then I dine, drink a bottle, go to
Will's, go behind the fcenes, make love in the *Green-
Room,* take a benefit-ticket, ferret the boxes, ftraddle
into the pit; *Green-Room* again; do the fame at both
houfes, and ftay at neither.

Sir *Sol.* Hah! a pretty life: do you never ftudy, Sir?

Saun. Um—in a morning a little, while my man draws
on my fhoes, I hum over a preface, or fo: Then turn to
the conclufion, and give my judgment accordingly.—I hate
fatigue; a gentleman fhou'd only have a tafte of every
thing.

Sir *Sol.* But do you never ftudy yourfelf neither?

Saun. O yes, Sir, that I never fail to do, at least three hours in a glafs every morning.

Sir *Sol.* Provoking dog! [*Afide.*] Well, Sir, and what other powerful reafons have you, to encourage my niece's coming into your family?

Saun. Why none fo great, Sir, as my family itfelf; 'tis as ancient as any in *England*. The Saunterers, Sir, came in with King *Stephen* the conqueror. And a man of honour, Sir, always values a good family beyond fortune.

Sir *Sol.* Ay, but fome fools don't, Sir; and I fhall not blufh to tell you, I am one of thofe. And let me tell you, Sir, he that out-lives his fortune, will have much ado fometimes to make his family own him. Poverty at court, Sir, is like wit in the city, always counted illegitimate.—Well, gentlemen, I have heard you all: And I won't marry my kinfwoman to this gentleman, becaufe, his prudent confcience, as he calls it, will let him fpend but a penny a day: Nor to this gentleman, becaufe, as far as I find, he has not that to fpend: Nor to the noble captain here, becaufe he fpends more than he has.

Capt. Why then, Sir, I'll ftick to my punk, and a pipe of mundungus.

Sir *Squab.* And as for Sir *Squabble Splithair*,—know, Sir, that now I won't take under a thoufand pound more with your niece; and fo your friend, and fervant.

Saun. And for me, Sir.————

Sir *Sol.* O fweet Mr. *Nothing to do!*

Saun. Know, Sir, that the noble family of the Saunterers fhall never be ftain'd with the bafe blood of a put, Sir; and fo your fervant again, Sir.   [*Exeunt.*

Sir *Sol.* Ha! ha! ha! Well, I fee there are other monfters in the world befide cuckolds, and full as ridiculous. But now to my own affairs. I'll ftep into the *Park*, and fee if I can meet with my hopeful fpoufe there! I warrant, engag'd in fome innocent freedom, (as fhe calls it,) as walking in a mafk; to laugh at the impertinence of fops that don't know her; but 'tis more likely, I'm afraid, a plot to intrigue with thofe that do. Oh! how many torments lie in the fmall circle of a Wedding-Ring!   [*Exit.*

ACT II. SCENE I.

Clarinda's Apartment.

Enter Clarinda *and* Sylvia.

CLARINDA.

HA! ha! poor *Sylvia!*

Syl. Nay, pr'ythee, don't laugh at me. There's no accounting for inclination: For if there were, you know, why shou'd it be a greater folly in me, to fall in love with a man I never saw but once in my life, than it is in you to refist an honeft gentleman, whofe fidelity has deferv'd your heart an hundred times over.

Clar. Ah, but an utter ftranger, coufin, and one that for aught you know, may be no gentleman.

Syl. That's impoffible; his converfation could not be counterfeit. An elevated wit, and good breeding, have a natural luftre that's inimitable. Befide, he fav'd my life at the hazard of his own; fo that part of what I give him, is but gratitude.

Clar. Well, you are the firft woman that ever took fire in the middle of the *Thames,* fure. But fuppofe now he is marry'd, and has three or four children!

Syl. Pfha! pr'ythee don't teaze me with fo many ill-natur'd objections: I tell you he is not marry'd, I am fure he is not: for I never faw a face look more in humour in my life.—Befide, he told me himfelf, he was a country gentleman, juft come to town upon bufinefs: And I'm refolv'd to believe him.

Clar. Well! well! I'll fuppofe you both as fit for one another then as a couple of Tallies. But ftill, my dear, you know there's a furly old father's command againft you; he is in articles to marry you to another: And tho' I know, love is a notable contriver, I can't fee how you'll get over that difficulty.

Syl. 'Tis a terrible one, I own; but with a little of your affiftance, dear *Clarinda*, I am ftill in hopes to bring it to an even wager, I prove as wife as my father.

Clar. Nay, you may be fure of me: You may fee by the management of my own amours, I have fo natural a compaffion for difobedience, I fha'n't be able to refufe you any thing in diftrefs.—There's my hand;—tell me how I can ferve you.

Syl. Why thus;—becaufe I wou'd not wholly difcover myfelf to him at once, I have fent him a note to vifit me here, as if thefe lodgings were my own.

Clar. Hither! to my lodgings! 'Twas well I fent Col. *Standfaft* word I fhou'd not be at home.   [*Afide.*

Syl. I hope you'll pardon my freedom, fince one end of my taking it too, was to have your opinion of him before I engage any farther.

Clar. O! it needs no apology; any thing of mine is at your fervice.—I am only afraid, my troublefome lover Mr. *Clerimont*, fhould happen to fee him, who is of late, fo impertinently jealous of a rival, tho' from what caufe I know not————not but I lie too.   [*Afide.* I fay, fhould he fee him, your country gentleman wou'd be in danger, I can tell you.

Syl. O! there's no fear of that; for I have order'd him to be brought in the back way: When I have talk'd with him a little alone, I'll find an occafion to leave him with you; and then we'll compare our opinions of him.

Enter Servant to Clarinda.

Ser. Madam, my Lady *Sadlife.*

Syl. Pfhah! fhe here!

Clar. Don't be uneafy; fhe fhan't difturb you; I'll take care of her.

Enter Lady Sadlife.

Lady *Sad.* O my dears, you have loft the fweeteft morning fure that ever peep'd out of the firmament, the park never was in fuch perfeÑion.

Clar. 'Tis always fo when your ladyfhip's there.

Lady *Sad.* 'Tis never fo without my dear *Clarinda.*

Syl. How civilly we women hate one another.   [*Aside.*
Was there a good deal of company, madam ?

Lady *Sad.* Abundance! and the beſt I have ſeen this
ſeaſon : for 'twas between twelve and one, the very hour
you know, when the mob are violently hungry. O ! the
air was ſo inſpiring ! ſo amorous ! and to compleat the
pleaſure, I was attack'd in converſation, by the moſt
charming, modeſt, agreably inſinuating young fellow,
ſure, that ever woman play'd the fool with.

Clar. Who was it ?

Lady *Sad.* Nay, Heav'n knows ; his face is as entirely
new, as his converſation. What wretches our young
fellows are to him !

Syl. What ſort of a perſon ?

Lady *Sad.* Tall, ſtreight, well-limb'd, walk'd firm, and
a look as chearful as a *May-day* morning.

Syl. The picture's very like : pray heav'n it is not my
gentleman's.   [*Aside.*

Clar. I wiſh this don't prove my Colonel.   [*Aside.*

Syl. How came you to part with him ſo ſoon ?

Lady *Sad.* O name it not ! that eternal damper of all
pleaſure, my huſband Sir *Solomon*, came into the *Mall* in
the very criſis of our converſation——I ſaw him at a
diſtance, and complain'd that the air grew tainted, that
I was ſick o'th' ſudden, and left him in ſuch abruptneſs
and confuſion, as if he had been himſelf my huſband.

Clar. A melancholy diſappointment indeed !

Lady *Sad.* Oh ! 'tis a huſband's nature to give 'em.

A Servant whiſpers Sylvia.

Syl. Deſire him to walk in——Couſin, you'll be at
hand.

Clar. In the next room——come, Madam, *Sylvia* has
a little buſineſs. I'll ſhew you ſome of the ſweeteſt,
prettieſt-figur'd china.

Lady *Sad.* My dear, I wait on you.

[*Exeunt Lady* Sad. *and* Clar.

Enter Atall, *as Mr.* Freeman.

Syl. You find, Sir, I have kept my word in ſeeing you;
'tis all you yet have aſk'd of me ; and when I know 'tis
in my power to be more obliging, there's nothing you
can command in honour, I ſhall refuſe you,

At. This generous offer, madam, is so high an obligation, that it were almost mean in me to ask a farther favour. [*Aside.*] Death! what a neck she has! But 'tis a lover's merit to be a miser in his wishes, and grasp at all occasions to enrich 'em——I own I feel your charms too sensibly prevail, but dare not give a loose to my ambitious thoughts, 'till I have pass'd one dreadful doubt that shakes 'em,

Syl. If 'tis in my power to clear it, ask me freely.

At. I tremble at the trial; and yet methinks my fears are vain: But yet to kill or cure 'em once for ever, be just and tell me; are you married?

Syl. If that can make you easy, no.

At. 'Tis ease indeed——nor are you promis'd, nor your heart engag'd?

Syl. That's hard to tell you: But to be just, I own my father has engag'd my person to one I never saw, and my heart I fear's inclining to one he never saw.

At. O yet be merciful, and ease my doubt; tell me the happy man that has deserv'd so exquisite a blessing.

Syl. That, Sir, requires some pause; 'tis the only secret yet I can refuse you: first tell me why you're so inquisitive, without letting me know the condition of your own heart.

At. In every circumstance my heart's the same with yours; 'tis promis'd to one I never saw, by a commanding father, who by my firm hopes of happiness I am resolv'd to disobey, unless your cruelty prevents it.

Syl. But my disobedience would beggar me.

At. Banish that fear, I'm heir to a fortune will support you like yourself——may I not know your family?

Syl. Yet you must not.

At. Why that nicety? Is not it in my power to enquire whose house this is when I am gone?

Syl. And be never the wiser: These lodgings are a friend's, and are only borrowed on this occasion: But to save you the trouble of any farther needless questions, I will make you one proposal. I have a young lady here within, who is the only confident of my engagements to you: On her opinion I rely; nor can you take it ill, if I make no further steps without it: 'Twould be miserable indeed shou'd we both meet beggars. I own your actions and appearance merit all you can defire ; let her be as well fatisfied of your pretenfions and condition, and you fhall find it fha'n't be a little fortune fhall make me ungrateful.

At. So generous an offer exceeds my hopes.

Syl. Who's there ?

Enter Servant.

Defire my Coufin *Clarinda* to walk in.

At. Ha! *Clarinda !* if it fhou'd be my *Clarinda* now, I'm in a fweet condition—by all that's terrible the very fhe ; this was finely contriv'd of fortune.

Enter Clarinda.

Clar. Defend me ! Col. *Standfaft !* fhe has certainly difcover'd my affairs with him, and has a mind to infult me by an affected refignation of her pretenfions to him —I'll difappoint her, I won't know him.

Syl. Coufin, pray, come forward ; this is the gentleman I am fo much oblig'd to—Sir, this lady is a relation of mine, and the perfon we are fpeaking of.

At. I fhall be proud to be better known among any of your friends.   [*Salutes her.*

Clar. So ! he takes the hint, I fee, and feems not to know me neither : I know not what to think—perhaps fhe's only jealous of him, and had a mind that my feeing her engagement with him, fhou'd occafion a breach between him and me—I am confounded ! I hate both him and her. How unconcern'd he looks ! confufion ! he addreffes her before my face.   [*Afide.*

Lady Sadlife *peeping in.*

Lady *Sad.* What do I fee ? the pleafant young fellow that talk'd with me in the *Park* juft now ! This is the luckieft accident ! I muft know a little more of him.
                                                [*Retires.*

Syl. Coufin, and Mr. *Freeman*——I think I need not make any apology——you both know the occafion of my leaving you together——in a quarter of an hour I'll wait on you again.   [*Exit* Syl.

B

At. So, I'm in a hopeful way now, faith; but buff's the word: I'll ſtand it.

Clar. Mr. *Freeman!* So, my gentleman has chang'd his name too! how harmleſs he looks————I have my ſenſes ſure, and yet the demureneſs of that face looks as if he had a mind to perſuade me out of 'em. I cou'd find in my heart to humour his aſſurance, and ſee how far he'll carry it————won't you pleaſe to ſit, Sir?

[They ſit.

At. What the devil can this mean? ſure ſhe has a mind to counterface me, and not know me too—with all my heart: If her ladyſhip won't know me, I'm ſure 'tis not my buſineſs at this time to know her.

Clar. Certainly that face is cannon proof.   [*Aſide.*

At. Now for a formal ſpeech, as if I had never ſeen her in my life before.—Madam—a hem! Madam, I— a hem!

Clar. Curſe of that ſteady face.   [*Aſide.*

At. I ſay, Madam, ſince I am an utter ſtranger to you, I am afraid it will be very difficult for me to offer you more arguments than one to do me a friendſhip with your couſin; but if you are, as ſhe ſeems to own you, her real friend, I preſume you can't give her a better proof of your being ſo, than pleading the cauſe of a ſincere and humble lover, whoſe tender wiſhes never can propoſe to taſte of peace in life without her.

Clar. Umph!——I'm choak'd.   [*Aſide.*

At. She gave me hopes that when I had ſatisfied you of my birth and fortune, you wou'd do me the honour to let me know her name and family.

Clar. Sir, I muſt own you are the moſt perfect maſter of your art that ever enter'd the liſts of aſſurance.

At. Madam!

Clar. And I don't doubt but you'll find it a much eaſier taſk to impoſe upon my couſin, than me.

At. Impoſe, Madam! I ſhould be ſorry any thing I have ſaid could diſoblige you into ſuch hard thoughts of me: Sure, Madam, you are under ſome miſinformation.

Clar. I was indeed, but now my eyes are open—— for 'till this minute I never knew that the gay Col. *Standfaſt* was the demure Mr. *Freeman.*

At. Col. *Standfaſt!* This is extremely dark, Madam.

Clar. This jeſt is tedious, Sir——Impudence grows dull, when 'tis ſo very extravagant.

At. Madam, I am a gentleman—but not yet wiſe enough, I find, to account for the humours of a fine Lady.

Clar. Troth, Sir, on ſecond thoughts I begin to be a little better reconcil'd to your aſſurance; 'tis in ſome ſort modeſty to deny yourſelf; for to own your perjuries to my face, had been an inſolence tranſcendently provoking.

At. Really, Madam, my not being able to apprehend one word of all this is a great inconvenience to my affair with your couſin : but if you will firſt do me the honour to make me acquainted with her name and family, I don't much care if I do take a little pains afterwards to come to a right underſtanding with you.

Clar. Come, come, ſince you ſee this aſſurance will do you no good, you had better put on a ſimple honeſt look, and generouſly confeſs your frailties : The ſame ſlyneſs that deceiv'd me firſt, will ſtill find me woman enough to pardon you.

At. That bite won't do. [*Aſide.*] Sure, Madam, you miſtake me for ſome other perſon.

Clar. Inſolent audacious villain ! I am not to have my ſenſes then ! [*Aſide.*

At. No.

Clar. And you are reſolved to ſtand it to the laſt ?

At. The laſt extremity. [*Aſide.*

Clar. Well, Sir, ſince you won't know yourſelf, 'tis poſſible at leaſt you may have ſome ſmall acquaintance with the perſon I take you for : it can do you no harm, I preſume, to own you know Col. *Standfaſt.*

At. By all that's binding, I know no more of him than you know of me.

Clar. If you know as much, 'tis enough.

At. Never ſaw or heard of any ſuch perſon, ſince I was born.

Clar. Nay ! that's hard ! And I muſt tell you Sir, ſince you will own nothing to me, I'll own ſomething to my couſin for you : I'll take care ſhe ſhall know you perfectly.

At. Be not so barbarous, Madam, without a cause to misrepresent me, where my soul most languishes to be clearly known-: Upon my knees I beg you do not in a rash error of my person so apparent, blindly ruin me with the only creature in whom my humble heart has treasur'd up its future hopes of happiness.

Clar. Poor little malice, you think this stings me now : but you shall find—I'm not so little mistress of my heart, but I can still recall it—and since you are so much a stranger to Colonel *Standfast,* I'll tell you where to find him, and tell him this from me ; I hate him, scorn, detest, and loath him : I never meant him but at best for my diversion, and should he ever renew his dull addresses to me, I'll have him used as his vain insolence deserves. Now, Sir, I have no more to say, and I desire you would leave the house immediately.

At. I would not willingly disoblige you, Madam, but 'tis impossible to stir 'till I have seen your cousin, and clear'd myself of these strange aspersions.

Clar. Don't flatter yourself, Sir, with so vain a hope, for I must tell you once for all, you've seen the last of her : And if you won't be gone, you'll oblige me to have you forc'd away.

At. I'll be even with you. [*Aside.*] Well, Madam, since I find nothing can prevail upon your cruelty, I'll take my leave : But as you hope for justice on the man that wrongs you, at least be faithful to your lovely friend, and when you have nam'd to her my utmost guilt, yet paint my passion as it is, sincere. Tell her what tortures I endur'd in this severe exclusion from her sight, that 'till my innocence is clear to her, and she again receives me into mercy,

A madman's frenzy's Heav'n to what I feel;
The wounds you give, tis she alone can heal.   [*Exit.*

Clar. Most abandon'd impudence ! And yet I know not which vexes me most, his out-facing my senses, or his insolent owning his passion for my cousin to my face :

'Tis impoſſible ſhe could put him upon this, it muſt be all his own ; but be it as it will, by all that's woman I'll have revenge.　　　　　　　　　　　　　*[Exit.*

　　· *Re-enter* Atall *and Lady* Sadlife *at the other ſide.*

At. Hey-dey! is there no way down ſtairs here ? Death ! I can't find my way out ! This is the oddeſt houſe.

Lady *Sad.* Here he is—I'll venture to paſs by him.

At. Pray, Madam, which is the neareſt way out ?

Lady *Sad.* Sir ! out———1———

At. O my ſtars! is't you, Madam, this is fortunate indeed—I beg you tell me, do you live here, Madam ?

Lady *Sad.* Not very far off, Sir : But this is no place to talk with you alone—indeed I muſt beg your pardon.

At. By all thoſe kindling charms that fire my ſoul, no conſequence on earth ſhall make me quit my hold, 'till you have given me ſome kind aſſurance that I ſhall ſee you again, and ſpeedily : I'gad I'll have one out of the family at leaſt.

Lady *Sad.* O good, here's company !

At. O do not rack me with delays, but quick, before this dear ſhort-liv'd opportunity's loſt, inform me where you live, or kill me : To part with this ſoft white hand is ten thouſand daggers to my heart.　*[Kiſſing it eagerly.*

Lady *Sad.* O lud ! I am going home this minute : And if you ſhou'd offer to dog my chair, I proteſt I——— was ever ſuch uſage———Lord———ſure ! oh———Follow me down then.　　　　　　　　　　　　　*[Exeunt.*

　　　　Re-enter Clarinda, *and* Sylvia.

Syl. Ha ! ha ! ha !

Clar. Nay, you may laugh, Madam, but what I tell you is true.

Syl. Ha ! ha ! ha !

Clar. You don't believe me then ?

Syl. I do believe, that when ſome women are inclin'd to like a man, nothing more palpably diſcovers it, than their railing at him; ha! ha!——Your pardon, coufin; you know you laugh'd at me juft now upon the fame occafion.

Clar. The occafion's quite different, Madam; I hate him. And, once more I tell you, he's a villain; you're impos'd on. He's a colonel of foot, his regiment's now in *Spain,* and his name's *Standfaft.*

Syl. But pray, good coufin, whence had you this intelligence of him?

Clar. From the fame place that you had your falfe account, Madam, his own mouth.

Syl. Ay, pray when?

Clar. This day feven-night.

Syl. Where?

Clar. In the next room.

Syl. How came you to fee him there?

Clar. Becaufe there was company in this.

Syl. What was his bufinefs with you?

Clar. Much about the fame as his bufinefs with you——love.

Syl. Love! to you!

Clar. Me, Madam! Lord! what am I? Old! or a monfter! is it fo prodigious that a man fhould like me?

Syl. No; but I'm amaz'd to think, if he had lik'd you, he fhould leave you fo foon for me!

Clar. For you! leave me for you! No, Madam, I did not tell you that neither! ha! ha!

Syl. No! what made you fo violently angry with him then? Indeed, coufin, you had better take fome other fairer way; this artifice is much too weak to make me break with him. But, however, to let you fee I can be ftill a friend; prove him to be what you fay he is, and my engagements with him fhall foon be over.

Clar. Look you, Madam, not but I flight the tendereft of his addreffes; but to convince you that my vanity was not miftaken in him, I'll write to him by the name of Col. *Standfaft,* and do you the fame by that of *Freeman;* and let's each appoint him to meet us at my Lady *Sadlife's* at the fame time: If thefe appear

two different men, I think our difpute's eafily at an
end ; if but one, and he does not own all I've faid of
him to your face, I'll make you a very humble curt'fy,
and beg your pardon.

Syl. And if he does own it, I'll make your Ladyfhip
the fame reverence, and beg your's.

Enter Clerimont.

Clar. Pfha ! he here !

Cler. I am glad to find you in fuch good company,
Madam.

Clar. One's feldom long in good company, Sir.

Cler. I am forry mine has been fo troublefome of
late ; but I value your eafe at too high a rate, to difturb
it.   [*Going.*

Syl. Nay, Mr. *Clerimont,* upon my word, you fhan't
ftir.   Hark you—[*Whifpers.*] Your pardon, coufin.

Clar. I muft not loofe him neither.—Mr. *Clerimont's*
way is to be fevere in his conftruction of people's
meaning.

Syl. I'll write my letter, and be with you, coufin. [*Ex.*

Cler. It was always my principle, Madam, to have
an humble opinion of my merit ; when a woman of
fenfe frowns upon me, I ought to think I deferve it.

Clar. But to expect to be always receiv'd with a
fmile, I think, is having a very extraordinary opinion of
one's merit.

Cler. We differ a little as to fact, Madam : For thefe
ten days paft, I have had no diftinction, but a fevere
refervednefs. You did not ufe to be fo fparing of your
good-humour ; and while I fee you gay to all the world
but me, I can't but be a little concern'd at the change.

Clar. If he has difcover'd the Colonel now, I'm undone ! he cou'd not meet him, fure.——I muft humour
him a little. [*Afide.*] Men of your fincere temper,
Mr. *Clerimont,* I own, don't always meet with the ufage
they deferve : but women are giddy things, and had we
no errors to anfwer for, the ufe of good-nature in a lover
wou'd be loft. Vanity is our inherent weaknefs: You

muſt not chide, if we are ſometimes fonder of your paſſions than your prudence.

Cler. This friendly condeſcenſion makes me more
your ſlave than ever.   O! yet be kind, and tell me, have
I been to tur'd with a groundleſs jealouſy?

Clar. Let your own heart be judge————But don't
take it ill if I leave you now:—I have ſome earneſt
buſineſs with my couſin *Sylvia*,—But to-night at my Lady
Dainty's I'll make you amends; you'll be there.

Cler. I need not promiſe you.

Clar. Your ſervant.—Ah! how eaſily is poor ſincerity
impos'd on!   Now for the Colonel.   [*Aſide.*
                                                                [*Exit.*

Cler. This unexpected change of humour more ſtirs
my jealouſy than all her late ſeverity.—I'll watch her
cloſe.

For ſhe that from a juſt reproach is kind,
Gives more ſuſpicion of a guilty mind,
And throw her ſmiles, like duſt, to ſtrike the lover blind.

ACT III. SCENE I.

Lady Dainty's *apartment : A table, with phials, gallipots, glasses, &c.*

Lady Dainty, *and* Situp, *her woman.*

Lady *DAINTY.*

SItup! Situp!

Sit. Madam!

Lady *D.* Thou art strangely slow; I told thee the *hartshorn!* I have the vapours to that degree————

Sit. If your Ladyship would take my advice, you should e'en fling your physic out of the window; if you were not in perfect health in three days, I'd be bound to be sick for you.

Lady *D.* Peace, Goody Impertinence! I tell thee, no woman of quality is, or should be in perfect health—Huh! huh! [*Coughs faintly.*] To be always in health, is as vulgar as to be always in humour, and would equally betray one's want of wit and breeding; 'tis only fit for the clumsy state of a citizen.—I am ready to faint under the very idea of such a barbarous life.—Where are the fellows?

Sit. Here, Madam.

Lady *D. Cæsar!*————run to my Lady *Roundsides*; desire to know how she rested; and tell her the violence of my cold is abated: Huh! huh! *Pompey,* step you to my Lady *Killchairman's*; give my service; say, I have been so embarrass'd with the spleen all this morning, that I am under the greatest uncertainty in the world, whether I shall be able to stir out, or no—And d'ye hear! desire to know how my Lord does, and the new monkey———— [*Exeunt Footmen.*

Sir. In my confcience, thefe great Ladies make themfelves fick to make themfelves bufinefs; and are well or
ill, only in ceremony to one another.   [*Afide.*

Lady *D.* Where's t'other fellow ?

Sir. He is not return'd yet, Madam.

Lady *D.* 'Tis indeed a ftrange lump, not fit to carry
a difeafe to any body: I fent him t'other day to the
Duchefs of *Diet-Drink* with the *cholic,* and the brute
put it into his own *tramontane* language, and call'd
it the *belly-ach* :—Never was creature under fuch
confufion fure! At my next vifit, half the company faluted me upon it.—I was forc'd to explain the
booby's meaning, left they fhould have fuppofed the delicacy of my conftitution capable of fo vulgar a difeafe:
A huh! huh!

Sir. I wifh your Ladyfhip had not occafion to fend for
any, for my part——

Lady *D.* Thy part?—Pr'ythee, thou wert made of
the rough mafculine kind;—'tis betraying our fex not
to be fickly, and tender.—All the families I vifit, have
fomething deriv'd to 'em from the elegant nice ftate
of indifpofition; you fee, even in the men, a genteel
(as it were) ftagger, or twine of the bodies; as if
they were not yet confirm'd enough for the rough
laborious exercife of walking, a lazy faunter in their
motion, fomething of quality! and their voices fo foft
and low, you'd think they were falling afleep, they
are fo very delicate.

Sir. But methinks, Madam, it would be better if the
men were not altogether fo tender.

Lady *D.* Indeed, I have fometimes wifh'd the creatures were not, but that the nicenefs of their frame fo
much diftinguifhes 'em from the herd of common people: Nay, ev'n moft of their difeafes, you fee, are not
prophan'd by the crowd: The *apoplexy,* the *gout,* and
vapours, are all peculiar to the nobility.—Huh! huh!
and I could almoft wifh, that *colds* were only ours;—
there's fomething in 'em fo genteel,——fo agreeably
difordering——Huh! huh!

Sir. That, I hope, I fhall never be fit for 'em—Your
Ladyfhip forgot the *fpleen.*

Lady *D.* Oh !——my dear *spleen,*——I grudge that ev'n to fome of us,

Sit. I knew an ironmonger's wife in this city that was mightily troubled with it.

Lady *D.* Foh ! what a creature haft thou nam'd ! An ironmonger's wife have the *spleen !* Thou might'ft as well have faid her hufband was a fine gentleman ; not but thofe wretches give themfelves the air of following us in every thing; they drefs, game, vifit, hate their hufbands, keep chaplains, and go on as far as fimple nature can : But then the creatures are fo fond of noife, and merry-making, that the delicacy of the *spleen* can't bear their barbarity ; and, therefore, never does 'em the honour to vifit 'em. I profefs—I feel it, while I commend it—Give me fomething.

Sit. Will your Ladyfhip pleafe to take any of the *fteel-drops ?* or the *bolus ?* or the *electuary ?* or——

Lady *D.* This wench will fmother me with queftions, —huh ! huh ! Bring any of 'em—Thefe healthy fluts are fo boifterous, they fplit one's brains : I fancy myfelf in an inn, while fhe talks to me——I muft have fome decay'd perfon of quality about me : For the commons of *England* are the ftrangeft creatures—— huh ! huh !

Enter Servant.

Ser. Mrs. *Sylvia,* Madam, is come to wait upon your Ladyfhip.

Lady *D.* Defire her to walk in ;—let the phyfic alone: —I'll take a little of her company; fhe's mighty good for the *spleen.*

Enter Sylvia.

Syl. Dear Lady *Dainty !*

Lady *D.* My good creature, I'm over-joy'd to fee you——huh ! huh !

Syl. I am forry to fee your Ladyfhip wrapt up thus ; I was in hopes to have had your company to the *Indian* houfe.

Lady *D.* If any thing could tempt me abroad, 'twou'd be that place, and fuch agreeable company : but how came you, dear *Sylvia,* to be reconcil'd to any thing

B 6

in an *Indian* houfe?　You us'd to have a moft barbarous inclination for our own odious manufactures.

Syl. Nay, Madam, I am only going to recruit my *tea-table:* As to the reft of their trumpery, I am as much out of humour with it as ever.

Lady *D.* How can a woman of tafte, as you are, be pleas'd with any thing that's common?　There is a peculiar air in every thing that's foreign.

Syl. I fancy your Ladyfhip hates your own country, as fome women do their hufbands, only for being too near 'em.

Lady *D.* And is not that a very good reafon? For don't you find, it holds from moft hufbands to their wives too: I hate any thing that's to be had like a pound of *fugar* at every grocer's: I am ready to fwoon at the fulfome fhops upon *Ludgate-hill*; and wou'd no more have my equipage in an *Englifh* drefs, than of an *Englifh* birth or education.

Syl. Now, I think, our own habits and fervants are as proper and ufeful as any.

Lady *D.* Ufeful!　O deplorable! What a tradesman's reafon, my dear, do you give? How infipid would life be, if we had nothing about us but what was neceffary? can you fuppofe fo many women of quality wou'd run mad after monkeys, fquirrels, parroquets, *Dutch* dogs, and eunuchs, but that they are of no manner of ufe in the world!

Syl. Now for that reafon, I like none of 'em all.

Lady *D.* How! Why, are not you ftruck with the magnificence of a foreign equipage? as *Swifs* porters, *French* cooks and footmen, *Italian* fingers, *Turkifh* coachmen, and *Indian* pages?

Syl. Very geographical indeed!

Lady *D.* Does not my Lord *Outfides* touch you?

Syl. It did furprize me at firft, I own: For his frightful *Blackmoor* coach-man, with his flat nofe, and great filver collar, made me fancy they had drefs'd up a *Dutch* maftiff, and I expected every minute to hear him bark at his horfes.

Lady *D.* Well, thou art a pleafant creature, thy diftafte is fo diverting.

Syl. And your Ladyſhip is ſo expenſive, that really I am not able to come into it.

Lady *D.* Now it is to me prodigious! how ſome women can muddle away their money upon houſewifry, children, books, and charities, when there are ſo many well-bred ways, and foreign curioſities, that more elegantly require it—I have every morning the rarities of all countries brought to me, and am in love with every new thing I ſee—Are the people come yet, *Situp?*

Sit. They have been below, Madam, this half hour.

Lady *D.* Diſpoſe 'em in the parlour, and we'll be there preſently. [*Exit* Sit.

Syl. How can your Ladyſhip take ſuch pleaſure in being cheated with the baubles of other countries?

Lady *D.* Thou art a very infidel to all finery.

Syl. And you are a very bigot——

Lady *D.* A perſon of all reaſon, and no complaiſance.

Syl. And your Ladyſhip all complaiſance, and no reaſon.

Lady *D.* Follow me, and be converted [*Exeunt.*

Re-enter Situp, *a Woman with* china-ware; *an* Indian-man *with* ſcreens, tea, *&c. a* Birdman *with a* paroquet, monkey, *&c.*

Sit. Come! come into this room.

Chin. W. I hope your Ladyſhip's Lady won't be long coming.

Sit I don't care if ſhe never comes to you.—It ſeems you trade with the Ladies for old clothes, and give 'em *china* for their gowns and petticoats—I'm like to have a fine time on't with ſuch creatures as you indeed..

Chi. Alas! Madam, I'm but a poor woman, and am forc'd to do any thing to live: Will your Ladyſhip be pleas'd to accept of a piece of *china?*

Sit. Poh! no;—I don't care.—Tho' I muſt needs ſay, you look like an honeſt woman. [*Looks on it.*

Chi. Thank you, good Madam.

Sit. Our places are like to come to a fine paſs indeed, if our Ladies muſt buy their *china* with our perquiſites: At this rate, my Lady ſha'n't have an old fan, or a glove; but——

Chi. Pray, Madam, take it.

Sit. No, not I; I won't have it, especially without a saucer to't. Here, take it again.

Chi. Indeed you shall accept of it.

Sit. Not I, truly——Come, give it me, give it me; here's my Lady.

Enter Lady Dainty *and* Sylvia.

Lady *D.* Well, my dear, is not this a pretty fight now?

Syl. It's better than fo many doctors and apothecaries, indeed.

Lady *D.* All trades muft live you know; and thofe no more than thefe could fubfift, if the world were all wife, or healthy.

Syl. I'm afraid our real difeafes are but few to our imaginary, and doctors get more by the found than the fickly.

Lady *D.* My dear, you're allow'd to fay any thing——but now I muft talk with the people.——Have you got any thing new there?

Chi.
Ind.
Arm. } Yes, an't pleafe your Ladyfhip.
Bird.

Lady *D.* One at once.——

Bird. I have brought your Ladyfhip the fineft monkey——

Syl. What a filthy thing it is!

Lady *D.* I now think he looks very humorous and agreeable—I vow in a white periwig he might do mifchief; cou'd he but talk, and take fnuff, there's ne'er a fop in town would go beyond him.

Syl. Moft fops would go farther if they did not fpeak; but talking, indeed, makes 'em very often worfe company than monkeys.

Lady *D.* Thou pretty little picture of man——how very *Indian* he looks! I cou'd kifs the dear creature.

Syl. Ah! don't touch him, he'll bite.

Bird. No, Madam, he is the tameft you ever faw, and the leaft mifchievous.

Lady *D.* Then take him away, I won't have him, for mifchief is the wit of a monkey, and I would not give a farthing for one that wou'd not break me three or four pounds worth of china in a morning. O! I am in love with thefe *Indian* figures—do but obferve what an innocent natural fimplicity there is in all the actions of 'em.

Chi. Thefe are pagods, Madam, that the *Indians* worfhip.

Lady *D.* So far I am an *Indian.*

Syl. Now to me they are all monfters.

Lady *D.* Prophane creature——I wou'd fain buy fomething of the *Armenians*; but amber necklaces are fuch odd things; they are the only people that come fo far, and bring no rarieties with 'cm————Oh! here *Situp* fhall wear one.

Sit. Lord! dear Madam, I fhall make fuch a figure, people will think I am going to dine with my Lady Mayorefs.

Chi. Is your Ladyfhip for a piece of right *Flanders* lace?

Lady *D.* Um—no, I don't care for it now it is not prohibited

Ind. Will your Ladyfhip be pleafed to have a pound of fine tea?

Lady *D.* What filthy odious *Bohea,* I fuppofe?

Ind. No, Madam, right *Kappakawawa.*

Lady *D.* Well, there's fomething in the very found of that name, that makes it irrefiftable——What is't a pound?

Ind. But fix guineas, Madam.

Lady *D.* How infinitely cheap! I'll buy it all. *Situp,* take the man in and pay him, and let the reft call again to-morrow.

Omnes. Blefs your Ladyfhip.

Exeunt Chi. Ind. Arm. *and* Bird.

Lady *D.* Lord! how feverifh I am—the leaft motion does fo diforder me——do but feel me.

Syl. No really, I think you are in very good temper.

Lady *D.* Burning indeed, child.

Enter Servant, Doctor *and* Apothecary.

Serv. Madam, here's *Doctor Bolus* and the *Apothecary.*

Lady *D.* Oh! Doctor, I'm glad you're come, one is not sure of a moment's life without you.

Dr. How did your ladyship rest, madam?

[*Feels her pulse.*

Lady *D.* Never worse, indeed doctor: I once fell into a little slumber indeed, but then was disturb'd by the most odious frightful dream: I dreamt there was an impudent fellow that came into my chamber with his sword drawn, and swore he would marry me whether I wou'd or no; and so methought I flew out of the room, and the horrid creature pursu'd me to a vast great thorny wood, and the briars did so stick in my cloaths, and I pull'd and was so out of breath; and then methought upon a sudden he chang'd into a great roaring mad bull, and then methought I ran, and ran, and ran, and my legs did so ach, that if the fright had not waken'd me, I had certainly perish'd in my sleep with the apprehension.

Dr. A certain sign of a disorder'd brain, madam, but I'll order something that shall compose your ladyship.

Lady *D.* Mr. *Rheubarb,* I must quarrel with you—— you don't disguise your medicines enough, they taste all physic; in a little time you'll bring me to take plain jallap. huh! huh!

Rheub. To alter it more might offend the operation, madam.

Lady *D.* I don't care what is offended, so my taste is not.

Dr. Hark you, Mr. *Rheubarb,* withdraw the medicine rather than not make it pleasant; I'll find a reason for the want of its operation.

Rheub. But, Sir, if we don't look about us she'll grow well upon our hands.

Dr. Never fear that, she's too much a woman of quality to dare to be well without her doctor's opinion.

Rheub. Sir, we have drain'd the whole catalogue of diseases already, there is not another left to put in her head.

Dr. Then I'll make her go 'em over again.

Enter Carelefs.

Care. So! here's the old levee! *Doctor* and *Apothecary* in clofe confultation: Now will I demolifh the quack and his medicines before her face—Mr. *Rheubarb,* your fervant, pray what have you got in your hand there?

Rheub. Only a julep and a compofing draught for my lady, Sir.

Care. Have you fo, Sir—pray let me fee—I'll prefcribe to day—Doctor you may go—the lady fhall take no phyfic at prefent but me.

Dr. Sir—

Care. Nay, if you won't believe me—

[*Breaks the phials.*

Lady *D.* Ah!——— [*Frighted and leaning upon* Syl.

Dr. Come away, Mr. *Rheubarb*—he'll certainly put her out of order, and then fhe'll fend for us again.

[*Ex.* Doctor *and* Apoth.

Care. You fee, madam, what pains I take to come into your favour.

Lady *D.* You take a very prepofterous way I can tell you, Sir.

Care. I can't tell how I fucceed, but I am fure I endeavour right, for I ftudy every morning new impertinence to entertain you; for fince I find nothing but dogs, doctors and monkeys are your favourites, it's very hard if your ladyfhip won't admit me as one of the number.

Lady *D.* When I find you of an equal merit with my monkey, you fhall be in the fame ftate of favour: I confefs, as a proof of your wit, you have done me as much mifchief here: But you have not half pug's judgment, nor his fpirit; for that creature will do a world of pleafant things, without caring whether one likes 'em or not.

Care. Why truly, madam, the little gentleman, my rival, I believe is much in the right on't; and if you obferve, I have taken as much pains of late to difoblige, as to pleafe you.

Lady *D.* You fucceed better in one than t'other, I can tell you, Sir.

Care. I am glad on't—for if you had not me now and then to plague you, what wou'd you do for a pretence to be chagrine, to faint, have the fpleen, the vapours, and all thofe modifh diforders that fo nicely diftinguifh a woman of quality?

Lady D. I am perfectly confounded! certainly there are fome people too impudent for our refentment.

Care. Modefty's a ftarving virtue, madam, an old threadbare fafhion of the laft age, and wou'd fit as oddly upon a lover now as a picked beard and muftachoes.

Lady D. Moft aftonifhing!

Care. I have try'd fighing and looking filly a great while, but 'twou'd not do—nay, had you had as little wit as good-nature, fhou'd have proceeded to dance and fing—tell me but how, what face or form can worfhip you, and behold your votary.

Lady D. Not, Sir, as the *Perfians* do the fun, with your face towards me: the beft proof you can give me of your horrid devotion, is never to fee me more. Come, my dear.   [*Ex. with* Sylvia.

Syl. I'm amaz'd fo much affurance fhou'd not fuc-ceed.   [*Exit.*

Care. All this fhan't make me out of love with my virtue—impudence has ever been a fuccefsful quality—and 'twou'd be hard indeed if I fhou'd be the firft that did not thrive by it.   [*Exit.*

S C E N E, Clerimont's Lodgings.

Enter Atall, *and* Finder *his Man.*

At. You are fure you know the houfe again?

Fin. Ah! as well as I do the upper gallery, Sir: 'Tis Sir *Solomon Sadlife's*, at the two glafs lanthorns, within three doors of my Lord Duke's.

At. Very well, Sir, then take this letter, enquire for my Lady *Sadlife's* woman, and ftay for an anfwer.

Fin. Yes, Sir.   [*Exit.*

At. Well, I find 'tis as ridiculous to propofe pleafure in love without variety of miftreffes, as to pretend to be a keen fportfman without a good ftable of horfes: We may talk what we will, but I say we love as we hunt, for pleasure; and he's likeliest to see most of the sport I'm sure that has a good led nag in the field: How this lady may prove I can't tell, but if she is not a deedy tit at the bottom, I'm no jockey.

Re-enter Finder.

Fin. Sir, here are two letters for you.

At. Who brought 'em ?

Fin. A couple of footmen, and they both desire an answer.

At. Bid 'em stay, and do you make haste where I order'd you.

Fin. Yes, Sir.   [*Exit.*

At. To Col. *Standfast*—that's *Clarinda*'s hand——to Mr. *Freeman*——that must be my *Incognita.* Ah ! I have most mind to open this first: But if t'other malicious creature shou'd have perverted her growing inclinations to me, 'twou'd put my whole frame in a trembling. Hold, I'll guess my fate by degrees—this may give me a glimpse of it. [*Reads* Clar. *Letter.*] Um—um—um—ha ! *to meet her at my Lady* Sadlife's *at seven o'clock to-night,* and takes no manner of notice of my late disowning myself to her—something's at the bottom of all this—now to solve the riddle. [*Reads t'other Letter.*] *My cousin* Clarinda *has told some things of you that very much alarm me ; but I am willing to suspend my belief of them 'till I see you, which I desire may be at my Lady* Sadlife's *at seven this evening.*

The devil ! the same place !

As you value the real friendship of your Incognita.

So now the riddle's out, the rival queens are fairly come to a reference, and one or both of 'em I must lose, that's positive !——Hard !

Enter Clerimont.

Hard fortune ! now poor impudence, what will become of thee ! O *Clerimont !* such a complication of adventures since I saw thee, such sweet hopes, fears, and unaccountable difficulties, sure never poor dog was surrounded with.

Cler. O, you are an induſtrious perſon, you'll get over 'em. But pray let's hear.

At. To begin then in the climax of my misfortunes : in the firſt place, the private lodgings that my *Incognita* appointed to receive me in, prove to be the very individual habitation of my other miſtreſs, whom (to compleat the blunder of my ill-luck) ſhe civilly introduced in perſon to recommend me to her better acquaintance.

Cler. Ha! ha! Death! how cou'd you ſtand 'em both together ?

At. The old way——Buff——I ſtuck like a burr to my name of *Freeman*, addreſs'd my *Incognita* before the other's face, and with a moſt unmov'd good breeding, harmleſly faced her down I had never ſeen her in my life before.

Cler. The pretttieſt modeſty I ever heard of. Well, but how did they diſcover you at laſt?

At. Why faith, the matter's yet in ſuſpenſe, and I find by both their letters they don't yet well know what to think ; (but to go on with my luck) you muſt know they have ſince both appointed me, by ſeveral names, to meet 'em at one and the ſame place at ſeven o'clock this evening.

Cler. Ah!

At. And laſtly to crown my fortune, (as if the devil himſelf moſt triumphantly rode a ſtraddle upon my ruin) the fatal place of their appointment happens to be the very houſe of a third lady, with whom I made an acquaintance ſince morning, and had juſt before ſent word I wou'd viſit near the ſame hour this evening.

Cler. O! murder! poor *Atall*! thou art really fallen under the laſt degree of compaſſion.

At. And yet, with a little of thy aſſiſtance, in the middle of their ſmall ſhot, I don't ſtill deſpair of holding my head above water.

Cler. You muſt think me barbarous indeed, if in ſuch diſtreſs I ſhou'd not throw out a rope to ſave you——not that I can imagine what you propoſe; for I dare ſwear thou doſt not deſign to marry any one of 'em.

At. Shou'd my *Incognita*'s birth prove equal to her beauty, I tremble to tell thee what might become of me.

Cler. Why then you had as good quit her friend, now.

At. No, no, that is not safe neither—and if I don't keep in with her, intimacy will certainly give her opportunities of spoiling my market with her rival.

Cler. Death! but you can't meet 'em both, you must lose one of 'em, unless you can split yourself.

At. Pr'ythee don't suspect my courage or my modesty, for I'm resolv'd to go on, if you will stand by me.

Cler. Faith, my very curiosity would make me do that ——but what can I do?

At. You must appear for me upon occasion in person.

Cler. With all my heart——What else?

At. I shall want a queen's messenger in my interest, or, rather one that can personate one.

Cler. That's easily found——but what to do?

At. Come along, and I'll tell you——for first I must answer their letters.

Cler. Thou art an original, faith.   [*Exeunt.*

The S C E N E *changes to* Sir Solomon's.

Enter Sir Solomon *leading Lady* Sadlife, *and* Wishwell
her woman.

Sir *Sol.* There, Madam, let me have no more of these airings————no good I'm sure, can keep a woman five or six hours abroad in a morning.

Lady *Sad.* You deny me all the innocent freedoms of life.

Sir *Sol.* Hah! you have the modish cant of this end of the town, I see: Intriguing, gaming, gadding, and party-quarries with a pox to 'em, are innocent freedoms, forsooth.

Lady *Sad.* I don't know what you mean, I'm sure I have not one acquaintance in the world that does an' ill thing.

Sir *Sol.* They must be better look'd after than your Ladyship then; but I'll mend my hand as fast as I can: Do you look to your reputation henceforward, and I'll take care of your person.

Lady *Sad.* You wrong my virtue with these unjust suspicions.

Sir Sol. Ay, it's no matter for that; better I wrong it than you. I'll secure my doors for this day at leaft. [*Ex.*

Lady Sad. O, *Wifhwell!* what fhall I do?

Wifh. What's the matter, Madam?

Lady Sad. I expect a letter from a gentleman, every minute, and if it fhould fall into Sir *Solomon's* hands, I'm ruin'd paft redemption.

Wifh. He won't fufpect it, Madam, fure, if they are directed to me, as they us'd to be.

Lady Sad. But his jealoufy's grown fo violent of late, there's no trufting to it now; if he meets it I fhall be lock'd up for ever.

Wifh. O dear Madam! I vow your Ladyfhip frights me——Why, he'll kill me for keeping counfel.

Lady Sad. Run to the window, quick, and watch the meffenger. [*Exit* Wifh.] Ah! there's my ruin near. ——I feel it——[*A knocking at the door.*] What fhall I do?——Be very infolent, or very humble, and cry. I have known fome women, upon thefe occafions, out-ftrut their hufband's jealoufy, and make 'em afk pardon for finding 'em out——O Lud! here he comes——I can't do't, my courage fails me——I muft ev'n ftick to my handkerchief, and truft to nature.

Re-enter Sir Solomon, *taking a letter from* Finder.

Sir Sol. Sir, I fhall make bold to read this letter; and if you have a mind to fave your bones, there's your way out.

Find. O terrible! I fhan't have a whole one in my fkin when I come home to my mafter.——[*Exit* Finder.

Lady Sad. [*Afide.*] I'm loft for ever.

Sir Sol. [*Reads.*] " Pardon, moft divine creature,
                    " the impatience of my heart;

Very well! thefe are her innocent freedoms! ah,
Cockatrice!   " which languifhes for an oppor-
                   " tunity to convince you of its fin-
                   " cerity——

O the tender——fon of a whore!
                   " which nothing cou'd relieve but
                   " the fweet hope of feeing you this
                   " evening.

Poor Lady! whofe virtue I have wrong'd with unjuft
fufpicions!

Lady *Sad.* I'm ready to fink with apprehenfion!

Sir *Sol.* ————————" To night at feven expeſt your
" dying *Strephon.*

Die, and be damn'd; for I'll remove your comforter,
by cutting her throat————I cou'd find in my heart to
ram his impudent letter into her windpipe————Ha!
what's this!   " To Mrs. *Wifhwell,* my Lady
" *Sadlife's* woman."

Ad, I'm glad of it with all my heart————————What a
happy thing 'tis to have one's jealoufy difappointed!
————Now have I been curfing my poor wife for the
miftaken wickednefs of that trollop—'Tis well I kept my
thoughts to myfelf: for the virtue of a wife, when
wrongfully accus'd, is moft unmercifully infolent—come,
I'll do a great thing—I'll kifs her, and make her amends
————what's the matter, my dear? has any·thing frighted you?

Lady *Sad.* Nothing but your hard ufage.

Sir *Sol.* Come! come! dry thy tears, it fhall be fo
no more————but, hark ye! I have made a difcovery
here—your *Wifhwell* I'm afraid is a flut—fhe has an
intrigue.

Lady *Sad.* An intrigue! heavens, in our family!

Sir *Sol.* Read there—I wifh fhe be honeft—

Lady *Sad.* How!—if there be the leaft ground to
think it, Sir *Solomon,* pofitively fhe fhan't ftay a minute
in the houfe—impudent creature—have an affair with a
man!

Sir *Sol.* But hold my dear—don't let your virtue cenfure too feverely neither.

Lady *Sad.* I fhudder at the thoughts of her.

Sir *Sol.* Patience, I fay, how do we know but his
courtfhip may be honourable?

Lady *Sad.* That, indeed, requires fome paufe.

Wifh.————————[*Peeping in.*] So! all's fafe I fee————
He thinks the letter's to me————O good madam—that
letter was to me the fellow fays————I wonder, Sir, how
you cou'd ferve one fo; if my fweetheart fhou'd hear you

had open'd it, I know he wou'd not h;
wou'd not.

Sir *Sol.* Never fear that, for if he is in
he's too much a fool to value being laugh

Lady *Sad.* If it be your's, here take y
next time bid him take better care, th;
letters fo publicly.

Wifh. Yes, Madam ; but now your Lac
it, I'd feign beg the honour of Sir *Solom*
for me; for I can't write.

Lady *Sad.* Not write!

Sir *Sol.* Nay, he thinks fhe's above t'
for be calls her divine creature—a pretty p
truly——But come, my Dear——Egad,
for her. Here's paper—you fhall do it.

Lady *Sad.* I, Sir *Solomon!* Lard, I
fellows, not I——I hope he won't tal
word.

Sir *Sol.* Nay, you fhall do it—come,
good hufband.

Wifh. Ay, pray good Madam, do——
Sir *Sol.* Ah! how eager the jade is !—
Lady *Sad.* I can't tell how to write to
you, my dear.

Sir *Sol.* Well! well! I'll dictate
begin——
Lady *Sad.* Lard! this is the oddeft fan

. Sir *Sol.* Come! come! Dear Sir; (f
loving as he for his ears.)

Wifh. No, pray, Madam, begin dea1
deareft angel.

Lady *Sad.* Out! you fool! you muft n
Dear Sir is very well.

. Sir *Sol.* Ay, ay, fo 'tis! but thefe y(
for fetting out at the top of their fpeed-
Wifhwell, what is thy lover? for the ft
may ferve for a countefs.

Wifh. Sir, he's but a butler at pref
good fchollard, as you may fee by his

and in time may come to be a steward; and then we shan't be long without a coach, Sir.

Lady *Sad.* Dear Sir——what must I write next?

Sir *Sol.* Why——   [*Musing.*

Wish. Hoping you are in good health, as I am at this present writing.

Sir *Sol.* You puppy, he'll laugh at you.

Wish. I'm sure my mother us'd to begin all her letters so.

Sir *Sol.* And thou art every inch of thee her own daughter, that I'll say for thee.

Lady *Sad.* Come, I have done't. [*Reads.*] " Dear " Sir, she must have very little merit that is insensible " of your's.

Sir *Sol.* Very well, 'faith! write all yourself.

Wish. Ay, good Madam, do; that's better than mine. ————But pray, dear Madam, let it end with, *So I rest your dearest loving friend, 'till death us do part.*

Lady *Sad.* [*Aside.*] This absurd flut will make me laugh out.

Sir *Sol.* But hark you, huffy; suppose now you shou'd be a little scornful and insolent to shew your breeding, and a little ill-natur'd in it to shew your wit.

Wish. Ay, Sir, that is if I design'd him for my gallant: But since he is to be but my husband, I must be very good-natur'd and civil before I have him; and huff him and shew my wit after.

Sir *Sol.* Here's a jade for you! [*Aside.*] But why must you huff your husband, huffy?

Wish. O, Sir, that's to give him a good opinion of my virtue; for you know, Sir, a husband can't think one cou'd be so very domineering, if one were not very honest.

Sir *Sol.* 'Sbud! this fool on my conscience, speaks the sense of the whole sex.   [*Aside.*

Wish. Then, Sir, I have been told, that a husband loves one the better, the more one hectors him, as a Spaniel does the more one beats him.

Sir *Sol.* Hah! thy husband will have a blessed time on't.

Lady *Sad.* So! I have done.

Wiſh. O pray, Madam, read it.

Lady *Sad.* [*Reads.*] " Dear Sir——ſhe muſt have
" very little merit that is inſenſible of your's; and
" while you continue to love, and tell me ſo,
" expect whatever you can hope from ſo much wit,
" and ſuch unfeign'd ſincerity—At the hour you
" mention, you will be truly welcome to your
" paſſionate——

Wiſh. Oh, Madam! it is not half kind enough; pray put in ſome more dears.

Sir *Sol.* Ay, ay, ſweeten it well—let it be all ſyrup—with a pox to her.

Wiſh. Every line ſhould have a *dear ſweet Sir* in it; ſo it ſhould——He'll think I don't love him elſe.

Sir *Sol.* Poor Moppet!——

Lady *Sad.* No, no, 'tis better now——Well, what muſt be at the bottom to anſwer *Strephon?*

Sir *Sol.* Pray let her divine ladyſhip ſign——*Abigail.*

Wiſh. No; pray Madam, put down *Liſpamintha.*

Sir *Sol. Liſpamintha!*

Lady *Sad.* No, come——I'll write *Cælia.* Here, go in and ſeal it.

Sir *Sol.* Ay, come—I'll lend you a wafer, that he mayn't wait for your divinityſhip.

Wiſh. Pſhah! you always flout one ſo.

[Exit Sir Sol. and Wiſh.

Lady *Sad.* So! this is luckily over—Well! I ſee a woman ſhould never be diſcourag'd from coming off at the greateſt plunge: For tho' I was half dead with the fright, yet now I'm a little recovered, I find——

That apprehenſion does the bliſs endear;
The real danger's nothing to the fear.   [*Exit.*

ACT IV. SCENE I.

Sir Solomon*'s.*

Enter Lady Sadlife, Atall, *and* Wishwell, *with lights.*

Lady *S A D L I F E.*

THIS room, I think is pleasanter; if you please, we'll sit here, Sir——*Wishwell!* Shut the door, and take the key o'th' inside, and set chairs.

Wish. Yes, Madam.

Lady *Sad.* Lard! Sir, what a strange opinion you must have of me, for receiving your visits upon so slender an acquaintance.

At. I have a much stranger opinion, Madam, of your ordering your servant to lock herself in with us.

Lady *Sad.* O! you would not have us wait upon ourselves.

At. Really, Madam, I can't conceive that two lovers alone have much occasion for attendance.   [*They sit.*

Lady *Sad.* Lovers! Lard! how you talk! Can't people converse without that stuff?

At. Um!—yes, Madam, people may; but without a little of that stuff, conversation is generally very apt to be insipid.

Lady *Sad.* Pooh! why we can say any thing without her hearing, you see.

At. Ay, but if we should talk ourselves up to an occasion of being without her, it would look worse to send her out, than to have let her wait without when she was out.

Lady *Sad.* You are pretty hard to please, I find, Sir: some men, I believe, would think themselves well us'd, in so free a reception as your's.

At. Hah! I see, this is like to come to nothing this time; so I'll e'en put her out of humour, that I may get off in time to my *Incognita.* [*Aside.*] Really, Madam, I can never think myself free, where my hand and my tongue are ty'd.   [*Pointing to* Wiſhwell.

Lady *Sad.* Your converſation, I find, is very different from what it was, Sir.

At. With ſubmiſſion, Madam, I think it very proper for the place we are in. If you had ſent for me, only to ſip tea, to ſit ſtill, and be civil, with my hat under my arm, like a ſtrange relation from *Ireland,* or ſo, why was I brought hither with ſo much caution and privacy ?

Lady *Sad.* Suppoſe I had a favourable thought of you ; does that give you a title to treat mê as if it was not in my power to refuſe you any thing ?

At. Come, Madam, I'll be plain with you—I wou'd not have you to think me ignorant of all the tendereſt forms that ought to approach a lady's favours ; but when a woman breaks the ſeeming promiſe of her eyes, with me ſhe loſes all pretence to 'em. (Your woman's being with us is ridiculous ;) I had a lover's honeſt reaſon, to expect you here alone ; but ſhe that thinks to make me dance attendance to her pride, to ſit at a diſtance, and tamely talk myſelf to a ſubmiſſive flame for her ; while ſhe with eyes infenſible receives it, and e'en ſwells her ſated vanity, to a deſpiſing of her eaſy conqueſt, before ſhe enjoys it ; let me tell you, Madam, in very conciſe terms, that woman—is moſt confumedly miſtaken.

Lady *Sad.* You have a very odd way of treating people ; you men are the ſtrangeſt creatures ! Is there no ſuch thing as patience in your compoſition ?

At. O yes, Madam, abundance ; for if you pleaſe but to order Madamoiſelle to get the tea ready, to boil it a great while, and ſtay 'till it's done, you ſhall find I can yet change the air of my approaches.

Lady *Sad.* I don't know how to make her do any ſuch thing, not I ; Lard ! ſhe knows I have had tea juſt now.

At. I have not ; and ſo your humble ſervant, Madam.

Lady *Sad.* Hold !

At. Really, Madam, my ſtomach won't ſtay; and if your Ladyſhip's tea is not ready, I muſt beg leave to take a diſh at the coffee-houſe.

            [*As he is going, Sir* Solomon *knocks at the door.*

Wiſh. O heav'ns! my maſter, Madam.

Sir *Sol.* Open the door, there, (within.)

Lady *Sad.* What ſhall we do?

At. Nothing now, I'm ſure.

Lady *Sad.* Open the door, and ſay, the gentleman came to you.

Wiſh. O lud! Madam, I ſhall never be able to manage it at ſo ſhort a warning——We had better ſhut the gentleman into the cloſet, and ſay, he came to no-body at all.

Lady *Sad.* In! in then, for mercy's ſake, quickly, Sir!

At. Soh; this is like to be a very pretty buſineſs! Oh, ſucceſs! and impudence! thou haſt quite forſaken me.   [*Enters the cloſet.*

Wiſh. Do you ſtep into your bed-chamber, Madam, and leave my maſter to me.   [*Exit Lady* Sadlife.

            [Wiſhwell *opens the door,* &c.

Enter Sir Solomon.

Sir *Sol.* What's the reaſon, miſtreſs, I am to be lock'd out of my wife's apartment.

Wiſh. Sir, my Lady was waſhing her——her——Neck, Sir, and I could not come any ſooner.

Sir *Sol.* I'm ſure I heard a man's voice. [*Aſide.* Bid your Lady come hither.——He muſt be here-abouts; 'tis ſo! all's out, all's over now: The devil has done his worſt, and I am a cuckold in ſpight of my wiſdom. 'Sbud now an *Italian* would poiſon his wife for this, a *Spaniard* would ſtab her, and a *Turk* would cut off her head with a ſcimitar; but a poor dog of an *Engliſh* cuckold now, can only ſquabble and call names.——Hold! here ſhe comes.——I muſt ſmother my jealouſy that her guilt mayn't be upon its guard.

Enter Lady Sadlife, *and* Wishwell.

Sir Sol. My dear! how do you do? Come hither, and kiss me.

Lady Sad. I did not expect you home so soon, my dear.

Sir Sol. Poor rogue———I don't believe you did ———with a pox to you. [*Aside.*] *Wishwell*, go down, I have business with your Lady.

Wish. Yes, Sir———but I'll watch you: For I'm afraid this good humour has mischief at the bottom of it——— [*Retires.*

Lady Sad. I scarce know whether he's jealous or not.

Sir Sol. Now dare not I go near that closet door, least the murderous dog should poke a hole in my guts thro' the key-hole.———Um—I have an old thought in my head—ay! and that will discover the whole bottom of her affair———'Tis better to seem not to know one's dishonour, when one has not courage enough to revenge it.

Lady Sad. I don't like his looks, methinks.

Sir Sol. Odso! what have I forgot now—Pr'ythee, my dear, step into my study, (for I am so weary!) and in the upermost parcel of letters, you'll find one that I receiv'd from *Yorkshire* to-day, in the scrutore; bring it down, and some paper; I will answer it while I think on't.

Lady Sad. If you please to lend me your key—but had not you better write in your study, my dear?

Sir Sol. No! no! I tell you, I'm so tir'd, I am not able to walk.———There! make haste.

Lady Sad. Wou'd all were well over. [*Exit Lady* Sad.

Sir Sol. 'Tis so by her eagerness to be rid of me. Well, since I find I dare not behave myself like a man of honour in this business, I'll at least act like a person of prudence, and penetration: For say, I should clap a brace of slugs now in the very bowels of this rascal, it may hang me; but if it does not, it can't divorce me:———No, I'll e'en put out the candles, and in a soft, gentle whore's voice, desire the gentleman to walk about his bufinefs; and if I can get him out before my wife returns, I'll fairly poft myfelf in his room; and fo, when fhe comes to fet him at liberty, in the dark, I'll humour the cheat, 'till I draw her into fome cafual confeffion of the faft; and then this injur'd front fhall bounce upon her, like a thunderbolt.

[*Puts out the candle.*

Wifh. [*Behind.*] Say you fo, Sir? I'll take care my Lady fhall be provided for you. [*Exit.*

Sir Sol. Hift! hift! Sir! Sir!

Enter Atall *from the clofet.*

At. Is all clear? may I venture, Madam?

Sir Sol. Ay! ay! quick! quick! make hafte before Sir *Solomon* returns. A ftrait-back'd dog, I warrant him. [*Afide.*] But when fhall I fee you again?

At. Whenever you'll promife me to make a better ufe of an opportunity.

Sir Sol. Ha! then 'tis poffible he mayn't yet have put the finifhing ftroke to me.

At. Is this the door?

Sir Sol. Ay! ay! away! [*Exit* Atall.] Soh! now the danger of being murder'd is over; I find, my courage returns: And if I catch my wife but inclining to be no better than fhe fhould be, I'm not fure that blood wo'n't be the confequence.

[*He goes into the clofet, and* Wifhwell *enters.*

Wifh. Soh! my Lady has her cue; and, if my wife mafter can give her no better proofs of his penetration than this, fhe'd be a greater fool than he, if fhe fhou'd not do what fhe has a mind to. Sir! Sir! Come! you may come out now. Sir *Solomon*'s gone.

Enter Sir Solomon *from the clofet.*

Sir Sol. So! now for a foft fpeech, to fet her impudent blood in a ferment, and then let it out with my penknife. [*Afide.*] Come, dear creature, now let's make the kindeft ufe of our opportunity.

Wiſh. Not for the world! if Sir *Solomon* ſhou'd come again, I ſhould be ruin'd——Pray be gone——I'll ſend to you to-morrow.

Sir *Sol.* Nay, now you love me not——You would not let me part elſe thus unſatisfied.

Wiſh. Now you're unkind. You know I love you, or I ſhould not run ſuch hazards for you.

Sir *Sol.* Fond whore! [*Aſide.*] But I'm afraid you love Sir *Solomon,* and lay up all your tenderneſs for him.

Wiſh. O ridiculous! how can ſo ſad a wretch give you the leaſt uneaſy thought? I loach the very ſight of him.

Sir *Sol.* Damn'd infernal ſtrumpet——I can bear no longer—Lights! lights! within there.   [*Seizes her.*

Wiſh. Ah! [*Shrieks.*] Who's this, help! murder!

Sir *Sol.* No, traitreſs, don't think to 'ſcape me; for now I've trapp'd thee in thy guilt, I could find in my heart to have thee flea'd alive, thy ſkin ſtuff'd, and hung up in the middle of *Guild-Hall,* as a terrible con-ſequence of cuckoldom to the whole city—Lights there!

Enter Lady Sadlife *with a light.*

Lady *Sad.* O heav'ns! what's the matter!
        [*Sir* Solomon *looks aſtoniſhed.*
Ha! what do I ſee! my ſervant on the floor, and Sir *Solomon* offering rudeneſs to her! O! I can't bear it! oh!   [*Falls into a chair.*

Sir *Sol.* What has the devil been doing here?

Lady *Sad.* This the reward of all my virtue! O re-venge! revenge!

Sir *Sol.* My dear! my good virtuous injur'd dear, be patient; for here has been ſuch wicked doings.——

Lady *Sad.* O torture! do you own it too! 'tis well my love protects you——but for this wretch! this monſter! this ſword ſhall do me juſtice on her.
        [*Runs at* Wiſhwell *with Sir* Solomon's *ſword.*

Sir *Sol.* O hold! my poor miſtaken dear!—This horrid jade, the gods can tell, is innocent for me; but ſhe has had, it ſeems, a ſtrong dog in the cloſet here:

which I fufpecting, put myfelf into his place, and had almoft trap'd her in the very impudence of her iniquity.

Lady *Sad.* How!—I'm glad to find he dares not own 'twas his jealoufy of me———— [*Afide.*

Wifh. [*Kneeling.*] Dear Madam, I hope your Ladyfhip will pardon the liberty I took in your abfence, in bringing my lover into your Ladyfhip's chamber; but I did not think you wou'd come home from prayers fo foon, and fo I was forc'd to hide him in that clofet: but my mafter fufpecting the bufinefs, it feems, turn'd him out unknown to me, and then put himfelf there, and fo had a mind to difcover whether there was any harm between us; and fo becaufe he fancy'd I had been naught with him.—

Sir *Sol.* Ay, my dear; and the jade was fo confoundedly fond of me, that I grew out of all patience, and fell upon her like a fury.

Lady *Sad.* Horrid creature, and does fhe think to ftay a minute in the family, after fuch impudence!

Sir *Sol.* Hold, my dear—for if this fhould be the man that is to marry her—you know there may be no harm done yet.

Wifh. Yes, it was he indeed, Madam.

Sir *Sol.* [*Afide.*] I muft not let the jade be turn'd away, for fear fhe fhou'd put it in my wife's head, that I hid myfelf to difcover her ladyfhip, and then the devil wou'd not be able to live in the houfe with her.

Wifh. Now, Sir, you know what I can tell of you.

[*Afide to Sir* Solomon.

Sir *Sol.* Mum! that's a good girl! there's a guinea for you.

Lady *Sad.* Well upon your interceffion, my dear, I'll pardon her this fault; but pray, miftrefs, let me hear of no more fuch doings, I am fo diforder'd with this fright——fetch my prayer-book, I'll endeavour to compofe myfelf. [*Exit Lady* Sadlife.

Sir *Sol.* Ay, do fo! that's my good dear—what two bleffed efcapes I have had! to find myfelf no cuckold at laft, and, which had been equally terrible, my wife not know I wrongfully fufpected her.—Well! at length I am fully convinc'd of her virtue—and now if I can but cut off the abominable expence, that attends some of her impertinent acquaintance, I shall shew myself a *Machiavel.*

Re-enter Wishwell.

Wish. Sir, here's my Lady *Dainty* come to wait upon my lady.

Sir *Sol.* I'm sorry for't with all my heart—why did you say she was within?

Wish. Sir, she did not ask if she was; but she's never deny'd to her.

Sir *Sol.* Gad so! why then if you please to leave her ladyship to me, I'll begin with her now.

Wishwell *brings in Lady* Dainty.

Lady *D.* Sir *Solomon,* your very humble servant.

Sir *Sol.* Your's, your's, madam.

Lady *D.* Where's my lady!

Sir *Sol.* Where your ladyship very seldom is—at prayers.

Lady *D.* Huh! huh! you keep your old humour still I see of endeavouring to speak home truths; but I think you commonly guess wrong: For you must know that I have bought me the prettiest atlas cushions with gold tassels on purpose to kneel upon.

Sir *Sol.* Not unlikely madam: you fine ladies have a great many fine things, that you never use—for I don't remember I have seen you, or your cushions, at church these three weeks.

Lady *D.* Never miss, never miss, if I am in any sort of condition to, huh, huh, endure the air: Tho' indeed a *Sunday* is very apt to give one the spleen, or the vapours——but if I am not there myself, I constantly send my woman to see how the fashions alter.

Sir *Sol.* I cry your mercy, Madam, I did not know that was your mode-market day before.

Lady *D.* Sir, the greatest distinction of people of quality is, that they make every thing easy to 'em.

Sir *Sol.* Yes, yes, being in the mode, I see, will let one into notable priviledges.

Enter Lady Sadlife.

Lady *Sad.* My dear Lady *Dainty.*

Lady *D.* Dear Madam, I am the happieft perfon alive in finding your Ladyfhip at home.

Sir *Sol.* So ! now for a torrent of impertinence.

Lady *Sad.* Your Ladyfhip does me a great deal of honour.

Lady *D.* I'm fure I do myfelf a great deal of plea-fure : I have made at leaft twenty vifits to-day, and not above five of them were at home : and meeting with a reafonable creature at laft, is like the pleafure of unla-cing, after being fqueez'd up in a ftrait pair of ftays at a birth-day.

Lady *Sad.* Some vifits are indeed ftrangely fatiguing.

Lady *D.* O! I'm quite dead! not but my coach is very eafy——yet fo much perpetual motion—you know.

Sir *Sol.* Ah, pox of your diforder——if I had the providing your equipage, ods-zooks you fhould rumble to your vifits in a wheel-barrow.　　　　　*[Afide.*

Lady *Sad.* Was you at my Lady Dutchefs's ?

Lady *D.* A little while.

Lady *Sad.* Had fhe a great circle ?

Lady *D.* Extream—I was not able to bear the breath of fo much company.

Lady *Sad.* Pray who had you ?

Lady *D.* Every body—my Lady *Toilet,* Lady *Patchit,* Mrs. *Peepers,* Lady *Whitewafh,* Mrs. *Layiton,* Lady *Steinkirk,* both the Miftrefs *Favourites,* Lady *Jumps,* and the Dutchefs of *Falbala.*

Lady *Sad.* You did not dine there ?

Lady *D.* Oh! I can't touch any body's dinner but my own—and I have almoft kill'd myfelf this week for want of my ufual glafs of *Tokay* after my *Ortalans,* and *Mufcovy* duck eggs.

Sir *Sol.* 'Sbud if I had the feeding of you, I'd bring you in a fortnight to neck-beef, and a pot of plain bub.　　　　　*[Afide.*

Lady *D.* Then I have been fo furfeited with the fight of a hideous city entertainment to-day at my

C 6

Lady *Cormorant's*, who knows no other happiness, or way of making one welcome, than eating, or drinking; I was ready to swoon at the sight of her table, being just come out of the fresh air.

Lady *Sad.* Pray how was it fill'd, Madam?

Lady *D.* At the upper end sat her Ladyship, and at each elbow a daughter, with arms like ploughmen, freckled like Turkey-eggs, and cheeks like catherine pears—they were enough to beat one down with the coarse pores of their skin! Huh! huh!

Lady *Sad.* O, frightful!—but pray go on.

Sir *Sol.* On my conscience, their daily conversation is made up of nothing but impudent fleering at honest people, that don't know as many ways of being foppishly vicious as themselves.   [*Aside.*

Lady *D.* At the lower end was an unlick'd thing, she call'd son—I suppose by her first venter; that sat all the while with his mouth gaping wide, not having from nature wit enough to fetch his breath through his nose.

Lady *Sad.* Ha, ha!

Lady *D.* The table, or rather larder, was fill'd with hams, roasted pullets, and Turkey-pyes, with a great *Cheshire* cheese in the middle, that rivall'd every one in bulk but her Ladyship; and a large tankard of strong beer, nutmeg and sugar, enough to fuddle a grand jury, or carry an interest at a election.

Lady *Sad.* A true *English* home-bred family.

Lady *D.* In every circumstance: for tho' she saw I was just fainting at her vast limbs of butchers meat—yet the civil savage forc'd me to sit down, and heap'd enough upon my plate to victual a fleet for an *East-India* voyage.

Lady *Sad.* How could you bear it? ha! ha!

Sir *Sol.* 'Sbud! I han't patience—pray, Madam, is it among the rules of your this end of the town breeding, to laugh at your friends for making you heartily welcome?

Lady *D.* Sir *Solomon!* 'tis impossible to see the titles of quality join'd with such mob dispositions, without easing one's spleen a little: And nothing distinguishes the commons fo much as their grofs feeding : I never knew a true *plebeian*, that had not an odious vaft fto-mach——huh ! huh !

Sir *Sol.* Your Ladyfhip knows the elegance of life.

Lady *Sad.* Does your Ladyfhip never go to the play ?

Lady *D.* Never but when I befpeak it myfelf, and then not to mind the actors ; for it's common to love fights : My great diverfion is in a repos'd pofture to turn my eyes upon the galleries, and blefs myfelf to hear the happy favages laugh——or when an aukward citizen crouds herfelf in among us, 'tis an unfpeakable pleafure to contemplate her airs and drefs——And they never 'fcape me—for I am as apprehenfive of fuch a creature's coming near me, as fome people are when a cat is in the room——but the play is begun, I believe, and if your Ladyfhip has an inclination, I'll wait upon you.

Lady *Sad.* I think, Madam, we can't do better; and here comes Mr. *Carelefs,* moft opportunely to fquire us——

Sir *Sol. Carelefs!* I don't know him, but my wife does, and that's as well!

Enter Carelefs.

Care. Ladies, your fervant—feeing your coach at the door, Madam, made me not able to refift this oppor-tunity to——to——you know, Madam, there's no time to be loft in love. Sir *Solomon,* your fervant——

Sir *Sol.* O yours ! yours, Sir ! A very impudent fel-low, and I'm in hopes will marry her.   [*Afide.*

Lady *D.* The affurance of this creature almoft grows diverting ; all one can do, can't make him the leaft fen-fible of a difcouragement.

Lady *Sad.* Try what compliance will do ; perhaps that may fright him.

Lady *D.* If it were not too dear a remedy—one wou'd almoft do any thing to get rid of his company.

Care. Which you never will, Madam, till you marry me, depend upon't : Do that, and I'll trouble you no more.

Sir *Sol.* This fellow's abominable!   He'll certainly
have her.   [*Aside.*

Lady *D.* There's no depending upon your word, or
elfe I might : for the laft time I faw you, you told me
then you would trouble me no more.

Care. Ay, that's true, Madam ; but to keep one's
word, you know, looks like a tradefman.

Sir *Sol.* Impudent rogue ! but he'll have her—[*Aside.*

Care. And is as much below a gentleman, as paying
one's debts.

Sir *Sol.* If he is not hang'd firft.———   [*Aside.*

Care. Befides, Madam ; I confider'd that my abfence
might endanger your conftitution, which is fo very tender, that nothing but love can fave it, and fo I would
e'en advife you to throw away your juleps, your cordials, and flops, and take me all at once.

Lady *D.* No, Sir, bitter portions are not to be taken
fo fuddenly.

Care. Oh! to chufe, Madam ; for if you ftand making
of faces, and kecking againft it, you'll but encreafe your
averfion, and delay the cure. Come, come, you muft
be advis'd.   [*Preſſing her.*

Lady *D.* What mean you, Sir ?

Care. To banifh all your ails, and be myfelf your
univerfal medicine.

Sir *Sol.* Well faid ! he'll have her.

Lady *D.* Impudent robuft man ; I proteft did not I
know his family, I fhou'd think his parents had not liv'd
in chairs and coaches, but had us'd their limbs all their
lives—Huh ! huh ! but I begin to be perfuaded health
is a great bleffing.   [*Aside.*

Care. My limbs, Madam, were convey'd to me from
before the ufe of chairs and coaches, and it might
leffen the dignity of my anceftors, not to ufe them as
they did.

Lady *D.* Was ever fuch a rude underftanding ? to value himfelf upon the barbarifm of his fore-fathers———
Indeed I have heard of kings that were bred to the
plough, and I fancy you might defcend from fuch a
race ; for you court as if you were behind one—

Huh! huh! huh! To treat a woman of quality like an exchange-wench, and exprefs your paffion with your arms; unpolifh'd man!

Care. I was willing, Madam, to take from the vulgar the only defirable thing among 'em, and fhew you— how they live fo healthy——for they have no other remedy.

Lady *D.* A very rough medicine! huh! huh!

Care. To thofe that never took it, it may feem fo—

Lady *D.* Abandon'd ravifher! Oh!   [*Struggling.*

Sir *Sol.* He has her, he has her.   [*Afide.*

Lady *D.* Leave the room, and fee my face no more.

Care. [*Bows and is going*]

Lady *D.* And, hark ye, Sir, no bribe, no mediations to my woman.

Care. [*Bows and fighs.*]

Lady *D.* Thou profligate! to hug! to clafp! to em- brace and throw your robuft arms about me like a vulgar, and indelicate! Oh! I faint with apprehenfion of fo grofs an addrefs.   [*She faints, and* Care. *catches her.*

Care. O my offended fair.

Lady *D.* Inhuman! ravifher! Oh!

                    [Care. *carries her off.*

Sir *Sol.* He has her! fhe's undone! he has her!

                    [*Exit after them.*

Lady *Sad.* This is one of the moft extraordinary love- fcenes I ever faw: I never could find a woman's fan- tafk would run high enough to oppofe her fecret incli- nation before: But I fancy by this time her Ladyfhip's delicacy would be glad to compound for a little of the vulgar.   [*Exit.*

Enter Clarinda *and* Sylvia.

Clar. Well, coufin, what do you think of your gentle- man now?

Syl. I fancy, Madam, that would be as proper a quef- tion to afk you: for really I don't fee any great reafon to alter my opinion of him yet——

Clar. Now I could dafh her at once, and fhew it her under his own hand that his name's *Standfaft,* and he'll be here in a quarter of an hour——but let her go on a little.   [*Aside.*

Syl. Pray, coufin, have you any particular reafon to be fo chearful?

Clar. You'll pardon me if I own a little of my fex's malice, my dear.: for a woman that won't be convinc'd of the infidelity of her lover, when her friend affures her of it from her own knowledge, is to me the moft unfortunate figure in nature! Ha! ha! ha!

Syl. I have two or three lines in my pocket that wou'd ftrangely damp this pertnefs; but I rather think it affected, and won't fhew it 'till I'm fure——[*Afide*] Methinks, coufin, we need not either of us give ourfelves any of thefe violent airs; for I fancy the gentleman's next appearance will extremely take down the vanity of one of us.

Clar. Ha! ha! Ay! ay! that it will, I'm pofitive.

Syl. You muft certainly be deceiv'd into fome fecret reafon for your being fo very pofitive.

Clar. Deceiv'd, Madam! If I had no reafon but what's writ in my face, I fancy, with fubmiffion to your Ladyfhip's beauty, that alone might juftify my confidence.

Syl. Your face——And have you really no better fecurity?

Clar. Better! ha! ha! Yes, yes: I have a better, Madam, I have your face————Look but in the honeft glafs, and tell me what I fhonld be afraid on? Ha! ha! ha!

Syl. No, Madam, I need not do that; I remember enough of my face to know it is not in any one charm like yours—Thanks to indulgent nature.

                    [*Lifting up her hands and eyes.*

Clar. Really, coufin, you have one quality I envy you for: For to be extravagantly vain, is certainly the firft ftate of happinefs.

Syl. Really I think fo too, and therefore won't undeceive your vanity, becaufe 'twou'd be giving my friend too barbarous a mortification.

Clar. Well! we are ftrangely good-natur'd: for let

me die, child, if I have not juſt the ſame tenderneſs for you.

Syl. Lard! how ſhall we do to requite one another ?

Clar. I vow I don't think I ought to refuſe you any ſervice in my power; therefore if you think it worth your while not to be out of countenance when the Colonel comes, I would adviſe you to withdraw now; for if you dare take his own word for it, he will be here in three minutes, as this may convince you.

[Gives a letter.

Syl. What's here? a letter from Colonel *Standfaſt ?* —Really, couſin, I have nothing to ſay to him—Mr. *Freeman*'s the perſon I'm concern'd for, and I expeᴄt to ſee him here in a quarter of an hour.

Clar. Then you don't believe them both the ſame perſon ?

Syl. Not by their hands or ſtyle, I can aſſure you, as this may convince you.   [*Gives a letter.*

Clar. Ha! The hand is different indeed——I ſcarce know what to think, and yet I'm ſure my eyes were not deceiv'd.

Syl. Come, couſin, let's be a little cooler; 'tis not impoſſible but we may have both laught at one another to no purpoſe—for I am confident they are two perſons.

Clar. I can't tell that, but I'm ſure here comes one of 'em.

Enter Atall, as Colonel Standfaſt.

Syl. Ha!

At. Hey! bombard, (there they are, faith!) bid the chariot ſet up, and call again about one or two in the morning—You ſee, Madam, what 'tis to give an impudent fellow the leaſt encouragement: I'm reſolv'd now to make a night on't with you.

Clar. I am afraid, Colonel, we ſhall have much ado to be good company, for we are two women to one man, you ſee; and if we ſhould both have a fancy to have you particular, I doubt you'd make but bungling work on't.

At. I warrant you we will pafs our time like Gods: two ladies and one man; the prettieft fet for ombre in the univerfe——Come! come! cards! cards! cards! and tea, that I infift upon.

Clar. Well, Sir, if my coufin will make one, I won't balk your good-humour.　　[*Turning* Syl. *to face him.*

At. Is the lady your relation, Madam?——I beg the honour to be known to her.

Clar. O, Sir! that I'm fure fhe can't refufe you—— coufin, this is Colonel *Standfaft.* [*Laughs afide.*] I hope now fhe's convinc'd.

At. Your pardon, Madam, if I am a little particular in my defire to be known to any of this lady's rela-tions.　　[*Salutes.*

Syl. You'll certainly deferve mine, Sir, by being al-ways particular to that lady——

At. Oh, Madam! Tall, lall.　[*Turns away, and fings.*

Syl. This affurance is beyond example.　　[*Afide.*

Clar. How do you do, coufin?

Syl. Beyond bearing—but not incurable.　[*Afide.*

Clar. [*Afide.*] Now can't I find in my heart to give him one angry word for his impudence to me this morn-ing; the pleafure of feeing my rival mortified makes me ftrangely good-natur'd.

At. [*Turning familiarly to* Clar.] Upon my foul you are provokingly handfome to-day. Ay gad! why is not it high treafon for any beautiful woman to marry.

Clar. What, would you have us lead apes?

At. Not one of you, by all that's lovely——Do you think we could not find you better employment? Death! what a hand is here!——Gad! I fhall grow foolifh!

Clar. Stick to your affurance, and you are in no danger.

At. Why then, in obedience to your commands, pry'thee anfwer me fincerely one queftion—How long do you really defign to make me dangle thus?

Clar. Why really I can't juft fet you a time; but when you are weary of your fervice, come to me with a fix-pence and modefty, and I'll give you a difcharge.

At. Thou infolent, provoking handfome tyrant.

Clar. Come! let me go——this is not a very civil way of entertaining my coufin, methinks.

At. I beg her pardon indeed. [*Bowing to* Sylv.] But lovers you know, Madam, may plead a fort of excufe for being fingular when the favourite fair's in company. ——but we were talking of cards, Ladies.

Clar. Coufin, what fay you?

Syl. I had rather you would excufe me, I am a little unfit for play at this time.

At. What a valuable virtue is affurance! Now am I as intrepid as a lawyer at the bar. [*Afide.*

Clar. Blefs me! you are not well?

Syl. I fhall be prefently———Pray, Sir, give me leave to afk you a queftion.

At. So! now it's a coming. [*Afide.*] Freely, Madam.

Syl. Look on me well: Have you never feen my face before?

At. Upon my word, Madam, I can't recollect that I have.

Syl. I am fatisfied.

At. But pray, Madam, why may you afk?

Syl. I'm too much diforder'd now to tell you——But if I'm not deceiv'd, I'm miferable. [*Weeps.*

At. This is ftrange——How her concern tranf-ports me!

Clar. Her fears have touch'd me, and half perfuade me to revenge 'em———Come, coufin, be eafy; I fee you are convinc'd he is the fame, and now I'll prove myfelf a friend.

Syl. I know not what to think——my fenfes are confounded: Their features are indeed the fame; and yet there's fomething in the air, their drefs and manner, ftrangely different: But be it as it will, all right to him in prefence I difclaim, and yield to you for ever.

At. O charming! joyful grief! [*Afide.*

Clar. No, coufin, believe it, both our fenfes cannot be deceiv'd, he's individually the fame; and fince he dares be bafe to you, he's miferable indeed, if flatter'd with a diftant hope of me; I know his perfon and his falfhood both too well; and you fhall fee will, as becomes your friend, refent it.

At. What means this ftrangenefs, Madam?

Clar. I'll tell you, Sir; and to ufe few words, know then, this Lady and myfelf have borne your faithlefs infolence and artifice too long: But that you may not think to impofe on me, at leaft, I defire you would leave the houfe, and from this moment never fee me more.

At. Madam! what! what is all this? Riddle me riddle me re,

> *For the devil take me,*
> *For ever from thee,*
> *If I can divine what this riddle can be!*

Syl. Not mov'd! I'm more amaz'd.

At. Pray, Madam, in the name of common fenfe, let me know in two words what the real meaning of your laft terrible fpeech was; and if I don't make you a plain, honeft, reafonable anfwer to it, be pleas'd the next minute to blot my name out of your table-book, never more to be enroll'd in the fenfelefs catalogue of thofe vain coxcombs, that impudently hope to come into your favour.

Clar. This infolence grows tedious: What end can you propofe by this affurance?————

At. Hey-dey!

Syl. Hold, coufin————one moment's patience: I'll fend this minute again to Mr. *Freeman,* and if he does not immediately appear, the difpute will need no farther argument.

At. Mr. *Freeman!* Who the devil's he! what have I to do with him?

Syl. I'll foon inform you, Sir.

[*Going, meets* Wifhwell *entering.*

Wifh. Madam, here's a footman mightily out of breath, fays he belongs to Mr. *Freeman,* and defires very earneftly to fpeak with you.

Syl. Mr. *Freeman!* Pray bid him come in——What can this mean?

At. You'll fee prefently.   [*Afide.*

Re-enter Wifhwell *with* Finder.

Clar. Ha!

Syl. Come hither, Friend; do you belong to Mr. *Freeman ?*

Find. Yes, Madam, and my poor mafter gives his humble fervice to your ladyfhip, and begs your pardon for not waiting on you according to his promife; which he would certainly have done, but for an unfortunate accident.

Syl. What's the matter ?

Find. As he was coming out of his lodgings to pay his duty to you, madam, a parcel of fellows fet upon him, and faid they had a warrant againft him; and fo, becaufe the rafcals began to be faucy with him, and my mafter knowing he did not owe a fhilling in the world, he drew to defend himfelf, and in the fcuffle the bloody villains run one of their fwords quite through his arm; but the beft of the jeft was, madam, that as foon as they got him into a houfe, and fent for a furgeon, he prov'd to be the wrong perfon; for their warrant it feems was againft a poor fcoundrel, that happens they fay to be very like him, one Colonel *Standfaft.*

At. Say you fo, Mr. Dog—if your mafter had been here I wou'd have given him as much.

[*Gives him a box on the Ear.*

Find. O Lord! pray, madam, fave me—I did not fpeak a word to the gentleman—O the devil! this muft be the devil in the likenefs of my mafter.

Clar. I am ftartled!

Syl. Is this gentleman fo very like him, fay you?

Find. Like, madam! ay, as one box of the ear is to another; only I think, madam, my mafter's nofe is a little, little higher.

Syl. Now, ladies, I prefume the riddle's folv'd.

At. Hark you, where is your mafter, rafcal ?

Find. Mafter, rafcal! fir, my mafter's name's *Freeman,* and I'm a free-born *Englifhman;* and I muft tell you, Sir, that I don't ufe to take fuch arbitrary focks

of the face from any man that does not pay me
and so my master will tell you too when he come

Syl. Will he be here then ?

Find. This minute, madam; he only stays
his wound drefs'd.

At. I'm refolv'd I'll stay that minute out, if
not come 'till midnight.

Find. A pox of his mettle——when his hanc
makes no difference between jest and earnest,
——if he does not pay me well for this, 'egad
tell the next for himself

Find. Has your ladyship any commands to my
madam ?

Syl. Yes, pray give him my humble fervice,
forry for his misfortune ; and if he thinks 'twi
wound no harm, I beg by all means he may be
hither immediately.

Find. 'Shah ! his wound, madam, I know]
not value it of a rufh; for he'll have the devil
of actions against the rogues for falfe imprifonm(
fmart-money—ladies, I kifs your hands——Sir
thing at all——

At. [*Afide.*] The dog has done it rarely ; fo
upon the stretch I don't know a better rafcal in *E*

Enter an Officer.

Off. Ay ! now I'm fure I'm right——Is not yo
Colonel *Standfaft*, Sir ?

At. Yes, Sir ; what then ?

Off. Then you are my prifoner, Sir——

At. Your prifoner ! who the devil are you ? a]
I don't owe a fhilling.

Off. I don't care if you don't, Sir ; I have a \
against you for high treafon, and I muft have yo
this minute.

At. Look you, Sir, depend upon't, this is bi
impertinent malicious profecution: You may
to stay a quarter of an hour I'm fure; I have
bufinefs here till then that concerns me nearer tl
life——

Clar. Have but fo much patience, and I'll fati
for your civility.

Off. I cou'd not ftay a quarter of an hour, madam, if you'd give me five hundred pound.

Syl. Can't you take bail, Sir ?

Off. Bail! no! no!

Clar. Whither muft he be carried ?

Off. To my houfe, 'till he's examin'd before the council.

Clar. Where is your houfe ?

Off. Juft by the Secretary's office; every body knows Mr. *Lockum* the meffenger—come, Sir.

At. I can't ftir yet, indeed, Sir.

[*Lays his hand on his fword.*

Off. Nay, look you, if you are for that play—come in gentlemen, away with him,

[*Enter Mufqueteers, and force him off.*

Syl. This is the ftrangeft accident; I am extremely forry for the Colonel's misfortune, but I am as heartily glad he is not Mr. *Freeman.*

Clar. I'm afraid you'll find him fo—I fhall never change my opinion of him 'till I fee 'em face to face.

Syl. Well, coufin, let 'em be two, or one, I'm refolv'd to ftick to Mr. *Freeman*; for to tell you the truth, this laft fpark has too much of the confident rake in him to pleafe me, but there is a modeft fincerity in t'other's converfation that's irrefiftible.

Clar. For my part I'm almoft tir'd with his impertinence either way, and cou'd find in my heart to trouble myfelf no more about him; and yet methinks it provokes me to have a fellow out face my fenfes.

Syl. Nay, they are ftrangely alike I own; but yet if you obferve nicely, Mr. *Freeman*'s features are more pale and penfive than the Colonel's.

Clar. When Mr. *Freeman* comes, I'll be clofer in my obfervation of him——in the mean time, let me confider what I really propofe by all this buftle I make about him: fuppofe, (which I can never believe) they fhould prove two feveral men at laft, I don't find that I'm fool enough to think of marrying either of 'em; nor (whatever airs I give myfelf) am I yet mad enough to do worfe with 'em——Well! fince I don't defign to come to a clofe engagement myfelt, then, why fhou'd I

not generously stand out of the way, and make room for
one that wou'd? no, I can't do that neither—I want,
methinks to convict him first of being one and the same
person, and then to have him convince my cousin, that
he likes me better than her——Ay, that wou'd do! and
to confess my infirmity, I still find (tho' I don't care this
for the fellow) while she has the assurance to nourish the
least hope of getting him from me, I shall never be heartily easy, 'till she's heartily mortified. [*Aside*.

Syl. You seem very much concern'd for the Colonel's
misfortune, cousin.

Clar. His misfortunes seldom hold him long, as you
may see; for he comes.

Enter Atall, as Mr. Freeman.

Syl. Bless me!

At. I am sorry, madam, I cou'd not be more punctual
to your obliging commands: But the accident that prevented my coming sooner, will, I hope, now give me
a pretence to a better welcome than my last; for now,
Madam, [*to* Clar.] your mistake's set right, I presume,
and I hope you won't expect Mr. *Freeman* to answer for
all the miscarriages of Colonel *Standfast*.

Clar. Not in the least, Sir: The Colonel's able to
answer for himself, I find! ha! ha! ha!

At. Was not my servant with you, madam?
[To Sylvia.

Syl. Yes, yes, Sir, he has told us all. I'll seem to
believe any thing rather than not engage him from
her. [*Aside.*] And I am sorry you have paid so dear
for a proof of your innocence: Had you come two minutes sooner, you would have been as much surpriz'd as
we; for the Colonel, that strange image of you, was
here.

At. O dear madam, why would you part with him,
when I had sent you word before, I wou'd be with you
as soon as my wound was dreft.

Syl. 'Twas not in our power to keep him, Sir; for
it seems the same officer that mistook you for him, pursu'd him hither, and hurried him away to prison.

At. I'd give the world methinks to see him! What

fay you, Madam, have you curiofity enough to take coach immediately, and carry me to him?

Syl. You'll excufe me if I don't defire to bring you together; efpecially while the fmart of the wound you receiv'd upon his account is fo frefh upon you; I wou'd not hazard you in a new quarrel.

Clar. Lard! how happy the creature is.   [*Afide.*

At. O fy! Madam, upon my faith, I have not the leaft malice in the world to the gentleman.

Clar. Nor the gentleman to you, I dare fwear, Sir! ha! ha! ha! for affurance and credulity—I thank my ftars I never faw a couple better match'd in my life before! ha! ha! Why won't you go to the meffenger's, coufin, and prove me in the wrong? you'll fee no danger of a new quarrel, take my word for't; for I'm ftrangely afraid that the only way in nature to bring this gentleman and the Colonel face to face, is to hold him a looking glafs! ha! ha!

At. I hope, madam, you won't take it ill, if the fury of this accufation fhou'd not raife me to a defire of convincing you of my innocence; while this lady's fatisfy'd of it, you'll pardon me, if I am not under the leaft degree of concern about it.

Syl. And for me, coufin, I fhall make but few words with you; you may endeavour as much as you pleafe, to amufe and confound me with fears, doubts, and jealoufies of perfons, but neither all the truth, or artifice under heaven, will be able to convince me, that this gentleman is not this gentleman—and therefore unlefs you can prove him to be nobody at all, I'd advife you to fet your heart at reft; for what I defign, you'll find, I fhall come to a fpeedy refolution in.

At. O generous refolution!

Clar. Well, madam, fince you are fo tenacious of your conqueft, I hope you'll give me the fame liberty; and not expect the next time you fall a crying, at the Colonel's gallantry to me, that my good-nature fhou'd give you up my pretenfions to him. And for you, Sir, ——I fhall only tell you, this laft plot was not fo clofely laid, but that a woman of a very slender capacity, you'll find, has wit enough to discover it.   [*Exit* Clar.

At. So! she's gone to the messenger's, I suppose—but, poor soul, her intelligence there will be extreamly small. [*Aside.*] Well, madam, I hope at last your scruples are over.

Syl. You can't blame me, Sir, if now we are alone, I own myself a little more surpris'd at her positiveness, than my woman's pride wou'd let me confess before her face; and yet methinks there is a native honesty in your look, that tells me I am not mistaken, and may trust you with my heart.

At. O! for pity still preserve that tender thought, and save me from despair.

Enter Cleriment.

Cler. Ha! *Freeman* again! is it possible?

At. How now, *Clerimont*, what are you surpriz'd at?

Cler. Why to see thee almost in two places at one time; 'tis but this minute, I met the very image of thee with the mob about a coach, in the hands of a messenger, whom I had the curiosity to stop and call to; and had no other proof of his not being thee, but that the spark wou'd not know me!

Syl. Strange! I almost think I'm really not deceiv'd.

Cler. 'Twas certainly *Clarinda* I saw go out in a chair just now——it must be she——the circumstances are too strong for a mistake.   [*Aside.*

Syl. Well, Sir, to ease you of your fears, now I dare own to you, that mine are over.   [*To* Atall.

Cler. What a Coxcomb have I made myself, to serve my Rival e'en with my own Mistress? but 'tis at least some ease to know him: All I have to hope is, that he does not know the ass he has made of me—that might indeed be fatal to him.   [*Aside.*

Enter Sylvia's *Aunt.*

Aunt. O, my dear Niece, I'm glad I've found you: your father and I have been hunting you all the town over.

Syl. My father in town?

Aunt. He waits below in the coach for you : He muſt needs have you come away this minute; and talks of having you married this very night to the fine Gentleman he ſpoke to you of.

Syl. What do I hear ?

At. If ever ſoft compaſſion touch'd your ſoul, give me a word of comfort in this laſt diſtreſs, to ſave me from the horrors that ſurround me.

Syl. You ſee we are obſerved—but yet depend upon my faith, as on my life—in the mean time, I'll uſe my utmoſt power to avoid my father's haſty will : In two hours you ſhall know my fortune and my family—Now don't follow me, as you'd preſerve my friendſhip.   Come—madam.   [*Exit with* Aunt.

At. Death ! how this news alarms me ! I never felt the pains of love before.

Cler. Now then to eaſe, or to revenge my fears—this ſudden change of your countenance, Mr. *Atall*, looks as if you had a mind to banter your friend into a belief of your being really in love with the lady that juſt now left you.

At. Faith, *Clerimont*, I have too much concern upon me at this time, to be capable of a banter; or if I were, I don't ſee any uſe it would be of in this affair : but to deal at once ſincerely with you, there's ſomething in this creature's beauty and ſoft temper, that ſtirs my very reaſon into a tenderneſs, that all her glittering ſex could never raiſe me to.

Cler. Ha ! he ſeems really touch'd, and I begin now only to fear *Clarinda*'s conduct—Well, Sir, if it be ſo, I'm glad to ſee a convert of you ; and now in return to the little ſervices I have done you, in helping you to carry on your affair with both theſe ladies at one time, give me leave to aſk a favour of you—Be ſtill ſincere, and we may ſtill be friends.

At. You ſurpriſe me—but uſe me as you find me.

Cler. Have you no acquaintance with a certain lady, whom you have lately heard me own I was unfortunately in love with ?

At. Not that I know of, I'm ſure not as the lady you are in love with: but pray why do you aſk ?

Cler. Come, I'll be sincere with you too: Because I have strong circumstances, that convince me 'tis one of those two you have been so busy about.

At. Not she you saw with me, I hope.

Cler. No, I mean the other——But, to clear the doubt at once, is her name *Clarinda?*

At. I own it is: But had I the least been warn'd of your pretences—

Cler. Sir, I dare believe you, and tho' you may have prevailed even against her honour, your ignorance of my passion for her makes you stand at least excus'd to me.

At. No, by all the solemn protestations tongue can utter, her honour is untainted yet for me; nay, even unattempted: Nor had I ever an opportunity, that cou'd encourage the most distant thought against it.

Cler. You own she has receiv'd your gallantries at least!

At. Faith, not to be vain, she has indeed taken some pains to pique her cousin about me; and if her beautiful cousin had not fallen in my way at the same time, I must own 'tis very possible, I might have endeavour'd to push my Fortune with her: But since I now know your heart, put my friendship to a trial.

Cler. Only this——If I shou'd be reduc'd to ask it of you, promise to confess your imposture, and your passion to her cousin, before her face.

At. There's my hand,—I'll do't, to right my friend and mistress. But, dear *Clerimont*, you'll pardon me, if I leave you here: For my poor *Incognita*'s Affairs at this time are in a very critical condition.

Cler. No ceremony——I release you.——

At. Adieu.

Cler. Women! What crazy vessels do we trust our fortunes in?

Now will I reproach her, humble her into shame;
Despise and leave her to her vanities for ever.
Ha! she's here.

Enter Clarinda.

Clar. I am more confounded now than ever.——I scarce know what to think——The messenger confesses

the colonel is ſtill his priſoner, but that his orders are
to give no ſoul admittance to him——Ha! *Clerimont!*
pray Heav'n he has not diſcovered me!

Cler. You ſeem diſorder'd, Madam——— ſome cruel
diſappointment has, I fear, befallen you.

Clar. 'Tis ſo! I ſee by his aſſurance—O guilt! what
cowards doſt thou make. of us————But let him not
inſult too far.   [*Aſide.*

Cler. What! not a word? Are you conſcious of any
wrong you have done me, Madam, that you ſtand thus
confounded at the ſight of me?

Clar. You have a very familiar way of expreſſing
yourſelf, Sir!

Cler. 'Twas my opinion of your virtue, Madam,
that kept me humble: But now that's loſt, methinks,
you ſhou'd expeɛt to be treated as you are————

Clar. What do you mean!

Cler. That two lovers and reputation are incon-
ſiſtent.

Clar. What! has your vanity then flatter'd you, to
ſuppoſe I receiv'd you for one?

Cler. Oh! Why truly, Madam, conſidering the converſation that has paſs'd between us, I do ſtill inſiſt,
that I might pretend to the poſt: But in love, as in
war, a man of honour can't ſee another put over his
head, without laying down his commiſſion at leaſt:
For, 'twere as infamous to ſerve you now, as 'twould
have once been. glorious.

Clar. 'Tis falſe! you never thought ſo——The man
that really loves, wou'd not dare to ſee the faults you
tax me with; much leſs with ſuch malicious inſolence
to tell me of 'em.

Cler. Come! Come! you know I lov'd you to a folly, or you had never dar'd to uſe me thus.

Clar. The man that ſcorns to ſtand a woman's idle
trial of his temper, gives better proofs of diſcerning
malice, than his paſſion.

Cler. He that fears to upbraid a woman for abandon'd liberties, like yours, may by his ſilence (whatever her pretence is) encourage her to make a real uſe
of 'em.   D 3

Cler. A Good-nature would at leaft impute the fault rather to want of judgment, than of virtue: But I am glad I am fo early warn'd againft your temper; had I never try'd it, my trufting it too far, as once my folly thought to do, might have made me miferable for ever.

Cler. How fubtilly that foft thought melts down my anger! I dare not look on her.   [*Afide.*

Enter Wifhwell.

Wifh. Madam, Sir *Solomon* defires to fpeak with you, he has juft received a letter out of *Yorkfhire* from the gentleman's father, that is propos'd to marry you.

Clar. Coming.   [*Exit* Wifh.

Cler. You muft not, fhall not————cannot ftir on this occafion.

Clar. I'll go, by all the injuries I have borne from you—I'll do at leaft a juftice to my fame, and wed the groffeft fool alive, rather than not revenge me on the fancy jealoufy that durft attaint it.

Cler. Hear me but one word.

Clar. Never, but for your greater torment know— You've loft a heart that wounds itfelf for you.   [*Exit.*

Cler. O cruel kindnefs! why fo late confefs'd? What wou'd not this fecret told in gentler terms have wrought me to! But 'tis the fex's nature to be vainly cruel.

Thefe kind Thoughts own'd in fpite, too plainly prove,
Revenge with them has fweeter charms than love.

[Exit.

ACT V. SCENE I.

The SCENE *continues.*

Enter Clerimont *and* Carelefs.

Cler. AND fo you took the opportunity of her fainting, to carry her off: Pray how long did her fit laft?

Care. Why, faith, I fo humour'd her affectation, that 'tis hardly over yet; for I told her, her life was in danger, and fwore, if fhe wou'd not let me fend for a Parfon to marry her, before fhe died, I'd that minute fend for a fhroud, and be buried alive with her in the fame coffin: But, at the apprehenfion of fo terrible a thought, fhe pretended to be frightened into her right fenfes again; and forbid me her fight for ever——fo that in fhort, my impudence is almoft exhaufted, her affectation is as unfurmountable as another's real virtue, and I muft e'en catch her that way, or die without her at laft.

Cler. How do you mean?

Care. Why, if I find I can't impofe upon her by humility, which I'll try, I'll e'en turn rival to myfelf in a very fantaftical figure, that I'm fure fhe won't be able to refift, &c. You muft know fhe has of late been flatter'd that the *Mufcovite* Prince *Alexander* is dying for her, though he never fpoke to her in his life.

Cler. I underftand you: fo you'd firft venture to pique her againft you, and then let her marry you in another perfon, to be reveng'd of you.

Care. One of the two ways, I am pretty fure to fucceed.

Cler. Extravagant enough! Pr'ythee, is Sir *Solomon* in the next room?

Care. What, you want his affiftance? *Clarinda*'s in her airs again!

Cler. Faith, *Carele/s,* I am almoſt aſhamed to tell you, but I muſt needs ſpeak with him.

Care. Come along then.   [*Exeunt.*

Enter Supple, *and Captain* Strutt.

Sup. If you pleaſe to walk in, Sir, my Maſter will wait upon you preſently————Here he is—

Enter Sir Solomon.

Capt. Your ſervant, Sir.

Sir *Sol.* Oh! yours, Sir. Have you any commands for me?

Capt. Sir, I hear you are a man of honour, and un-derſtand a ſword.

Sir *Sol.* Sir, I know a little of the law, and I believe that's as well.

Capt. But men of honour are above law, Sir, and I have been once with you before, Sir; and I come now to tell you, once for all, that if I don't marry your niece, you muſt meet me behind *Montagu Houſe.*

Sir *Sol.* Meet you! for what, Sir?

Capt. With your ſword in hand, Sir.

Sir *Sol.* By gingo, captain, but I won't——I don't like your company ſo well.

Capt. Then, Sir, I'll poſt you for a coward.

Sir *Sol.* Then, Sir, you'll poſt yourſelf for a mad-man——.For I'm a citizen of *London,* have fined for alderman, and will fight with ne'er a beggarly rake of you all.

Capt. Then, I muſt tell you, Sir, you are a pitiful putt, and have neither honour nor courage.

Sir *Sol.* And I muſt tell you, Sir, I have both; for I pay my debts, and fear no bailiff alive, Sir————which I believe, is more than you can ſay, moſt terrible captain.

Capt. Look you, Sir, I'll ſpoil her fortune, I'll fol-lew her to the church, and the play-houſe; I'll knock every man down that looks at her, and cut every cox-comb's throat that pretends to her.

Sir *Sol.* Sir, if you talk at this rate to me, I'll ſwear

the peace againſt you, and bind you to a ſtrange com-
panion, your good behaviour.

Enter Clerimont.

Cler. What's the matter, Sir *Solomon?*

Sir·*Sol.* Why, here's an impertinent beggarly fellow,
ſwears he'll have my niece, or cut my throat.

Cler. How, Sir !

Capt. Sir, I'm in love with his niece, among the reſt
of the great fortunes of the town : Sir, I have followed
her at a diſtance theſe twelve months, and have ſpent an
hundred pounds after her in fair perriwigs, red ſtockings,
and ſword knots.

Cler. Did you ever ſpeak to her, Sir ?

Capt. No, Sir, but I have done all that's neceſſary,
or uſual with ſoldiers. I have toaſted her, bow'd to her,
walk'd with my arms acroſs, and ogled her.

Cler. [*Looking nearly on him*] Hum ! is not your name
Strutt ?

Capt. Ay, Sir, Capt. *Strutt,* and as good a family—

Cler. As ever was kick'd, Sirrah ! Was not you my
father's footman at the revolution ? I'll cool your love,
Mr. Dog.   [*Kicks him.*

Sir *Sol.* By Gingo, Captain, I did not know you
would take a beating——There——now, ha'n't I courage, Captain ?

Capt. Sir, as I was your father's footman, I take
theſe blows ; but as a I am a Captain of the militia——

Cler. You'll take 'em better, I know—[*Kicks him again.*

Capt. Blood ! Sir——don't think, Sir,——damme,
Sir, I ſhall expeſt ſatisfaſtion.   [*Exit.*

Sir *Sol.* O dear Mr. *Clerimont,* I'm perſuaded he'll
fight yet.

Cler. Never apprehend it, Sir. I vow I did not know
the rogue, he was ſo alter'd.

Sir *Sol.* Really, Sir, my niece and I are extreamly
oblig'd to you for this : and to ſhew you I'm in earneſt,
if you like the conditions I told you of, ſhe's your's.

Cler. That indeed was my buſineſs to you now, Sir,
and if you pleaſe——

D 5

Sir *Sol.* Here's company, come into the next room.
[*Exeunt.*

Enter Lady Dainty, *Lady* Sadlife *and* Carelefs.

Lady *D.* This rude boifterous man has given me a thoufand diforders; the cholick, the fpleen, the palpitation of the heart, and convulfions all over—huh! huh! —I muft fend for the doctor.

Lady *Sad.* Come, come, madam, e'en pardon him, and let him be your phyfician—do but obferve his penitence fo humble he dares not fpeak to you.

Care. [*Folds his arms and fighs.*] Oh!

Lady *Sad.* How can you hear him figh fo?

Lady *D.* Nay let him groan—for nothing but his pangs can eafe me.

Care. [*Kneels and prefents her his drawn Sword; opening his breaft.*] Be then at once moft barbaroufly juft, and take your vengeance here.

Lady *D.* No, I give thee life to make thee miferable; live, that my refenting eyes may kill thee every hour.

Care. Nay then, there's no relief but—this—
[*Offering at his fword, Lady* Sadlife *holds him.*
Lady *Sad.* Ah! for mercy's fake—barbarous creature, how can you fee him thus?

Lady *D.* Why, I did not bid him kill himfelf: but do you really think he wou'd ha' don't?

Lady *Sad.* Certainly, if I had not prevented it.

Lady *D.* Strange paffion! but 'tis its nature to be violent, when one makes it defpair.

Lady *Sad.* Won't you fpeak to him?

Lady *D.* No, but if your—is enough concern'd to be his friend, you may tell him—not that it really is fo— but you may fay—you believe I pity him.

Lady *Sad.* Sure love was never more ridiculous on both fides.

Enter Wifhwell.

Wifh. Madam, here's a page from Prince *Alexander,* defires to give a letter into your ladyfhip's own hands.

Lady *D.* Prince *Alexander!* what means my heart? I come to him.

Lady *Sad.* By no means, madam, pray let him come in

Care. Ha! Prince *Alexander!* nay, then I have found out the secret of this coldness, madam.

Enter Page.

Page. Madam, his Royal Highness Prince *Alexander,* my master, has commanded me on pain of death, thus [*kneeling*] to deliver this, the burning secret of his heart.

Lady D. O grace of grandeur! happy, happy, climate! where such respect, and high distinctions are familiar.

Reads.

" *Most Divine Lady,*

   " *THE fiery fate that's darted from the Cannon's*
" *mouth, is not so sure or sudden, as the subtile lightning*
" *of your refulgent eyes :* (Enchanting) *like death, you level*
" *Princes with the peasant :* (Irresistible) *I beg the imme-*
" *diate ease, and honour of kissing your fair hands in person,*
" *that I may silence at once all saucy rivals hopes, and own*
" *the passion of a Prince, whose wounds are only worthy the*
" *relief of such immortal beauty.*

Transcendent glory! this is indeed a conquest, worthy my sex's highest pride!

Care. So! she bites rarely.

Lady *Sad.* She'll swallow all, ne'er doubt it. [*Aside.*

Lady *D.* Where is the Prince ?

Page. Repos'd in private on a mourning pallat, 'till your commands vouchsafe to raise him.

Lady *Sad.* By all means receive him here immediately, I have the honour to be a little known to his Highness.

Lady *D.* The favour, Madam, is too great to be re-sisted : Pray tell his Highness then, the honour of the visit he designs me, makes me thankful, and impatient! huh! huh!   [*Exit* Page.

Care. Are my sufferings, madam, so soon forgot then! was I but flatter'd with the hope of pity ?

Lady *D.* The happy have whole days, and those they choose. [*resenting.*] The unhappy have but hours, and those they lose.   [*Exit repeating.*

 Lady *Sad.* Don't you lose a minute then.

D 6

Care. I'll warrant you—ten thoufand thanks, dear madam, I'll be transform'd in a fecond—

[*Exeunt feverally.*

Enter Clarinda *in Man's Habit.*

Clar. So! I'm in for't now! how I fhall come off, I can't tell : 'twas but a bare faving game I made with *Clerimont* ; his refentment had brought my pride to its laft legs, diffembling : And if the poor man had not lov'd me too well, I had made but a difmal humble figure———I have us'd him ill, that's certain, and he may e'en thank himfelf for't—he would be fincere, and I faw I was fure of him—which was more than I cou'd fay by my double-fac'd Colonel, whom confequently I was in fear of lofing : Befide, I cou'd not bear to let another drefs up her vanity in any lover of mine, tho' I did not defign to wear him myfelf—Well, (begging my fex's pardon) we do make the fillieft tyrants—we had better be reafonable ; for to do 'em right) we don't run half the hazard in obeying the good fenfe of a lover ; at leaft, I'm reduc'd now to make the experiment—Here they come.

Enter Sir Solomon *and* Clerimont.

Sir *Sol.* What have we here ! another captain ? if I were fure he were a coward now, I'd kick him before he fpeaks—Is your bufinefs with me, Sir ?

Clar. If your name be Sir *Solomon Sadlife.*

Sir *Sol.* Yes, Sir, it is, and I'll maintain it, as antient as any, and related to moft of the families in *England.*

Clar. My bufinefs will convince you, Sir, that I think well of it.

Sir *Sol.* And what is your bufinefs, Sir ?

Clar. Why, Sir—you have a pretty kinfwoman call'd *Clarinda.*

Cler. Ha !

Sir *Sol.* And what then, Sir——fuch a Rogue as t'other.   [*Afide.*

Clar. Now, Sir, I have feen her, and am in love with her.

Cler. Say you fo, Sir!—I may chance to cure you of it.   [*Aside.*

Clar. And to back my pretenfions, Sir, I have a good fifteen hundred pounds a year eftate, and am, as you fee, a pretty fellow into the bargain.

Sir Sol. She that marries you, Sir, will have a choice bargain indeed.

Clar. In fhort, Sir, I'll give you a thoufand guineas to make up the match.

Sir Sol. Hum—[*Aside.*] But, Sir, my niece is provided for.

Cler. That's well.   [*Aside.*

Sir Sol. But if fhe were not, Sir, I muft tell you, fhe is not to be caught with a fmock face and a feather, Sir ——and——and——let me fee you an hour hence. [*Aside.*

Clar. Well faid, Uncle. [*Aside.*]—But, Sir, I'm in love with her, and pofitively will have her.

Sir Sol. Whether fhe likes you or no, Sir?

Clar, Like me! ha! ha! I'd feign fee a woman that diflikes a pretty fellow with fifteen hundred pounds a year, a white wig, and black eye-brows.

Cler. Hark you, young gentleman, there muft go more than all this, to the gaining of that lady.

[*Takes* Clarinda *afide.*

Sir Sol. [*Aside*]. A thoufand guineas! that's five hundred more than I propos'd to get of Mr. *Clerimont*—but my honour is engag'd—ay, but then here's a thoufand pounds to releafe it—now fhall I take the money, it muft be fo—coin will carry it.

Clar. Oh, Sir, if that be all, I'll foon remove your doubts and pretenfions——Come, Sir, I'll try your courage.

Cler. I am afraid you won't, young gentleman.

Clar. As young as I am, Sir, you fhall find I fcorn to turn my back to any man——   [*Exeunt* Clar. *and* Cler.

Sir Sol. Ha! they are gone to fight—with all my heart—a fair chance at leaft for a better bargain: For if the young fpark fhou'd let the air into my friend *Clerimont*'s midriff now, it may poffibly cool his love too, and then there's my honour fafe, and a thoufand guineas   [*Exit.*

Enter Lady Dainty, *and Lady* Sadlife.

Lady *D.* Don't you think the Prince long ? But great perſons are diſtinguiſh'd by a peculiar ſlowneſs in their motion.

Lady *Sad.* Now am I ſurpris'd at your curioſity : For I'm confident you won't like him when you ſee him.

Lady *D.* I have ſeen him *en paſſant* from my window, and if the diſtance did not deceive me, I thought there was ſomething ſo agreeably *bizarre* in his appearance.

Lady *Sad.* Extremely *bizarre* indeed, for he has a fierce tawny face, and odious whiſkers.

Lady *D.* Which in ſome countries are allow'd the moſt diſtinguiſhing marks of beauty.

Lady *Sad.* But your ladyſhip, I know, allows no beauty, without a certain delicacy and tenderneſs of perſon.

Lady *D.* Um—that's partly true; but the idea I have conceiv'd of the Prince's figure, has in ſome meaſure—remov'd that ſickly weakneſs of my taſte.

Lady *Sad.* I am glad to find your ladyſhip a little reconcil'd to the uſeful beauties of a lover—but here comes the Prince.

Enter Careleſs *as Prince* Alexander.

Lady *D.* Your highneſs, Sir, has done me honour in this viſit

Care. Madam—   [*Salutes her.*
Lady *D.* A captivating perſon !

Care. May the days be taken from my life, and added to yours !—moſt incomparable beauty ! whiter than the ſnow, that lies the year about unmelted on our *Ruſſian* mountains.

Lady *D.* How manly his expreſſions are—we are extremely oblig'd to the *Czar* for not taking your highneſs home with him.

Care. He left me, madam, to learn to be a Ship-Carpenter.

Lady *Sad.* A very politic accompliſhment !

Lady *D.* And in a prince entirely new.

Care. All his nobles, Madam, are masters of some useful science, and most of our arms are quarter'd with mechanical instruments, as hatchets, hammers, pickaxes, and hand-saws.

Lady *D.* I admire the manly manners of your court.

Lady *Sad.* Oh! so infinitely beyond the soft idleness of ours.

Care. 'Tis the fashion, ladies, for the eastern princes to profess some trade or other——The last Grand Seignior was a locksmith——

Lady *D.* How new his conversation is?

Care. Too rude I fear, madam, for so tender a composition as your divine ladyship's

Lady *D.* Courtly to a softness too!

Care. Were it possible, Madam, that so much delicacy cou'd endure the martial roughness of our manners and our country, I cannot boast; but if a province at your feet cou'd make you mine, that province and its master shou'd be yours.

Lady *D.* Ay! here's grandeur with address; an odious native lover now, wou'd have complain'd of the taxes perhaps, and have haggled with one for a scanty jointure out of his horrid lead-mines, in some uninhabitable mountains, about an hundred and fourscore miles from unheard of *London.*

Care. I am inform'd, Madam, there is a certain poor distracted *English* fellow, that refus'd to quit his saucy pretensions to your all-conquering beauty, tho' he had heard I had myself resolv'd to adore you. *Careless*, I think, they call him.

Lady *D.* Your highness wrongs your merit, to give yourself the least concern for one so much below your fear.

Care. When I first heard of him, I on the instant order'd one of my retinue to strike off his head with a scimitar; but they told me the free laws of *England* allow'd of no such power: so that, tho' I am a prince of the blood, Madam, I am oblig'd only to murder him privately.

Lady *D.* 'Tis indeed a reproach to the ill-breeding of our constitution, not to admit your power with your person. But if the pain of my entire neglect can end him, pray be easy.

Care. Madam, I'm not revengful; make him but miferable——I'm fatisfy'd.

Lady *D.* you may depend upon't.

Care. I'm in ftrange favour with her ——— [*Afide.*
Pleafe you, ladies, to make your fragrant fingers familiar
with this box.

Lady *D.* Sweet or plain, Sir?

Care. Right *Mofco*, Madam, made of the fculls of
conquer'd enemies.

Lady *Sad.* Gunpowder, as I live?

Lady *D.* Every thing manly.

Lady *Sad.* Will your highnefs pleafe to amufe yourfelf
with a difh of tea.

Care. Excufe me, Madam, 'tis a liquor I never heard
of, and in my own country I am fam'd for regularity in
my diet; even after a meal I never exceed a gentle pint
glafs of burnt Brandy or Geneva.

        [*A noife of dogs barking without.*

Lady *D.* Ah! what noife is that?

Care. Your pardon, Madam; only a harmlefs entertainment after my own country fafhion, that I defign'd
myfelf the honour of prefenting your incomparable ladyfhip.

Lady *Sad.* I hope he'll bring in the bears upon her.

        [*Afide.*

Lady *D.* Pray, Sir, what is it?

Care. Madam, a fet of *Ruffian* ladies lap-dogs, that
dance to admiration.

Lady *D.* By all means admit 'em——I'm taken with
the humour. We have had fomething like 'em here in
England, Sir; and all people of fafhion grew ftrangely
fond of 'em.

Care. They cou'd not be *Englifh* then——I have feen
all your *Englifh* dancing——Madam, but I obferv'd
that's generally perform'd——by——fad dogs——pleafe
you fit, ladies.

A Dance to an odd Tune, imitating Mr. Pinkethman's
famous dancing Dogs.

Lady *D.* Infinitely new, and humourous——but this
room's exceeding hot———I'm fainting.

Care. Let this arm fupport you, Madam.

Lady *Sad.* The next is cooler; if your highnefs pleafes we'll withdraw.

Care. Madam, I am but the needle to this northern ftar: I wait on you.   *[Exeunt.*

The S C E N E *changes to the Field.*

Enter Clarinda *and* Clerimont.

Cler. Come, Sir, we are fair enough.

Clar. I only wifh the lady were by, Sir, that the conqueror might carry her off the fpot: I warrant fhe'd be mine.

Cler. That, my talking hero, we fhall foon determine.

Clar. Not that I think her handfome, or care a rufh for her.

Cler. You are very mettled, Sir, to fight for a woman you don't value!

Clar. Sir, I value the reputation of a gentleman, and I don't think any young fellow ought to pretend to it till he has talk'd himfelf into a lampoon, loft his two or three thoufand pounds at play, kept his mifs, and kill'd his man.

Cler. Very gallant indeed, Sir; but if you pleafe to handle your fword, you'll foon go through your courfe.

Clar. Come on, Sir——I believe I fhall give your miftrefs a truer account of your heart than you have done. I have had her heart long enough, and now will have your's.

Cler. Ha! does fhe love you then?

[Endeavouring to draw.

Clar. I leave you to judge that, Sir. But I have lain with her a thoufand times; in fhort, fo long, till I'm tir'd of it.

Cler. Villain, thou lyeft! draw, or I'll ufe you as you deferve, and ftab you.

Clar. Take this with you firft——*Clarinda* will never marry him that murders me.

Cler. She may the man that vindicates her honour—— therefore be quick, or I'll keep my word——I find your fword is not for doing things in hafte.

Clar. It flicks to the scabbard fo; I believe I did not wipe off the blood of the laft man I fought with.

Cler. Come, Sir! this trifling fhan't ferve your turn; here give me yours, and take mine.

Clar. With all my heart, Sir——Now have at you.

Cler. Death! you villain, do you ferve me fo!

[Cler. *draws, and finds only a hilt in his hand.*

Clar. In love and war, Sir, all advantages are fair; fo we conquer, no matter whether by force or ftratagem: come quick, Sir! your life or miftrefs——

Cler. Neither——————Death! you fhall have both or none: here drive your fword; for only through this heart you reach *Clarinda.*

Clar. Death! Sir, can you be mad enough to die for a woman that hates you?

Cler. If that were true, 'twere greater madnefs than to live.

Clar. Why to my knowledge, Sir, fhe has us'd you bafely, falfly, ill, and for no reafon.

Cler. No matter, no ufage can be worfe than the contempt of poorly, tamely, parting with her——She may abufe her heart by happy infidelities; but 'tis the pride of mine to be even miferably conftant.

Clar. Generous paffion—You almoft tempt me to refign her to you.

Cler. You cannot, if you wou'd—I wou'd indeed have won her fairly from you with my fword, but fcorn to take her as your gift. Be quick, and end your infolence——

Clar. Yes, thus—moft generous *Clerimont*—you now indeed have fairly vanquifh'd me. [*Runs to him.*] My woman's follies and my fhame be buried ever heie.

Cler. Ha! *Clarinda!* is't poffible! my wonder rifes with my joy—How came you in this habit?

Clar. Now you indeed recall my blufhes, but I had no other veil to hide 'em, while I confefs'd the injuries I had done your heart, in fooling with a man I never meant on any terms to engage with. Befide, I knew from our late parting, your fear of lofing me wou'd reduce you to comply with Sir *Solomon*'s demands, for his intereft in your favour: therefore, as you faw, I was refolv'd to ruin his

market by feeming to raife it; for he fecretly took the
offer I made him.

Cler. 'Twas generoufly and timely offer'd, for it really
prevented my figning articles to him ; but if you wou'd
heartily convince me that I fhall never more have need
of his intereft, e'en let us fteal to the next prieft, and honeftly put it out of his power ever to part us.

Clar. Why, truely confidering the trufts I have made
you, 'twou'd be ridiculous now, I think, to deny you
any thing——and if you fhould grow weary of me after
fuch ufage, I can't blame you.

Cler. Banifh that fear; my flame can never wafte,
For love fincere refines upon the tafte.   [*Exeunt,*

Enter Sir Solomon, *with old Mr.* Willful : *Lady* Sadlife,
and Sylvia *weeping.*

Sir *Sol.* Troth, my old friend, this is a bad bufinefs
indeed; you have bound yourfelf in a thoufand pound
bond, you fay, to marry your daughter to a fine gentleman, and fhe in the mean time, it feems, is fallen in
love with a ftranger.

Will. Look you, Sir *Solomon,* it does not trouble me
o'this : for I'll make her do as I pleafe, or I'll ftarve her.

Lady *Sad.* But, Sir, your daughter tells me that the
gentleman fhe loves is in every degree in as good circumftances as the perfon you defign her for: and if he does
not prove himfelf fo before to-morrow morning, fhe will
chearfully fubmit to whatever you'll impofe on her.

Will. All fham! all fham ! only to gain time——I
expect my friend and his fon here immediately, to demand performance of articles; and if her ladyfhip's nice
ftomach does not immediately comply with 'em, as I told
you before, I'll ftarve her.

Lady *Sad.* But confider, Sir, what a perpetual difcord
muft a forc'd marriage probably produce.

Will. Difcord! pfhaw! waw ! one man makes as good
a hufband as another——A month's marriage will fet all
to rights, I warrant you—You know the old faying Sir
Solomon, lying together makes pigs love. Difcord, quotha!
No! no! Young women are like fiddles, if they are well

play'd upon, they muſt make good muſic whether they will or no.

Lady *Sad*. [*To* Sylvia] What ſhall we do for you? there's no altering him——Did not your lover promiſe to come to your aſſiſtance?

Syl. I expect him every minute—but can't foreſee from him the leaſt hope of my redemption——This is he!

Enter Atall *undiſguis'd.*

At. My *Sylvia!* dry thoſe tender eyes, for while there's life there's hope.

Lady *Sad*. Ha! is't he? but I muſt ſmother my confuſion!

Will. How, now, Sir! pray who gave you commiſſion to be ſo familiar with my daughter?

At. Your pardon, Sir; but when you know me right, you'll neither think my freedom or my pretenſions familiar or diſhonourable.

Will. Why, Sir, what pretenſions have you to her?

At. Sir, I ſav'd her life at the hazard of my own: that gave me a pretence to know her; knowing her, made me love, and gratitude made her receive it.

Will. Ay, Sir, and ſome very good reaſons, beſt known to myſelf, make me refuſe it—Now what will you do?

At. I can't tell yet, Sir—But if you'll do me the favour to let me know thoſe reaſons——

Will. Sir, I don't think myſelf oblig'd to do either; but I'll tell you what I'll do for you, ſince you ſay you love my daughter, and ſhe loves you, I'll put you in the neareſt way to get her.

At. Don't flatter me! I beg you, Sir.

Will. Not I, upon my ſoul, Sir, for look you—'tis only this—get my conſent, and you ſhall have her.

At. I beg your pardon, Sir, for endeavouring to talk reaſon to you. But to return your raillery, give me leave to tell you, when any man marries her but myſelf, he muſt extremely aſk my conſent.

Will. Before *George*, thou art a very pretty impudent fellow, and I'm ſorry I can't puniſh her diſobedience by throwing her away upon thee.

At. You'll have a great deal of plague about this bufinefs, Sir; for I fhall be mighty difficult to give up my
pretenfions to her.

Will. Ha! 'tis a thoufand pities I can't comply with
thee: thou wilt certainly be a thriving fellow; for thou
doft really fet the beft face upon a bad caufe that ever I
faw fince I was born.

At. Come Sir—once more raillery apart; fuppofe I
prove myfelf of equal birth and fortune to deferve her?

Will. Sir, if you were eldeft fon to the *Cham* of *Tar-
tary*, or had the dominions of the *Great Mogul* entail'd
upon you and your heirs for ever; it wou'd fignify no
more than the bite of my thumb—The girl's difpos'd of,
I have match'd her already upon a thoufand pound forfeit, and faith fhe fhall fairly run for't, though fhe's
yerk'd and flea'd from the creft to the crupper.

At. Confufion!

Syl. What will become of me?

Will. And if you don't think me in earneft now, here
comes one that will convince you of my fincerity.

At. My father! Nay then my ruin is inevitable.

Enter Sir Harry Atall.

Sir *Har.* [*To* At.] O fweet Sir, have I found you at
laft! Your very humble fervant: what's the reafon pray,
that you have had the affurance to be almoft a fortnight
in town, and never come near me; efpecially when I fent
you word I had bufinefs of fuch confequence with you.

At. I underftood your bufinefs was to marry me, Sir,
to a woman I never faw; and to confefs the truth, I durft
not come near you, becaufe I was at the fame time in
love with one you never faw.

Sir *Har.* Was you fo, Sir—why then, Sir, I'll find a
fpeedy cure for your paffion—Brother *Wilful*—Hey,
Fiddles there!

At. You may treat me, Sir, with what feverity you
pleafe; but my engagements to that lady are too powerful and fix'd, to let the utmoft mifery diffolve 'em.

Sir *Har.* What does the fool mean?

At. That I can fooner die than part with her.

Will. Hey !—why, is this your fon, Sir *Harry ?*

Sir *Har.* Hey-dey ! why, did not you know that be-fore ?

At. O Earth ! and all you ftars ! is this the lady you defign'd me, Sir ?

Syl. O fortune ! is it poffible ?

Sir *Har.* And is this the lady, Sir, you have been making fuch a buftle about ?

At. Not life, health or happinefs are half fo dear to me.

Sir *Sol.* [*Joining* At. *and* Sylvia's *hands.*—] loll ! loll, leroll !

At. O tranfporting joy ! [*Embracing* Sylvia.]

Sir *Har.* ⎰   [*Joining in the tune, and danc ing about*
and *Will.* ⎱   *'em*] loll ! loll !

Sir *Sol.* Hey ! within there ! [*Calls the fiddles*] by jingo we'll make a night on't.

Enter Clarinda *and* Clerimont.

Clar. Save you, fave you, good people ! I'm glad uncle, to hear you call fo chearfully for the fiddles, it looks as if you had a hufband ready for me.

Sir *Sol.* Why, that I may have by to-morrow night, madam ; but in the mean time, if you pleafe, you may wifh your friends joy.

Clar. Dear *Sylvia !*

Syl. Clarinda.

At. O *Clerimont,* fuch a deliverance

Cler. Give you joy, joy, Sir.

Clar. I congratulate your happinefs—and am pleas'd our little jealoufies are over : Mr. *Clerimont* has told me all, and cur'd me of curiofity for ever.

Syl. What married ?

Clar. You'll fee prefently ! but Sir *Solomon,* what do you mean by to-morrow ! why do you fancy I have any more patience than the reft of my neighbours ?

Sir *Sol.* Why truly, madam, I don't fuppofe you have; but I believe to-morrow will be as foon as their bufinefs can be done, by which time I expect a jolly fox-hunter

from *Yorkſhire,* and if you are reſolv'd not to have patience till next day, why the ſame Parſon may toſs you
up all four in a diſh together.

Clar. A filthy fox-hunter ?

Sir *Sol.* Odzooks ! a mettled fellow, that will ride
you from day-break to ſun-ſet ! none of our flimſy *London* raſcals, that muſt have a chair to carry 'em to their
coach, and a coach to carry 'em to a trapes, and a con-
ſtable to carry both to the round-houſe.

Clar. Ay, but this fox-hunter, Sir *Solomon,* will come
home dirty and tir'd as one of his Hounds, he'll be always
aſleep before he's a-bed, and on horſeback before he's
awake ; he muſt riſe early to follow his ſport, and I ſit
up late at cards for want of better diverſion—put this
together my wiſe uncle.

Sir *Sol.* Are you ſo high fed, madam, that a country
gentleman of fifteen hundred pounds a year won't go
down with you.

Clar. Not ſo, Sir, but you really kept me ſo ſharp, that
I was e'en forc'd to provide for myſelf, and here ſtands
the fox-hunter for my money

[*Claps* Cler. *on the ſhoulder.*

Sir *Sol.* How !

Cler. Even ſo, Sir *Solomon*—hark in your ear, Sir ! you
really held your conſent at ſo high a price, that to give
you a proof of my good huſbandry, I was reſolv'd to ſave
charges, and e'en marry her without it.

Sir *Sol.* Hell ! and—

Clar. And hark you in t'other ear, Sir—becauſe I
wou'd not have you expoſe your reverend age by a miſtake
—Know, Sir, I was the young ſpark with the ſmooth
face and a feather, that offer'd you a thouſand guineas
for your conſent, which you wou'd have been glad to
have taken.

Sir *Sol.* The devil ! if ever I traffick in women's fleſh
again, may all the bank-ſtocks fall when I have bought
'em, and riſe when I have ſold 'em.——Hey dey ! what
have we here ! more cheats !

Cler. Not unlikely, Sir——for I fancy they are married.

Enter Lady Dainty *and* Carelefs.

Lady *Sad.* That they are, I can affure you—I give your highnefs joy, madam.

Lady *D.* Lard! that people of any rank fhou'd ufe fuch vulgar falutations—Tho' methink highnefs has fomething of grandeur in the found.

Enter Servant.

Serv. Sir, the mufic's come.

Lady *Sad.* Let 'em play.

Lady *D.* Well! there's nothing fhews fo vifibly the remaining footfteps of our primitive barbarity, as our odious noife at weddings! huh! huh!

Care. It ferves, madam, to recommend the pleafures that fucceed, and makes us tafte the joys of filence with a higher relifh.

Lady *D.* But fo much dancing and tumult, is fo like the mob folemnities of a *May*-day——huh! huh! and the poor bride is us'd juft like their pole, for all the town to dance round her.

Lady *Sad.* Ah! but there's yet a groffer part of the ceremony to come, madam, and that is throwing the ftocking.

Lady *D.* That indeed is a thing that infults us fo near, that I wonder the men have not thought it their intereft to lay it down——But I was in hopes, good people, that confident fellow *Carelefs* had been among you.

Care. What fay you, madam, (to divert the good company) fhall we fend for him by way of mortification?

Lady *D.* By all means; for your fake, methinks, I ought to give him full defpair.

Care. Why then, to let you fee, that 'tis a much eafier

thing to cure a fine lady of her fickly tafte, than a lover of his impudence————There's *Carelefs* for you, without the leaft tincture of defpair about him.

[*Difcovers himfelf.*

All. Ha! *Carelefs!*

Lady *D.* Abus'd! undone!

All. Ha! ha!

Cler. Nay, now, madam, we wifh you a fuperior joy; for you have married a man, inftead of a mon-fter.

Care. Come! come, madam, fince you find you were in the power of fuch a cheat—you may be glad it was no greater, you might have fallen into a rafcal's hands: but you know, I am a gentleman, my fortune no fmall one, and if your temper will give me leave, will deferve you.

Lady *Sad.* Come! e'en make the beft of your fortune : for take my word, if the cheat had not been a very agreeable one, I wou'd never have had a hand in't—you muft pardon me if I can't help laugh-ing.

Lady *D.* Well! fince it muft be fo, I pardon all ; only one thing let me beg of you, Sir—that is your promife to wear this habit one month for my fatis-faction.

Care. O, madam! that's a trifle! I'll lie in the fun a whole fummer for an olive complexion, to oblige you.

Will. Odzooks, here's a great deal of good company, ho! and 'tis a fhame the fiddles fhould be idle all this while.

Care. Oh! by no means! come ftrike up, gentle-men.

They Dance.

Lady *D.* Well! Mr. *Carelefs,* I begin now to think bet-ter of my fortune, and look back with apprehenfion of the efcape I have had; you have already cur'd my folly, and were but my health recoverable, I should think my-self completely happy.

Care. For that, madam, we'll venture to save you doctor's fees,

And trust to Nature: Time will soon discover,
Your best Physician is a favour'd Lover.

Exeunt.

EPILOGUE.

WELL, Sirs, I know not how the play may pass,
    But in my humble fenfe—our Bard's an afs;
For, had he ever known the leaft of nature,
H'had found his Double Spark *a difmal creature:*
To pleafe two ladies, he two forms puts on,
As if the thing in fhadows cou'd be done :
The women really two, and he, poor foul! but one.
Had he revers'd the hint, h' had done the feat,
Had made th' impoftor credibly compleat ;
A fingle miftrefs——might have ftood the cheat.
She might to feveral lovers have been kind,
Nor ftrain'd your faith, to think both pleas'd and blind.
Plain fenfe had known, the fair can love receive,
With half the pains your warmeft vows can give.

    But, hold!——I'm thinking I miftake the matter ;
On fecond thoughts :——The hint's but honeft fatire ;
And only meant t'expofe their modifh fenfe,
Who think the fire of love's——but impudence.
Our fpark was really modeft ;——when he found
Two female claims at once, he one difown'd ;
Wifely prefuming, tho' in ne'er fuch hafte,
One wou'd be found enough for him at laft.
So that to fum the whole—I think the play
Deferves the ufual favours on his day ;
If not he fwears he'll write the next to mufick,
In Doggrel *rhymes wou'd make or him, or you, fick.*
His groveling fenfe, Italian *air fhall crown,*
And then, he's fure, ev'n nonfenfe will go down.
But, if you'd have the world fuppofe the ftage
Not quite forfaken in this airy age,
Let your glad Votes our needlefs fear confound,
And fpeak in claps as loud for fenfe, as found.

XXXXXXXXXXXXXXXXXXXXXXXXXXXXXXXXX

X I M E N A:

OR, THE

HEROICK DAUGHTER.

A

TRAGEDY.

—————————*Face nuptiali*
Digna, & in omne Virgo
Nobilis Ævum.   .HOR.

XXXXXXXXXXXXXXXXXXXXXXXXXXXXXXXXX

E 3

XIMENA:

OR THE

HEROICK DAUGHTER.

A

TRAGEDY.

Dublin, ...

To the READER.

THE *Cid* of *Monsieur Corneille* (from whence the following scenes are drawn) has made such an *eclat* on all the theatres of *Europe*, that were I to be wholly silent on the side of the *Heroick Daughter*, the great liberties I have taken in altering the conduct of his fable, might be more imputed to a vain opinion of my own judgment, than any foundations in reason, or nature: but I hope I shall stand upon better terms with the impartial, and the curious. I am not insensible what vast odds will be offer'd against me, while I am entering the lists with so fam'd an author, as *Corneille*: but that shall not discourage me: for I look upon truth in an argument, to be like courage in a combat, the best advantage a man can have over his antagonist; 'tis not his fame ought to fright me; for let mine be never so obscure, if I am in the right, his being in the wrong will be no more a wonder, than that a watchman's plain staff should foil the sword of a field-officer.

But I have a farther view, that while I am comparing the two plays, I may give the lovers of the *theatre* some insight into the merit, and difficulty of forming a good fable; and that even our common spectators, who find themselves unaccountably pleas'd with a pathetick scene, may be more pleas'd, by knowing they have reason to be so.

It may perhaps be expected, I should offer some excuse for not publishing this piece till seven years after its first appearance on the stage; and you will probably answer,

E 4

I had as good have said nothing about it, as to tell you it has been little better than idleness, or indifference: for it having done my business, when acted, I confess I wanted the modern appetite for fame, that authors usually think follows them into the country, after publication. But if I had any real cause to defer it, it was from an observation I had made that most of my plays (except the first, the *Fool in Fashion)* had a better reception from the publick, when my interest was no longer concern'd in them: I therefore supposed this might have a fairer chance for favour, when the author had no farther stake upon it: and I hope I may be allowed the honest vanity of this complaint, while I have (to my cost) so many facts to support it——Every auditor, whose memory will give him leave, cannot but know, that *Richard the Third,* which I altered from *Shakespear,* did not raise me five pounds on the third day, though for several years since, it has seldom or never fail'd of a crowded audience— The *Fop's Fortune* lagg'd on the fourth day, and only held up its head by the heels of the *French Tumblers,* who it seems had so much wit in their limbs, that they forced the town to see it, till it laugh'd itself into their good graces.—The *Kind Impostor* did not pay the charges on the sixth day, tho' it has since brought me, as a sharer, more than I was then disappointed of as author. 'Twas at first a moot point whether the *Careless Husband* should live or die; but the houses it has since filled have reproach'd the former coldness of its auditors—The *Wife's Resentment* is another, tho' not an equal, instance of the same nature.

But not to take the particularity of this treatment wholly to myself, I confess it has sometimes been the fate of the better authors: nor ought we so much to wonder at it, if we consider, that there is in human nature a certain low latent malice to all laudable undertakings, which never dares break out upon any thing, with so much licence, as on the fame of a dramatick writer: for even the lavish applause, that is usually heaped upon his first labours, is not perhaps so entirely owing to their real admiration of the work itself, as the mean pleasure they take in swelling him up to rival the reputation of others, that have writ well before him : if he succeeds in a first play, let him look well to the next, for then he is enter'd the herd, as a common enemy, and is to know that they, who gave him fame, can take it away; he is then to be allowed no more merit or mercy, than the rest of his brethren; of which nothing can be a stronger instance, than the torrent of applause, that was deservedly thrown in upon the *Old Bachelor*, and the boisterous cavils that the next year unreasonably over-run the same author's play of the *Double-Dealer :* and I am apt to believe that after the success of the *Funeral*, it was the same caprice that deserted the *Tender Husband :* and that all this is not mere conjecture only, I beg leave to relate a matter of fact, that perhaps will better incline you to my opinion. When the *Heroick Daughter* was first acted, I had the curiosity (not having then any part in it) sometimes to slip unseen into the side-boxes, where I met with the highest mixture of pleasure, and mortification: the pleasure was in observing the generality of the audience, in a silent, fix'd attention, never failing by their looks or gestures, to discover those pleasing emotions of the mind, which I was always confident would rise from so elevated a subject: the mortification was from a set of well-dress'd merry-making criticks, that call themselves the *Town*, whose private wit was continually insulting the publick diversion, by their waggish endeavours to burlesque every thing, that seem'd to have a serious effect on their neighbours; and treating the poor rogue the author (who stood with his hat over his eyes at their elbow) with the utmost insults, scandal, and malevolence: and when the play was over, some of the same persons, (which had like to have made me laugh) came and wish'd me joy of its success: but I have since seen frequent instances, that the same sort of auditors, with a little management, have been made as enterprizing friends to other authors, as they were then enemies to me: for with some leading men of the town, or celebrated wit at the head of them, they have been often known, by their over bearing manner of applause, to make a wretched sickly play stand ſtoutly upon its legs for ſix days together : but (as in mine, and moſt caſes) when they are not ſo engaged and marſhall'd, they naturally run riot into miſchief and cruelty. Upon the whole, till this accident convinc'd me, I never could believe, that to bring a play upon the ſtage, was ſo invidious a taſk ; and as it was with great reluctance, that I from hence reſolv'd never to trouble the town with another, ſo I found it neceſſary, (while I was a player at leaſt) not to put people of mere pleaſure and fortune in mind, that I durſt pretend to any talent that their footmen might not be equally maſters of : and if in breach of this reſolution, I have ſince attempted in the *Non-juror* to expoſe the enemies of our conſtitution, and liberties, it was becauſe I knew the friends of the government would ſecure me a fair hearing, and from all ſuch apprehenſions of being diſturbed, by the wanton malice of a few *Petits Maitres*; not but I flatter myſelf, that even its enemies will allow, I gave their principles fair play in the characters of Sir *John Woodville*, and *Charles*, who were no where ſhewn in a contemptible light; and I hope it was no great malice to make them amiable in their converſation—If therefore I have not juſtly accounted for the neglect, or diſcouragement, which moſt of my other plays met with at firſt ; I ſhall however beg leave of the world to comfort myſelf with ſuppoſing, that their preſent ſucceſs is now, one way or other, owing to their merit. But I have rambled too far from my firſt deſign, which was to give you

An EXAMEN of the *Cid*, and the *Heroick Daughter*.

THE great beauties of the *French* play, are in the tender compaſſion that riſes from the misfortunes of the two lovers *Rodrigue*, and *Chimene*; but ſhould we not be much more ſenſible of their diſtreſs, if before we ſaw them unfortunate, we were firſt rais'd to a proper admiration of their perſons and virtues ? They may indeed, as in the *Cid*, move us ſimply, as lovers; but as *ſuch* lovers, their ſorrows would certainly ſtrike deeper into the

hearts of an audience. In this point *Corneille* seems de-
fective: for he opens his play with a cold conversation
between *Chimene,* and her *Suivante,* whom *Chimene* desires
to repeat, what reason she had to suppose, the Count
her father was inclin'd to prefer her favour'd lover *Rodrigue* to his rival Don *Sanchez?* By the way she owns in
the same scene, she has heard all this before; but when
an author wants to acquaint his audience with a necessary
fact, nothing is so common, as to make some person in
the play improbably desirous to hear it over again; a
poor shift! we see thro' it, 'tis lazy——He could not
but know, that *Artis est celare Artem.* After *Chimene* is
inform'd, that her father has allow'd *Rodrigue* the person most worthy of her, she thinks the news too good to
be true, and is still, (tho' she can't very well tell why)
afraid it will come to nothing, and so quaintly walks off,
to as little purpose as she came on.

In all this scene, *Chimene* utters no one sentiment that
can possibly draw to her the least esteem from the audience; we only as yet see her a marriageable young woman, that is willing to have a husband—A poor setting
out for the heroine of a tragedy; the hero indeed is less
faultily manag'd, for he never appears till he enters at
once into his distress of being oblig'd to revenge the
blow, his father had just receiv'd, upon the father of his
mistress, who gave it. This incident is doubtless of uncommon beauty: but had we been better acquainted with
the merit, and dignity of his passion for the daughter of
his enemy, before his critical entrance on that occasion,
our imagination would have had a much higher alarm,
at the first sight of them; and this was palpably evident
from the different surprize his sudden appearance
gave in the *Heroick Daughter* at *London,* to what I observ'd it had in the same scene of the *Cid,* when acted
at *Paris.*

In the *English* play more care is taken to make the audience sure, the son brings with him the highest senti-
ments of courage, love and honour, that must make a
sensible heart tremble at the immediate distress, in which
his first appearance shews him involv'd.

The second scene in the *Cid*, breaks into the apartment of the Infanta, who is secretly in love with *Rodrigue*, but her honour combating with the inequality of his birth, she resolves to sacrifice her passion to her glory, and in order to it, uses her utmost endeavours to advance his marriage with her rival *Chimene:* there is something so romantick, so cold, and inactive in this episode, and so very little conducive to the main design, that I have left it quite out of the *Heroick Daughter*, and supply'd the vacancy with the character of *Belzara*, to whom I have given a more natural interest to advance the marriage of *Ximena*, which is to make Don *Sanchez* (whom *Belzara* is contracted to) despair of her. *Corneille* seems even in this scene too, to have lost a fair occasion of heightening the character of *Rodrigue*, and preparing the audience in his favour; but the Infanta, in no part of it, mentions the least motive to her passion for him, unless that he is a *Jeune Cavalier*.

The next scene introduces the Quarrel, and the blow given to the father of *Rodrigue*, by the father of his mistress, and this is the first scene of the *Cid*, that is made use of in the *Heroick Daughter:* this quarrel seems too sudden and unprepared, and wants the terror that would naturally arise from it, if, as I observ'd, the audience were prepossess'd with a proper admiration of the lovers, whose approaching ruin they would then be more nearly concern'd for; and this concern I have attempted to give by the preparation of a whole first act in the *Heroick Daughter*, which is entirely unborrow'd, and previous to the first opening *beauties* of the *Cid:* the heroick obligations, that have pass'd between the two lovers, (whom I call *Carlos* and *Ximena*) before they secretly entertain or publickly avow their passion; the gentle manner of *Ximena*'s first softening the prejudice of *Alvarez*; the solemn interposition of the king to heal the hereditary feud of their families, and his crowning their reconcilement with the immediate union of the lovers, were all intended to give a dignity to their passion, and consequently to move the audience with a quicker sense of their ensuing calamities, than if (as they are in the *Cid*) they had been only shewn

in their mere lawful defire of being virtuous bed-
fellows.

Though terror feems the favourite paffion of *Corneille*,
and what he ufually paints in much more lively colours
than his objects of pity; yet the fatal rupture that ruins
the happinefs of thefe lovers, lofes half its force and
beauty for want of art or pains in preparing it. For
terror muft certainly rife in proportion to the object it
menaces; and we cannot be as much concern'd for the mif-
fortunes of merit unknown, as for what is evident and
confpicuous; and till that rupture happens, we are (in
the *Cid*) utter ftrangers to the merit of *Rodrigue* and
Chimene.

But befides all this, the quarrel itfelf feems an accident meerly arifing from the brutal temper of the Count,
and the fpectator might as well expect, from the beginning of the fcene, that it was to end in a friendly conclufion of their childrens marriage, as their fo unforefeen
and violent enmity: and tho' furprize is a neceffary part
of tragedy, yet that furprize is never to be abrupt: for
when it is fo, it is more apt to fhock than delight us;
we do not love to be ftartled into a pleafure: as an audience ought never to be wholly let into the fecret defign
of a play, fo they ought not to be entirely kept out of
it, you may fafely leave room for the imagination to
guefs at the nature of the thing you intend, and are only
to furprize them with your manner of bringing it about:
as in the fecond act of *Dryden*'s *All for Love*; where *Marc
Antony* feems confirm'd in his refolution to part with
Cleopatra; yet when he once confents to expoftulate with
her in perfon, tho' you eafily forefee the conteft is to
end to her advantage, yet you are far from lofing the
pleafure of your furprize, while it is fo artfully executed;
nay, you have a farther delight, from the private ap-
plaufe you give to your own judgment, in fo rightly fore-
feeing the conclufion; and to this reafon may be attri-
buted the fuccefs of moft allegorical writings——But
here (in this fcene of the quarrel in the *Cid*) is an important action brought about, and you know not what it
means, till it is over. Then indeed you fee—What?

why, that the hopes of the young couple's wedding are
all blown up; like enough, but the audience have as yet
no great reafon to be concern'd at it, they know very
little of them.   Befide the fcene is half over before you
know who the old men are, or what their quarrelling can
fignify; fo that your admiration cannot go along with
the performance, and your attention is either loft, or in
pain, till the author explains himfelf; which is afterwards
too late, your imagination is not at leifure to look fo far
back for the propriety of what's paft; you are then to be
intent upon what is to come, or elfe what you *have* feen,
is but an interruption to what you *are* to fee; the cafe of
many a modern play; this lazinefs, or want of fkill in
an author, does not give an auditor fair play for his money, it will not let him fee all the play; nor is it enough
to fay, the fcene is notwithftanding natural—If you cannot fay it has art, as well well as nature, you praife it
but by halves.

I cannot omit another objection to the character of the
Count, who is fo infolent, fierce, and turbulently vain of
his merit, that he is below the dignity of the fubject :
nor will his being a *Spaniard* excufe it, they are all *Spani-
ards* in the play; and tho' a ridiculous pride is natural to
the nation, we are not by that rule to fhew a *Frenchman*
dancing, or a *Dutchman* drunk in a tragedy.   In fhort,
he is a mere *Miles Gloriofus*, and makes fo difagreeable a
figure, that we have much ado to think him an object
worthy of that filial regard and duty which *Chimene* pays
to his memory.   I therefore thought it neceffary, in
higher juftification of her forrows, and virtue, to make
him more civilized and rational in the *Heroick Daughter*;
his honourable and open reconcilement to *Alvarez*; his
generous compaffion for the diftrefs of *Carlos*, whom he
had reduc'd to the neceffity of fighting him : his humanity and honour (in cafe he fell by his fword) in bequeath-
ing him his daughter, were all attempted to give the audience, as well as *Ximena*, a more juftifiable regret for
the lofs of him—The only reafon *Corneille* feems to have
for making him fo brutal, is to introduce an unreafonable quarrel, from whence all the diftrefs of the play was

to rife : I have likewife attempted to remove that objection, by grounding the jealoufy and refentment of the
Count upon the fubtile infinuations of *Sanchez*, it being
the immediate (tho' difhonourable) intereft of his love
to *Ximena*, by any artifice to obftruct her marriage with
Carlos : This expedient I thought would make the Count
more excufable in his violent meafures, and might remove the odium that lay hard upon him in the *Cid*, by
throwing it upon *Sanchez*, whofe character here may
better endure it.

The next fcene of moment that follows the quarrel, is
the challenge which is delivered with fo vaunting a boaft
by *Rodrigue*, that one would imagine he thought it firft
prudent to frighten his enemy, before he fought him ;
and truly, by the behaviour of the Count, he feems to
have carried his point; for after the challenge is made,
the Count as pleafantly evades it, by pretending to be
offended with *Rodrigue's* prefumption in calling him to
an account. In fhort they debate fo heartily, that you
begin to lofe your apprehenfion of its coming to mifchief; for even after they feem both determin'd, and
going out, the Count is refolv'd to have t'other chance
for refuming the debate, and fays brifkly to *Rodrigue*
———*Art thou fo weary of thy life?* But I think nothing
can better expofe the abfurdity of the queftion, than the
fhrewd anfwer, that is made to it, viz. *What are you
afraid to die?* There is reafon in the anfwer, but (between two men of honour) there could be none for the
queftion.

This fort of behaviour I could not be reconcil'd to, and
have taken the liberty, in the firft fix lines of the fcene,
to get the challenge accepted with the plain language of
a man determined: and tho' I could not allow them to
expoftulate, while their courage was only in queftion,
yet I could not help thinking the lover in fome part of the
fcene, owed a figh or two to the terrors of his miftrefs,
and the certain mifery his honour was then going to reduce her to, which would have been ftill unqueftionable,
tho' his regard to her had here fhewn its laft effort to
right his injuries with a bloodlefs reparation : for tho'

he had before debated himself into a resolution of reveng-
ing them, yet nothing is more natural, than to see love
turn back and back again, for another last adieu. I
shall here beg leave to quote a few lines from the scene
itself, as the shortest way of explaining how I have conducted it———When the place of meeting is just going
to be appointed, *Carlos* stops short,—and says to the
Count,

One moment's respite for Ximena's *sake,*
She has not wrong'd me, and my heart would spare her;
We both, without a stain to either's honour,
May pity her distress, and pause to save her.
Nor need I blush, that I suspend my cause,
Since with its vengeance her sure woes are blended;
O! lay not on her innocence, the grief
Of a mourn'd father, or a lover's blood!
O! spare her sighs, prevent her streaming tears,
Stop this effusion of my bleeding honour,
And heal, if possible, its wounds with peace.

To all which, when the Count is immoveable, and
grows at last impatient of his reproaches;   then *Carlos*
recovers to his honour and breaks out as follows———

O! give me back that vile submissive shame,
That I may meet thee with retorted scorn,
And right my honour with untainted vengeance;
Yet no—withold it! take it to acquit my love,
That Sacrifice was to Ximena *due:*
Her helpless sufferings claim'd that pang; and since
I cannot bring dishonour to her arms,
Thus my rack'd heart pours forth its last adieu,
And makes libation of its bleeding peace:
Farewel, dear injured Softness—Follow me.

After the place of meeting is appointed, *Carlos* trou-
bles you with no more of his love, than by uttering with
a sigh, as he goes out,

Poor Ximena !——

Which had fo compaffionate an effect upon our *Englifh*
hearers, that if his love was then a weaknefs, it was at
leaft fuch a one as they heartily forgave him.

'The next fcene of the *Infanta,* (who is always dropping in, like cold water, upon the heat of the main
action) is for that reafon again left out; our difference
otherwife is not material, till the King receives notice of
the Count's being killed by *Rodrigue*; which is fo flightly
related, or, to ufe *Corneille's* own words, *Sans aucune nar-
ration touchante,* and received with fo little furprife, or
curiofity to know any circumftances of the action, that
upon my firft reading the *French* play, I fcarce knew
whether I was to believe him dead, or no. I have therefore endeavour'd, in the *Heroick Daughter,* to awa-
ken the audience, by making that relation more folemn
and particular, and to prepare the probability of the *Cataf-
trophe,* which I fhall better account for in its place: But
in the laft fcene of this fecond act it muft be allow'd,
the *Cid* begins to feize upon the heart of the fpectator,
and this is one of thofe great beauties that have fo juftly
given rife to its fame: The fluctuating pity, that is fo
finely perplex'd between the tears of a pious daughter,
and the venerable forrows of a father: The happy fkill
of throwing them both, in the fame inftant, at the
King's feet for juftice and mercy; and with pretenfions
fo equally laudable, is an incident which few tragedies,
either ancient or modern, can boaft of. The only liberty I have taken with this fcene, is in making the father
plead with more refignation, and rather to truft his caufe
to its fimple merits, than thofe of his own paft fervices.

The next act opens with *Rodrigue's* appearing in the
apartment of his miftrefs, where he leffens his character,
by juftifying his honour to her fervant: After *Chimene*
too is left alone with the fame fervant *Elvire,* fhe throws
away a great many fine fentiments upon that prating
creature, who has no fenfe of them, but endeavours to
comfort her by vulgar advice, which makes *Chimene* in-
excufable to hear; befides the main action cools in the

converfation : This is avoided in the *Heroick Daughter*, by making *Belzara* the third perfon in thefe two fcenes, who has an intereft in ferving *Carlos*, yet never is mean or difhonourable in her attempting it. But the next fcene makes us ample amends for all we may have juftly found fault with.

The meeting of *Rodrigue* and *Chimene*, throws us in-to a tendernefs that is irrefiftible: This incident gives the *Cid* as fair an affurance of being immortal, as any modern poetry can hope for. There is fomething fo amiable in the defpair of *Rodrigue*, in his natural difre-gard of his fafety, for the refiftlefs pleafure of feeing his miftrefs; and we are apt to be fo feiz'd with the inftant idea of her tender paffion breaking through her filial ob-ligations to purfue him, that at the firft fight of them it is impoffible, for an attentive auditor, not to feel the moft agreeable tranfport and aftonifhment: And fince the incident is *Corneille*'s and not mine, it may be no vanity to fay, this effect was evident from the hurry and bufy murmur that ran through the audience at its firft prefentation in *London*. And it would indeed be a re-flection on our *Englifh* tafte, to fuppofe we could be lefs fenfible than our neighbours, of fo palpable an excellence: For *Corneille* fpeaking of the reception of this fcene in *Paris*, fays,

Qu'alors que ce malheureux amant fe prefentoit devant elle, il s'elevoit un certain Fremiffement dans l'Affemblée qui mar-quoit une Curofite merveilleufe, & un redoublement d'atten-tion pour ce qu'ils avoient à fe dire ans un eftat fi pitoy-able.

But allowing it all this admiration, I have fome rea-fons to offer (to better judgment) why the conduct of this fcene in the *Heroick Daughter*, is not implicitly form'd upon the model of that in the *Cid:* I cannot but think, that *Rodrigue*'s entering with an anfwer to the laft words of *Chimene*, muft be unnatural, if you don't fuppofe him to have liften'd at the door to her private difcourfe; and tho' 'tis poffible moft of our modifh criticks may own they would have liften'd in his condition, yet that is no proof, that lift'ning, especially in another perfon's houfe, is not always the effect of meannefs, ill-manners, or treachery; I therefore thought it more reafonable to let him approach her in a mute fubmiffive addrefs, and to give him time for it, have thrown *Ximena* into a reproach-ful aftonifhment the moment fhe fees him; *Corneille*, after fome fine touches of their diftrefs, fuffers him to proceed in excufe of his offence, in which he feems too fond of fhewing the man of Honour, and the harfh terms he ufes in his juftification, are too choquant for the ear of an in-jured miftrefs.   Thefe are his words.

“ *Car enfin n'attens pas de mon Affection,*
“ *Un lache repentir d'une bonne Action.*

And a little farther:

“ *Je le ferois encour, fi j'avois à le faire.*

This laft line is omitted in the *Heroick Daughter*, and the firft are foften'd by only faying,

“ ——*How fhall I repent me of a crime,*
“ *Which uncommitted had deferv'd thy fcorn?*

I have endeavour'd in the fame fpeech to make his crime more pitiful, by his pleading the regard he had to her peace, in firft endeavouring to reduce her father into a temper, that might have ended their difference with a lefs fatal reparation; and it feems to heighten the diftrefs of *Ximena*, when you fee her heart is full, and confcious of the obligation.

After *Chimene* has anfwer'd his plea, in the moft fub-lime fentiments of her filial duty to purfue him for her father's death, *Rodrigue* infifts, that her own hand alone ought to fatisfy her vengeance; I have here made bold to fhorten their arguments upon this point, which feem a little too near the romantick, and have fubftituted one, that I thought more agreeable to nature, where *Carlos* says,

> *Let not the wretch once honour'd with thy love,*
> *Thy* Carlos, *once thought worthy of thy arms,*
> *Be dragg'd a publick spectacle to justice,*
> *To draw the irksome pity of a croud,*
> *Who may, with vulgar reason, call thee cruel;*
> *My death from thee will elevate thy vengeance,*
> *And shew, like mine, thy duty scorn'd assistance.*

But the greatest omission in this scene, is, that *Chimene* so far forgets her filial duty, as to take no precaution, not so much as his word of honour, that *Rodrigue* shall appear to answer his crime to the law; she is indeed concern'd for her reputation, and on that account only desires him to leave her; her last concern, when they part at the end of the scene, is,

" ———*Et sur tout Garde bien, qu'on Te voye.*

This makes their meeting look too like a modern intrigue, I have therefore endeavour'd to give her a better reason for releasing him; when he reproaches her with want of love, in refusing his desire to fall by her hand, she replies—

> *Can hate have part in interviews like this?*
> *Art thou not now within my power to seize?*
> *Yet I'll release thee,* Carlos, *on thy word,*
> *Give me thy word, that on the morrow's noon*
> *Before the king in person thou wilt answer,*
> *And take the shelter of the night to leave me.*

I do not see how the scene could possibly be said to have a just conclusion, but by this mutual discharge of their duty for the present: and when *Carlos* had given his honour to appear, then indeed there is a more pardonable and natural excuse for the tenderness they fall into;

which tho' the *reader* must be charm'd with in the original, I have ventur'd to alter, to make them more agreeable to the *spectator*.

The next scene breaks into the street, where the father of *Rodrigue* is wandering up and down alone, in search of his son; a very slender mark of his wisdom, and puts one in mind of a vulgar saying—*To look for a needle*, &c. —Nay, he does all this, tho' he has five hundred friends in his house (whom he had drawn together to vindicate the cause of his honour) waiting for him; and there is no excuse appears for his leaving them alone, or why some do not attend him abroad: where he entertains the audience with a long account (which he gives to himself) of his condition, in pointed conceits, and quaint Antithesis, that would be much prettier in an epigram—At last he meets with his son, with whom he falls into a tedious argument; and to comfort his sorrow for the loss of his mistress, tells him there are more women than *Ximena*, and would have him shew the greatness of his heart, in shaking off its weakness for her: this seems unpardonable, and stains the character of the father; for to suppose him capable of changing his mistress, takes away half the merit of the son's having reveng'd his honour; which, had he not inviolably loved her, had only shewn his courage in common with other men. The answer the son makes him, indeed is truly great, which it might easily be, when he had so dishonourable a thought to oppose; so that the one speech is only fine from the other's being improper, I might say unnatural: this scene seems extremely cold, after the spirit and warm passion in the preceding one : care should be always taken in such cases not to suffer the attention to languish, but (as *Horace* says—*Semper ad eventum festinet*) when the subject will not suffer us to exceed what is gone before, we should at least keep our hearers awake, by being busy about new matter and action, plainly necessary to carry on the story of the play. All that seems useful in this scene, is the last speech of it, which is the only one, that is taken into the *Heroick Daughter:* There *Alvarez* appears at the head of his friends in his own house,

where his fon may be fuppos'd with more probability to
come to him.   But *Corneille* honeftly tells us in his *Ex-
amen* of the *Cid*, that the reafon why he did not bring
on Don *Diegue* with his friends about him, was becaufe
thofe perfonages are generally fupplied by aukward fellows, and candle-fnuffers—a miferable fign of the low-
nefs of the *French* Theatre, when fo great an author is
forc'd to reftrain his fancy, and to commit an abfurdity,
to make his play fit for the ftage—But this not being our
cafe here, I had the liberty of writing as well as I could.
After *Corneille* has done his fcene, I have given the
fon a foliloquy, that I thought would be a new motive to the compaffion of the audience; if your curiofity is as warm as my vanity could wifh it, you
will now turn to it at the end of the fourth act.

The two laft acts of the *Cid*, though in nature, they
may be finely written, lofe half their force for want of
art : All thofe great fentiments which *Chimene* utters to
the *Infanta* in the beginning of the fourth act, are improper in that place ; for fhe is not only arguing her
cafe with one that has nothing to do with it, but fhe is
merely talking while fhe fhould be *doing*; we are impatient for the iffue of her appeal to the King, and it is
no excufe to the hearer, that the king's daughter ftops
her by the way, when it was in the poet's choice to have
fent the King's daughter to prayers, or any other employment in the mean time——In fhort, the author
feems to want matter for two acts more, and is reduced
to thefe fhifts to give the audience full meafure for their
money : But the *Heroick Daughter*, having a whole fifft
act added before the action of the *Cid* begins, of confequence transfers the third act of the *French* play
into the fourth of the *Englifh*, by which expedient, the
neceffary matter of the two laft acts of the one, are
eafily contain'd in the fingle fifth act of the other.

The next prolixity the *Cid* entertains us with, is
the King's folemn reception of *Rodrigue* after his defeat
of the *Moors* ; which let it be never fo juftly due to the
merit of the action, yet *Non nunc erat his locus*. All

this moves not, and might have been ſuppos'd or related only, that the more immediate buſineſs of the play, might have come forward, as is attempted in the *Heroick Daughter.*

Beſide, the making *Rodrigue* to give an account of his own victory, muſt either leſſen the action, or his character——Any friend, that was a well-wiſher to his intereſt, muſt certainly have been a more proper herald of his fame : I have therefore made *Alonzo* give the particulars of this glorious ſervice to his country, and I thought the audience would be better pleas'd if it were given to *Ximena,* that they might at the ſame inſtant ſee the new conflict it muſt naturally raiſe between her paſſion and her duty : for tho' the *King* is in the play the perſon moſt concern'd to hear it, yet the *Spectator* is moſt concern'd that *Ximena* ſhould hear it ; and it offends not either manners, or probability, that the king is ſuppos'd to have heard it before.

When *Chimene* returns to court for juſtice, the king, in hopes to appeaſe her, has a mind firſt to make a diſcovery of her paſſion, and cunningly tells her, that her deſire of vengeance is anſwer'd, for *Rodrigue* is dead of his wounds ; at which *Chimene* fainting, his Majeſty fairly bites her, owns he is alive, and that he is now convinc'd ſhe has no mind to hurt him——— This. *Fineſſe* is needleſs, and ill becomes the gravity of the ſubject : There is nothing of it in the *Heroick Daughter.*

Well ! when all will not do, when ſhe finds it is ſo hard to make the King more ſenſible of her private wrongs, than of her lover's late ſervice to the publick, it is indeed time to make her loſe her ſenſes, for then, poor Lady ! ſhe demands the combat, and is forced to call her vanity and falſhood to the aſſiſtance of her duty, by propoſing her perſon as a reward to any gentleman that would be the champion of her cauſe, if he prov'd victorious : This is ſacrificing her

paffion to her duty with a vengeance: What an in-
confolable figure would fhe have made, if nobody had
taken up the cudgels! 'tis well fhe knew fhe was
handfome, or that might really have been the cafe;
but to be ferious——

I thought it much more decent and natural, when
fhe was in this extremity, to let *Sanchez,* who had
before offered his fervice, take this fair occafion of
ftepping in to her affiftance; 'tis he, therefore, that
in *Ximena*'s name demands the combat, and that
fhe might not have the guilt of flattering him with
the leaft hope, as a lover, he is made even to difguife
the motive to it with his pretended friendfhip for her
late father: The King's granting the combat and the
neceffary orders about it, conclude the fourth act of
the Cid.

The fifth act begins with *Rodrigue*'s abruptly vi-
fitting *Chimene,* without leave or excufe, before he
was going to the lifts. And tho' in her firft words
fhe pretends to be fhock'd at his appearance, yet he
takes no notice of it, but goes on with his bufinefs,
and fhe as infenfibly finks into mildnefs and temper
to hear it: Here they feem too declamatory, and
romantick, which I have endeavour'd to avoid, by
giving a more fpirited turn to the paffions, and re-
ducing them nearer to common life; and the expedient
that introduces the interview itfelf, is, I hope, upon
a more pardonable foundation: For to make thefe two
acts into one, in the *Heroick Daughter,* it was but to
contrive this fcene naturally to follow the laft, without leaving the ftage vacant, which is effected by the
King's giving *Carlos* leave to take his farewel of
Ximena before his going to the combat; and thus her
hearing him, while her friend *Belzara* is prefent, and
in the court, feems more excufable, than her receiving his vifit in open day, in her private apartment: And that your patience might not languifh,

the combat immediately follows his parting from her; and tho' you see nothing of that engagement on the stage, yet your imagination all the while enjoys it in the alarms and terrors of *Ximena*, which upon every distant sound of the trumpet she is differently thrown into: And I have always observed, that when any thing of moment is heard to be doing from behind, that has a warm effect upon the actors in fight, it seems to give a double delight to the audience: This incident is entirely my own, and yet I flatter myself, not the least artful in that play. The return of *Sanchez* from the combat too, is here prepared with such circumstances, as might more probably lead *Ximena* into the mistake of his being the victor; but all this is languidly interrupted in the *Cid*, by making the infanta's melancholy passion break into the warmest connection of the story; and *Chimene* too, for want of having her imagination stirr'd with such various notice of the combat, which the trumpet gives her, falls again into an inactive and declamatory account of her calamities, which in a last act ever surfeits the attention.

After the combat she accosts the king with a long argument, on a supposition that *Rodrigue* is dead, wherein she begs to be releas'd from her obligation to marry *Sanchez* as the victor, and barters to reward him with her fortune, which she is willing to settle upon *Sanchez* for his trouble, provided she may have leave to dispose of her person in a nunnery—All this the king hears without undeceiving her as to *Rodrigue*'s being alive, which is not only improbable, but needlefsly carries her mistake farther than it will bear to be beautiful. In the *Heroick Daughter*, the very instant she hints at the death of *Carlos*, the king rectifies her mistake: Which prevents that odd project of compromizing the matter with *Sanchez*, and lets the hearer sooner into matter of more importance: The king too here is only an advocate, not a tyrant for *Carlos*; and *Ximena* having made no promise to marry the victor, avoids that violation of her duty, which, in the *Cid*, the absolute power of the king would impose on her.

But here he is fo tender of her virtue, that he even fuffers not *Carlos* to approach her, without leave— And now we come to the laft conflict of her heart, which concludes in a refolution not to truft her love in fight of him that had killed her father, but to fhut her forrows from the world in a cloifter: And I am of opinion, it was impoffible under fuch misfortunes to difpofe of her otherwife, without breaking into the laws of honour and virtue. Well! but tho' you grant me this, we are here ftill at a lofs; this can be no abfolute conclufion of the play, the matter ftands juft as it did three acts ago, the lovers were parted then, and all we have done with them fince comes to no more. *Corneille* feems to be plunged in this difficulty, and in my humble opinion had much better have parted them for ever, than have brought them together with fo wretched a violation of *Chimene*'s character: In fhort, his expedient comes to no more than this, that the king gives her leave, for decency's fake, to be virtuous a year longer, but after that's expir'd, he obliges her (and fhe tacitly confents) to marry the man that has killed her father. As if a difhonourable action could be juftify'd, by our ftaying a year before we commit it.

'There feemed therefore to me but one way in nature, to bring them decently together, which was by removing the fundamental caufe of their feparation : If therefore, without offending nature or probability, we can make the father of *Ximena* recover of his wounds, I fee no reafon, why every auditor might not in honour congratulate their happinefs : By this expedient their ftory is inftructive, and thefe heroick lovers ftand at laft two fair examples of rewarded virtue : But it is now time to conclude.

Notwithftanding all our critical amendments, it muft be allowed, that the firft happinefs of a tragick writer depends on his choice of a proper fubject, without that his art and genius are but mifemployed : If therefore there be any thing more than my not being a fufficient mafter of ftyle, that could make the *Heroick Daughter* lefs fuccefsful than the *Cid*, I can allow it might be likewife owing to the fubject, of which perhaps the chief characters are too feverely virtuous for the home-fpun morals of our *Englifh* audience: Whereas the *French* run into the other extreme; with them your hero muft be virtuous even to romance, or he is infuffer-able; but good-nature is fo diftinguifhing a characte-riftic of the *Englifh*, that the *French* have no word to exprefs it: And the perfons that *we* often *pity* in our plays, a *French* critick would tell you ought to be *banged* by poetical juftice. But we are fo tender-hearted, that let the characters of our tragedies be never fo cri-minal, yet if you can but make them penitent, and miferable, refign'd and humble in their afflictions, we forget all their old faults, take them immediately into favour, and the handkerchiefs of a whole audience fhall be wet with their misfortunes: This effect is frequent at the tragedy of *Venice Preferv'd*, where *Jaffeir*, after having been a confpirator againft his country from a private revenge; after his betraying that confpiracy, and the life of his deareft friend, from the importunities of a wife, whom his weaknefs could not refift, yet makes his peace with the audience at laft, and dies furrounded with their compaffion: I am therefore con-vinc'd, that criminal characters, fo artfully conducted, have much the advantage of the perfect and blamelefs; and perhaps it is the narrownefs of the *French* genius, that would never let their beft authors attempt to raife compaffion upon fuch bold and natural foundations. But on the other fide, it would be hard to infer from hence, that characters nearer to perfection ought not as well to appear the principals of tragedy: Both *Carlos* and *Ximena* have their imperfections, and I allow are moft to be pity'd, when they are leaft able to refift them; I cannot therefore but infift, that the *Cid* has all the greatnefs, dignity and diftrefs in the fubject, that tragedy requires; and though it may have had too many hearers of an uncultivated tafte, who think it inclines to the romantick; yet if filial duty, love, and honour in the higheft inftances of felf-denial, are not imaginary virtues, then certainly all its ſtructures are upon exalted nature : Let the common practice of mankind be what it will, it is not unnatural to be virtuous ; and it ought to be more commendable to pity the misfortunes of the virtuous, than of thoſe who owe their diſtreſs to their immediate criminal conduct. But I am notwith-ſtanding willing to compound for the inference, by granting, that when a capable genius ſets himſelf to work, there may juſtly be room for ſucceſs upon either foundation.

PROLOGUE.

*A*S oft in form'd affemblies of the fair,
  The ftrait-lac'd prude will no loofe paffion bear,
Beyond fet bounds no lover muft addrefs,
But fecret flame in diftant fighs exprefs ;
Yet if by chance fome gay coquette fails in,
A joyous murmur breaks the filent fcene;
Each heart, reliev'd by her enliv'ring fire,
Feels eafy hope, and unconfin'd defire ;
Then fhuddering prudes with fecret envy burn,
And treat the fops, they could not catch, with fcorn.
So plays are valued ; not confin'd to rules,
Thofe Prudes, *the criticks call them, feafts for fools ;*
And if an audience 'gainft thofe rules is warm'd,
Or by the lawlefs force of genius charm'd,
Their whole confederate body is alarm'd :
Then every feature's falfe, though ne'er fo taking,
The heart's deceiv'd, though 'tis with pleafure aking.
They'll prove your charmer's not agreeable :
Thus far'd it with the Cid *of fam'd* Corneille.
In France *'twas charg'd with faults were paft enduring,*
But ftill had beauties that were fo alluring,
It rais'd the envy of the grave Richlieu,
And fpite of his remarks, *cram'd houfes drew :*
Of this affertion if the truth you'll know,
Two lines will prove it from the great Boileau :
En vain contre le *Cid* un miniftre fe ligue,
Tout *Paris* pour *Chimene* a les yeux de *Rodrigue.*
In vain againft the *Cid* the ftatefman arms,
Paris with *Rodrick* feels *Ximena's* charms.
This proves, when paffion truly wrought appears,
In plays imperfect, 'twill command your tears :
Yet think not from what's faid, we rules defpife ;
To raife your wonder from abfurdities ;
As France *improv'd it from the* Spanifh *pen,*
We hope, now Britifh, *'tis improv'd again :*
And though loft tragedy has long feem'd dead,
Yet having lately rais'd her awful head,

PROLOGUE.

To-night with pains and cost we humbly strive
To keep the spirit of that taste alive:
But if like Phaëton, in Corneille's carr,
Th' unequal muse unhappily should err,
At least you'll own from glorious heights she fell,
And there's some merit in attempting well.

Dramatis Personæ.

MEN.

Don *Ferdinand*, King of *Castile*.   Mr. *Mills.*

Don *Alvarez*, his late General, and Father of Don *Carlos*.   } Mr. *Cibber.*

Don *Gormaz*, Count of *Gormaz*, the present General, and father of *Ximena*.   } Mr. *Booth.*

Don *Carlos*, in love with *Ximena*.   Mr. *Wilks.*

Don *Sanchez*, his secret Rival, tho' lately betroth'd to *Belzara*.   } Mr. *Elrington.*

Don *Alonzo*, Don *Garcia*, officers of the court.   } Mr. *Thurmond.* Mr. *Bowman.*

A *Page*.

WOMEN.

Ximena, daughter to *Gormaz*.   Mrs. *Oldfield.*

Belzara, her friend forsaken by Don *Sanchez*.   } Mrs. *Porter.*

The SCENE, the Royal Palace in *Seville.*

THE

THE
HEROICK DAUGHTER.

ACT I.

Alvarez *and* Carlos;

Alv. A Lliance! ha! and with the race of *Gormaz* !
My mortal foe! The king enjoins it, faidſt
thou ?
Let me not think thou couldſt defcend to aſk it :
Take heed, my fon, nor let the daughter's eyes
Succeed in what the father's fword has fail'd ;
Since I to age have ſtood his hate unmov'd,
Be not thou vanquiſh'd by her female wiles,
Nor ſtain thy honour with infulted love.
   Car. O taint not with fo hard a thought her virtues,
Which ſhe has prov'd fincere, from obligations :
'Tis to her fuit I owe my late advancement.
You know, my lord, the fortune of this fword
Redeem'd her from the *Moors*, when late their captive;
For which, at her return to court, ſhe fwell'd
The action with fuch praifes to the king,
He bad her name the honours cou'd reward it ;
She, confcious of our houfes hate, furpriz'd,
And yet difdaining that her heart ſhou'd fall
In thanks below the benefit receiv'd,
Warm'd with th'occafion, begg'd his royal favour
Wou'd rank me in the field, the next her father.
The king comply'd, and with a fmile infiſted,
That from her own fair hand I ſhou'd receive
The grace. This forc'd me then to vifit her :
To fay what follow'd from our interview,
Might tire, at leaſt, if not offend your ear.
   Alv. Not fo, my *Carlos*, but proceed.
   Car. In brief ;
The queen, who now in higheſt favour holds

F 4

The fair *Ximena*, foon perceiv'd our paffion,
Approv'd and cherifh'd it; our houfes difcord,
She knew of old, had often fhook the ftate;
Whereon fhe kindly to the king propos'd
This happy union, as the fole expedient
To cure thofe wounds, and fortify his throne:
Nay, fhe, *Ximena*, if I know her thoughts,
Chiefly to that regard refigns her heart.
O! fhe difclaims, contemns her beauty's power,
And builds no merit but on ftable virtue.

Alv. If fo, I fhou'd indeed applaud her fpirit.

Car. Oh! had you fearch'd her foul like me, you would
Repofe your life, your fame upon her truth.

Alv. On thee at leaft I'm fure I may; I know
Thou lov'ft thy honour equal to *Ximena*,
And to that guard I dare commit thy love,
Keep but that union facred :——

Car. When I break it,
May your difpleafure, and *Ximena*'s fcorn,
Unite their force to torture me with fhame:
But fee! fhe comes! her eye, my lord, has reach'd you,

Ximena enters.

Mark her concern, the fofnefs of her fear,
O'ercaft with doubt and diffidence to meet you;
One gentle word from you wou'd chafe the cloud,
And let forth all the luftre of her foul.

Alv. Hail, fair *Ximena*—beauteous brightnefs, hail,
Propitious be this meeting to us all!
With equal joy and wonder I furvey thee.
How lovely's virtue in fo bright a form!.
Thy father's fiercenefs all is loft in thee:
Well have thy eyes reproach'd our houfes' jars,
And calm'd the tempefts that have wreck'd our peace;
What we with falfe refentments but inflam'd,
Thy nobler virtues have appeas'd with honour.

Ximena. Thefe praifes, from another mouth, my lord,
Might dye thefe glowing cheeks with crimfon fhame;
But as they flow thus kindly from *Alvariz*,
From the heroick fire of my deliverer,
As you beftow 'em, my exulting heart,
Tho' undeferv'd, receives with joy the found:

But for thofe virtues you afcribe to me,
Alas! they are but copy'd all from thence;
Carlos, I faw, was brave, victorious, great,
Compaffionate——I am at beft, but grateful————
Cou'd I be lefs reduc'd with obligations?
Cou'd I retain our houfe's ancient hate,
When *Carlos*' deeds fo greatly had forgot it?
If heav'n had will'd our feuds fhou'd never end,
It would have chofe fome other arm to fave me:
But if its kinder providence decrees,
Ximena's yielded heart fhou'd cure thofe ills,
And bind our paffions in the chains of peace;
Be witnefs that, all gracious heav'n, I've gain'd
The end, the heav'n of my hopes on earth,
And fill'd the proudeft fails of my ambition.

   Alv. O *Carlos! Carlos!* we are both fubdu'd!
Where can fuch heavenly fweetnefs find a foe?
What *Gormaz* may refolve, his heart can tell,
But mine no longer can refift fuch virtue;
His pride perhaps may triumph o'er my weaknefs,
And wrong *Ximena* to infult *Alvarez:*
Be mine that fhame, but then be mine this glory,
                    [*He joins their hands.*
That I furrender to his daughter's merit
All that her heart demands, or mine can give:
If he's obdurate, let her wrongs reproach him.
            [*Don* Sanchez *and* Alonzo *obferving them.*
No thanks, my fair; for both or neither are
Oblig'd: Whatever may be due to me,
Let love, and mutual gratitude repay.
   D. San. Death to my eyes! *Alvarez* joins
        their hands!
   Alon. Forbear! is this a time for jealoufy?   *Apart.*
   D. San. Thou that haft patience then, re-
     lieve my torture.
   Car. O *Ximena!* how my heart's oppref'd with fhame!
Thou giv'ft me a confufion equal to
My joy. I yet am laggard in my duty;
I muft defpair to reach with equal virtues
Dread *Gormaz*' heart, as thou haft touch'd *Alvarez.*
   Xim. That hope we muft to providence refign;
F 5

The king intends this day to found his temper,
Which, tho' severe, I know is generous,
In honour great, as in resentments warm,
Fierce to the proud, but to the gentle yielding ;
The goodness of *Alvarez* must subdue him.
  Alon. My lord, I heard the king enquiring for you.
  Alv. Sir, I attend his majesty—I thank you.
  Xim. Saw you the count, my father, in the presence ?
  Alon. Madam, I left him with the king this instant,
Withdrawn to th' window, and in conference.
  Xim. "Twas his command I shou'd attend him there.
  Alv. Come, fair Ximena, *if thy father's ear*
        Inclines, like mine, unprejudic'd to hear :
        His hate subdu'd will publick good regard,
        And crown thy virgin virtues with reward.
                              [*Ex.* Alv. Car. Xim.
  D. *San.* Help me, *Alonzo,* help me, or I sink,
Th'oppression is too great for nature's frame,
And all my manhood reels beneath the load;
Oh rage ! oh torment of successless love !
  Alon. Alas ! I warn'd you of this storm before,
Yet you, incredulous and deaf, despis'd it ;
But since your hopes are blasted in their bloom,
Since vow'd *Ximena* never can be yours,
Forget the folly, and resume your reason :
Recover to your vows your love betroth'd,
Return to honour, and the wrong'd *Belzara.*
  D. *San.* Why dost thou still obstruct my happiness,
And thwart the passion that has seiz'd my soul ?
A friend shou'd help a friend in his extremes,
And not create, but dissipate his fears.
'Tis true I see *Ximena's* heart is given,
But then her person's in a father's power ;
He, I've no cause to fear, will slight my offers.
Thou know'st, the aversion that he bears *Alvarez*
Bars like a rock her wishes from their harbour :
While *Carlos* has a fear, shall I despair ?
Has not the count his passions too to please,
And will he starve his hate to feed her love ?
May I not hope he rather may embrace
The fair occasion of my timely vows,

To torture *Carlos* with a sure despair,
And force *Ximena* to assist his triumph ?
Nay, she perhaps, when his commands are fix'd,
In pride of virtue may resist her love,
Suppress the passion, and resign to duty.
  Alon. Why will you tempt such seas of wild disquiet,
When honour courts you in a calm to joy ?
Belzara's charms are yielded to your hopes,
Contracted to your vows, and warm'd to love ;
Ximena scarce has knowledge of your flame,
Without reproach she racks you with despair,
And must be perjur'd cou'd her heart relieve you.
  D. *San.* Let her relieve me, I'll forgive the guilt,
Forget it, smother in her arms the thought,
And drown the charming falshood in the joy.
  Alon. What wild extravagance of youthful heat
Obscures your honour, and destroys your reason ?
  D. *San.* I am not of that lifeless mould of men,
That plod the beaten road of virtuous love :
With me 'tis joyous.   Beauty gives desire,
Desire by nature gives instinctive hope;
  The phœnix woman sets herself on fire,
  Hope gives us love, our love makes them desire,
  And in the flames they raise, themselves expire :
  Alon. Not love, nor hope can give you here success.
  D. *San.* Let those despair, whose passions have their
      bounds,
Whose hopes in hazards, or in dangers die :
Shew me the object worthy of my flame,
Let her be barr'd by obligations, friends,
By vows engag'd, by pride, aversion, all
The common lets that give the virtuous awe ;
My love wou'd mount the tow'ring falcon's height,
Cut thro' them all, like yielding air, my way,
And downwards dart me rapid on the quarry.
  Alon. Farewel, my lord, some other time perhaps
This rapture may subside, and want a friend ;
I shall be glad t'advise, when you can hear.
But see, *Belzara* comes, with eyes confus'd,
That speak some new disorder in her heart.
Wou'd you be happy, friend, be just ; preserve

Inviolate the honeſt vows you've made her.
Farewel, I leave you to embrace th'occaſion.   [*Exit.*

Enter Belzara.

Bel. I come, Don *Sanchez*, to inform you of
A wrong, that near concerns our mutual honour;
'Tis whiſper'd thro' the court, that you retraƈt
Your ſoleinn vows by contraƈt ſeal'd to me,
And with a perjur'd heart purſue *Ximena.*
Such falſe reports ſhou'd periſh in their birth.
I've done my honeſt part, and diſbeliev'd them;
Do yours, and by your vows perform'd deſtroy them.

D. *San.* Madam, this tender care of me deſerves
Acknowledgemeats beyond my power to pay;
But virtue always is the mark of malice,
Contempt the beſt return that we can make it.

Bel. Virtue ſhou'd have ſo ſtriƈt a guaid, as not
To ſuffer ev'n ſuſpicion to approach it.
For tho', Don *Sanchez*, I dare think you juſt,
Yet while the envious world believes you falſe,
I feel their inſults, and endure the ſhame.

D. *San.* Malice ſucceeds when its report's believ'd;
Seem you to ſlight it, and the monſter's mute.

Bel. I could have hop'd ſome cauſe to make me ſlight it.
This cold concern to ſatisfy my fears,
Proclaims the danger, and confirms them true.

D. *San.* Then you believe me falſe?

Bel. Believe it! Heav'n!
Am I to doubt, what ev'n your looks, your words,
Your faint evaſions faithleſly confeſs?
Ungrateful man! when you betray'd my heart,
You ſhou'd have taught me too to bear the wrong.

D. *San.* When tears with menaces relieve their grief,
They flow from pride, not tenderneſs diſtreſt.

Bel. Inſulting, horrid thought! Am I accus'd
Of pride, complaining from a breaking heart?

D. *San.* Behold th' unthrifty proof of woman's love!
Purſue you with the ſighs of faithful paſſion,
You ſtarve our pining hopes with painted coyneſs;
But if our honeſt hearts diſdain the ycke,
Or ſeek from ſweet variety, relief,

Alarm'd to lofe what you defpis'd fecure,
Your tremb'ling pride retracts its haughty air,
And yields to love, purfuing when we fly.
Thefe lavifh tears, when I deferv'd your heart,
Had held me fighing to be more your flave;
But to beftow them when that heart's broke loofe,
When more I merit your contempt than love,
Arraigns your juftice, and acquits my falfhood.
    Bel. Injurious, falfe, and barbarous reproacht.
Have I with-held my pity from your fighs,
Or us'd with rigour my once boundlefs power?
Am I not fwo:n by teftify'd confent,
By folemn vows contracted, yielded yours?
But what avails the force of truth's appeal,
Where the offender is himfelf the judge?
But yet remember, tyrant. while you triumph,
I am Don *Henrick*'s daughter, whom you dare betray;
Henrick, whofe fam'd revenge of injur'd honour,
Dares ftep as deep in blood, as you in provocations.
    D. *San.* Since then your feeming grief's with rage
        reliev'd,
Hear me with temper, madam, once for all.
You urge our folemn contract fworn : I own
The fact, but muft deny the obligation.
'Twas not to me, but to a father's will,
To *Henrick*'s dread commands your pride fubmitted:
Since then your merit's to obedience due,
Seek your reward from duty, not from *Sanchez:*
Your flights to me live yet recorded here,
Nor can your forc'd fubmiffions now remove them:
Ximena's fofter heart has rais'd me to
A flame, that gives at once revenge and rapture.
How far Don *Henrick* may refent the change,
I neither know, nor with concern fhall hear.
Nay, truft your injur'd patience to inflame him.
    Bel. Inhumane, vain provoker of my heart,
I need not urge the ills that muft o'ertake thee;
Thy giddy paffions will, without my aid,
Punifh their guilt, and to themfelves be fatal.
Ximena's heart is fixt as far above
Thy hopes, as truth and virtue from thy foul.

To her avenging scorn I yield thy love;
There, faithless wretch, indulge thy vain desires,
And starve, like tortur'd *Tantalus*, in plenty;
  Gaze on her charms forbidden to thy taste,
  Famisht and pining at the tempting feast,
  Still rackt, and reaching at the flying fair,
  Pursue thy falshood, and embrace despair. [*Exit.*
 D. *San.* So raging winds in furious storms arise,
Whirl o'er our heads, and are when past forgotten.

Enter Alonzo.

 Alon. Why, *Sanchez*, are you still resolv'd on ruin?
I met *Belzara* in disorder'd haste;
At sight of me she stopt, and wou'd have spoke,
But grief, alas! was grown too strong for words:
When turning from my view her mournful eyes,
She burst into a show'r of gushing tears,
And in the conflict of her shame retir'd.
O yet collect your temper into thought,
And shun the precipice that gapes before you:
A moment hence, convinc'd, your eyes will see
Ximena parted from your hopes for ever.
 D. *San.* Why dost thou double thus my new disquiets?
For pains foreseen are felt before they come.

Enter King, Gormaz, Alvarez, Carlos, Ximena.

 Alon. Behold the king, *Alvarez*, and her father.
Be wise, tho' late, and profit from the issue.
 King. Count *Gormaz* you, and you *Alvarez*, hear:
Tho' in the camp your swords, in court your counsel,
Have justly rais'd your fame to envy'd heights,
Yet let me still deplore your race and you,
That from a long descent of lineal heat,
Your private feuds as oft have shook the state.
And what's the source of this upheld defiance?
Alas! the stubborn claim of ancient rank,
Held from a two days antedated honour,
Which gave the younger house pre-eminence.
How many valiant lives have eas'd our foes
Of fear, destroy'd by this contested title!
And what's decided by this endless valour?

Whose honour yet confesses the superior ?
While both dare die, the quarrel is immortal :
Or say that force on one part has prevail'd,
Is there such merit in unequal strength ?
If violence is virtue, brutes may boast it :
Lions with lions grapple and dispute ;
But men are only great, truly victorious,
When with superior reason they subdue.
Can you then think you are in honour bound
To heir the follies of your anceſtors ?
Since they have left you virtues and renown,
Tranſmit not to poſterity their blame.
 Alv. and *Gor.* My gracious lord——
 King. Yet hold, I'll hear you both.
Of your compliance, *Gormaz*, I've no doubt ;
This quarrel in your nobler breaſt was dying,
Had not, *Alvarez*, you reviv'd it.
 Alv. I ?
Wherein, my gracious lord, ſtand I ſuſpected ?
 King. What elſe cou'd mean that ſullen gloom you
That conſcious diſcontent ſo ill conceal'd   [wore,
In your abrupt retirement from our court,
When late the valiant Count was made our general ?
Was't not your own requeſt, you might reſign it ?
Which tho' 'tis true you long had fill'd with honour,
Was it for you to circumſcribe our choice ?
T' oppoſe from private hate the publick good,
And in his caſe, whoſe mĕrit had preferr'd him ?
When his fierce temper, from reflection calm,
Inclin'd to let the embers of his heat expire,
Was it well done thus to revive the flame,
To wake his jealous honour to reſentment,
And ſhake that union we had laid to heart ?
If thou haſt ought to urge, that may defend
Thy late behaviour, or accuſe his conduct,
Unfold it free, we are prepar'd to hear.
 Alv. Alas, my lord, the world misjudges me ;
My hate ſuppos'd is not ſo deeply rooted ;
Age has allay'd thoſe fevers of my honour,
And weary nature now wou'd reſt from paſſions.
The noble Count, whoſe warmer blood may boil,

Perhaps is still my foe: I am not his,
Nor envy him those honours of his merit.
Where virtue is, I dare be just, and see it.
Your majesty has spoke your wisdom in
Your choice, for I have seen his arm deserve it.
In all the sieges, battles, I have won,
I knew not better to command, than he
To execute. Those wreaths of victory
That flourish still upon this hoary brow,
Impartial I confess, his active sword
Has lopt from heads of *Moors*, and planted there.

    King. How has report, my *Gormaz*, wrong'd this man!

    Alv. Nor was the cause of my retirement more
Than that I found it time to ease my age,
Unfit for farther action, and bequeath
My son the needless pomp of my possessions.

    King. Is't possible? Coud'st thou conceal this goodness?
Cou'd secret virtue take so firm a root,
While slander like a canker kill'd its beauties?
Gormaz, if yet thou art not passion's slave,
Take to thyself the glory to reward him.

    Gor. My lord, the passions that have warm'd this breast,
Yet never stirr'd but in the cause of honour.
Honour's the spring that moves my active life,
And life's a torment, while that right's invaded.
Shew me the man whose merit claims my love,
Whose milder virtues modestly assail me,
And honour throws me at his feet submissive.
In proof of this, there needs but now to own,
The generous advances of *Alvarez*
Have turn'd my fierce resentments into shame.
What can I more? My words but faintly speak me.
But since my king seems pleas'd with my conversion,
My heart and arms are open to embrace him.

    King. Receive him, soldier, to thy heart, and give
Your king this glory of your mutual conquest.
[They embrace.

    Xim. Auspicious omen!

    Car. O transporting hope!

    D. San. Adders and serpents mix in their embraces!
[Apart.

King. O *Gormaz!* O *Alvarez!* stop not here,
Confine not to yourselves your stinted virtue,
But in this noble ardour of your hearts,
Secure to your posterity your peace.
       [*Carlos* and *Ximena* kneel.
Behold the lifted hands that beg the blessing,
The hearts that burn to ratify the joy,
And to your heirs unborn transmit the glory.
 Gor. Receive her, *Carlos,* from a father's hand,
Whose heart by obligations was subdu'd.
 Alv. Accept, *Ximena,* all my age holds dear,
Not to my bounty, but thy merit due.
 King. O manly conquest! O exalted worth!
What honours can we offer to applaud it?
To grace this triumph of *Ximena*'s eyes,
Let public jubilee conclude the day.
Sound all our sprightly instruments of war,
Fifes, clarions, trumpets, speak the general joy.
 Alv. Raise high the clangor of your lofty notes,
Sound peace at home——
 Gor. And terror to our foes.
 King. Let the loud cannon from the ramparts roar.
 Gor. And make the frighted shores of Africk *ring,*
 Car. Long live! and ever glorious live, the king!
     [*Trumpets and volleys at a distance.*
 Alv. O may this glorious day for ever stand
Fam'd in the rolls of late recorded time!
 King. This happy union fixt, my lords, we now
Must crave your counsel in our state's defence——
Letters this morn alarm us with designs
The *Moors* are forming to invade our realms;
But let them be, we're now prepar'd to meet them.
  The prince that wou'd sit free from foreign fears,
  Shou'd first with peace compose intestine jars;
  Of hearts united, while secure at home,
  His rash invaders to their graves must come. [*Exeunt.*

ACT II.

Enter Don Sanchez.

RElentlefs fortune! thou haft done thy part,
  Neglected nothing to oppofe my love;
But thou fhalt find, in thy defpight, I'll on.
Wert thou not blind indeed, thou had'ft forefeen
The honour done this hour to old *Alvarez.*
His being nam'd the prince's governor,
(Which I well know the ambitious *Gormaz* aim'd at)
Muft, like a wildfire's rage, embroil their union,
Rekindle jealoufies in *Gormaz*' heart,
Whofe fatal flame muft bury all in afhes.
But fee, he comes, and feems to ruminate
With penfive grudge the king's too partial favour.

Gormaz on *the other fide.*

Gor. The king methinks is fudden in his choice.——
'Tis true, I never fought (but therefore is
Not lefs the merit) nor obliquely hinted,
That I defir'd the office—He has heard
Me fay, the prince his fon I thought was now
Of age to change his prattling female court,
And claim'd a governor's inftructive guidance——
Th' advice, it feems, was fit—but not th' advifer——
Be't fo—why is *Alvarez* then the man?
He may be qualify'd—I'll not difpute——
But was not *Gormaz* too of equal merit?
Let me not think *Alvarez* plays me foul—
That cannot be—he knew I wou'd not bear it——
And yet why he's fo fuddenly preferr'd——
I'll think no more on't—Time will foon refolve me.

   D. San. Not to difturb, my lord, your graver thought
May I prefume——.
   Gor. Don *Sanchez* may command me.
This youthful lord is fworn our houfe's friend;
If there's a caufe for jealous thought, he'll find it. [*Afid*

   D. San. I hear, my lord, the king has frefh advic
Of a defign'd invafion from the *Moors.*   [receiv'
Holds it confirm'd, or is it only rumour?

Gor. Such new alarms indeed his letters bring,
But yet their grounds feem'd doubtful at the council.
    D. San. May it not prove fome policy of ftate?
Some bugbear danger of our own creating?
The king I have obferv'd is fkill'd in rule,
Perfect in all the arts of tempering minds,
And—for the public good—can give alarms
Where fears are not, and hufh them where they are.
    Gor. 'Tis fo! he hints already at my wrongs.   [*Afide.*
    D. San. Not but fuch prudence well becomes a prince:
For peace at home is worth his deareft purchafe.
Yet he that gives his juft refentments up,
Tho' honour'd by the royal mediation,
And fees his enemy enjoy the fruits,
Muft have more virtues than his king, to bear it—
Perhaps, my lord, I am not underftood,
Nay, hope my jealous fears have no foundation;
But when the tyes of friendfhip fhall demand it,
Don *Sanchez* wears a fword that will revenge you. [*Going.*
    Gor. Don *Sanchez*, ftay—I think thou art my friend;
Thy noble father oft' has ferv'd me in
The caufe of honour, and his caufe was mine.
What thou haft fajd fpeaks thee *Belthazar's* fon;
I need not praife thee more———If I deferve
Thy lpve, refufe not what my heart's concern'd
To afk; fpeak freely of the king, of me,
Of old *Alvarez*, of our late alliance,
And what has followed fince: then fum the whole,
And tell me truly, where th' account's unequal.
    D. San. My lord, you honour with too great a truft
The judgment of my unexperienc'd years;
Yet for the time I have obferv'd on men,
I've always found the generous open heart
Betray'd, and made the prey of minds below it.
O! 'tis the curfe of manly virtue, that
Cowards, with cunning, are too ftrong for heroes;
And fince you prefs me to unfold my thoughts,
I grieve to fee your fpirit fo defeated,
Your juft refentments by vile arts of court
Beguil'd, and melted to refign their terror.
Your honeft hate, that had for ages ftood,

Unmov'd, and firmer from your foes defiance,
Now fapp'd, and undermin'd by his fubmiffion.
Alvarez knew you were impregnable
To force, and chang'd the foldier for the ftatefman;
While you were yet his foe profefs'd,
He durft not take thefe honours o'er your head;
Had you ftill held him at his diftance due,
He wou'd have trembled to have fought this office.
When once the king inclin'd to make his peace,
I faw too well the fecret on the anvil,
And foon foretold the favour that fucceeded.
Alas! this project has been long concerted,
Refolv'd in private 'twixt the king and him,
Laid out and manag'd here by fecret agents.
While he, good man, knew nothing of the honour,
But from his fweet repofe was dragg'd t'accept it.
O! it inflames my blood to think his fear
Shou'd get the ftart of your unguarded fpirit,
And proudly vaunt it in the plumes he ftole
From you.

 Gor. O! *Sanchez*, thou haft fir'd a thought,
That was before but dawning in my mind.
O! now afrefh it ftrikes my memory,
With what diffembled warmth the artful king
Firft charg'd his temper with the gloom he wore,
When I fupply'd his late command of general.
Then with what fawning flattery to me,
Alvarez' fear difguis'd his trembling hate,
And footh'd my yielding temper to believe him.

 D. San. Not flattery, my lord; tho' I muft grant,
'Twas praife well tim'd, and therefore fkilful.

 Gor. Now on my foul, from him 'twas loathfom
I take thy friendfhip, *Sanchez*, to my heart; [daubing
And were not my *Ximena* rafhly promis'd——

 D. San. Ximena's charms might grace a monarch's be
Nor dares my humble heart admit the hope,
Or, if it durft, fome fitter time fhou'd fhew it.
Refults more preffing now demand your thought;
Firft eafe the pain of your depending doubt,
Divide this fawning courtier from the friend.

 Gor. Which way fhall I receive, or thank thy love?

D. *San.* My lord, you over-rate me now—but fee,
Alvarez comes—row probe his hollow heart,
Now while your thoughts are warm with his deceit,
And mark how calmly he'll evade the charge.
My lord, I'm gone.   [*Exit.*
    Gor. I am thy friend for ever.

Enter Alvarez.

    Alv. My lord, the king is walking forth to fee
The prince, his fon, begin his horfemanfhip;
If you're inclin'd to fee him, I'll attend you.
    Gor. Since duty calls me not, I've no delight
To be an idle gaper on another's bufinefs.
You may indeed find pleafure in the office,
Which you've fo artfully contriv'd to fit.
    Alv. Contriv'd, my lord! I'm forry fuch a thought
Can reach the man, whom you've fo late embrac'd.
    Gor. Men are not always what they feem: Th's honour,
Which in another's wrong you've barter'd for,
Was at the price of thofe embraces bought.
    Alv. Ha! bought? For fhame fupprefs this poor fufpi-
For if you think, you can't but be convinc'd,   [cion;
The naked honour of *Alvarez* fcorns
Such bafe difguife——yet paufe a moment——
Since our great mafter with fuch kind concern
Himfelf has interpos'd to heal our feuds,
Let us not thanklefs rob him of the glory,
And undeferve the grace by new falfe fears.
    Gor. Kings are, alas! but men, and form'd like us,
Subject alike to be by men deceiv'd;
The blufhing court from this rafh choice will fee,
How blindly he o'erlooks fuperior merit.
Cou'd no man fill the place but worn *Alvarez?*
    Alv. Worn more with wounds and victories than age,
Who ftands before him in great actions paft?
But I'm to blame to urge that merit now,
Which will but fhock what reafoning may convince.
    Gor. The fawning flave! O *Sanchez!* how I thank
            thee!—   [*Afide.*
    Alv. You have a virtuous daughter, I a fon,
Whofe fofter hearts our mutual hands have rais'd

E'en to the summit of expected joy ;
If no regard to me, yet let at least
Your pity of their passions rein your temper.
  Gor. O needless care! to nobler objects now
That son be sure in vanity pretends.
While his high father's wisdom is preferr'd
To guide and govern our great monarch's son,
His proud aspiring heart forgets *Ximena;*
Think not of him, but your superior care ;
Instruct the royal youth to rule with awe
His future subjects trembling at his frown ;
Teach him to bind the loyal heart in love,
The bold and factious in the chains of fear ;
Join to these virtues too your warlike deeds.
Inflame him with the vast fatigues you've born,
But now are past, to shew him by example,
And give him in the closet safe renown :
Read him what scorching suns he must endure;
What bitter nights must wake, or sleep in arms,
To counter-march the foe, to give th'alarm,
And to his own great conduct owe the day.
Mark him on charts the order of the battle,
And make him from your manuscripts a heroe.
  Alv. Ill-temper'd man ! thus to provoke the heart,
Whose tortur'd patience is thy only friend.
  Gor. Thou only to thyself can'st be a friend ;
I tell thee, false *Alvarez*, thou hast wrong'd me,
Hast basely robb'd me of my merit's right,
And intercepted our young prince's fame ;
His youth with me had found the active proof,
The living practice of experienc'd war ;
This sword had taught him glory in the field,
At once his great example, and his guard ;
His unfledg'd wings from me had learnt to soar,
And strike at nations trembling at my name ;
This I had done, but thou, with servile arts,
Hast fawning crept into our master's breast,
Elbow'd superior merit from his ear,
And, like a courtier, stole his son from glory.
  Alv. Hear me, proud man—for now I burn to spea
Since neither truth can sway, nor temper touch thee ;

Thus I retort with scorn thy sland'rous age;
Thou! thou the tutor of a kingdom's heir!
Thou guide the passions of o'er-boiling youth,
That can'st not in thy age yet rule thy own!
For shame retire, and purge th'imperious heart,
Reduce thy arrogant, self-judging pride,
Correct the meanness of thy groveling soul,
Chase damn'd suspicion from thy manly thoughts,
And learn to treat with honour thy superior.
   Gor. Superior, ha! dar'st thou provoke me, traitor?
   Alv. Unhand me, ruffian! left thy hold prove fatal.
   Gor. Take that! audacious dotard.   [*Strikes him.*
   Alv. O! my blood!
Flow forward to my arm to chain this tyger.
If thou art brave, now bear thee like a man,
And quit my honour of this vile disgrace.   [*They fight.*
                       [Alvarez *is disarm'd.*
O feeble life! I have too long endur'd thee.
   Gor. Thy sword is mine, take back th'inglorious trophy,
Which wou'd disgrace thy victor's thigh to wear;
Now forward to thy charge, read to the prince
This martial lecture of thy fam'd exploits,
And from this wholesome chastisement, learn thou
To tempt the patience of offended honour.   [*Exit.*
   Alv. O rage! O wild despair! O helpless age!
Wert thou but lent me to survive my honour?
Am I with martial toils worn gray, and see
At last one hour's blight lay waste my laurels?
Is this fam'd arm to me alone defencelefs?
Has it so often prop'd this empire's glory,
Fenc'd like a rampart the *Castilian* throne,
To me alone disgraceful! to its master uselefs!
O sharp remembrance of departed glory!
O fatal dignity too dearly purchas'd!
Now, haughty *Gormaz*, now guide thou my prince;
Insulted honour is unfit t'approach him.
And thou, once glorious weapon, fare thee well,
Old servant worthy of an abler master;
Leave now for ever his abandon'd side,
And to revenge him, grace some nobler art.
My son!

Enter Carlos.

O *Carlos!* can'ft thou bear difhonour!

Car. What villain dares occafion, fir, the queftion?
Give me his name, the proof fhall anfwer him.

Alv. O juft reproach! O prompt refentful fire!
My blood rekindles at thy manly flame,
And glads my labouring heart with youth's return.
Up, up, my fon——I cannot fpeak my fhame——
Revenge, revenge me!

Car. O my rage! of what?

Alv. Of an indignity fo vile, my heart
Redoubles all its tortuie to repeat it.
A blow! a blow! my boy.

Car. Diftraction! fury!

Alv. In vain, alas, this feeble arm affail'd
With mortal vengeance the aggreffor's heart:
He dally'd with my age, o'erborn, infulted;
Therefore to thy young arm for fure revenge
My foul's diftrefs commits my fword and caufe:
Purfue him, *Carlos,* to the world's laft bounds,
And from his heart tear back our bleeding honour.
Nay, to inflame thee more, thou'lt find his brow
Cover'd with laurels, and far fam'd his prowefs;
Oh! I have feen him dreadful in the field,
Cut thro' whole fquadrons his deftructive way,
And fnatch the gore-dy'd ftandard from the foe.

Car. O rack not with his fame my tortur'd heart,
That burns to know him, and eclipfe his glory.

Alv. Tho' I forefee, 'twill ftrike thy foul to hear it,
Yet fince our gafping honour calls for thy
Relief—O *Carlos,* 'tis *Ximena's* father——

Car. Ha!

Alv. Paufe not for a reply—I know thy love,
I know the tender obligations of thy heart,
And even lend a figh to thy diftrefs.
I grant, *Ximena* dearer than thy life;
But wounded honour muft furmount them both.
I need not urge thee more; thou know'ft my wrong,
'Tis in thy heart, and in thy hand the vengeance:
Blood only is the balm for grief like mine,
Which till obtain'd, I will in darknefs mourn,
Nor lift my eyes to light, till thy return.

But haste, o'ertake this blaster of my name,
Fly swift to vengeance, and bring back my fame. [*Exit.*
 Car. Relentlefs heav'n! is all thy thunder gone ?
Not one bolt left to finifh my defpair?
Lie ftill, my heart, and clofe this deadly wound ;
Stir not to thought, for motion is thy ruin.
But fee, the frighted poor *Ximena* comes,
And with her tremblings ftrikes thee cold as death.
My helplefs father too, o'erwhelm'd with fhame,
Begs his difmiffion to his grave with honour.
Ximena weeps, heart-pierc'd *Alvarez* groans :
Rage lifts my fword, and love arrefts my arm ;
O ! double torture of diftracting woe.
Is there no mean betwixt thefe fharp extremes ?
Muft honour perifh, if I fpare my love ?
O ignominious pity ! fhameful foftnefs !
Muft I, to right *Alvarez*, kill *Ximena?*
O cruel vengeance ! O heart-wounding honour !
Shall I forfake her in her foul's extremes,
Deprefs the virtue of her filial tears,
And bury in a tomb our nuptial joy ?
Shall that juft honour that fubdu'd her heart,
Now build its fame relentlefs on her forrows ?
Inftruct me, heav'n, that gav'ft me this diftrefs,
To chufe, and bear me worthy of my being !
O love ! forgive me, if my hurry'd foul
Shou'd act with error in this ftorm of fortune !
For heav'n can tell what pangs I feel to fave thee !
But hark ! the fhrieks of drowning honour call !
'Tis finking, gafping, while I ftand in paufe.
Plunge in, my heart, and fave it from the billows.
It will be fo——the blow's too fharp a pain,
And vengeance has at leaft this juft excufe,
That e'en *Ximena* blufhes, while I bear it :
Her generous heart, that was by honour won,
Muft, when that honour's ftain'd, abjure my love.
     O peace of mind, farewel ! Revenge, I come !
     And raife thy altar on a mournful tomb.   [*Exit.*

ACT III.

Garcia *and* Gormaz.

Gor. THE king is mafter of his will and me.
But be it as it may—what's done's irrevo-
cable.

Gar. My lord, you ill receive this mark of favour,
And while thus obftinate, inflame your fault.
When fovereign power defcends to afk of fubjects
The due fubmiffion, which its will may force,
Your danger's greater from fuch flighted mildnefs,
Than fhou'd you difobey its full commands.

Gor. The confequence, perhaps, may prove it fo.

Gar. Have you no fear of what his frown may do?

Gor. Has he no fear of what my wrongs may do?
Men of my rank are not in hours undone;
When I am crufh'd, I fall with vengeance round me.

Gar. The rafh indignity you've done *Alvarez,*
Without fome proof of wrong, bears no excufe.

Gor. I am myfelf the judge of what I feel;
I feel him falfe, and feeling muft refent.

Gar. Shall it be deem'd a falfhood to accept
A dignity by royal hands confer'd?

Gor. He fhou'd have wav'd it; firft confulted me.
He might have held me ftill his friend fincere;
Have fhar'd my fortunes, as a friend intreating;
But bafelefs, thus to out me of my right,
By treacherous acts to do me private wrong,
Is what I never can forgive, and have refented.

Gar. But in this violence you offend the king,
The fanction of whofe choice claim'd more regard.

Gor. Why am I fretted with thefe chains of honour,
Lefs free than others in my juft refentments?
Who unprovok'd myfelf, do no man wrong,
But injur'd, am as ftorms implacable.

Gar. My lord, this ftubborn temper will undo you.

Gor. Then, Sir, *Alvarez* will be fatisfy'd.

Gar. Be yet perfuaded, and compofe this broil.

Gor. My refolution's fix'd; let's wave the fubject.

Gar. Will you refuse all terms of reparation?

Gor. All! all! that are not from my honour due!

Gar. Dare you not trust that honour with your king?

Gor. My life's my king's! my honour is my own.

Gar. What's then in short your answer? For the king
Expects it on my first return.

Gor. 'Tis this;
That I dare die, but cannot bow to shame.

Gar. My lord, I take my leave.

Gor. Don *Garcia*'s servant.   [*Exit* Garcia.
Who fears not death, smiles at the frowns of power.

Enter Carlos.

Car. My lord, your leave to talk with you.

Gor. Be free.
I did expect you on this late occasion.

Car. I'm glad to find you do my honour right,
And hope you'll not refuse it wrong'd *Alvarez*.

Gor. He had a sword to right himself.

Car. That sword is here.

Gor. 'Tis well; the place—and let our time be short.

Car. One moment's respite for *Ximena*'s sake,
She has not wrong'd me, and my heart wou'd spare her;
We both, without a stain to either's honour,
May pity her distress, and pause to save her.
Nor need I blush, that I suspend my cause,
Since with its vengeance her sure woes are blended:
Not for myself, but for her tender sake,
I bend me to the earth, and beg for mercy.
Let not her virtues suffer for her love;
O! lay not on her innocence the grief
Of a mourn'd father's, or a lover's blood;
O! spare her sighs, prevent her streaming tears;
Stop this effusion of my bleeding honour,
And heal, if possible, its wounds with peace.

Gor. What you have offer'd for *Ximena*'s sake,
Will, in her gratitude, be full repaid;
And for the peace you ask, that's yours to give.
Submission 'tis in vain to hope, for know,
I have this hour refus'd it to the king.
Thy father's arts betray'd my friendship's faith;

G 2

I felt the wrong, and, as I ought, reveng'd it.
We're now on equal terms : but if his cause
So deep is in thy heart, that thou resolv'st,
With fruitless vengeance, to provoke my rage,
Then thou, not I, art author of thy ruin.

   Car. Support me now, *Ximena,* guard my heart,
And bar this pressing provocation's entrance.   [*Aside.*
Have I, my lord, in person wrong'd you?

   Gor. No.

   Car. Why then these fatal cruelties to me,
That I must lose, or wrong *Ximena*'s love ?
For she must scorn me, shou'd I bear my shame;
Or fly me, though my honour should revenge it

   Gor. Place that to thy misfortune, not to me.

   Car. Not to you?
Am I not forc'd by wrongs, I blush to name,
To prosecute this fatal reparation ?
Which, had you temper, or a feeling here;
Had you the spirit to confess your error,
Your heart's confusion had subdu'd *Alvarez,*
And thrown you at his injur'd feet for pardon.

   Gor. If thou com'st here to talk me from my sense,
Or think'st with words t'extenuate his guilt,
Thou offer'st to the winds thy forceless plea.
I will not bear the mention of his truth;
His falshood's here, 'tis rooted in my heart,
And justifies a worse revenge than I have taken.

   Car. O patience, heav'n ! O tortur'd rage ! Not speak !
The pious pangs of my torn soul insulted !
Have I for this bow'd down my humble knee,
To swell thy triumph o'er my father's wrongs,
And hear him tainted with a traytor's practice ?
O give me back that vile submissive shame,
That I may meet thee with retorted scorn,
And right my honour with untainted vengeance.
Yet no—with-hold it, take it to acquit my love !
That sacrifice was to *Ximena* due,
Her helpless sufferings claim'd that pang : And since
I cannot bring dishonour to her arms,
Thus my rack'd heart pours forth its last adieus,

And makes libation of its bleeding peace :
Farewell, dear injur'd softnefs——Follow me.
   Gor. Lead on——yet hold ! fhou'd we together forth,
It may create fufpicion, and prevent us :
Propofe the place, I'll take fome different circle.
   Car. Behind the ramparts, near the *Weftern* gate.
   Gor. Expect me on the inftant.
   Car. Poor *Ximena !*   [*Exit.*
   Gor. Deep as refentment lodges in my heart,
It feels fome pity there for *Carlos'* paffion——
It fhall be fo—his brave refentment's juft ;
                                       [*Writes in Tablets.*

   And hard his fate—both ways—this legacy
   Shall right my honour and my enemy.   [*Exit.*

              Enter Belzara, *and* Ximena.

   Bel. Look up, *Ximena*, and fupprefs thy fears.
What tho' a tranfient cloud o'ercaft thy joy,
Shall we conclude from thence a wreck muft follow ?
   Xim. Can I refift the fears that reafon forms ?
Have I not caufe to tremble in the ftorm ?
While horror, ruin, and defpair's in view ?
Can I fupport the good *Alvarez'* fhame,
Whofe generous heart took pity on our love,
And not let fall a grateful tear to mourn it ?
Can I behold fierce *Carlos*, ftung with his difgrace,
Breaking like fire from thefe weak-holding arms,
And not fink down with terror at his rage ?
Muft I not tremble, for the blood may follow ?
If by his arm my haplefs father falls,
Am I not forc'd with rigour to revenge him ?
If *Carlos* by my father's fword fhou'd bleed,
Am I not bound with double grief to mourn him ?
One gave me life, fhall I not revere him ?
The other is my life, can I furvive him ?
   Bel. Her griefs have fomething of fuch mournful force,
That, tho' not equal to my own, I feel them.
   Xim. *Carlos* you fee too fhuns my fight ; no news,
No tidings yet arrive, tho' I have fent
My fwifteft fears a thoufand ways to find him.
Who can fupport thefe terrors of fufpenfe ?
                          G 3

Bel. Be not thus torn with wild uncertain fears:
Carlos may yet arrive, and save your peace;
He is too much a lover to resist
The tender pleadings of *Ximena*'s sorrow.
One word, one sigh from you arrests his arm,
And makes the tempest of his rage subside.

Xim. And say that I cou'd conquer him; with tears,
And terrors cou'd subdue his piteous heart,
To yield his honour and its cause to love,
What will the world not say of his compliance?
Can I be happy in his fame's disgrace?
Can love subsist on shame, that sprung from honour?
Shall I reduce him to such hard contempt,
And raise on infamy our nuptial joy?
Ah no! no means are left for my relief:
Let him resist, or yield to my distress,
Or shame, or sorrow's sure to meet me.

Bel. *Ximena* has, I see, a soul refin'd,
Too great, too just, too noble to be happy:
True virtue must despair from this vile world
To crown its days with unallay'd reward.
But see, your servant is return'd! good news,
Kind heav'n!

Enter a Page.

Xim. Speak quickly, hast thou seen Don *Carlos?*
Page. Madam, where your commands directed me,
I've made the strictest search in vain to find him.
Xim. Now, now *Belzara*, where's that hope thou
       gav'st me?
Has no one seen him pass, or heard of him?
Bel. Nor hast thou gain'd no knowledge of his steps?
Page. As I return'd, the centinel, that guards
The gate, inform'd me, that he saw him scarce
Ten minutes hence pass in disorder'd haste
From out this very house alone.
Bel. Alone?
Page. Alone; and after soon my lord, wrapt in
His cloak, without a servant, follow'd him.
Xim. O Heav'n!
Bel. No servant, said'st thou?

Page. None.—And as
My lord came forth, the foldier ftanding to
His arms, he fign'd forbiddance, and reply'd,
Be fure you faw me not.

   Xim. Then ruin's fure——
They are engag'd, and fatal blood muft follow:
    Excufe, my dear, this hurry of my fate,
    One moment loft may prove an age too late.   [Exit.

   Bel. Howe'er my own afflictions prefs my heart,
I bear a part in poor *Ximena's* grief,
Tho' e'en the worft that can befall her hopes,
May better be endur'd than what I feel!
O! nothing can deftroy her lover's truth;
Carlos may prove unhappy, not inconftant:
Whate'er difafters may obftruct her joy,
The comfort of his truth is fure to find her.
That thought ev'n pains of parting may remove,
Or fill up all the fpace of abfence with delight.
But I, alas! am left to my defpair alone,
Confin'd to figh in folitude my woes,
Or hide with anguifh what I blufh to bear.
In vain the woman's pride refents my wrongs,
Unconquer'd love maintains his empire ftill,
And with new force infults my heart's refiftance.

Enter Alonzo *haftily.*

   Alon. Your pardon, madam——Have you feen lord
    Gormaz?
I come to warn him that he ftir not hence,
The guards are order'd to attend his doors.

   Bel. Alas, they are too late! *Carlos* and he
Are both gone forth, 'tis fear'd with fatal purpofe;
And poor *Ximena* drown'd in tears has follow'd 'em.

   Alon. Then 'tis indeed too late: I wifh my friend,
The rafh Don *Sanchez,* has not blown this fire.
Be not concern'd, madam, I know your griefs,
And, as a friend, have labour'd to prevent 'em.
You have not told *Ximena* of his falfhood?

   Bel. Alas! I durft not; knowing that her friendfhip
Would, for my fake, fo coldly treat his vows,
That 'twou'd but more provoke him to infult me.

G 4

Alon. You judge him right; patience will yet recall him.
'Tis not his love, but pride pursues *Ximena*;
A youthful heat, that with the toil will tire.
Be comforted, I'll still observe his steps,
And when I find him staggering, catch him back
To love, and warm him with his vows of honour.
But duty calls me to the king——Shall I
Attend you, Madam?

Bel. Sir, I thank your care:
My near concern for poor *Ximena*'s fate,
Keeps me impatient here, 'till her return.   [*Exeunt.*

Enter King, Garcia, Sanchez, *Attendants.*

King. Since mild intreaties fail, our power shall
          force him :
Cou'd he suppose, his insult to our person offer'd,
His outrage done within our palace walls,
Deserv'd the lenity we've deign'd to shew him ?
Is yet *Alonzo* with our orders gone ?

Gar. He is, my lord, but not return'd.

D. San. Dread Sir,
For what the Count has offer'd to *Alvarez,*
I dare not plead excuse; but as his friend,
Wou'd beg your royal leave to mitigate
His seeming disobedience to your pleasure ;
Restraint, however just, oppos'd against
The tide of passion, makes the current fiercer,
Which of itself in time had ebb'd to reason ;
Your will surpriz'd him in his heart's emotion,
Ere thought had leisure to compose his mind.
Great souls are jealous of their honour's shame,
And bend reluctant to enjoin'd submission.
Had your commands oblig'd him to repair
Alvarez' wrongs with hazards in your service,
Were it to face the double-number'd foe,
To pass the rapid stream thro' showers of fire,
To force the trenchment, or to storm the breach,
I'll answer he'd embrace with joy the charge,
And march intrepid in commands of honour.

King. We doubt not of his daring in the field ;
But he mistakes, if he concludes from thence,

That to perfift in wrong is height of fpirit,
Or to have acted wrong is always bafe:
Perfection's not the attribute of man,
Nor therefore can a fault confeft degrade him:
The loweft minds have fpirit to offend,
But few can reach the courage to confefs it.
Submitting to our will, the count had loft
No fame, nor can we pardon his refufa'.
What you have faid, Don *Sanchez*, fpeaks the friend;
What we refolve, 'tis fit fhou'd fpeak the king:
We both have faid enough——The public now
Requires our thought. We are inform'd ten fail
Of warlike veffels, mann'd with our old foes
The *Moors*, were late difcover'd off our coaft,
And fteering to the river's mouth their courfe.

   Gar, The lives, Sir, they have loft in like attempts
Muft make them cautious to repeat the danger;
This is no time to fear them.

   King. Nor contemn;
Too full fecurity has oft' been fatal.
Confider with what eafe the flood at night
May bring them down t'infult our capital.
Let at the port, and on the walls, our guards
Be doubled; till the morn that force may ferve.
Gormaz has tim'd it ill to be in fault,
When his immediate prefence is requir'd.

   Gar. My liege, *Alonzo* is return'd.

Enter Alonzo.

   King. 'Tis well!
Have you obey'd us? Is the Count confin'd?
   Alon. Your orders, Sir, arriv'd unhappily
Too late; the Count, with *Carlos*, was before
Gone forth, to end their fatal difference.
As I came back, I met the gathering croud
In fright, and hurrying to the weftern gate,
To fee, as they reported, in the field
The body of fome murder'd nobleman.
Struck with my fears I hafted to the place,
Where, to my fenfe's horror, when arriv'd,
I found them true, and *Gormaz* juft expir'd;

G 5

While fair *Ximena*, to adorn the woe,
Bath'd his pale breathlefs body with her tears,
Calling with cries for juftice on his head,
Whofe rueful hand had done the barb'rous deed.
The pitying crowd took part in her diftrefs,
And join'd her moving plaints for due revenge;
While fome, in kinder feeling of her griefs,
Remov'd the mournful object from her eyes,
And to the neighbouring convent bore the body,
Which when committed to the abbot's care,
I left the preffing throng to tell the news.

   King. *Ximena*'s griefs are follow'd with our own,
For tho' in fome degree the haughty count
Drew on himfelf the fon's too juft revenge,
We cannot lofe without a deep concern
So true a fubject, and fo brave a foldier:
However pity may for *Carlos* plead,
Death ends his failings, and demands our grief.

   Alon. Sir, here in the tablets of the unhappy count,
In his own hand thefe written lines were found.

   King. ' *Alvarez* wrong'd me in my mafter's favour:
' *Carlos* is brave, and has deferv'd *Ximena*.' [*Reading.*
Strange, generous fpirit, now we pity thee.

   Alon. Behold, Sir, where the loft *Ximena* comes,
O'erwhelm'd with forrow, to demand your juftice.

Enter Ximena.

   Xim. O facred Sir! forgive my grief's intrufion,
Behold a helplefs orphan at your feet,
Who for a father's blood implores your juftice

Enter Alvarez, *haftily.*

   Alv. O! turn, dread royal mafter, turn your eyes
See on the earth your faithful foldier proftrate,
Whofe honour's juft revenge intreats your mercy.
   Xim. O godlike monarch, hear my louder cries!
   Alv. O be not to the old and helplefs deaf!
   Xim. Revenge yourfelf, your violated laws.
   Alv. Support not violence in rude aggreffors.
   Xim. Be greatly good, and do the injur'd juftice.
   Alv. Be greater ftill, and fhew the valiant mercy.

Xim. O Sir, your crown's support and guard is gone,
The impious *Carlos*' sword has kill'd my father——
Alv. And like a pious son aveng'd his own.
King. Rise, fair *Ximena*, and *Alvarez*, rise!
With equal sorrow we receive your plaints.
Both shall be heard apart——proceed, *Ximena;*
Alvarez, in your place you speak, be patient.
Xim. What can I say? But miseries like mine
May plead with plainest truths their piteous cause.
Is he not dead? Is not my father kill'd?
Have not these eyes beheld his ghastly wound,
And mixt with fruitless tears his streaming blood?
That blood which in his royal master's cause
So oft has sprung him thro' your foes victorious?
That blood, which all the raging swords of war
Cou'd never reach, a young presumptuous arm
Has dar'd within your view to sacrifice?
These eyes beheld it stream——Excuse my grief,
My tears wil better than my words explain me.
King. Take heart, *Ximena*, we're inclin'd to hear thee.
Xim. O shall a life so faithful to the king
Fall unreveng'd, and stain his glory?
Shall merit so important to the state
Be left expos'd to sacrilegious rage,
And fall the sacrifice of private passion?
Alvarez says his honour was insulted;
Yet, be it so, was there no king to right it?
Who better cou'd protect it than the donor?
Shall *Carlos* wrest the sceptre from your hand,
And point the sword of justice whom to punish?
O! if such outrage may escape with pardon,
Whose life's secure from his self judging rage?
O where's protection, if *Ximena*'s tears,
And tender passion cou'd not save her father?
King. *Alvarez*, answer her.
Alv. My heart's too full:
Divided, torn, distracted with its griefs,
How can I plead poor *Carlos*' cause, when I
Am toucht with pity of *Ximena*'s woe?
Her suffering piety has caught my soul,
And only leaves me sorrow to defend me.

Ximena has a grief I cannot difallow,
Nor dare I hope for pardon, but your pity;
Carlos even yet may merit fome compaffion.
Perhaps I'm partial to his piety,
And fee his deeds with a fond father's eye;
But that I ftill muft leave to royal mercy!
O Sir, imagine what the brave endure,
When the chafte front of honour is infulted,
Her fame abus'd, and ravifh'd by a blow.
Oh piercing, piercing muft the torture be,
If foft *Ximena* wanted power t'appeafe it.
Pardon this weaknefs of o'erflowing nature;
I cannot fee fuch filial virtue perifh,
And not let fall a tear to mourn its hardfhip.

   Xim. O my divided heart! oh poor *Alvarez!* [*Afide.*
   King. Compofe thy griefs, my good old friend, we
     feel them.

   Alv. If *Gormaz'* blood muft be with blood reveng'd,
O do not, facred Sir, mifplace your juftice;
Mine was the guilt, and be on me the vengeance:
Carlos but acted what my fufferings prompted;
The fatal fword was not his own, but mine:
I gave it with my wrongs into his hand,
Which had been innocent had mine been able.
On me your vengeance will be juft and mild!
My days, alas! are drawing to their end;
But *Carlos* fpar'd, may yet live long to ferve you:
Preferve my fon, and I embrace my fate.
Since he has fav'd my honour from the grave,
O lay me gently there to reft for ever.

   King. Your mutual plaints require our tend'reft thought,
Our counfel fhall be fummon'd to affift us——
Look up, my fair, and calm thy forrows;
Thy king is now thy father, and will right thee:
Alvarez on his word has liberty:
Be *Carlos* found to anfwer to his charge.
Sanchez, wait you *Ximena* to her reft,
Whom on the morrow's noon we full will anfwer.

   Hard is the tafk of juftice, where diftrefs
   Excites our mercy, yet demands redrefs.   [*Exeunt.*

ACT IV.

Belzara *alone, in* Ximena's *apartment.*

Bel. SURE some ill-boding planet must preside
    Malignant to the peace of tender lovers!
Undone *Ximena!* O relentless honour!
That first subdu'd thy generous heart, then rais'd
Thy lover's fatal arm to pierce it through
Thy father's life, and make thy virtue wretched:
The haplefs *Carlos* too is loft for ever!
Condemn'd to fly an exile from her fight,
In whom he only lives! Oh heav'n! he's here,
His miferies have made him defperate.

Enter Carlos.

Carlos, what wild diftraction has poffeft thee,
That thus thou feek'ft thy fafety in thy ruin?
Is this a place to hide thy wretched head,
Where juftice, and *Ximena's* fure to find thee?
  Car. I would not hide me from *Ximena's* fight.
Banifht from her, I every moment die:
Since I muft perifh, let her frowns deftroy me,
Her anger's fharper than the fword of juftice.
  Bel. Alas, I pity thee, but would not have
Thee tempt the firft emotions of her heart,
While duty and refentment yet tranfport her:
I wait each moment her return from court,
Which now, be fure, will be with friends attended:
O fly, for pity's fake, regard her fame;
Shou'd you be feen, what muft the world conclude?
Wou'd you encreafe her miferies, to have
Malicious tongues report her love conceal'd
Beneath her roof her father's murderer?
But fee, fhe comes! O hide thee but a moment!
Kill not her honour too, let that perfuade thee.
                        [*Exit* Carlos.
Don *Sanchez* here! Oh heav'ns! how I tremble! [*retires.*

Enter Sanchez *and* Ximena.

D. *San.* This noble conqueft, madam, of your love,

To after-ages muſt record your fame.
Juſt is your grief, and your reſentment great,
And great the victim that ſhould fall before it,
But words are empty ſuccours to diſtreſs;
Therefore command my actions to relieve you.
Wou'd you have ſure revenge, employ this ſword;
My fortune and my life is yours to right you;
Accept my ſervice, and you over-pay it.

   Bel. O faithleſs barb'rous man! but I'll divert
Thy cruel aim, and uſe my power for *Carlos.* [*Apart.*
   Xim. O miſerable me!
   Bel. Take comfort, madam.
   D. *San. Belzara* here! then I have loſt th' occaſion.
                                    [*Aſide.*
Yet I may urge enough to give her pain:
Commanding me, you make your vengeance ſure.
   Xim. That were t'offend the king, to whom I have
Appeal'd, and whence I now muſt only wait it.
   D. *San.* Revenge from juſtice, madam, moves ſo ſlow,
That oft' the watchful criminal eſcapes it.
Appeal to your reſentment, you ſecure it.
Carlos, you found, wou'd truſt no other power,
And 'tis but juſt you quit him, as he wrong'd you.
   Bel. Alas, Don *Sanchez,* madam, feels not love;
He little thinks how *Carlos* fills your heart;
What ſhining glory in his crime appears;
What pangs it coſt him to take part with honour:
That you muſt hate the hand that could deſtroy him.
Sanchez, to ſhew the real friend, would uſe
His ſecret int'reſt with the king to ſpare him;
For tho' you're bound in duty to purſue him,
Yet love, alas! wou'd with a conſcious joy,
Applaud the power that cou'd unbid preſerve him.
   Xim. O kind *Belzara!* how thou feel'ſt my ſufferings!
Yet I muſt think, Don *Sanchez* means me well.
   D. *San.* Confuſion! how her ſubtle tongue has foil'd
    me————   [*Aſide.*
Madam, ſome other time I'll beg your leave
To wait your ſervice, and approve my friendſhip.
   Xim. Oh! every friend, but *Carlos,* is at hand,
To help me! Grief, Sir, is unfit to thank you.

D. San. Oh! if such beauties 'midst her sorrows shine,
What darting charms must point her smiling eyes ! [*Exit.*
  Xim. At length I'm free, at liberty to think,
And give my miseries a loose of sorrow.
O *Belzara!* *Carlos* has kill'd my father !
Weep! weep my eyes, pour down your baleful show'rs,
He that in grief shou'd be my heart's support,
Has wrought my sorrows, and must fall their victim.
When *Carlos* is destroy'd, what comfort's left me?
Spite of my wrongs he still inhabits here :
O still his fatal virtues plead his cause ;
His filial honour charms my woman's heart,
And there ev'n yet he combats with my father.
  Bel. Restrain these headstrong sallies of your heart,
And try with slumbers to compose your spirits.
  Xim. O! where's repose for misery like mine ?
How grievous, heav'n! how bitter is my portion !
O shall a parent's blood cry unreveng'd ?
Shall impious love suborn my heart to pay
His ashes but unprofitable tears,
And bury in my shame the great regards of duty ?
  Bel. Alas, that duty is discharg'd ; you have
Appeal'd to justice, and shou'd wait its course.
Nor are you bound with rigour to enforce it ;
His hard misfortunes may deserve compassion.
  Xim. O! that they do deserve, it is my griefs
Cou'd I withdraw my pity from his cause,
Were falshood, pride, or insolence his crime,
My just revenge, without a pang, shou'd reach him,
But as he is supported with excuse,
Defended by the cries of bleeding honour,
Whose cruel laws none but the great obey ;
My hopeless heart is tortur'd with extreams,
It mourns in vengeance, and at mercy shudders.
  Bel. O what will be at last the dire resolve
Of your afflicted soul ?
  Xim. There is but one.
Can end my sorrows, and preserve my fame ;
  The sole resource my miseries can have,
  Is to pursue, destroy; then meet him in the grave.
                        [*Going.*

Carlos *meets her.*

Amazement, horror! have my eyes their fenfe?
Or do my raving griefs create this phantom?
Support me! help me! hide me from the vifion!
For 'tis not *Carlos* come to brave my forrows.

         [Carlos *kneels.*

 Bel. O turn your eye, in pity of his griefs,
Refign'd, and proftrate at your feet for mercy.
 Xim. What will my woes do with me?
 Bel. Now!
Now, conqu'ring love, fhoot all thy fires to fave him;
Now fnatch the palm from cruel honour's brow;
Maintain thy empire and relieve the wretched:
O hang upon his tongue thy thrilling charms,
To hold her heart, and kill the hopes of *Sanchez.* [*Exit.*
 Car. O pierce not thus, with thy offended eyes,
The wretched heart that of itfelf is breaking.
 Xim. Can I be wounded, and not fhrink with pain?
Can I fupport, with temper, him that fhed
My father's blood, triumphant in my ruin?
O *Carlos! Carlos!* was thy heart of ftone?
Was nothing due to poor *Ximena's* peace?
O! 'twas not thus I felt new pains for thee,
When at my feet thy fighs of love were pity'd,
And all hereditary hate forgotten!
Tho' bound in filial honour, to infult
Thy flame; I broke thro' all to crown thy vows,
And bore the cenfure of my race to fave thee:
-And am I thus requited? left forlorn?
The tender paffion of my heart defpis'd!
Cou'd not my terrors move one fpark of mercy?
No mild abatement of thy ftern revenge,
T' excufe thy crime, or juftify my love?
 Car. O hear me but a moment.
 Xim. O my heart!
 Car. One mournful word!
 Xim. Ah! leave me to defpair!
 Car. One dying laft adieu, then wreak thy vengeance:
Behold the fword that has undone thee.
 Xim. Ah! ftain'd with my father's blood! O rueful object!

Car. O *Ximena!*

Xim. Take hence that horrid steel,
That, while I bear thy sight, arraigns my virtue,

  Car. Endure it rather to support resentment,
T'enflame thy vengeance, and to pierce thy victim.
I am more wretched than thy rage can wish me.

  Xim. O cruel *Carlos!* in one day thou hast kill'd
The father with thy sword, the daughter with
Thy sight——O yet remove that fatal object;
I cannot bare the glare of its reproach;
If thou wou'dst have me hear thee, hide the cause,
That wounds reflection to our mutual ruin.

  Car. Thus I obey————but how shall I proceed?
What words can help me to deserve thy hearing?
How can I plead my wounded honour's cause,
Where injur'd love and duty are my judges?
Or how shall I repent me of a crime,
Which, uncommitted, had deserv'd thy scorn?
Yet think not, O I conjure thee! think not,
But that I bore a thousand racks of love,
While my conflicting honour press'd for vengeance.
O I endur'd! submitted ev'n to shame,
Begg'd, as for life, for peaceful reparation!
But all in vain! like water sprinkled on
A fire, those drops but made him burn the more,
And only added to thy father's fiercenefs.
Reduc'd, at last, to these extremes of torture,
That I must be, or infamous, or wretched,
I sav'd my honour, and refign'd to ruin.
Nor think, *Ximena,* honour had prevail'd,
But that thy nobler soul oppos'd thy charms,
And told my heart, none but the brave deserv'd thee.
Now having thus difcharg'd my honour's debt,
And wash'd my injur'd father's stains away,
What yet remains of life is due to love.
Behold the wretch, whose honour's fatal fame
Is founded on the ruin of thy peace:
Receive the victim, which thy griefs demand,
Prepar'd to bleed, and bending to the blow.

  Xim. O *Carlos,* I must take thee at thy word,
But must with equal justice too difcharge

My ties of love, as fatal bonds of duty.
O think not, tho' enforc'd to thefe extremes,
My heart is yet infenfible to thee!
O! I muft thank thee for thy painful paufe;
The generous fhame thy tortur'd honour bore,
When at my father's feet my fuff'rings threw thee.
Can I prefent thee in that dear confufion,
And not with grateful fighs of pity mourn thee?
I can lament thee, but I dare not pardon;
Thy duty done, reminds me of my own;
My filial piety, like thine diftrefs'd,
Compels me to be miferably juft,
And afks my love a victim to my fame:
Yet think not duty cou'd o'er love prevail,
But that thy nobler foul affures my heart,
Thou wou'd'ft defpife the paffion that cou'd fave thee.

 Car. Since I muft die, let that kind hand deftroy me.
Let not the wretch once honour'd with thy love,
Thy *Carlos,* once thought worthy of thy arms,
Be dragg'd a public fpectacle to juftice;
To draw the irkfome pity of a crowd,
Who may with vulgar reafon call thee cruel.
My death from thee will elevate thy vengeance,
And fhew, like mine, thy duty fcorn'd affiftance.

 Xim. Shall I then take affiftance? and from thee?
Accept that vengeance from thy heart's defpair?
No, *Carlos,* no!
I will not judge, like thee, my private wrongs,
But to the courfe of juftice truft my duty,
Which fhall, in every part, untainted flow,
Unmix'd with gain'd advantage o'er thy love,
And from its own pure fountain raife my glory.

 Car. O can my death with fhame advance that glory?
Can I do more than perifh to appeafe thee?
Can my misfortunes too have reach'd thy hate?

 Xim. Can hate have part in interviews like this?
Nay, can I give thee greater proof of love,
Than that I truft my vengeance with thy honour?
Art not thou now within my power to feize?
Yet I'll releafe thee, *Carlos,* on thy word;
Give me thy word, that on the morrow noon,

Before the king in perſon thou wilt anſwer,
And take the ſhelter of the night to leave me.
  Car. O! thou haſt found the way to fix my ruin!
It muſt be ſo, thou ſhalt have ample vengeance;
Purſu'd by thee, my life's not worth the ſaving;
But then that fatal honour, my engagement,
That at the hour propos'd, I'll meet my fate——
But muſt we part, *Ximena*, like ſworn foes?
Has love no ſenſe of all its periſh'd hopes?
Diſmiſs my miſeries, at leaſt, with pity:
May I not breathe upon this injur'd boſom
One parting ſigh, to eaſe my wounded ſoul,
And looſe the anguiſh of a broken heart?
  Xim. Support me, heav'n—we meet again to-morrow.
  Car. To-morrow we muſt meet, like enemies,
Thy piercing eyes, relentleſs in revenge,
And all the ſoftneſs of thy heart forgotten;
This only moment is our life of love.
O take not from this little interval,
The poor expiring comfort that is left me.
                       [Ximena *weeps.*
My heart's confounded with thy ſoft compaſſion,
And doats upon the virtue that deſtroys me.
  Xim. O! I ſhall have the ſtart of thee in woe;
Thou can'ſt but fall for her thou lov'ſt; but what
Muſt ſhe endure that loves thee——and deſtroys thee?
Yet, *Carlos*, take this comfort in thy fate——
That if the hand of juſtice ſhou'd o'ertake thee,
Thy mournful urn ſhall hold *Ximena's* aſhes.
  Car. O miracle of love!
  Xim. O mortal ſorrow!
But haſte, O leave me while my heart's reſolv'd;
Fly, fly me, *Carlos*, leſt thou taint my fame;
Leſt in this ebbing rigour of my ſoul
I tell thee, th' I proſecute thy fate,
My ſecret wiſh is, that my cauſe may fail me.
  Car. O ſpirit of compaſſion! O *Ximena!*
What pangs and ruin have our parents coſt us!
  Farewel, thou treaſure of my ſoul——O ſtay!
  Take not at once my ſhort-liv'd joys away.

While thus I fix me on thy mournful eyes,
Let my diftreffes to extreams arife.
Thy victim's now fecure; for thus to part,
I fate thy vengeance with a broken heart. [*Exeunt.*

Enter Alvarez with Noblemen, Officers, and others.

1*ft. Nob.* Thefe few, my lord, are on my part engag'd.
In half an hour Don *Henrique de Las Torres,*
With fixty more, will wait upon your caufe,
Refolv'd, and ready, all like us, to right you:
Since the juft quarrel of your houfe muft live,
Since the brave blood of *Carlos* is purfu'd,
The race of *Gormaz* fhall attend his afhes.

Alv. My lord, this mark of your exalted honour
Will bind me ever grateful to your friendfhip;
Tho' I ftill hope the mercy of the king
Will fpare the criminal, whofe guilt is honour.
The fervice I have done the ftate has found
A bounteous mafter always to reward it;
Nor am I yet fo wedded to my reft,
But that I ftill can on occafion break it.
The *Moors* are anchor'd now within the river,
And, as I'm told, near landing to infult us——
Wherefore I wou'd entreat you at this time,
To wave my private danger for the public.
Since chance has form'd us to fo brave a body,
Let us not part inactive in our honour;
Let's feize this glad occafion of th' alarm,
Let's chafe thefe robbers in our king's defence,
And bravely merit, not demand his mercy.

1*ft. Nob. Alvarez* may command us, who is ftill
Himfelf, and owns no caufe unmix'd with honour.

Alv. How now! the news.

Enter a fervant, who whifpers Alvarez.

Juft enter'd, and alone!
O heav'n, my prayers are heard! my noble friends,
Something to our prefent purpofe has occurr'd;
Let me intreat you, forward to the garden,
Where you will find a treble number of
Our forces affembled on the like occafion;

Myself will in a moment bring you news,
That will confirm and animate our hopes. [*Exeunt Nob.*

Enter Carlos.

My *Carlos !* O do I live once more t'embrace thee,
Prop of my age, and guardian of my fame !
Nor think, my champion, that my joy's thus wild,
For that thou only haft reveng'd my honour,
(Tho' that's a thought might blefs me in the grave)
No, no, my fon, for thee am I tranfported ;
Alas ! I am too fenfible what pains
Thy heart muft feel from anguifh of thy love ;
And had I not new hopes that will fupport thee,
Some prefent profpect of thy pain's relief,
My fenfe of thy afflictions would deftroy me.
   Car. What means this kind compaffion of my griefs }
Is there, on earth, a cure for woes like mine ?
O, Sir, you are fo tenderly a father,
So good, I can't repent me of my duty :
Be not however jealous of my fame,
If yet I mix your tranfports with a figh,
For ruin'd love, and for the loft *Ximena :*
For fince I drag, with my defpair, my chain ;
Her fated vengeance only can relieve me.
   Alv. No more deprefs thy fpirit with defpair,
While glory and thy country's caufe fhould wake it ;
The *Moors*, not yet expected, are arriv'd ;
The tide and filent darknefs of the night
Land, in an hour, their forces at our gates :
The court's difmay'd, the people in alarm,
And loud confufion fills the frighted town.
But fortune, ere this public danger reach'd us,
Had rais'd five hundred friends, the foes of *Gormaz*,
Whofe fwords refolve to vindicate thy vengeance,
And here without expect thee at their head.
Forward, my fon, their numbers foon will fwell,
Suftain the brunt and fury of the foe.
And if thy life's fo painful to be borne,
Lay it at leaft with honour in the duft.
Caft it not fruitlefs from thee ; let thy king

First know its value, ere his laws demand it;
But time's too precious to be talk'd away.
  Advance, my son, and let thy master see,
  What he has lost in Gormaz, is redeem'd in thee.
  Car. Relenting heav'n at last has found the means
To end my miseries with guiltless honour.
Why shou'd I live a burden to myself,
A trouble to my friends, a terror to *Ximena?*
Not all the force of mercy, or of merit,
Can wash a father's blood from her remembrance,
Or reconcile the horror to her love.
Yet I'll not think her duty so severe,
But that to see me fall my country's victim
Wou'd please her passion, tho' it shock'd her vengeance:
It must be so——dying with honour I
Discharge the son, the subject, and the lover:
O! when this mangled body shall be found
A bare and undistinguish'd carcass 'midst the slain,
Will she not weep in pity of my wounds,
And own her wrongs have ample expiation?
  Her duty then may, with a secret tear,
  Confess her vengeance great, and glorious my despair.
                                    [Exit,

A C T V.

Belzara *alone.*

Bel. VIctorious *Carlos,* now resume thy hopes,
    Demand thy life, and silence thy *Ximena.*
Hard were thy fate indeed, if she alone
Should be the bar to triumphs nobly purchas'd.
But see, she comes, with mournful pomp of woe,
To prosecute this darling of the people,
And damp, with ill-tim'd griefs, the public joy.

Enter Ximena, *in mourning, attended.*

Ximena! Oh! I more than ever now
Deplore the hard afflictions that pursue thee;
While thy whole native country is in joy,

Art thou the only object of despair?
Is this a time to profecute thy caufe,
When public gratitude is bound t'oppofe thee?
When on the head of *Carlos*, which thy griefs
Demand, fortune has pour'd protection down?
The *Moors* repuls'd, his country fav'd from rapine,
His menac'd king confirm'd upon his throne,
From every heart but thine, will find a voice
To lift his echo'd praifes to the heav'ns.

   Ximena, Is't poffible? Are all thefe wonders true?
Am I the only mark of his mifdoing?
Cou'd then his fatal fword tranfpierce my father;
Yet fave a nation to defeat my vengeance?
Still as I pafs, the public voice extols
His glorious deeds, regardlefs of my wrongs;
The eye of pity, that but yefternight
Let fall a tear in feeling of my caufe,
Now turns away, retracting its compaffion,
And fpeaks the general grudge at my complaining.
But there's a king, whofe facred word's his law;
Supported by that hope, I ftill muft on,
Nor, till by him rejected, can be filent.

   Bel. Your duty fhou'd recede, when publick good
Muft fuffer in the life your caufe purfues.

   Xim. But can it be? Was it to *Carlos'* fword
The nation thus tranfported owes its fafety?
O let me tafte the pleafure, and the pain!
Tell me, *Belzara*, tell me all his glory,
O! let me furfeit on the guilty joy,
Delight my paffion, and torment my virtue.

   Bel. *Alonzo*, who was prefent, will inform us.

Enter Alonzo.

'Lonzo, if your bufinefs will permit.

   Alon. The Abbot, at whofe houfe Count *Gormaz* lies,
Has fent in hafte to fpeak with me, I guefs,
To fix the order of his funeral.   [*Apart to* Belz.

   Bel. Spare us at leaft a moment from th' occafion;
Ximena has not yet been fully told
The action of our late deliverance;
The fame of *Carlos* may compofe her forrows.

Alon. Permit the action then to praife itfelf;
Late in the night at lord *Alvarez'* houfe,
Five hundred friends were gather'd in his caufe,
T'oppofe the vengeance, that purfu'd his fon;
But in the common danger, braye *Alvarez*,
With valiant *Carlos* at their head, preferr'd
The publick fafety to their private honour,
And march'd with fwords determin'd 'gainft the *Moors.*
This brave example, ere they reach'd the harbour,
Increas'd their numbers to three thoufand ftrong.
  Bel. Were the *Moors* landed ere you reach'd the port?
  Alon. Not till fome hours after; when we arriv'd,
Our troops were form'd, *Ximena* was the word,
And *Carlos* foremoft to confront the foe.
The *Moors* not yet in view, he order'd firft
Two thirds of our divided force to lie
Conceal'd i'th' hatches of our fhips in harbour;
The reft, whofe numbers every moment fwell'd,
Halted with *Carlos*, on the fhore, impatient,
And filent on their arms repofing, pafs'd
The ftill remainder of the wafting night.
At length the brightnefs of the moon prefents
Near twenty fail approaching with the tide;
Our order ftill obferv'd, we let them pafs;
Nor at the port, or walls, a man was feen.
This deadnefs of our filence wings their hope
To feize th' occafion, and furprize us fleeping.
And now they difembark, and meet their fate;
For at the inftant they were half on fhore,
Uprofe the numbers in our fhips conceal'd,
And to the vaulted heaven thunder'd their huzza's,
Which *Carlos* echo'd from his force on fhore:
At this, amaz'd confufion feiz'd their troops,
And ere their chiefs cou'd form them to refift,
We prefs'd them on the water, drove them on
The land, then fir'd their fhips to ftop their flight:
Howe'er at length their leaders, bravely rallying,
Recover'd them to order, and a while
Suftain'd their courage, and oppos'd our fury:
But, when their burning fhips began to flame,
The dreadful blaze prefenting to their view.

Their flaughter'd heaps that fell where *Carlos* fought,
(For oh! he fought, as if to die were victory)
Their fruitlefs courage then refign'd their hopes;
And now their wounded king, defpairing, call'd
Aloud, and hail'd our general to furrender,
Whom *Carlos* anfwering receiv'd his prifoner:
At this, the reft had on fubmiffion quarter;
Our trumpets found, and fhouts proclaim our victory:
While *Carlos* bore his captive to his father,
Whofe heart, tranfported at the royal prize,
Dropt tears of joy, and to the king convey'd him,
Where now he's pleading for his fon's diftrefs,
And afks but mercy for his glorious triumph.　　*[Exit.*

　Xim. Too much! it is too much, relentlefs heaven!
Th' oppreffion's greater than my foul can bear!
O wounding virtue! O my tortur'd heart!
Art only thou forbidden to applaud him?
Cannot a nation fav'd appeafe thy vengeance?
Why! why, juft heaven, are his deeds fo glorious,
And only fatal to the heart that loves him?

　Bel. Compofe, *Ximena*, thy diforder, fee,
The king approaches, fmiling on *Alvarez*,
Whofe heart o'erflowing gufhes at his eyes,
And fpeaks his plea too ftrong for thy complaint.　*[him.*

　Xim. Then fleep, my love, and virtue arm t'oppofe
Let me look backward on his fatal honour,
Survey this mournful pomp of his renown,
Thefe woeful trophies of his conquer'd love,
That thro' my father's life purfu'd his fame,
And made me in his nuptial hopes an orphan:
O broken fpirit! would'ft thou fpare him now,
Think on thy father's blood! exert the daughter,
Supprefs thy paffion, and demand thy victim!

Enter King, Alvarez, Sanchez, &c.

　King. Difmifs thy fears, my friend, and man thy heart,
For while his actions are above reward,
Mercy's of courfe included in the debt.
Our ableft bounty's bankrupt to his merit.
Our fubjects refcu'd from fo fierce a foe,
The *Moors* defeated, ere the rude alarm

VOL. III.　　　　　　　　H

Allow'd us time to order our defence,
Our crown protected, and our sceptre fixt,
Are actions that secure acknowledgment.

Alv. My tears, Sir, better than my words will thank you.

Enter Garcia.

Gar. Don *Carlos*, Sir, without, attends your pleasure,
And comes surrender'd, as his word engag'd,
To answer the appeal of fair *Ximena.*

King. Attend him to our presence.

Xim. O my heart!

King. Ximena, with compassion we shall hear thee,
But must not have thy griefs arraign our justice,
If in his judge thou find'st an advocate:
Not less his virtues, than thy wrongs will plead.

Xim. O fainting cause! but thus my griefs demand him.
[Kneeling.

While the King raises Ximena, *enter* Alonzo,
and whispers Alvarez.

Alv. This instant, say'st thou? Can I leave my son?

Alon. The matter's more important than your stay.
Make haste, my lord.

Alv. What can thy transport mean?
Be plain.

Alon. We have no time to lose in words,
Away, I say.

Alv. Lead on, and ease my wonder.   [*Exeunt.*

Enter Carlos, *and kneels to the King.*

King. O rise, my warrior, raise thee to my breast,
And in thy master's heart repeat thy triumphs.

Car. These honours, Sir, to any sense but mine,
Might lift its transports to ambition's height;
But while *Ximena's* sorrows press my heart,
Forgive me, if, despairing of repose,
I taste no comfort in the life she seeks;
And urge the issue of her grief's appeal.

King. Ximena, 'tis most true, has lost a father,
But thou hast sav'd her country from its fate,

And the fame virtue that demands thy life,
Owes more than pardon to the public weal.
　Xim. My royal lord, vouchfafe my griefs a hearing.
O think not, Sir, becaufe my fpirits faint,
That the firm confcience of my duty ftaggers.
The criminal I charge, has kill'd my father ;
And, tho' his valour has preferv'd the ftate,
Yet every fubject is not wrong'd like me,
Therefore with eafe may pardon, what they feel not,
As he has fav'd a nation from its foes,
The thanks that nation owes him are but juft,
And I muft join the general voice t'applaud him :
But all the tribute, that my heart can fpare him,
Is tears of pity, while my wrongs purfue him.
What more than pity can thofe wrongs afford ?
What lefs than juftice can my duty afk ?
If public obligations muft be paid him,
Let every fingle heart give equal fhare :
(*Carlos* has prov'd that mine is not ungrateful)
But muft my duty yield fuch difproportion ?
Muft on my heart a father's blood be levy'd,
And my whole ruin pay the public thanks ?
If blood for blood might be before demanded,
Is it lefs due, becaufe his fame's grown greater !
Shall virtue, that fhou'd guard, infult your laws,
And tolerate our paffions to infringe 'em ?
If to defend the public, may excufe
A private wrong, how is the public fafe ?
How is a nation from a foe preferv'd,
If every fubject's life is at his mercy ?
My duty, Sir, has fpoken, and kneels for judgment.
　Car. O noble fpirit, how thou charm'ft my fenfe,
And giv'ft my heart a pleafure in my ruin !　　*[Apart.*
　King. Raife thee, *Ximena*, and compofe thy thoughts.
As thou to *Carlos'* deeds haft fpoke impartial,
So to thy virtue, that purfues him, we
Muft give an equal plaudit of our wonder ;
But we have now our duty to difcharge,
Which, far from blaming, fhall exalt thy own :
If thy chafte fame, which we confefs fublime,
Compels thy duty to fupprefs thy love,
To raife yet higher than thy matchlefs glory,
H 2

Prefer thy native country to them both,
And to the public tears refign thy victim :
Where a whole people owe their prefervation,
Shall private juftice do a public wrong,
And feed thy vengeance with the general forrow ?
 Xim. Is then my caufe the public's victim ?
 King. No.
We've yet a hope to conquer thy refentment,
And rather wou'd compofe than filence it :
For if our arguments feem yet too weak
To guard thy virtue from the leaft reproach,
Behold the generous fanction that protects it,
Read there the pardon which thy father gives him,
And with his dying hand affigns thy beauties.
 Xim. My father's pardon !
 King. Read, and raife thy wonder.
 Xim. (Reads) ' *Alvarez* wrong'd me in my mafter's
  ' favour,
' *Carlos* is brave, and has deferv'd *Ximena !*'
 Car. O foul of honour ! now lamented victory !
 King. Now, fair *Ximena,* now refume thy peace,
Reduce thy vengeance to thy father's will,
And join the hand his honour has forgiven.
 Xim. All gracious heav'n ! have my fwol'n eyes their
             [fenfe ?
 D. San. O tottering hope ! but I have yet a thought,
That will compel her virtue to purfue him.
 Xim. Why did you fhew me, Sir, this wounding good-
This legacy, tho' fit for him to leave,   [nefs ?
Wou'd in his daughter be reproach to take ;
Honour unqueftion'd may forgive a foe,
But who'll not doubt it when it fpares a lover ?
If you propos'd to mitigate my griefs,
You fhou'd have hid this cruel obligation.
Why wou'd you fet fuch virtues in my view,
And make the father dearer than the lover ?
 King. Since with fuch rigour thou purfu'ft thy ven-
And what we meant fhou'd pacify, provokes it, [geance,
Attend fubmiffive to our laft refolve :
For fince thy honour's fo feverely ftrict,
As not to ratify thy father's mercy,
We'll right at once thy duty and thy lover :

Give thee the glory of his life purfu'd,
And feal his pardon to reward thy virtue.
  Xim. Avert it heav'n, that e'er my guilty heart
Shou'd impioufly infult a father's grave,
And yield his daughter to the hand that kill'd him.
  D. *San.* Unnatural thought! madam, fupprefs your
Your murder'd father was my deareft friend;   [tears,
Permit me therefore, in your finking caufe,
To offer an expedient may fupport it.
  Xim. Whatever right or juftice may, I'm bound
In duty to purfue, and thank your friendfhip.
  D. *San.* Thus then to royal juftice I appeal,
And in *Ximena's* right her advocate,
Demand from *Carlos* your reverfe of pardon.
  King. What means thy tranfport?
  D. *San.* Sir, I urge your laws;
And fince her duty's forc'd to thefe extreams,
There's yet a law from whence there's no appeal,
A right, which e'en your crown's oblig'd to grant her,
The right of combat, which I here demand,
And afk her vengeance from a champion's fword.
  Car. O facred Sir, I caft me at your feet,
And beg your mercy wou'd relieve my woes;
Since her firm duty is inflexible,
Confign her victim to the braver fword.
Grant this expedient to acquit my crime,
Or filence with my arm her heart's reproaches:
O, nothing is fo painful as fufpenfe:
This way our griefs are equally reliev'd,
Her duty's full difcharg'd, your juftice crown'd,
And conqueft muft attend fuperior virtue.
  King. This barb'rous law, which yet is unrepeal'd,
Has often againft right, grofs wrongs fupported,
And robb'd our ftate of many noble fubjects;
Nor ever was our mercy tempted more
T'oppofe its force, than in our care for *Carlos:*
But fince his peace depends upon his love,
And cruel love infifts upon its right,
We'll truft his virtues to the chance of combat,
And let his fate reproach, or win *Ximena.*
  Xim. What unforefeen calamities furround me!

King. Ximena! now no more complain, we grant
Thy suit ; but where's this champion of thy cause,
Whose appetite of honour is so keen,
As to confront in arms this laurell'd brow,
And dare the shining terrors of his sword ?
   D. San. Behold th'assailant of this glorious hero.
Your leave, dread Sir, thus to appel him forth. [*Draws.*
   Bel. Hold, heart, and spare me from the public shame.
                                [*Aside.*
   D. San. Carlos, behold the champion of *Ximena,*
Behold th'avenger of brave *Gormaz'* blood.
Who calls thee traitor to thy injur'd love,
Ungrateful to the sighs that pitied thee,
And proudly partial to thy father's falshood ;
These crimes my sword shall prove upon thy heart,
And to defend them dares thee to the combat.
   Car. Open the lists, and give th' assailant room,
There on his life my injur'd sword shall prove,
This arm ne'er drew it but in right of honour :
First, for thy slander, *Sanchez,* I defy thee,
And throwing to thy teeth the traitor's name,
Will wash the imputation with thy blood,
And prove thy virtue false as is thy spirit :
For not *Ximena's* cause, but charms have fir'd thee ;
Vainly thou steal'st thy courage from her eyes,
And basely stain'st the virtue that subdu'd her.
   D. San. O that thy fate in arms——
   King. Sanchez, forbear——
'Tis not your tongues must arbitrate your strife,
Let in the lists your vauntings be approv'd.
Whose arm, *Ximena,* shall defend your cause ?
   Xim. O force of duty ! Sir, the arm of *Sanchez.*
   D. San. My word's my gage.
   King. 'Tis well, the lists are set,——
Let on the morn the combatants be cited,
And, *Felix,* you be umpire of the field.
   Car. The valiant, Sir, are never unprepar'd.
O Sir, at once relieve my soul's suspense,
And let this instant hour decide our fate.
   D. San. This moment, Sir---I join in that with *Carlos,*

King. Since both thus prefs it, be it now decided.
Carlos, be ready at the trumpet's call.
You, *Felix,* when the combat's done, conduct
The victor to our prefence——Now, *Ximena,*
As thou art juft or cruel in thy duty,
Expect the iffue will reward or grieve thee:
Sanchez, fet forward—*Carlos,* we allow
Thy pitied love a moment with *Ximena.*

[Ex. King and train.

D. *San.* A fruitlefs moment that muft prove his laft.

[Exit.

Car. Ximena! O permit me, ere I die,
To tell thy heart, thy hard unkindnefs kills me.
   Xim. Ah *Carlos,* can thy plaints reproach my duty?
Nay, art thou more than *Sanchez* is in danger?
   Car. Or thou more injur'd than thy haplefs father,
Whofe greater heart forgave my fenfe of honour?
Thou can'ft not think I fpeak regarding life,
Which hopelefs of thy love's not worth my care.
But, oh! it ftrikes me with the laft defpair,
To think that lov'd *Ximena's* heart had lefs
Compaffion than my mortal enemy:
My life had then indeed been worth acceptance,
Had thy relenting throes of pity fav'd it;
But, as it is purfu'd to thefe extremes,
Thus made the victim of fuperfl'ous fame,
And doom'd the facrifice of filial rigour,
Thefe arms fhall open to thy champion's fword,
And glut the vengeance that fupports thy glory.
   Xim. Haft thou no honour, *Carlos,* to defend?

[Trembling.

   Car. How can I lofe what *Sanchez* cannot gain?
For where's his honour where there's no refiftance?
Is it for me to guard *Ximena's* foe,
Or turn outrageous on the friendly breaft,
Which her diftrefsful charms have warm'd to right her?
   Xim. O cruel *Carlos!* thus to rack my heart
With hard reproaches, that thou know'ft are groundlefs.
Why doft thou talk thus cruelly of death,
And give me terrors unconceiv'd before?
What tho' my force of duty has purfu'd thee,

H 4

Haſt thou not left thy courage to defend thee?
O! is thy quarrel to our race reviv'd?
Cou'dſt thou, to right thy honour, kill my father?
And now not guard it, to deſtroy *Ximena?*

  Car. O heavenly found, O joy unfelt before!

  Xim. O! Is my duty then not thought compulſive?
Can'ſt thou believe I'm pleas'd while I purſue thee?
Or think'ſt thou I'm not pleas'd the king preſerv'd thee?
And that thy courage yet may waſd my vengeance?
O if thou knew'ſt what tranſports fill'd my heart,
When firſt I heard the *Moors* had fled before thee,
Thy love wou'd feel confuſion for my ſhame,
And ſcarce forgive the paſſion thou reproacheſt.
O *Carlos,* guard thy life, and ſave *Ximena!*

  Car. And ſave *Ximena!* O thou haſt fir'd my heart
With animated love, and ſav'd thy *Carlos*——

[Sound trumpets.

But, hark! the trumpet calls me to the liſt!   [thee!

  Xim. May heav'n's high care, and all its angels guard

  Car. Words wou'd but wrong my heart, my ſword
Shall ſpeak it.
Sanchez, I come——impatient to chaſtiſe
Thy love, which makes thee now the criminal:
I might have ſpar'd thee, had the rival ſlept;
But boldly thus avow'd, thou'rt worth my ſword.
'Tis ſaid the lion, tho' diſtreſt for food,
Eſpying on the turf the huntſman ſleeping,
Reſtrains his hunger, and forbears the prey:
But when his rouſing foe, alarm'd and ready,
Uplifts his javelin brandiſht to aſſail him,
The generous ſavage then erects his creſt,
Grinds his ſharp fangs, and with fierce eyes inflam'd,
Surveys him worthy of his rage defy'd,
Furious uprearing ruſhes on the game,
And crowns at once his vengeance and his fame.   [*Exit.*

  Xim. O glorious ſpirit! O hard-fated virtue!
With what reluctance has my heart purſu'd thee!

  Bel. Was ever breaſt like mine with woe divided?
I fear the dangers of the faithleſs *Sanchez,*
And tremble more for his dread ſword's ſucceſs.

Shou'd *Carlos* fall——What ſtops him from *Ximena?*
Keep down, my ſighs, or ſeem to riſe for her.
   Xim. Tell me, *Belzara*, was my terror blameful?
Might not his paſſion make my heart relent,
And feel at ſuch a time a pang to ſave him?
   Bel. So far was your compaſſion from a crime,.
That 'tis the exalted merit of your duty.
Had *Carlos* been a ſtranger to your heart,
Where were the virtue that your griefs purſu'd him?
Were it no pain to loſe him, where the glory?
The ſacrifice that's great muſt firſt be dear;
The more you love, the nobler is your victim.
   Xim. Thy partial friendſhip ſees not ſure my fault,
I doubt my youthful ignorance has err'd,
And the ſtrict matron, rigidly ſevere,
May blame this weakneſs of my woman's heart:.
But let her feel my trial firſt, and if
She blames me then, I will repent the crime.
                            [*Sound trumpet at diſtance,*
Hark, hark, the trumpet! O tremendous ſound!
Belzara! O the combat is begun,
The agonizing terror ſhakes my ſoul:.
Help me, ſupport me with thy friendly comforts;.
O tell me what my duty owes a parent,
And warm my wiſhes in his champion's favour——
Oh heaven! it will not, will not be! my heart
Rebels, and ſpite of me inclines to *Carlos*,.
Who now again, in *Sanchez*, fights my father..
Now he attacks him, preſſes, now retreats;
Again recovers, and reſumes his fire,
Now grows too ſtrong, and is at laſt triumphant!
   Bel. Reſtrain thy thoughts, collect thy conſtancy,
Give not thy heart imaginary wounds,.
Thy virtue muſt be providence's care;
   Xim. O guard me heav'n—Help me to ſupport it! ah!
                            [*Trumpets and ſhouts.*.
'Tis done, thoſe dreadful ſhouts proclaim the victor;
If *Carlos* conquers, ſtill I've loſt a father;
And if he periſhes, then—die *Ximena.*
   Bel. Conquer who may, no hope ſupports *Belzara,*

H 5.

Enter Garcia.

Came you, Don *Garcia*, from the combat ?
  Gar. Madam,
The king, to fhew he difapproves the cuftom,
Forbad his own domefticks to be prefent. [*Shouts nearer.*
But I prefume 'tis done, thefe fhouts confirm it ;
Hence from this window we may guefs the victor.
  Xim. O tell me quickly, while I have fenfe to hear thee ?
  Gar. O heav'n, 'tis *Sanchez*, I fee him with his fword
In triumph preffing thro' the crowd his way.
  Xim. Sanchez ! thou'rt fure deceiv'd. O better yet
Inform thy dazzled eyes.
  Gar. 'Tis certain he !
For now he ftops, and feems to warn them back ;
The crowd retires, I fee him plain, and now
He mounts the fteps that lead to this apartment.
  Xim. Then, fatal vengeance, thou art dearly fated.
Now love unbounded may o'erflow my heart,
And *Carlos'* fate without a crime be mourn'd:
O *Sanchez*, if poor *Carlos* told me true,
If 'twas thy love, not honour fought my caufe,
Thy guilt has purchas'd with thy fword my fcorn,
And made thy paffion wretched as *Ximena*.
  Bel. O heav'n, fupport her nobler refolution—
But fee, he comes to meet the difappointment.

Enter Don Sanchez, *and lays his fword at* Ximena's *feet*.

  D. San. Madam, this fword, that in your caufe was
     drawn—
  Xim. Stain'd with the blood of *Carlos*, kills *Ximena*.
  D. San. I come to mitigate your griefs.
  Xim. Avant, avoid me, wing thee from my fight !
O thou haft given me for revenge, defpair,
Has ravifht with thy murderous arm my peace,
And robb'd my wifhes of their deareft object.
  D. San. Hear me but fpeak.
  Xim. Can'ft thou fuppofe 'twill pleafe me,
To hear thy pride triumphant, paint my ruin,
Vaunt thy vain prowefs, and reproach my forrows ?
  D. San. Thofe forrows, wou'd you hear my ftory—

Xim. Hence,
To regions diftant, as thy foul from joy,
Fly, and in gloomy horrors wafte thy life :
Remorfe, and pale affliction wait thee to
Thy reft, repofe forfake thee, frightful dreams
Alarm thy fleeps, and in thy waking hours
May woes like mine purfue thy fteps for ever!

   Bel. O charming rage ! how cordially fhe hates him !

Enter King.

   King. What ftill in tears, *Ximena ?* Still complaining!
Cannot thy duty's full difcharge content thee ?
Repin'ft thou at the act of providence ?
And think'ft thy caufe ftill wrong'd in heav'n's decree ?

   Xim. O far, Sir, from my foul be fuch a thought,
I bow fubmiffive to high heav'n's appointment.
But is affliction impious in its forrow ?
Tho' vengeance to a father's blood was due,
Is it lefs glorious that I priz'd the victim ?
Has nature loft its privilege to weep,
When all that's valuable in life is gone ?
O *Carlos, Carlos !* I fhall foon be with thee.

   King. Are then thefe tears for *Carlos*—O *Ximena !*
The vanquifh'd *Sanchez* has deceiv'd thy grief,
And made this trial of thy generous heart ;
For know thy *Carlos* lives, and lives t' adore thee.

   Xim. What means my royal lord ?

   King. Inform her, *Sanchez.*

   D. *San.* The fortune of the combat I had told before,
Had, Sir, her fright endur'd my fpeech.
I wou'd have told you, madam, as oblig'd
In honour to the conquering fword of *Carlos,*
How nobly, for your fake, he fpar'd your champion ;
When on the earth fuccumbent, and difarm'd,
I lay : ' Live *Sanchez*, faid the generous victor,
' The life that fights *Ximena's* caufe is facred ;
' Take back thy fword, and at her feet prefent
' The glorious trophy which her charms have won,
' The laft oblation that defpair can make her.'
Toucht with the noble fullnefs of his heart,
I flew to execute the grateful charge ;

H 6

But, madam, your affright miftook the victor,
And your impatient griefs refus'd me audience.
   King. Now think *Ximena*, one moment think for *Carlos.*
   Xim. O love! O perfecuted heart!
Inftruct me heav'n to fupport my fame,
To right my paffion, and revere my father.
   D. *San.* And now with juft confufion, Sir, I own
In me 'twas guilty love, that drew my fword;
But fince th' event has crown'd a nobler paffion,
I plead the merit of that fword's defeat,
Regret the error, and intreat for pardon.
   King. Sanchez, thy crime is punifht in itfelf.
We late have heard of thy retracted vows,
Which, on thy ftrict allegiance, we enjoin
Thy honour inftantly to ratify.
Supprefs thy tears, *Belzara,* he fhall right thee.
   Xim. 'Tis fixt; a beam of heav'nly light breaks forth,
And fhews my ruin'd peace its laft refource.
   Gar. Don *Carlos,* Sir, attends your royal pleafure.
   King. Has he your leave, *Ximena,* to approach?
   Xim. O Sir, yet hold, I dare not fee him now.
While my depending juftice was my guard,
I faw him fearlefs from affaults of love:
But now my vanquifht vengeance dreads his merit,
And confcious duty warns me to avoid him;
Since then my heart's impartial to his virtues,
O do not call me cruel to his love,
If I, in reverence to a father's blood,
Shou'd fhut my forrows ever from his fight;
For tho' you raife above mankind his merit,
And I confefs it——ftill he has kill'd my father——
Nay, tho' I grant the fact may plead for mercy,
Yet 'twould in me be impious to reward it;
My eyes may mourn, but never muft behold him more;
Yet, ere I part, let, Sir, my humble fenfe
Applaud your mercy, and confefs your juftice.
Hence to fome facred cloifter I'll retire,
And dedicate my future days to heav'n——
'Tis done—O *lead me to my peaceful cell,*
One figh for Carlos—*Now, vain world, farewel.*

As Ximena *is going off,* enter Alvarez *and* Alonzo.

Alv. Turn, turn, *Ximena*, O prepare to hear
A ftory will diftract thy fenfe with joy,
Drive all thy forrows from thy finking heart,
And crown thy duty with triumphant love.
Pardon, dread Sir, this tumult of my foul,
That carries in my rudenefs my excufe;
O prefs me not to tell particulars,
But let my tidings leap at once the bounds
Of your belief, and in one burft of joy
Inform my royal mafter, that his crown's fupport,
My vanquifh'd friend, thy father, *Gormaz*, lives;
He lives in health confirm'd from mortal danger,   [him.
Thefe eyes have feen him, thefe bleft arms embrac'd
The means, th' occafion of his death fuppos'd,
Wou'd afk more words than I have breath to utter;
Alonzo knows it all——O where's my *Carlos?*
   King. Fly *Sanchez!* make him with this news, thy friend,
   Alv. O lead me, lead me, to his heart's relief.——
                                                    [*Exeunt.*
   Xim. O heav'n! *Alvarez* wou'd not fure deceive me.
   King. Proceed, *A'onzo,* and impart the whole.
Whence was his death fo firmly credited,
And his recovery not before reveal'd?
   Alon. My liege, the great effufion of his blood
Had fuch effect on his deferted fpirits,
That I, who faw him, judg'd him quite expir'd:
But when the abbot, at whofe houfe he lay,
With friendly forrow wafh'd his hopelefs wound,
His heaving breaft difcover'd life's return:
When calling ftrait for help, on ftricter fearch,
His wound was found without a mortal fymptom:
And when his fenfes had refum'd their function,
His firft words fpoke his generous heart's concern
For *Carlos,* and *Ximena;-* when being told
How far her filial vengeance had purfu'd him,
Is't poffible, he cry'd? Oh heav'n! then wept,
And begg'd his life might be one day conceal'd,
That fuch exalted merit of her duty
Might raife her virtue worthy of his love,

But, Sir, to tell you how *Alvarez* met him,
What generous reconcilements pafs'd between them,
Wou'd afk more time than public joy cou'd fpare.
Let it fuffice, the moment he had heard
Ximena had appeal'd brave *Carlos* to the lifts,
We flew with terror to proclaim him living——
But, Sir, fo foon the combat follow'd your
Decree, that breathlefs we arriv'd too late,
And had not his phyficians prefcrib'd
His wound repofe, himfelf had ventur'd forth
To throw his errors at your feet for pardon.

    King. Not only pardon, but our love fhall greet him.
Brave *Carlos* fhall himfelf be envoy of
Our charge, and gratulate his bleft recovery:
Has he your leave, *Ximena*, now t'approach you?

    Xim. My fenfes ftagger with tumultuous joy,
My fpirits hurry to my heart's furprize,
And finking nature faints beneath the tranfport.

Enter Alvarez, Sanchez, *and* Carlos.

    King. Look up, *Ximena*, and compleat thy joy.
    Xim. My *Carlos!* oh!
    Car. *Ximena!* oh my heart!   *[Embracing.*
    Alv. O *Carlos!* O *Ximena!* yet fupprefs
Thefe tranfports till kind *Gormaz*' hand confirms them:
Firft pay your duty there, hafte to his feet,
And let his fanction confecrate your love.

    King. Lofe not a moment from his fight! O fly!
Tell him his king congratulates his health,
And will with loads of honour crown his virtues.
Nor in his orifons let his heart forget
The hand of heav'n, whofe providential care
      Has order'd all the innocent to fave,
      To right the injur'd, and reward the brave.

EPILOGUE.

Spoken by XIMENA.

Well, Sirs!

I'M come to tell you, that my fears are over,
I've seen papa, and have secur'd my lover:
And troth I'm wholly on our author's side,
For had (as Corneille made him) Gormaz dy'd,
My part had ended as it first begun,
And left me still unmarried and undone,
Or, what were harder far than both—a nun.
The French, for form indeed, postpones the wedding,
But gives her hopes within a year of bedding.
Time could not tie her marriage knot with honour,
The father's death still left the guilt upon her:
The Frenchman stopt her in that forc'd regard,
The bolder Briton weds her in reward:
He knew your taste wou'd ne'er endure their billing
Shou'd be so long deferr'd, when both were willing:
Your formal Dons of Spain an age might wait,
But English appetites are sharper-set.
'Tis true, this diff'rence we indeed discover,
That though like lions you begin the lover,
To do you right, your fury soon is over.
Beside, the scene thus chang'd this moral bears,
That virtue never of relief despairs:
But while true love is still in plays ill-fated,
No wonder you gay sparks of pleasure hate it;
Bloodshed discourages what should delight you,
And from a wife, what little rubs will fright you!
And virtue not consider'd in the bride,
How soon you yawn, and curse the knot you've ty'd!
How oft the nymph, whose pitying eyes give quarter,
Finds in her captive she has caught a Tartar!
While to her spouse, that once so high did rate her,
She kindly gives ten thousand pounds to hate her.

EPILOGUE.

So on the other side some sighing swain,
That languishes in love whole years in vain,
Impatient for the feast, resolves he'll have her,
And in his hunger vows he'll eat for ever;
He thinks of nothing but the honey moon,
But little thought he could have din'd so soon:
Is not this true? Speak——Dearies of the pit,
Don't you find too, how horribly you're bit?
For the instruction therefore of the free,
Our author turns his just catastrophe:
Before you wed let love be understood,
Refine your thoughts, and chase it from the blood.
Nor can you then of lasting joys despair,
For when that circle holds the British fair,
Your hearts may find Heroick Daughters there.

THE
COMICAL LOVERS,

A

COMEDY,

Dramatis Personæ.

MEN.

Palamede, a Courtier,	Mr. *Wilks.*
Rhodophil, Captain of the Guard,	Mr. *Booth.*
Celadon, a Courtier, brother to *Doralice*,	Mr. *Cibber.*
Jasper, Servant to *Celadon.*	

WOMEN.

Melantha, an affected Lady,	Mrs. *Bracegirdle.*
Doralice, Wife to *Rhodophil*,	Mrs. *Porter.*
Florimel, a Maid of Honour,	Mrs. *Oldfield.*
Flavia, a Maid of Honour.	
Olinda, } Sisters.	
Sabina, }	
Melissa, Mother to *Olinda* and *Sabina.*	
Philotis, Servant to *Melantha.*	
Beliza, Servant to *Doralice.*	

THE
COMICAL LOVERS.

ACT I. SCENE I.

The SCENE *is Walks near the Court.*

Enter Celadon, Doralice, *meeting each other: He in a Riding Habit. They embrace.*

Cel. DEAR *Doralice!*

Dor. My dear brother! welcome! a thoufand welcomes. Methinks this year you have been abfent, has been fo tedious! I hope as you have made a pleafant voyage, fo you have brought your good humour back again to court.

Cel. I never yet knew any company I could not be merry in, except it were an old woman's.

Dor. Or at a funeral.

Cel. Nay, for that you fhall excufe me; for I was never merrier than I was at a creditor's of mine, whofe book perifh'd with him. But what new beauties have you at court? How do *Meliffa's* two fair daughters?

Dor. When you tell me which of them you are in love with, I'll anfwer you.

Cel. Which of them, naughty fifter! What a queftion's there? With both of 'em, with each and fingular of 'em.

Dor. Blefs me! you are not ferious!

Cel. You look as if it were a wonder, to fee a man in love: Are they not handfome?

Dor. Ay, but both together——

Cel. Ay, and both afunder too: Why, I hope, there are but two of 'em; the tall finging and dancing one, and the little innocent one?

Dor. But you can't marry both?

Cel. No, nor either of 'em, I truft in my conftitution: But I can keep them company, I can fing and dance with 'em, and treat 'em; and that, I take it, is fomewhat better than mufty marrying them: Marriage is

poor folks pleafure, that cannot go to the coft of variety :
But I am out of danger of that with thefe two, for I love
'em fo equally, I can never make choice between 'em :
Had I but one miftrefs, I might go to her to be merry,
and fhe perhaps be out of humour, there were a vifit
loft : But here, if one of 'em frowns upon me, the other
will be the more obliging, on purpofe to recommend
her own gaity ; befides a thoufand things I cou'd name.

Dor. And none of 'em to any purpofe.

Cel. Well, if you will not be cruel to a poor lover,
you might oblige me, by carrying me to their lodgings.

Dor. You know I am always bufy about the queen.

Cel. But once or twice only, till I am a little flufh'd
in my acquaintance with other ladies, and have learn'd
to play for myfelf. I promife you I'll make all the hafte
I can to end your trouble, by being in love fomewhere
elfe.

Dor. You would think it hard to be deny'd now.

Cel. And reafon good. Many a man hangs himfelf
for the lofs of one miftrefs; how do you think then I
fhould bear the lofs of two, efpecially in a court where I
think beauty is but thin fown ?

Dor. There's one *Florimel,* the queen's ward, a new
beauty, as wild as you, and a vaft fortune.

Cel. I am for her before the world; bring me to her,
and I'll releafe you of your promife for the other two.

Dor. Well, if I do promife, will you fwear not to attempt any other woman in the mean time ?

Cel. Swear! by all the——

Dor. Hold! before you fwear——What do you think
of thofe two mafk'd ladies, that are coming yonder ?

Cel. Why, I fay that a rafh oath is better let alone
than repented———Dear fifter, don't difturb my con-
templations.   [*Putting her by.*

Dor. Oh! your fervant, Sir.   [*Exit* Doralice.

Enter Phormio, *walking over the ftage haftily: After
him* Florimel *and* Flavia, *mafked.*

Fla. Phormio, Phormio, you will not leave us——
Phor. In faith, I have a little bufinefs—— [*Exit* Phor.
Cel. Cannot I ferve you in the gentleman's room, ladies?

Fla. Which of us wou'd you ferve?

Cel. Either of you, or both of you.

Fla. Why cou'd you not be conftant to one?

Cel. Conftant to one! I have been a courtier, a fol-dier, and a traveller to gocd purpofe, if I muft be con-ftant to one. Give me fome twenty, fome forty, fome a hundred miftreffes: I have more love than any one woman can turn her to.

Flor. Blefs us! let us be gone, coufin; we two are nothing in his hands.

Cel. Yet, for my part, I can live with as few mif-treffes as any man: I defire no fuperfluities, only for neceffary change, or fo, as I fhift my linen.

Flor. A pretty odd kind of a fellow this; he fits my humour rarely——— [*Afide.*

Fla. You are as unconftant as the moon.

Flor. You wrong him, he's as conftant as the fun, he would fee all the world round in twenty-four hours.

Cel. 'Tis very true, madam; but like him, I would vifit and away.

Flor. For what an unreafonable thing it were to ftay long, be troublefome, and hinder a lady of a frefh lover?

Cel. A rare creature this!———Befides, madam, how like a fool a man looks when, after all his eagernefs of two minutes before, he fhrinks into a faint fit, and a cold compliment!———Ladies both, into your hands I commit myfelf; fhare me betwixt you.

Fla. I'll have nothing to do with you, fince you can-not be conftant to one.

Cel. Nay, rather than lofe any of you, I'll do more; I'll be conftant to a hundred of you: Or (if you will needs fetter me to one) agree the matter between your-felves, and the moft handfome take me.

Flor. Tho' I am not fhe, yet fince my mafk's on, and you cannot convince me, have a good faith of my beauty, and for once I take you for my fervant.

Cel. And for once I'll make a blind bargain with you: ftrike hands; its a match, miftrefs.

Flor. Done, fervant.

Cel. Now I'm sure I have the worst on't; for you see the worst of me, and that I don't of you, 'till you shew your face——Yet now I think on't, you must be handsome——

Flor. What kind of beauty do you like?

Cel. Just such a one as yours.

Flor. What's that?

Cel. Such an oval face, clear skin, hazle eyes, thick brown eye-brows and hair, as you have, for all the world.

Fla. But I can assure you, she has nothing of all this.

Cel. Hold thy peace, *Envy*——Nay, I can be constant an' I set on't.

Flor. 'Tis very well, *Celadon*, you can be constant to one you have never seen, and have forsaken all you have seen.

Cel. It seems you know me then: Well, if thou should'st prove one of my cast mistresses, I would use thee most damnably, for offering to make me love thee twice.

Flor. You are i'th' right: An old mistress, or servant, is like an old tune, the pleasure on't is past when we have once learn'd it.

Fla. But what woman in the world would you wish her like?

Cel. I have heard of one *Florimel*, the queen's ward: would she were as like her for beauty, as she is for humour!

Fla. Do you hear that, cousin?—— [*To* Flor. *aside.*

Flo. *Florimel's* not handsome: Besides, she's unconstant, and only loves for some few days.

Cel. If she loves for shorter time than I, she must love by winter-days and summer-nights, i'faith.

Flor. When you see us together you shall judge: In the mean time adieu, sweet servant.

Cel. Why you won't be so inhuman, to carry away my heart, and not so much as to tell me where I may hear news on't.

Flor. I mean to keep it safe for you; for if you had it, you would bestow it worse: Farewel, I must see a lady.

Cel. So must I too, if I can pull off your mask.

Flor. You will not be fo rude, I hope?

Cel. By this light I will.

Flor. By this leg but you fhan't.

      [*Exeunt* Flor. *and* Fla. *running.*

Cel. Then by this hand, next time I fhall take better hold, Mrs. *Nimblefoot.*   [*Exit.*

     Enter Doralice *and* Beliza.

Dor. Beliza, bring the lute into this harbour; the walks are empty: I would hear the fong the princefs *Almaibea* bid me learn.   [*They go in and fing.*

Enter Palamede, *in a Riding-Habit, and hears the Song. Re-enter* Doralice *and* Beliza.

Bel. Madam, a ftranger.

Dor. I did not think to have had witneffes of my bad finging.

Pal. If I have err'd, madam, I hope you'll pardon the curiofity of a ftranger; for I may well call myfelf fo, after five years abfence from the court. But you have freed me from one error.

Dor. What's that, I befeech you?

Pal. I thought good voices and ill faces had been infeparable; and that to be fair, and to fing well, had been only the privilege of angels.

Dor. And how many more of thefe fine things can you fay to me?

Pal. Very few, madam; for if I fhould continue to fee you fome hours longer, you look fo killingly, that I fhould be mute with wonder.

Dor. This will not give you the reputation of a wit with me: You travelling *Monfieurs* live upon a ftock you have got abroad for the firft day or two: To repeat with a good memory, and apply with a good grace, is all your wit; and commonly your gullets are fow'd up like cormorants; when you have regorg'd what you have taken in, you are the leaneft things in nature.

Pal. Then, madam, I think you had beft make that ufe of me; let me wait on you for two or three days together, and you fhall hear all I have learnt of extraordinary in other countries; and one thing which I never faw ti!l I came home, that is a lady of a better voice, better face, and better wit than any I have feen abroad.   And after this, if I fhould not declare myfelf moft paffionately in love with you, I fhould have lefs wit than yet you think I have.

Dor. A very plain and pithy declaration.   I fee, Sir, you have been travelling in *Spain* or *Italy*, or fome of the hot countries, where men come to the point imme-diately.   But are you fure thefe are not words of courfe? for I would not give my poor heart an occafion of com-plaint againft me, that I engag'd it too rafhly, and then could not bring it off.

Pal. Your heart may truft itfelf with me fafely: I fhall ufe it very civilly while it ftays, and never turn it away, without fair warning to provide for itfelf.

Dor. Firft then, I do receive your paffion with as little confideration on my part, as ever you gave it me on yours: And now fee what a miferable wretch you have made yourfelf.

Pal. Who! I miferable? Thank you for that.   Give me love enough, and life enough, and I defy fortune.

Dor. Know then, thou man of vain imagination, know to thy utter confufion, that I am virtuous.

Pal. Such another word, and I give up the ghoft.

Dor. Then to ftrike you quite dead, know that I am marry'd too.

Pal. Art thou marry'd?   O thou horrible virtuous woman!

Dor. Yes, marry'd to a gentleman; young, hand-fome, rich, valiant, and with all the good qualities that will make you defpair and hang yourfelf.

Pal. Well, in fpite of all that, I'll love you: For-tune has cut us out for one another; for I am to be marry'd within thefe three days; marry'd paft redemption, to a young, fair, rich, and virtuous lady; and it fhall go hard but I will love my wife as little as I perceive you do your hufband.

Dor. Remember I invade no property: My fervant you are only till you are married.

Pal. In the mean time, you are to forget you have a hufband.

Dor. And you that you are to have a wife.

Bell. [*Aside to her lady.*] O madam, my lord's just at the end of the walks, and if you make not haste, will discover you.

Dor. Some other time, new servant, we'll talk farther of the premises; in the mean while break not my first commandment, that is not to follow me.

Pal. But where then shall I find you again?

Dor. At court. Yours for two days, Sir.

Pal. And nights, I beseech you, madam.

[*Exeunt* Dor. *and* Bel.

Pal. Well, I'll say that for thee, thou art a very dextrous executioner; thou hast done my business at one stroke; yet I must marry another——And yet I must love this; and if it leads me into some little inconveniencies, as jealousies, and duels, and death, and so forth; yet while sweet love is in the case, fortune do thy worst, and avant mortality.

Enter Rhodophil.

Rho. How, *Palamede!*   [*Sees* Palamede.

Pal. Rhodophil!

Rho. Who thought to have seen you in *Sicily?* What brought you home from travel?

Pal. The commands of an old rich father.

Rho. And the hopes of burying him.

Pal. Both together, as you see, have prevail'd on my good-nature. In few words, my old man has already married me, for he has agreed with another old man, as rich and as covetous as himself; the articles are drawn, and I have given my consent for fear of being disinherited; and yet know not what kind of woman I am to marry.

Rho. Sure your father intends you some very ugly wife, and has a mind to keep you in ignorance, till you have shot the gulf.

Pal. I know not that; but obey I will, and must.

Rho. Then I cannot chuse but grieve for all the good girls, and courtezans of *France* and *Italy*; they have lost the most kind-hearted, doating, prodigal humble servant in *Europe.*

Pal. All I could do in these three years I staid behind you, was to comfort the poor creatures for the loss of you. But what's the reason that in all this time a friend could never hear from you?

Rho. Alas, dear *Palamede*, I have had no joy to write, nor indeed to do any thing in the world to please me: The greatest misfortune imaginable is fallen upon me!

Pal. Pr'ythee, what's the matter?

Rho. In one word, I am marry'd; wretchedly marry'd; and have been above these two years. Yes, faith, the devil has had power over me, in spite of my vows and resolutions to the contrary.

Pal. I find you have sold yourself for filthy lucre; she's old, or ill-condition'd.

Rho. No, none of these: I am sure she's young; and for her humour, she laughs, sings and dances eternally; and, which is more, we never quarrel about it, for I do the same.

Pal. You're very unfortunate indeed: Then the case is plain, she's not handsome.

Rho. A great beauty too, as people say.

Pal. As people say! Why, you should know that best yourself.

Rho. Ask those that have smelt a strong perfume two years together what's the scent.

Pal. But here are good qualities enough for one woman.

Rho. Ay, too many, *Palamede:* If I could put 'em into three or four women, I should be content.

Pal. O, now I have found it, you dislike her for no other reason, but because she's your wife.

Rho. And is not that enough? All that I know of her perfections now, is only by memory: I remember indeed that about two years ago, I lov'd her passionately; but those golden days are gone, *Palamede:* yet I lov'd her a whole half year, double the natural term of any mistress, and I think in my conscience I could have held out another quarter; but then the world began to laugh at me, and a certain shame of being out of fashion seiz'd me: At last, we arriv'd at that point, and there was nothing left in us to make us new to one another. Yet still I set a good face upon the matter, and am infinite fond of her before company; but when we are alone, we walk like two lions in a room, she one way and I another: and we like with our backs to each other, so far distant, as if the fashion of great beds was only invented to keep husband and wife sufficiently asunder.

Pal. The truth is, your disease is very desperate; but though you cannot be cur'd, you may be patch'd up a little; you must get you a mistress, *Rhodophil:* That indeed is living upon cordials; but, as fast as one fails, you must supply it with another.

Rho. Truth is, I have been thinking on't, and have just resolv'd to take your counsel; and faith, considering the disadvantages of a marry'd man, I have provided well enough for an humble sinner, that is not ambitious of great matters.

Pal. What is she for a woman?

Rho. One of the stars of *Syracuse*, I assure you : young enough, fair enough, and, but for one quality, just such a woman as I could wish for; being a town lady, without any relation to the court: yet she thinks herself undone, if she be not seen three or four times a day with the princess: and for the king, she haunts and watches him so narrowly in a morning, that she prevents even the chymists, who beset his chamber, to turn their mercury into his gold.

Pal. Yet hitherto methinks, you are no very unhappy man?

Rho. With all this, she's the greatest gossip in nature; for, besides the court, she's the most eternal visiter of the town; and yet manages her time so well, that she seems ubiquitary. For my part, I can compare her to nothing but the sun; for, like him, she takes no rest, nor ever sets in one place, but to rise in another.

Pal. I confess she had need be handsome with these qualities.

Rho. No lady can be so curious of a new fashion, as she is of a new *French* word. She is the very mint of the nation, and as fast as any bullion comes out of *France*, coins it immediately into our language.

Pal. And her name is——

Rho. No naming; that's not like a cavalier: Find her if you can by my defcription; and I am not fo ill a painter, that I need write the name beneath the pictur.

Pal. Well then, how far have you proceeded in your love?

Rho. 'Tis yet in the bud, and what fruit it may bear, I cannot tell; for this infufferable humour of haunting the court is fo predominant, that fhe has hitherto broken all her affignations with me, for fear of miffing her vifit there.

Pal. That's the hardeft part of your adventure; but, for aught I fee, fortune has us'd us both a'ike; I have a ftrange kind of miftrefs too at court, befides her I am to marry.

Rho. You have made hafte to be in love then; for, if I am not miftaken, you are but this day arriv'd.

Pal. That's all one; I have feen the lady already who has charm'd me; feen her in thefe walks, courted her, and received for the firft time an anfwer that does not put me into defpair.

Rho. Have you feen your honourable miftrefs yet?

Pal. No—but I was juft going as I met you.

Rho. Then don't let me hinder you: for to tell you the truth, I have a fmall affair upon my hands.

Pal. Why then, dear *Rhodophil*——

Rho. No ceremony: We fhall meet, and compare notes.

Pal. Pofitively.

Rho. Adieu——   [*Exeunt feverally.*

Enter Melantha *looking in a pocket-glafs, and* Philotis.

Phil. Count *Rhodophil's* a fine gentleman indeed, madam; and I think deferves your affection.

Mel. Let me die but he is a fine perfon; he fings and dances *en François,* and writes the *billets doux* to a miracle.

Phil. And thofe are no fmall talents to a lady that underftands and values the *French* air, as your ladyfhip does.

Mel. How charming is the *French* air! and what a *etourdi bête* is one of our untravell'd iflanders! When he would make his court to me, let me die, but he is juft *Æfop's* afs, that would imitate the courtly *French* in his addreffes; but inftead of thofe, comes pawing upon me, and doing all things fo *mal adroitly.*

Phil. 'Tis great pity *Rhodophil's* a marry'd man, that you may not have an honourable intrigue with him.

Mel. Intrigue, *Philotis!* that's an old phrafe; I have laid that word by: Amour, Affair, founds better. But thou art heir to all my caft words, as thou art to my old ward-robe. Oh, Count *Rhodophil! Ah mon cher!* I could live and die with him.

Enter Palamede, *and a Servant.*

Serv. Sir, this is my lady.

Pal. Then this is fhe that is to be divine, and nymph, and goddefs, and with whom I am to be defperately in love.   [*Bows to her, delivering her a letter.* This letter, madam, which I prefent you from your father, has given me both the happy opportunity, and the boldnefs to kifs the faireft hands in *Sicily.*

Mel. Came you lately from *Palermo,* Sir?

Pal. But yefterday, madam.

Mel. [Reading the letter.] *Daughter, receive the bearer of this letter, as a gentleman whom I have chofen to make you happy;* (O *Venus,* a new fervant fent me! and let me die, but he has the air of a *gallant homme.) His father is the rich Lord* Cleodemus, *our neighbour. I fuppofe you will find nothing difagreeable in his perfon, or his converfe; both which he has improved by travel. The treaty is already concluded, and I fhall be in town within thefe three days; fo that you have nothing to do, but to obey your careful father.*

[*To Pala.*] Sir, my father, for whom I have a blind obedience, has commanded me to receive your paffionate addreffes; but you muft alfo give me leave to avow, that I cannot merit 'em from fo accomplifh'd a cavalier.

Pal. I want many things, madam, to render me accomplifh'd; and the firft and greateft of them is your favour.

I 3

Mel. Let me die, *Philotis*, but this is extremely *French*; but yet Count *Rhodophil*——A gentleman, Sir, that underſtands the *grande monde* ſo well, who has haunted the beſt converſations, and who, in ſhort, has Voyag'd, may pretend to the good graces of any lady.

Pal. [*Aſide.*] Hey-day! *Grande monde!* Converſation! Voyag'd! and Good graces! I find my miſtreſs is one of thoſe that run mad in new *French* words.

Mel. I ſuppoſe, Sir, you have made the tour of *France,* and, having ſeen all that's fine there, will make a conſiderable reformation in the rudeneſs of our court: For let me die, but an unfaſhion'd, untravell'd, mere *Sicilian*, is a *bête*; and has nothing in the world of an *honnête homme.*

Pal. I muſt confeſs, madam, that——

Mel. And what new minuets have you brought over with you? Their minuets are to a miracle! and our *Sicilian* jigs are ſo dull and ſad to 'em.

Pal. For minuets, madam——

Mel. And what new plays are there in vogue? And who danc'd beſt in the *grande ballet?* Come, ſweet ſervant, you ſhall tell me all.

Pal. [*Aſide.*] Tell her all! Why ſhe aſks all, and will hear nothing——To anſwer in order, madam, to your demands——

Mel. I am thinking what a happy couple we ſhall be! for you ſhall keep up your correſpondence abroad, and every thing that's new writ in *France*, and fine, I mean, all that's delicate, and *bien tourné*, we will have firſt.

Pal. But, madam, our fortune——

Mel. I underſtand you, Sir; you'll leave that to me: For the manage of a family, I know it better than any lady in *Sicily.*

Pal. Alas, madam, we——

Mel. Then we will never make viſits together, nor ſee a play, but always apart; you ſhall be every day at the king's *levee*, and I at the queen's; and we will never meet, but in the drawing-room.

Phil. Madam, the new prince is juſt paſs'd the end of the walk.

Mel. The new prince, fay'ſt thou ? Adieu, dear ſervant,
I have not made my court to him theſe two long hours.
Oh, 'tis the ſweeteſt prince! So *obligeant, charmant, ra-*
viſſant, that——Well, I'll make haſte to kiſs his hands;
and then make half a ſcore viſits more, and be with you
again in a twinkling.   [*Exit, running with* Phil.

Pal. [*Solus.*] Now, Love, of thy mercy bleſs me from
this tongue; it may keep the field againſt a whole army
of lawyers, and that in their own language, *French* gib-
beriſh. 'Tis true, in the day-time, 'tis tolerable when
a man has field-room to run from it; but to be ſhut up
in a bed with her, like two cocks in a pit, humanity
cannot ſupport it. I muſt kiſs all night in my own defence, and hold her down like a boy at cuffs; nay, and
give her the riſing blow every time ſhe begins to ſpeak.
                                           [*Exit.*

ACT II. SCENE I.

Enter Celadon, *meeting* Doralice.

Dor. BRother! what makes you here, about the
queen's apartments? Which of the ladies are
you watching for?

Cel. Any of 'em that will do me the good turn to
make me ſoundly in love.

Dor. Then I'll beſpeak you one; you will be deſpe-
rately in love with *Florimel.* So ſoon as the queen heard
you were return'd, ſhe gave you her for a miſtreſs.

Cel. Thank her majeſty: but to confeſs the truth, my
fancy lies partly another way.

Dor. That's ſtrange: *Florimel* vows you are in love
with her already——

Cel. She wrongs me horribly: If ever I ſaw or ſpoke
with this *Florimel!*

Dor. Well, take your fortune, I muſt leave you.
                                    [*Exit* Doralice.

Enter Florimel, *ſees him, and is running back.*

Cel. Nay faith, I am got betwixt you and home; you

are my pris'ner, Lady Bright, till you resolve me one question. [*She signs.*] Is she dumb? I-gad, I think, she is. What, a vengeance, dost thou at court with such a rare face, without a tongue to answer to a kind question? Art thou dumb indeed? Then thou can'st tell no tales——

[Goes to kiss her.

Flor. Hold, hold, you are not mad!

Cel. Oh, my Miss in a masque! have you found your tongue?

Flor. 'Twas time, I think; what had become of me, if I had not?

Cel. Methinks your lips had done as well.

Flor. Yes, if my masque had been over 'em, as it was when you met me in the walks.

Cel. Well, will you believe me another time? Did I not say you were intolerably handsome? They may talk of *Florimel* if they will, but i'faith she must come short of you.

Flor. Have you seen her then?

Cel. I look'd a little that way, but I had soon enough of her; she is not to be seen twice without a surfeit.

Flor. However, you are beholden to her; they say she loves you.

Cel. By fate she shall not love me; I have told her a piece of my mind already: Pox o' these coming women, they set a man to dinner, before he has an appetite.

[Flavid at the door.

Fla. *Florimel*, you are call'd within ——

Cel. I hope in the lord you are not *Florimel?*

Cler. Ev'n she at your service; the same kind and coming *Florimel*, you have described.

Cel. Why then we are agreed already; I am as kind and coming as you for the heart of you: I knew at first we two were good for nothing but one another.

Flor. But, without raillery, are you in love?

Cel. So horribly much, that, contrary to my own maxims, I think in my conscience I cou'd marry you.

Flor. No, no, 'tis not come to that yet: But if you are really in love, you have done me the greatest pleasure in the world.

Cel. That pleasure, and a better too, I have in store for you.

Flor. This animal called a lover, I have long'd to see these two years.

Cel. Sure you walk'd with your masque on all the while; for if you had been seen, you could not have been without your wish.

Flor. I warrant you mean an ordinary whining lover: but I must have other proofs of love ere I believe it.

Cel. You shall have the best that I can give you.

Flor. I would have a lover, that if need be, should hang himself, drown himself, break his neck, and poison himself, for very despair. He that will scruple this, is an impudent fellow, if he says he's in love.

Cel. Pray, madam, which of these four would you have your lover do? for a man's but a man, he cannot hang, and drown, and break his neck, and poison himself, all together.

Flor. Well then, because you are but a beginner, and I would not discourage you, any one of these shall serve your turn in a fair way.

Cel. I am much deceiv'd in those eyes of yours, if a treat, a song, and the fiddle, be not a more acceptable proof of love to you, than any of those tragical ones you have mention'd.

Flor. However, you will grant it is but decent you shou'd be pale, lean, and melancholy, to shew you are in love; and that I shall require of you when I see you next.

Cel. When you see me next! Why, you do not make a rabbit of me, to be lean at twenty-four hours warning? In the mean while, we burn day-light, lose time, and love.

Flor. Would you marry me without consideration?

Cel. Ay, to choose; for they that think on't, twenty to one, would never do it: hang fore-cast; to make sure of one good night is as much, in reason, as a man should expect from this ill world.

Flor. Methinks a few more years, and discretion, would do well; I do not like this going to bed so early, it makes one so weary before morning.

Cel. That's much, as your pillow is laid before you go to sleep.

L 5

Flor. Shall I make a propofition to you ? I will give you a whole year of probation to love me in, to grow referv'd, difcreet, fober, and faithful, and to pay me all the fervices of a lover.————

Cel. And at the end of it you'll marry me ?

Flor. If neither of us alter our minds before————

Cel. By this light, a neceffary claufe————but if I pay in all the aforefaid fervices before the day, you fhall be oblig'd to take me fooner into mercy.

Flor. Provided if you prove unfaithful, then your time of a twelvemonth to be prolong'd : fo many fervices, I will bate you fo many days or weeks; fo many faults, I will add to your 'prenticefhip fo much more : and of all this I only to be the judge. If you like it, follow me, captive.   [*She pulls him.*

Cel. March on, conqueror.   [*Exeunt* Cel. *and* Flore.

Enter Palamede *folus.*

Pal. 'Tis pretty odd, that my miftrefs fhould fo much refemble *Rhodophil's*! The fame news-monger, the fame paffionate lover of a court ; the fame, but Bafta!———— fince I muft marry her, I'll fay nothing of her, becaufe he fhall not laugh at my misfortune.

Enter Rhodophil.

Rho. Well, *Palamede*, how go the affairs of love ? You've feen your miftrefs ?

Pal. I have fo.

Rho. And how, and how ? Has the old *Cupid*, your father, chofen well for you ? Is he a good woodman ?

Pal. She's much handfomer than I could have imagin'd : In fhort, I love her, and will marry her.

Rho. Then you are quite off your old miftrefs ?

Pal. You are miftaken ; I intend to love 'em both, as a reafonable man ought to do. For fince all women have their faults and imperfections, 'tis fit that one of them fhould help the t'other.

Enter Doralice, *walking by and reading.*

Pal. Ods my life ! *Rhodophil*, will you keep my counfel !

Rho. Yes: Where's the fecret?

Pal. There 'tis. [*Shewing* Doralice.] I may tell you, as my friend *fub Sigillo,* &c. This is that very numerical lady, with whom I am in love.

Rho. By all that's virtuous, my wife.   [*Afide.*

Pal. You look ftrangely; how do you like her? Is fhe not very handfome?

Rho. Sure he abufes me. [*Afide.*] Why the devil do you afk my judgment?   [*To him.*

Pal. You are fo dogged now, you think no man's miftrefs handfome but your own. Come, you fhall hear her talk too; fhe has wit, I affure you.

Rho. This is too much, *Palamede.*   [*Going back.*

Pal. Pr'ythee do not hang back fo: Of an old try'd lover, thou art the moft bafhful fellow,

    [*Pulling him forwards.*

Dor. Were you fo near and would not fpeak, dear hufband?   [*Looking up.*

Pal. Hufband quoth-a! I have cut out a fine piece of work for myfelf.   [*Afide.*

Rho. Pray, fpoufe, how long have you been acquainted with this gentleman?

Dor. Who! I acquainted with this ftranger? To my beft knowledge, I never faw him before.

Enter Melantha *at the other end.*

Pal. Thanks, fortune, thou haft help'd me.   [*Afide.*

Rho. *Palamede,* this muft not pafs fo; I muft know your miftrefs a little better.

Pal. It fhall be your own fault elfe. Come, I'll introduce you.

Rho. Introduce me! Where?

Pal. There, to my miftrefs.   [*Pointing to* Melantha, who fwiftly paffes over the ftage.

Rho. Who! *Melantha!* O heavens, i did not fee her.

Pal. But I did; I am an eagle where I love: I have feen her this half hour.

Dor. [*Afide*] I find he has wit, he has got off fo readily; but it would anger me if he fhould love *Melantha.*

I 6

Rho. [*Aside.*] Now I could e'en wish it were my wife he lov'd, I find he is to be married to my mistress.

Pal. Shall I run after, and fetch her back again, to present you to her?

Rho. No, you need not; I have the honour to have some small acquaintance with her.

Pal. [*Aside.*] O *Jupiter!* What a blockhead was I, not to find it out? My wife that must be, is his mistress; I did a little suspect it before: Well, I must marry her, because she's handsome, and because I hate to be disinherited, for a younger brother, which I am sure I shall be if I disobey; and yet I must keep in with *Rhodophil,* because I love his wife.

[*To* Rhodo.] I must desire you to make my excuse to your lady, if I have been so unfortunate to cause any mistake, and withal to beg the honour of being known to her.

Rho. O, that's but reason. Hark you, spouse, pray look upon this gentleman as my friend; whom, to my knowledge, you have never seen before this hour.

Dor. I am so obedient a wife, Sir, that my husband's commands shall ever be a law to me.

Enter Melantha *again hastily, runs to embrace* Doralice.

Mel. O my dear, I was just going to pay my devoirs to you; I had not time this morning, for making my court to the king, and our new prince. Well, never nation was so happy, and all that, in a young prince; and he's the kindest person in the world to me, let me die if he is not.

Dor. He has been bred up far from court, and therefore——

Mel. That imports not: Tho' he has not seen the *Grande Monde,* and all that, let me die but he has the air of the court most absolutely.

Pal. But yet, madam, he——

Mel. O servant, you can testify, that I am in his good graces. Well, I cannot stay long with you, because I have promised him this afternoon——But hark you, my dear, I'll tell you a secret. [*Whispers to* Dor.

Rho. The devil's in me that I must love this woman.
[*Aside.*

Pal. The devil's in me that I muſt marry this woman.
[*Aſide.*

Mel. [*Raiſing her voice.*] So the prince and I——But you muſt make a ſecret of this, my dear, for I wou'd not for the world your huſband ſhould hear it, or my tyrant there that muſt be.

Pal. Well, fair impertinent, your whiſper is not loſt, we hear you. [*Aſide.*

Dor. I underſtand then, that——

Mel. I'll tell you my dear, the prince took me by the hand, and preſs'd it *à la derobée*, becauſe the king was near, made the *doux yeux* to me, and ſaid a thouſand gallantries, or let me die, my dear.

Dor. Then I am ſure you——

Mel. You are miſtaken, my dear.

Dor. What! before I ſpeak?

Mel. But I know your thoughts. You think, my dear, that I aſſum'd ſomething of *ficrté* into my countenance, to *rebuté* him; but quite contrary, I regarded him, I know not how to expreſs it in our dull *Sicilian* language, *d'un air enjoüe:* and ſaid nothing but *adautre, ádautre,* and that it was all *grimace,* and would not paſs upon me.

Enter Flavia, Melantha *ſees her, and runs away from* Doralice.

[*To* Flavia.] My dear, I muſt beg your pardon, I was juſt making a looſe from *Doralice,* to pay my reſpects to you: Let me die, if I ever paſs time ſo agreeably, as in your company; and if I would leave it for any ladies in *Sicily.*

Fla. Here's the new beauty, *Florimel,* is coming this way.

Enter Forimel, Melantha *runs to her.*

Mel. O dear madam! I have been at your lodgings, in my new galeche ſo often, to tell you of a new amour, betwixt two perſons whom you would little ſuſpect for it; that, let me die, if one of my coach-horſes be not dead, and another quite tir'd, and ſunk under the fatigue.

Flor. O, *Melantha!* I can tell you news ; the prince is coming this way.

Mel. The prince! O sweet prince! He and I are to——and I forgot it——Your pardon, sweet madam, for my abruptness. Adieu, my dears. Servant *Rhodophil*; servant, servant ; servant all. [*Exit. running.*

Rhodophil *goes to* Florimel *and* Flavia. [*Whispers.*

Dor. [*To* Pal.] Why do you not follow your miſtreſs, Sir ?

Pal. Follow her ! Why at this rate ſhe'll be at the *Indies* within this half hour.

Dor. However, if you can't follow her to-day, you'll meet her at night I hope.

Rho. [*To himſelf.*] I begin to hate this *Palamede*, be-cauſe he is to marry my miſtreſs : Yet break with him I dare not, for fear of being quite excluded from her company. 'Tis a hard caſe, when a man muſt go by his rival to his miſtreſs : But 'tis, at worſt, but uſing him like a pair of heavy boots in a dirty journey ; after I have foul'd him all day, I'll throw him off at night.——

Pal. But can you, in charity, ſuffer me to be mortified, without affording me ſome relief ? If it be but to puniſh that ſign of a huſband there ; that lazy matrimony, that dull inſipid taſte, who leaves ſuch delicious fare at home, to dine abroad on worſe meat, and to pay dear for't into the bargain.

Dor. All this is in vain : Aſſure yourſelf, I will never admit of any viſit from you in private.

Pal. That is to tell me in other words, my condition is deſperate.

Dor. I think you in ſo ill a condition, that I am re-ſolv'd to pray for you this very evening, in the cloſe walk behind the terras ; for that's a private place, and there I am ſure no body will diſturb my devotions. And ſo good-night, Sir. [*Exit.*

Pal. This is the neweſt way of making an appoint-ment I ever heard of : Let women alone to contrive the means : I find we are but dunces to 'em. Well, I will not be ſo prophane a wretch as to interrupt her devotions ; but to make 'em more effectual, I'll down upon my knees, and endeavour to join my own with 'em.

Fla. *Celadon!* What makes him here?

[*Exeunt all but* Flavia.

Enter to her Celadon, Olinda, Sabina ; *they walk over the stage together ; he seeming to court them.*

Olin. Nay, sweet *Celadon*————

Sab. Nay, dear *Celadon.*

Fla. O-ho! I see his business now, 'tis with *Melissa's* two daughters: Look, look, how he peeps about to see if the coast be clear ; like a hawk that will not plume if she be look'd on————

[*Exeunt* Celadon, Olinda, Sabina.

So————at last he has truss'd his quarry.

Enter Florimel.

Flor. Did you see *Celadon* this way?

Fla. If you had not ask'd the question, I should have thought you had come from watching him ; he is just gone off with *Melissa's* daughters.

Flor. *Melissa's* daughters! He did not court 'em I hope.

Fla. So busily, he lost no time : While he was teaching the one a tune, he was kissing the other's hand.

Flor. O a fine gentleman!

Fla. And they so greedy of him! Did you never see two fishes about a bait, tugging it this way and t'other way? For my part, I look'd at least he should have lost a leg or arm i'th' service————Nay, never vex yourself, but e'en resolve to break with him.

Flor. No, no, 'tis not come to that yet ; I'll correct him first, and then hope the best from time.

Fla. From Time! Believe me there's little good to be expected from him. I never knew the old gentleman with the scythe and the hour-glass bring any thing but grey hairs, thin cheeks, and loss of teeth : You see *Celadon* loves others.

Flor. There is the more hope he may love me amongst the rest : Hang't, I would not marry one of these solemn fops : Give me a servant that is an high-flyer at all games, that is bounteous of himself to many women ; and yet whenever I pleas'd to throw out the lure of

matrimony, should come down with a swinge, and by
the better at his own quarry.

Fla. But are you sure you can take him down when
you think good?

Flor. Nothing more certain.

Fla. What wager will you venture upon the trial?

Flor. Any thing.

Fla. My maidenhead to yours.

Flor. That's a good one: Who shall take the forfeit?

Fla. Well, I'll go and write a letter as from these
two sisters, to summon him immediately; it shall be
deliver'd before you. I warrant you see a strong combat betwixt the flesh and the spirit: If he leaves you to
go to them, you'll grant he loves them better?

Flor. Not a jot the more: A bee may pick of many
flowers, and yet like some one better than all the rest.

Fla. But then your bee must not leave his sting behind
him.

Flor. Well, make the experiment however: I hear
him coming, and a whole noise of fidler's at his heels.
Hey-day, what a mad husband shall I have!

Enter Celador.

Fla. And what a mad wife will he have! Well, I must
go a little way, but I'll return immediately and write
it: You'll keep him in discourse the while. [*Exit.* Fla.

Cel. Where are you, madam? What do you mean to
run away thus? Pray stand to't, that we may dispatch
this business. Caught! by all that's impudent. [*Aside.*

Flor. I think you mean to watch me, as they do
witches, to make me confess I love you. Lord, what
a bustle have you kept this afternoon! What with eating, singing, and dancing, I am so wearied, that I shall
not be in case to hear any more love this fortnight.

Cel. Nay, if you surfeit on't before trial, mercy on you
when I have marry'd you.

Flor. But what king's revenue do you think will maintain this extravagant expence?

Cel. I have an intolerable father, a rich old rogue, if
he would once die! Lord how long does he mean to make
it ere he dies?

Flor. As long as ever he can, I'll pafs my word for him.

Cel. I think then we had beft confider him as an obfti-nate old fellow, that is deaf to the news of a better world, and ne'er ftay for him.

Flor. But e'en marry and get him grand children in abundance, and great grand-children upon them, and fo inch him and fhove him out of the world by the very force of new generations.——If that be the way, you muft ex-cufe me.

Cel. But doft thou know what it is to be an old maid?

Flor. No, nor hope I fha'n't thefe twenty years.

Cel. But when that time comes, in the firft place thou wilt be condemn'd to tell ftories, how many men thou might'ft have had; and none believe thee: then thou groweft froward, and impertinently wearieft all thy friends to folicit man for thee.

Flor. Away with your old common-place wit: I am refolv'd to grow fat, and look young till forty, and then flip out of the world with the firft wrinkle, and the repu-tation of five-and-twenty.

Cel. Well, what think you now of a reckoning betwixt us?

Flor. How do you mean?

Cel. To difcount for fo many days of my years fervice, as I have paid in fince morning.

Flor. With all my heart.

Cel. Imprimis, for a treat: *Item,* for my glafs coach-: *Item,* for fitting bare, and playing with your fan: and laftly and principally, for my fidelity to you this long hour and half.

Flor. For this I bate you three weeks of your fervice: now hear your bill of faults; for your comfort, 'tis a fhort one.

Cel. I know it.

Flor. Imprimis, Item, and fum total, for keeping com-pany with *Meliffa*'s daughters.

Cel. How the deuce came you to know of that? Gad, I believe the devil plays booty againft himfelf, and tells you of my fins.   [*Afide.*

Flor. The offence being fo fmall, the punifhment fhall be proportionable; I will fet you back only half a year.

Cel. You're moſt unconſcionable : Why then do you think we ſhall come together ? There's none but the old patriarchs could live long enough to marry you at this rate. What, do you take me for ſome couſin of *Methuſa-lem's*, that I muſt ſtay an hundred years before I come to beget ſons and daughters ?

Flor. Here's an impudent lover ; he complains of me, without offering to excuſe himſelf ; *Item*, a fortnight more for that.

Cel. So there's another puff in my voyage has blown me back to the north of *Great-Britain*.

Flor. All this is nothing to your excuſe for the two ſiſters.

Cel. Faith, if ever I did more than kiſs 'em, and that but once————

Flor. What could you have done more to me ?

Cel. An hundred times more ; as thou ſhalt know, dear rogue, at time convenient.

Flor. You talk, you talk : Cou'd you kiſs 'em, tho' but once, and never think of me ?

Cel. Nay, if I had thought of thee, I had kiſs'd 'em over a thouſand times with the very force of imagination.

Flor. The gallants are mightily beholden to you ; you have found 'em out a new way to kiſs their miſtreſſes, upon other women's lips.

Cel. What wou'd you have ? You are my *Sultana* Queen, the reſt are but in the nature of your ſlaves : I may make ſome ſlight excurſion in the enemy's country for forage, or ſo, but I ever return to my head quarters.

Enter Boy with a Letter.

Cel. To me ?

Boy. If your name be *Celadon*.   [Celad. *reads ſoftly.*

Cel. [*To the Page.*] Child, come hither child, here's money for thee : So, be gone, quickly, good child, be-fore any body examines thee : Thou art in a dangerous place, child————[*Thruſts him out.*] Very good, the ſiſters ſend me word they will have the fiddles this afternoon, and invite me to ſup there————Now cannot I forbear, and I ſhou'd be hang'd, tho' I 'ſcap'd a ſcouring ſo lately for it. Yet I love *Florimel* better than both of 'em together,

——There's the riddle on't. But only for the sweet sake of variety. [*Aside.*]——Well, we must all sin, and all repent, and there's an end on't.

Flor. What is it that makes you fidge up and down so?

Cel. Faith I am sent for by a very dear friend, and 'tis upon a business of life and death.

Flor. On my life, some woman.

Cel. On my honour, some man; do you think I would lye to you?

Flor. But you engag'd to sup with me.

Cel. But I consider it may be scandalous to stay late in your lodgings. Adieu, dear creature, if ever I am false to thee again—— [*Exit* Celadon.

Flor. See what constant metal you men are made of! He begins to vex me in good earnest. Hang him, let him go and take enough of e'm; and yet methinks I can't endure he should neither. Lord, that such a mad-cap as I should ever live to be jealous! I must after him. Some ladies would discard him now, but I,

A fitter way for my revenge will find,
I'll marry him, and serve him in his kind. [Exit *Flor.*

ACT III.   SCENE I.

Enter Rhodophil *meeting* Doralice *and* Flavia. Rhodophil *and* Doralice *embrace.*

Rho. MY own dear heart!

Dor. My own true love! [*She starts back.*] I had forgot myself, to be so kind; indeed I am very angry with you, dear; you are come an hour after you appointed: If you had staid a minute longer, I was just considering whether I should stab, hang, or drown myself. [*Embracing him.*

Rho. Nothing but the king's business could have hinder'd me; and I was so vex'd, that I was just laying down my commission, rather than have fail'd my dear. [*Kissing her hand.*

Fla. Why, this is love as it should be, betwixt man

and wife ; such another couple would bring marriage into fashion again.   But is it always thus betwixt you ?

Rho. Always thus ! this is nothing.   I tell you there is not such a pair of turtles in all *Sicily* : there is such an eternal cooing and kissing betwixt us, that indeed it is scandalous before company.

Dor. Well, if I had imagin'd I should have been this fond fool, I would never have marry'd the man I lov'd : I marry'd to be happy, and have made myself miserable, by over-loving.   Nay, and now my case is desperate, for I have been married above these two years, and find myself every day worse and worse in love ; nothing but madness can be the end on't.

Fla. Doat on to the extremity, and you are happy.

Dor. He deserves so infinitely much, that the truth is, there can be no doating in the matter ; but to love well, I confess is a work that pays itself : 'tis telling gold, and after taking it for one's pains.

Rho. By that I should be a very covetous person, for I am ever pulling out my money, and putting it into my pocket again.

Dor. Oh dear *Rhodophil !*

Rho. Oh sweet *Doralice !*   [*Embracing each other.*

Fla. [*Aside.*] Nay, I'm resolv'd I'll never interrupt lovers : I'll leave 'em as happy as I found 'em.
                              [*Steals away.*

Rho. What, is she gone ?   [*Looking up.*

Dor. Yes, and without taking leave.

Rho. Then there's enough for this time.

Dor. Yes, sure, the scene's done, I take it.
        [*Parting from her. They walk contrary on the
           stage, he with his hands in his pocket, whistling,
           she singing a dull melancholy tune.*

Rho. Pox o' your dull tune, a man can't think for you.

Dor. Pox o' your damn'd whistling, you can neither be company to me yourself, nor leave me to the freedom of my own fancy.

Rho. Well, thou art the most provoking wife.

Dor. Well, thou art the dullest husband, thou art never to be provok'd.

Rho. I was never thought dull till I marry'd thee, and now thou haft made an old knife of me, thou haft whetted me fo long till I have no edge left.

Dor. I fee you are in the hufband's fashion, you referve all your good humour for your miftreffes, and keep your ill for your wives.

Rho. Pi'ythee leave me to my own cogitations; I am thinking over all my fins, to find for which of them 'twas I marry'd thee.

Dor. Whatever your fin was, mine's the punifhment.

Rho. My comfort is, thou art not immortal; and when that bleffed, that divine day comes, of this depar-ture, I am refolv'd I'll make one holy-day more in the almanack, for thy fake.

Dor. Ay, you had need make a holy-day for me, for I am fure you have made me a martyr.

Rho. Then fetting my victorious foot upon thy head, in the firft hour of thy filence, (that is, the firft hour thou art dead, for I defpair of it before) I will fwear by thy ghoft, an oath as terrible to me, as *Styx* is to the gods, never more to be in danger to the bonds of matrimory——

Dor. And I am refolv'd to marry the very fame day thou dy'ft, if it be to fhew how little I'm concern'd for thee.

Rho. Pr'ythee, *Doralice*, why do we quarrel thus, a-days? Ha! This is but a kind of heathenifh life, and does not anfwer the ends of marriage. If I have err'd, propofe what reafonable atonement may be made before we fleep, and I fhall not be refractory: But withal confider, I have been marry'd thefe three years, and be not too tyrannical.

Dor. Why fhould you talk of a peace, when you can give no fecurity for performance of articles?

Rho. Then fince we muft live together, and both of us ftand upon our terms, as to the matter of dying firft, let us ev'n make ourfelves as merry as we can with our misfortunes. Why there's the devil on't, if thou couldft make thy favours but a little lefs eafy, or but a little more unlawful, thou fhould'ft fee what a termagant lover I would prove. I have taken fuch pains to like thee *Doralice*, that I have fancy'd thee all the fine women in the town to help me out : But now there's none left for me to think on, my imagination is quite jaded. Thou art a wife and thou wilt be a wife, and I can make thee another no longer.   [*Exit.* Rho.

Dor. Well, since thou art a husband, and wilt be a husband, I'll try if I can't find out another that won't think me a wife.

Enter Melantha *and* Flavia *to her.*

Mel. Dear, my dear, pity me, I am so chagrin'd to-day, and have had the most signal affront at court! I went this afternoon to do my *devoir* to the princess, and help'd to make her court some half an hour : After which, she went to take the air, chose out two ladies to go with her, that came in after me, and left me most barbarously behind her.

Fla. You are the less to be pitied, *Melantha*, because you subject yourself to these affronts, by coming perpetually to court, where you have no business nor employment.

Mel. I declare I had rather of the two, be *railly'd*, nay *mal traitée* at court, than be deify'd in the town; for positively, nothing can be so *ridicule* as a mere town lady.

Fla. And therefore I would e'en advise you to quit the court, and live either wholly in the town; or, if you like not that, in the country.

Dor. In the country! nay, that's to fall beneath the town; for they live there upon our offals here : Their entertainment of wit is only the remembrance of what they had when they were last in town; they live this year upon last year's knowledge, as the cattle do all night, by chewing the cud of what they eat in the afternoon.

Mel. And then they tell for news such unlikely stories: A letter from one of us is such a present to 'em, that the poor souls wait for the carrier's day with such devotion, that they cannot sleep the night before.

Fla. No more than I can the night before I am to go a journey.

Dor. Or I, before I am to try on a new gown.

Mel. A fong that's ftale here, will be new there a twelvemonth hence: And if a man of the town by chance come amongft 'em, he's reverenc'd for teaching 'em the tune.

Dor. A friend of mine, who makes fongs fometimes, came lately out of the Weft, and vow'd he was fo put out of countenance with a fong of his: For at the firft country gentleman's he vifited, he faw three taylors crofs legg'd upon the table in the hall, who were tearing it out as loud as they could fing.

—After the pangs of a defperate lover, &c.

And all that day he heard nothing elfe, but the daughters of the houfe, and the maids, humming it over in every corner, and the father whiftling it.

Fla. Indeed I have obferv'd of myfelf, that when I am out of town but a fortnight, I am fo humble, that I would receive a letter from my taylor or mercer, for a favour.

Mel. When I have been at grafs in the fummer, and am new come up again, methinks I am to be turn'd into ridicule by all that fee me: But when I have been once or twice at court, I begin to value myfelf again, and to defpife my country acquaintance.

Fla. There are places where all people may be adored, and we ought to know ourfelves fo well as to chufe 'em. But I fee we fhall leave *Melantha* where we found her; for the town and country are become more dreadful to her than the court, where fhe was affronted. But you forget, we are to wait on the princefs. Come, *Doralice.*

Dor. Farewell, *Melantha.*

Mel. Adieu, my dear.

Fla. You are out of charity with her; and therefore I fhall not give your fervice.

Mel. Do not omit it, I befeech you; for I have fuch a tender for the court, that I love it even from the drawing room to the lobby, and can never be *rebutée,* by any ufage. But hark you, my dear, one thing I had forgot of great concernment.

Dor. Quickly then, we are in haste.

Mel. Do not call it my service, that's too vulgar; but do my *baise-mains* to the princess.

Dor. To do you service then, we will do your *baise-mains* to the princess.   [*Exeunt* Fla. *and* Dor.

Enter Philotis *with a paper in her hand.*

Mel. O, are you there, minion? And well, are not you a most precious damsel, to retard all my visits for want of language, when you know you are paid so well for furnishing me with new words for my daily conversation? Let me die, if I have not run the risque already, to speak like one of the vulgar; and if I have one phrase left in all my store that is not threadbare, and fit for nothing but to be thrown to peasants.

Phil. Indeed, madam, I have been very diligent in my vocation; but you have so drain'd all the *French* plays and romances, that they are not able to supply you with words for your daily expences.

Mel. Drain'd! What a word's there? *Epuisée*, you sot, you. Come, produce your morning's work.

Phil. 'Tis here, madam.   [*Shews the paper.*

Mel. O, my *Venus!* fourteen or fifteen words to serve me a whole day! Let me die, at this rate I cannot last till night. Come read your works: Twenty to one, half of them will not pass muster neither.

Phil. Sottises.   [*Reads.*

Mel. Sottises, *bon*, that's an excellent word to begin withal, as for example: He or she said a thousand *Sottises* to me. Proceed.

Phil. Figure: As what a figure of a man is there? *Naive* and *Naiveté.*

Mel. Naive; as how?

Phil. Speaking of a thing that was naturally said; it was so *naive*, or such an innocent piece of simplicity; 'twas such a *naiveté.*

Mel. Truce with your interpretations; make haste.

Phil. Foible, *chagrin*, grimace, *embarassé*, double entendre, equivoque, eclaircissement, suite, beveue, façon, penchant, coup d'etourdi, and ridicule.

Mel. Hold, hold; how did they begin?

Phil. They began at *Sottifes*, and ended *en Ridicule.*

Mel. Now give me your paper in my hand, and hold you my glafs, while I practife my airs for the day. [*Melantha laughs in the glafs.*] How does that laugh become my face ?

Phil. Sovereignly well, madam.

Mel. Sovereignly ! Let me die, that's not amifs, that word fhall not be yours, I'll invent it, and bring it up myfelf; my new head fhall be yours upon it : Not a word of the word, I charge you.

Phil. I am dumb, madam.

Mel. That glance, how fuits it with my face ?
[*Looking in the glafs again.*

Phil. 'Tis fo *languiffant.*

Mel. Languiffant ! That word fhall be mine too, and my laft *Indian gown* thine for't. That figh.
[*Looks again.*

Phil. 'Twill make many a man figh, madam, 'tis a mere *Incendiary.*

Mel. Take my blue petticoat for that truth. If thou haft any more of thefe phrafes, let me die, but I could give away all my wardrobe, and go naked for 'em.

Phil. Go naked! Then you would be a *Venus*, madam. O *Jupiter !* What had I forgot ? This paper was given me by *Rhodophil's* page.

Mel. [Reading the letter.]—*Beg the favour from you—Gratify my paffion—fo far—Affignation—in the—*Grotto, *—behind the* Terras—*Clock this evening.*—Well, for the *Billet-doux*, there's no man in *Sicily* muft difpute with *Rhodophil*; they are fo *French*, fo gallant, and fo *tendre*, that I cannot refift the temptation of the affignation. Now go you away, *Philotis*, it imports me to practife what I fhall fay to my fervant when I meet him.
[*Exit* Philotis.

Rhodophil, you'll wonder at my affurance to meet you here ; let me die, I am fo out of breath with coming, that I can render you no reafon for it. Then he will make this repartee ; Madam, I have no reafon to accufe you for that which is fo great a favour to me. Then I reply, But why have you drawn me to this folitary place ? Let me die, but I am apprehenfive of fome violence

from you. Then fays he, Solitude, madam, is moft fit
for lovers; but by this fair hand——Nay now, I vow
you're rude, Sir: O fie, fie, fie! I hope you'll be honourable?———You'd laugh at me if I fhou'd, madam——
What do you mean to ravifh a kifs by main force? Ha,
ha, ha!   [*Exit.*

Palamede and Doralice *meet; fhe with a book in her
hand feems to ftart at fight of him.*

Dor. 'Tis a ftrange thing that no warning will ferve
your turn; and that no retirement will fecure me from
your impertinent addreffes! Did I not tell you. that I
was to be private here at my devotions?

Pal. Yes; and you fee I have obferv'd my cue exactly: I am come to relieve you from them. Come,
fhut up, fhut up your book; the man's come who is to
fupply your neceffities.

Dor. Then it feems, you are fo impudent to think it
was an affignation? This I warrant was your lewd in-
terpretation of my innocent meaning.

Pal. Venus forbid that I fhould harbour fo unreafonable a thought of a fair young lady, that you fhould
lead me hither into temptation. I confefs I might think
indeed it was a kind of honourable challenge, to meet
privately without feconds, and decide the difference
betwixt the two fexes: But I hope you'll forgive me if
I thought amifs.

Dor. You thought too, I'll lay my life on't, that you
might as well make love to me, as my hufband does
to your miftrefs.

Pal. I was fo unreafonable to think fo too.

Dor. And then you wickedly inferr'd, that there was
fome juftice in the revenge of it: Or at leaft but little
injury; for a man to endeavour to enjoy that, which he
accounts a bleffing, and which is not valu'd as it ought
by the dull poffeffor. Confefs your wickednefs; did
you not think fo?

Pal. I confefs I was thinking fo, as faft as I could;
but you think fo much before me, that you will let me
think nothing.

ie very thing that I defign'd: I have fore-
 arguments, and left you without a word
l for mercy. If you have any thing far-
 ere fentence pafs———Poor animal! I
ither for my diverfion.

ou may have, if you'll make ufe of me
; but I tell thee, woman, I'm now paft

may be, I came hither to hear what fine
ld fay for yourfelf.
ould be very angry, to my knowledge,
: fo much time to fay many of 'em; and
ou would——

'alamede, I am a woman of honour.
ou are; you have kept touch with your
d before we part, you fhall find that I
ionour——yet I have one fcruple of con-

ant you will not want fome naughty argu-
to fatisfy yourfelf——I hope you are afraid
our friend?
traying my friend! I am more afraid of
l by you to my friend. You women now
he way of telling firft yourfelves: A man
are of his reputation will be loth to truft

u charge your faults upon our fex: You
ocks, you never make love, but you clap
nd crow when you have done.
rather you women are like hens; you
you cackle an hour after, to difcover your
'll venture it for once.
nvince you that you are in the wrong, I'll
e dark *grotto*, to my devotion, and make
that it fhall be impoffible for you to find me.
I do find you——
f you do find me——

       [*She runs in, and he after.*

Inter Rhodophil *and* Melantha.

ie die, but this folitude, and that grotto

re ſcandalous; I'll go no farther.: Beſides, you have a
ſweet lady of your own.

Rho. But a ſweet miſtreſs, now and then, makes my
ſweet lady ſo much more ſweet.

Mel. I hope you will not force me?

Rho. But I will if you deſire it.

Pal. [Within.] Where the devil are you, madam?
S'death I begin to be weary of this hide and ſeek: If
you ſtay a little longer, 'till the fit's over, I'll hide in
my turn, and put you to the finding of me.

       [He enters and ſees Rho. *and* Mel.
How, *Rhodophil* and my miſtreſs!

Mel. My ſervant to apprehend me! This is *ſurprenant
au dernier.*

Rho. I muſt on, there's nothing but impudence can
help me out.

Pal. Rhodophil, how came you hither in ſo good company?

Rho. As you ſee, *Palamde;* an effect of pure friendſhip; I was not able to live without you.

Pal. But what makes my miſtreſs with you?

Rho. Why, I heard you were here alone, and could
not in civility but bring her to you.

M.l. You'll pardon the effects of a paſſion, which I
may now avow for you, if it tranſported me beyond
the rules of *Bienſéance.*

Pal. But who told you I was here? They who told
you that, may tell you more for aught I know.

Rho. O, for that matter, we had intelligence.

Pal. But let me tell you, we came hither ſo privately,
that you could not trace us.

Rho. Us! what us? You are alone.

Pal. Us! The devil's in me for miſtaking. Me, I
meant: Or us; that is, you are me, or I you, as we
are friends, that's Us.

Dor. Palamede, Palamede!   *[Within.*

Rho. I ſhould know that voice: Who's within there,
that calls you?

Pal. Faith, I can't imagine; I believe that place is
haunted.

Dor. Palamede, Palamede!   *[Within.*

Rho. Lord, lord, what shall I do? Well, dear friend, to let you see I scorn to be jealous, and that I dare trust my mistress with you, take her back, for I would not willingly have her frighted; and I am resolv'd to see who's there? I'll not be daunted with a bug-bear, that's certain; pr'ythee dispute it not, it shall be so; nay, do not put me to swear, but go quickly; there's an effect of pure friendship for you now.

Enter Doralice, *and looks amaz'd, seeing them.*

Rho. Doralice! I am thunder-struck to see you here.

Pal. So am I, quite thunder-struck; was it you that call'd me within? (I must be impudent)

Rho. How came you hither, spouse?

Pal. Ay, how came you hither? And which is more, how could you be here without my knowledge?

Dor. [*To her husband.*] O, gentleman, have I caught you i'faith? Have I broke forth in ambush upon you? I thought my suspicions would prove true.

Rho. Suspicions! This is very fine, spouse. Pr'ythee what suspicions?

Dor. O, you feign ignorance: Why of you and *Me-lantha*; here have I staid these two hours, waiting with all the rage of a passionate loving wife, but infinitely jealous, to take you two together; for hither I was certain you would come.

Rho. But you are mistaken, spouse, in the occasion; for we came hither on purpose to find *Palamede,* on intelligence he was gone before.

Pal. I'll be hang'd then, if the same party, who gave you intelligence I was here, did not tell your wife you would come hither: Now I smell the malice out on both sides.

Dor. Was it so, think you? Nay, then I'll confess my part of the malice too. As soon as ever I sp.'d my husband and *Melantha* come together, I had a strange temptation to make him jealous in revenge; and that made me call *Palamede, Palamede,* as though there had been an intrigue between us.

Mel. Nay, I vow there was an appearance of an intrigue between us too.

Pal. To fee how things will come about !

Rho. And was it only thus, my dear *Doralice?*

[*Embraces.*

Dor. And did I wrong n'own *Rhodophil,* with a falfe fufpicion ?   [*Embracing him.*

Pal. [*Afide.*] Now I am confident we had all four the fame defign : 'Tis a pretty odd kind of game this, where each of us plays for double ftakes : This is juft thruft and parry with the fame motion; I am to get his wife, and yet to guard my own miftrefs. But I am vilely fufpicious, that, while I conquer in the right wing, I fhall be routed in the left: For both our women will certainly betray their party, becaufe they are each of them for gaining two, as well as we; and I much fear,

If their neceffities and ours were known,
They have more need of two, than we of one.

[*Exeunt, embracing one another.*

Enter Melifla, *after her* Olinda *and* Sabina.

Mel. I muft take this bufinefs up in time: This wild fellow begins to haunt my houfe again. Well, I'll be bold to fay, 'tis as eafy to bring up a young lion, without mifchief, as a maidenhead of fifteen, to make it tame for a hufband's bed : Not but that the young man is handfome, rich, and young; and I could be content he fhould marry one of them: But to feduce 'em both in this manner !——Well, I'll examine them apart ; and if I can find out which he loves, I'll offer him his choice——*Olinda,* come hither, child.——

Olin. Your pleafure, madam ?

Mel. Nothing but your good, *Olinda.* What think you of *Celadon ?*

Olin. Why, I think he's a very mad fellow; but yet I have fome obligements to him : He teaches me new airs on the *Guitarre,* and talks wildly to me, and I to him.

Mel. But tell me in earneft, do you think he loves you ?

Olin. Can you doubt it ? There were never two fo cut out for one another.: we both love finging, dancing, treats and mufick. In fhort, we are each others counter-part.

Mel. But does he love you ferioufly?

Olin. Serioufly.! I know not that; if he did, perhaps I fhould not love him: But we fit and talk, and
we wrangle and are friends: When we are together we
never hold our tongues, and then we have always a
noife of fiddles at our heels; he hunts me merrily as the
hound does the hare: and either this is love, or I know
it not.

Mel. Well, go back, and call *Sabina* to me. [*Olinda
goes behind*] This is a riddle paft my finding out: whether he loves her or no is the queftion; but this I am
fure of, fhe loves him.——O my little favourite, I muft
afk you a queftion concerning *Celadon:* Is he in love
with you?

Sab. I think indeed he does not hate me, at leaft if
a man's word may be taken for it.

Mel. But what expreffions has he made you?

Sab. Truly the man has done his part: he has fpoken
civilly to me, and I was not fo young but I underftood
him.

Mel. And you could be content to marry him?

Sab. I have fworn never to marry; befides, he's a
wild young man; yet to obey you, mother, I would be
content to be facrific'd.

Mel. No, no, we wou'd but lead you to the altar.

Sab. Not to put off the gentleman neither; for if I
have him not, I am refolv'd to die a maid; that's once,
mothe——

Mel. Both my daughters are in love with him, and I
cannot yet find he loves either of them.

Olin. Mother, mother, yonder's *Celadon* in the walks.

Mel. Peace, wanton, you had beft ring the bells for
joy. Well, I'll not meet him, becaufe I know not
which to offer him, yet he feems to like the youngeft
beft; I'll give him opportunity with her. *Olinda,* do
you make hafte after me.

Olin. This is fomething hard though.   [*Exit* Meliffa.

Enter Celadon.

Cel. You fee, ladies, the leaft breath of yours brings
K 4

me to you: I have been feeking you at your lodgings, and from thence came hither after you.

Sab. 'Tis well you found us.

Cel. I found you! Half this brightnefs betwixt you two was enough to have lighted me; I could never mifs my way: Here's fair *Olinda* has beauty enough for one family: Such a voice, fuch a wit, fo noble a ftature, fo white a fkin!

Olin. I thought he would be particular at laft.   [*Afide.*

Cel. And young *Sabina*, fo fweet an innocence; fuch a rofe-bud newly blown. This is my goodly palace of love, and that my little with-drawing room.———A word, madam———   [*To* Sab.

Olin. I like not this [*Afide.*] Sir, if you are not too bufy with my fifter I would fpeak with you.

Cel. I come, madam———

Sab. Time enough, Sir; pray finifh your difcourfe ———And as you were a faying, Sir———

Olin. Sweet, Sir———

Sab. Sifter, you forget my mother bid you make hafte.

Olin. Well, go you and tell her I am coming———

Sab. I can never endure to be the meffenger of ill news; but if you pleafe, I'll fend her word you won't come.———

Olin. Minion, minion, remember this———

[*Exit* Olinda.

Sab. She's horribly in love with you.

Cel. Lord, who could love that walking fteeple! fhe's fo high, that every time fhe fings to me, I am looking up for the bell, that tolls to church———Ha! give me my little fifth rate that lies fo fnug———She, hang her, a *Dutch*-built bottom; fhe's fo tall there's no boarding her. But we lofe time———Madam, let me feal my love upon your mouth. [*Kifs.*] Soft and fweet, by heaven! Sure you wear rofe-leaves between your lips!

Sab. Lord, lord, what's the matter with me! My breath grows fo fhort I can fcarce fpeak to you.

Cel. No matter, give me thy lips again, and I'll fpeak for thee.

Sab. You don't love me———

Cel. I warrant thee; sit down by me, and kiss again; ——— She warms faster than *Pigmalion*'s image.   [*Aside.*]
[*Kiss.*]———I marry, Sir, this was the original use of lips; talking, eating, and drinking came by the by———

Sab. Nay, pray be civil, will you be at quiet?

Cel. What would you have me sit still and look upon you like a little puppy dog, that's taught to beg with his fore-leg up.

Enter Florimel.

Flor. *Celadon* the faithful! in good time, Sir———

Cel. In very good, *Florimel*; for heaven's sake help me quickly.

Flor. What's the matter?

Dor. Do you not see here's a poor gentlewoman in a swoon! (Swoon away!) I have been rubbing her this half hour, and cannot bring her to her senses.

Flor. Alas! how came she so?

Cel. O barbarous, do you stay to ask questions? Run for charity.

Flor. Help, help, alas poor lady ———   [*Exit* Flor.

Sab. Is she gone?

Cel. Thanks to my wit that help'd me at a pinch: I thank heaven, I never pump'd for a lye in my life yet.

Sab. I am afraid you love her, *Celadon.*

Cel. Only as a civil acquaintance, or so: But however to avoid slander, you had best be gone before she comes again.

Sab. I can find a tongue as well as she———

Cel. Ay, but the truth is, I'm a kind of a scandalous person, and for you to be seen in my company——————— stay in the walks, by this kiss I'll be with you presently.   [*Exit* Sab.

Enter Florimel *running.*

Flor. Help, help, I can find no body.

Cel. 'Tis needless now, my dear, she's recovered and gone off, but so wan and weakly———

Flor. Umh! what was your business here, *Celadon?*

Cel. Charity, charity, christian charity; you saw I was labouring for life with her.

K 5

Flor. But how came you hither ? Not that I care——
But, only to be fatisfy'd.   [*Sings.*

Cel. You are jealous, in my confcience.

Flor. Who, I jealous! Then I wifh this figh may be
the laft that ever I may draw.

Cel. But why do you figh then ?

Flor. Nothing but a cold, I cannot fetch breath
well——But what will you fay, if I wrote the letter
you had to try your faith ?

Cle. Hey-day! this is juft the devil and the finner ;
you lay fnares for me, and then punifh me for being
taken ; here's trying a man's faith indeed : What, do
you think I had the faith of a flock or of a ftone ?
Nay, and you go to tantalize a man————'Gad, I love
upon the fquare, I can endure no tricks to be ufed to
me.   [Olinda *and* Sabina *at the door peeping.*

Olin. Sab. Celadon, Celadon !

Flor. What voices are thofe ?

Cel. Some comrades of mine that call me to play—
Pox on 'em, they'll fpoil all————   -   [*Afide.*

Flor. Pray let's fee 'em.

Cel. Hang 'em, tatter-de malions, they are not worth
your fight : Pray, gentlemen, be gone, I'll be with you
immediately.

Sab. No, I'll ftay here for you.

Flor. Do your gentlemen fpeak with treble voices?
I'm refolv'd to fee what company you keep.

Cel. Nay, good my Dear————[*He lays hold of her
                    to pull her back, fhe lays hold of* Olinda, *by whom*
                    Sabina *holds ; fo that he pulling, they all come in.*

Flor. Are thefe your comrades ? [*Sings.*] '*Tis* Stre-
ph*en calls, what would my love ?* Why do you not
roar out like a great bafs-viol, *Come follow to the My r-
tle grove.*---Pray, Sir, which of thefe fair ladies is it,
for whom you were to do the courtefy ? for it were un-
confcionable to leave you to 'em both. What, a man's
but a man, you know.

Olin. The gentleman may find an owner.

Sab. Though not of you.

Flor. Pray agree whofe the loft fheep is, and take him.

Cel. 'Slife, they'll cry me anon, and tell my marks.

Sab. Come away, fifter, we fhall be jeer'd to death elfe.

[*Exeunt* Olinda *and* Sabina.

Flor. What do you look that way for? You can't forbear leering after the forbidden fruit---But when e'er I take a wencher's word again——

Cel. A wencher's word! why fhould you fpeak fo contemptibly of the better half of mankind? I'll ftand up for the honour of my vocation.

Flor. You are in no fault, I warrant——

Cel. Not to give a fair lady the lye, I am in fault; but otherwife——Come let us be friends, and let ne wait upon you to your lodging.---

Flor. This impudence fhall not fave you from my table book. *Item,* A month more for this fault——

Cel. Pfhah! Pfhah! You fhall fee I will fo belabour you with conftancy and flames, and darts, and blank verfe, and foft things, and all that, that before I part with you, I will reduce that unmerciful long fcroll in your table book, to within two feconds of the critical minute.

Flor. Say you fo, Sir? I have a good mind to put you to a proof of your gallantry——What would you fay if I fhould make you an affignation at the mafque-rade to-night? But by the way, I have a mind to play deep there, and for fear I fhould baulk my fortune for want of a good fum, you fhall lend me two or three hundred piftoles.

Cel. Ah! dear madam, this is the leaft proof you could have made of me. I have juft that fum in my ftrong box, and the minute you meet me at the maf-querade, they are pofitively at your fervice---I'll bring 'em myfelf——But how fhall I know you?

Flor. O! I'll fhew you my face——But you promife not to mention the word Love to any woman before I come.

Cel. Fie, fie, doubt my conftancy! you might as well fufpect my honour.

Flor. Well, remember then I depend upon both——
Adieu, I am in hate.

Cel. One minute will break no squares, I'll warrant
you.

Flor. No, no, no more, I shall give you a surfeit of
my company.

Cel. A surfeit! why you have but tantalized me all
this while.

Flor. What would you have?

Cel. An hand, a lip, or any thing that you can
spare; when you have conjur'd up a spirit, you must
give him some employment, or he'll tear you to pieces.

Flor. Well, well, because I won't discourage your
constancy——there, there's a lock of my hair set in
diamonds to help your contemplation——Now not one
word or step farther, but take your leave in dumb shew,
and be gone.

Cel. Oh!   [*Bowing, and affecting a sigh.*
Flor. Oh impertinent!

So have I seen in tragick scenes a lover,
With dying eyes his parting pains discover,
While the soft nymph looks back to view him far,
And speaks her anguish with her handkercher:
Again they turn, still ogling as before,
Till each gets backward to the distant door,
Then, when the last, last look their grief betrays,
The Act is ended, and the musick plays.
                    [Exeunt, mimicking this.

ACT IV.   SCENE I.

Enter Palamede, Rhodophil, *in masquerade, with flam-*
beaux before them.

Pal. THIS masquerading, *Rhodophil,* is a most
glorious invention.

Rho. I believe it was invented first by some jealous
lover, to discover the haunts of his jilting mistress,
or by some distressed servant, to get an opportunity
with another man's wife.

Pal. No, no, it muſt be the invention of a woman, there's ſo much ſubtlety and love in it.

Rho. Let the invention be whoſe it will, I'm ſure 'tis extremely pleaſant; for to go unknown is the next degree to going inviſible. [*Enter* Beliza.] *Beliza,* What makes you here ?

Bel. Sir, my lady ſent me after you, to let you know ſhe finds herſelf a little indiſpos'd, ſo that ſhe cannot be at court, but is retired to reſt in her own apartment, where ſhe ſhall want the happineſs of your dear embraces to-night.

Rho. A very fine phraſe, *Beliza,* to let me know my wife deſires to lie alone.

Pal. I doubt, *Rhodophil,* you take the pains to inſtruct your wife's women in theſe elegancies.

Rho. Tell my dear lady, that ſince I muſt be ſo unhappy, as not to wait on her to-night, I will lament bitterly for her abſence: 'Tis true, I ſhall ſtay a little here at court to-night, but without her I ſhall take no divertiſſement.

Bel. I ſhall do your commands, Sir. [*Exit* Beliza.

Rho. She's ſick, as aptly for my purpoſe, as if ſhe had contriv'd it ſo.

Pal. Sick! and lies alone! Then it's poſſible ſhe may have contriv'd it for my purpoſe. Mum!

Rho. Well! if ever woman was a help-meet for a man, my ſpouſe is ſo; for within this hour I received a note from *Melantha,* that ſhe would be here in maſquerade in boy's habit, to rejoice with me before ſhe enter'd into fetters, for I find ſhe loves me better than *Palamede,* only becauſe he's to be her huſband: There's ſomething of antipathy in the word Marriage to the very nature of love: marriage is the mere ladle of affection, that cools it, when 'tis never ſo fiercely boiling over.

Pal. Dear *Rhodophil,* I muſt beg your pardon, there's an occaſion fall'n out, which I had forgot: I can't be at the maſquerade to-night.

Rho. Dear *Palamede,* I am ſorry we ſha'n't have one courſe together at the herd; but I find your game lies ſingle: Good fortune to you with your miſtreſs. [*Exit*

Pal. So, he has wish'd me good fortune with his wife; there's no sin in this, then. Here's fair leave given: Well, I must go visit the sick: I cannot resist the temptations of my charity. O what a difference will she find betwixt a dull resty-husband, and the free spirit of a lover! He sets out like a carrier's horse, plodding on because he knows he must, with the bells of matrimony chiming so melancholy about his neck, in pain till he's at his journey's-end, and despairing to get thither. [*Clashing of Swords.*] Hark! What noise is that? swords! nay then have with you.——   [*Exit.*

Re-enter Palamede *with* Rhodophil, *and* Doralice *in Man's Habit.*

Rho. Friend, your relief was very timely, otherwise I had been oppress'd.

Pal. What was the quarrel?

Rho. What I did, was in rescue of this youth.

Pal. What cause could he give 'em?

Dor. The common cause of fighting in masquerade; they were drunk, and I was sober.

Rho. Have they not hurt you?

Dor. No, but I'm exceedingly ill with the fright on't.

Pal. Let's lead him to some place, where he may refresh himself.

Rho. Do you conduct him then.

Pal. How cross this happens to my design of going to *Doralice!* for I'm confident she was sick on purpose that I should visit her. Hark you, *Rhodophil,* cou'd not you take care of this stripling? I am partly engag'd to-night.

Rho. You know I have business; but come, youth, if it must be so——

Dor. No, good Sir, don't give yourself that trouble; I shall be safer, and better pleas'd with your friend here.

Rho. Farewell then, once more I wish you a good adventure.

Pal. Damn this kindness! now must I be troubled with this young rogue, and miss my opportunity with *Doralice.* [*Exit.* Rhodophil *alone;* Palamede *with* Doralice.

*The Scene opens to the masquerade. Company of all sorts,
and some at play.* Celadon *looking on.*

Cel. Let me see, I am to lend *Florimel* three hundred
pistoles to night; and if she had press'd me for three
hundred and two, I must positively have borrow'd a
couple to have made up the sum: She was resolved to
leave me without a cross in my pocket, I find; wisely
presuming, that while I want money for my *Menu ple-
sieurs*, I shall the oftener come to her for consolation:——
Suppose now I should baulk her design, and fairly venture one hundred of them to win a couple more to 'em
—— Stay ——let me see—— I have the box, and throw
——A *Don* sets me ten pistoles, I nick him ——Ten
more——I sweep them too——Now in all reason he is
nettled and sets me twenty.——Um! Say you so,
my little *Don*, says I——Slap! I win them too. Now
he kindles, and butters me with forty——they are a
my own. In fine, he is vehement, and bleeds on to
fourscore, or an hundred: And I not willing to
tempt fortune, come away a moderate winner of about
two hundred pistoles——Ay! ay, exactly the sum I have
occasion for——Ha!

Enter Flavia *and* Florimel *in masquerade.*

I'gad, and here comes another thing; I have always
occasion for a fine woman, by *Jupiter.*

Flor. Do you think he won't know me?

Fla. Not if you keep your design of passing for an
African.

Flor. Well, now I shall make a fair tryal of him;
For I have a strange mind to know if his conscience
will let him be as great a rogue to *Melissa*'s daughters, as he has been to me.

Fla. I never doubt his conscience for any thing——
See, he is making to the bait already.

Cel. If your wit and face, madam, come up to what
the rest of your person promises, there's one heart gone
astray, to my knowledge.

Flor. 'Tis true, Sir, I have been flatter'd in my own
country with the reputation of a little handsomeness;
but how it will pass in *Sicily*, is a question.

Cel. Why, madam, are not you of *Sicily?*

Flor. No, Sir, of *Morocco;* I only came hither to fee fome of my relations, who are fettled here, and turn'd chriftians, fince the expulfion of my countrymen the *Moors.*

Cel. Are you then a *Mahometan?*

Flor. A *Muffulman,* at your fervice.

Cel. A *Muffulwoman,* fay you? I proteft by your voice I fhould have taken you for a certain Chriftian lady of my acquaintance.

Flor. It feems you are in love then; if fo, Sir, I have done with you: 'Twill be dangerous for a poor brown *African* to invade the dominions of a *Sicilian* complexion.

Cel. Pfhah! Some little liking I might have, but that was only a morning dew, 'tis drawn up by the funfhine of your beauty. I find your *African Cupid* is a much furer archer, than ours of *Europe*——Yet——wou'd I cou'd fee you——One look would fecure your conqueft.

Flor. No, no, I'll referve my face to gratify your imagination with——But in earneft, do you love me?

Cel. Ay, by *Alba,* do I moft intolerably: You have wit in abundance: by your motion I fee you dance to a miracle; by your voice, I'm fure you fing like an angel; and if one were but to fee your face, I'll warrant it looks like a *Cherubim.*

Flor. But can you be conftant upon occafion?

Cel. Conftant! Ay, by *Mahomet.*

Flor. You fwear like a *Turk,* Sir; but take heed, our prophet is a fevere punifher of promife-breakers.

Cel. Pfhah! Madam, your prophet is a *Cavalier,* I warrant; I honour him for the handfome provifion he has made for us lovers in the other world, as black eyes, young limbs, and frefh miftreffes every day in the week. Ah! go thy ways, little *Mahomet,* I'faith thou fhalt always have my good word.

Flor. Hold, hold, Sir, we are a little too particular; all the company are at play, you fee; if you have a mind to venture your money, I'll make one with you immediately——In the mean time, when you have an idle thought to throw away, beftow it on your fervant *Fatyma.*

Cel. This lady *Fatyma* pleafes me moft infinitely.

Fla. Falfe, or true, madam?

Flor. Falfe, as water; but by fire, air, and earth, I'll fit him for't. Have you the high dice about you?

Fla. I have 'em.

Flor. By your leave, Sir, what's your game?

Cel. Raffle, madam——Come, fet what you pleafe, 'tis no matter what I lofe; the greateft ftake, my heart, is gone already.

Flor. There.   [*She fets, and he throws.*

Cel. So, I have a good chance, two quarters and a fix.

Flor. Two fixes and a trey wins it. [*Sweeps the money.*

Cel. Very well, madam——Come, I'll try my fortune once again——What have I here? two fixes and a quatre—Come, an hundred piftoles more upon that throw.

Flor. I'm at you, Sir.——*Flavia,* the high dice.

Fla. There.

Flor. Three fives, I have won you, Sir.

Cel. Blood and furies! it would never have vex'd me to have loft my money to a *Chriftian,* but to a *Pagan!* an *Infidel!*——

Fla. Come, come, madam, e'en give over while you are a winner.

Cel. I hope the lady is not under the curb of a governefs, madam; you'll give her leave to do what fhe pleafes with her own, fure.

Flor. Since you are fo brifk, Sir, come, there's your hundred piftoles again, cover 'em and I am at you.

Cel. Stay, madam——I will cover you, tho' I'm ftrip'd for't; give me the box——Here——Frefh dice.

Flor. I'll throw with the old ones.

Cel. There, madam——Juft in, faith! Two fives and an ace.

Flor. Come on, Sir——Three fours——it's mine.

Cel. Umh!——Loll! loll! de doll! What the devil did I mean to play with this *Brunet* of *Afric?*

Fla. May the lady have leave to go now, Sir?

Cel. If your ladyfhip had never come hither, there wou'd have been no great lofs of your company. Come, madam, this diamond locket to twenty piftoles.

Flor. Some lady's favour, I prefume; I am loth to win it.

Cel. Upon honour, madam, my own hair, defign'd only for an old aunt that lives in the country.

Flor. Nay then, Sir, if it be your own, I won't undervalue it——There's thirty piftoles againft it : Have-at-it——Two fixes and a five——I ftand fair for't. [*He throws.*] 'Tis mine, Sir.

Cel. Confume and grind the fouls of thefe dice !—— Not one ftake in five : The devil——if ever I touch box again. Ah, plague of your jeft.

Flavia *fhakes the box at him, and goes out laughing at* Flor. A pretty figure I fhall make to *Florimel* by and by—— Now will I fteal into a corner, and laugh at myfelf moft unmercifully : For my condition is fo ridiculous, that 'tis paft curfing. [*Exit.*

The fcene changes into an eating houfe, bottles of wine on the table. Palamede, *and* Doraice *in men's habit.*

Dor. Now cannot I find in my heart to difcover my felf, though I long he fhould know me. [*Afide.*

Pal. I tell thee, boy, now I have feen thee fafe, I muft be gone; I have no leifure to throw away on thy raw converfation. I am a perfon that underftand better things, I—

Dor. Were I a woman, Oh how you'd admire me ! Cry up every word I faid, and fcrew your face into a fubmiffive fmile.

Pal. Ay, boy, there's dame Nature in the cafe : He who cannot find wit in a miftrefs, deferves to find nothing elfe, boy. But thefe are riddles to thee, child; and I have not leifure to inftruct thee ; I have affairs to difpatch, great affairs ; I am a man of bufinefs.

Dor. Come, you fhall not go ; you have no affair but what you may difpatch here, to my knowledge.

Pal. I now find thou art a boy of more underftanding than I thought thee ; a very lewd wicked boy.

Dor. You are miftaken, Sir, I would only have you fhew me a more lawful reafon why you would leave me, than I can why you fhould not, and I'll not ftay you ; for I am not fo young, but I underftand the preffing occafions of mankind as well as you.

Pal. A very forward and underftanding boy ! thou art

in great danger of a page's wit, to be brisk at fourteen, and dull at twenty. But I'll give thee no farther account, I muſt and will go.

Dor. My life on't, your miſtreſs is not at home.

Pal. This imp will make me very angry. I tell thee, young Sir, ſhe's at home, and at home for me ; and, which is more, ſhe is a-bed for me, and ſick for me.

Dor. For you only ?

Pal. Ay, for me only.

Dor. But how do you know ſhe's ſick a-bed ?

Pal. She ſent her huſband word ſo.

Dor. And are you ſuch a novice in love, to believe a wife's meſſage to her huſband ?

Pal. Why, what the devil ſhould be her meaning elſe?

Dor. It may be, to go in maſquerade as well as you; to obſerve your haunts, and keep your company without your knowledge.

Pal. Nay, I'll truſt her for that ; ſhe loves me too well to diſguiſe herſelf from me.

Dor. If I were ſhe, I would diſguiſe myſelf on pur-poſe to try your wit, and come to my ſervant like a riddle, read me and take me.

Pal. I cou'd know her in any ſhape ; my good genius would prompt me to find out a handſome woman. There's ſomething in her that would attract me to her without my knowledge.

Dor. Yet ſtill my mind gives me, that you have met her diſguis'd to-night, and have not known her.

Pal. This is the moſt pragmatical, conceited, little fellow, he will needs underſtand my buſineſs better than myſelf. I tell thee once more, thou doſt not know my miſtreſs.

Dor. And I tell you once more, that I know her better than you do.

Pal. The boy is reſolv'd to have the laſt word. I find I muſt go without a reply.   [*Exit.*

Dor. Ah, miſchief, I have loſt him with my fooling. *Palamede, Palamede;* 'tis I, *Doralice.* [*He returns, ſhe plucks off her peruke, and puts it on again, when he knows her.*]

Pal. O heavens! Is it you madam?

Dor. Now, where was your good genius, that wou'd prompt you to find me out?

Pal. Why, you see I was not deceiv'd; you yourself were my good genius.

Enter Rhodophil, *and* Melantha *in boy's habit.* Rhodophil *sees* Palamede *kissing* Doralice's *hand.*

Rho. Palamede! Again I am fallen into your quarters. What! engaging with a boy?

Pal. I was just chastizing this young villain; he was running away without paying his share of the reckoning.

Rho. Then I find I was deceived in him.

Pal. Yes, you are deceived in him: 'Tis the archest rogue, if you did but know him.

Mel. Good *Rhodophil,* let's go off *A-la-derobée,* for fear I should be discover'd.

Rho. There's no retiring now, I warrant you for discovery: Now have I the oddest thought to entertain you before your servant's face, and he never the wiser; 'twill be the prettiest juggling trick to cheat him when he looks upon us.

Mel. This is the strangest caprice in you.

Pal. [*To* Doralice.] This *Rhodophil's* the unluckiest fellow to me! This is now the second time he has barr'd the dice, when we were just ready to have nick'd him; but if ever I get the box again——

Dor. Do you think he will know me? Am I like myself?

Pal. No more than a picture in the hangings.

Dor. Nay, then he can never discover me, now the wrong side of the arras is turned towards him.

Pal. At least, 'twill be some pleasure to me to enjoy what freedom I can, while he looks on; I will storm the out-works of matrimony even before his face.

Rho. What wine have you here, *Palamede?*

Pal. Old *Chios,* or the rogue's damn'd that drew it.

Rho. Come to the most constant of mistresses; that I believe is yours, *Palamede.*

Dor. Pray spare your seconds; for my part, I am but a weak brother.

Pal. Now, to the truest of turtles; that is, your wife,

Rhodophil, that lies fick at home in the bed of honour.

Rho. Now let's have one common health, and fo have done.

Dor. Then, for once, I'll begin it. Here's to him that has the faireft lady in *Sicily* in mafquerade to-night.

Pal. This is fuch an obliging health, I'll kifs thee, dear rogue, for thy invention.   [*Kiffes her.*

Rho. He who has this lady, is a happy man, with-out difpute. [*Kiffes her.*]——I'm the moft concern'd in this I am fure.   [*Afide.*

Pal. Was it not well found out, *Rhodophil?*

Mel. Ay, this was *bien trouvé* indeed.

Dor. [*To* Melantha.] I fuppofe I fhall do you a kind-nefs, to enquire if you have been in *France,* Sir?

Mel. To do you fervice, Sir.

Dor. O, *Monfieur, votre valet bien humble.* [*Saluting her.*

Mel. Et votre efclave, Monfieur, de tout mon cœur.
        [*Returning the falute.*

Dor. I fuppofe, fweet Sir, you are the hope and joy of fome thriving citizen, who has pinch'd himfelf at home to breed you abroad, where you have learn'd your exercifes, as it appears, moft aukwardly, and are return'd, with the addition of a new lac'd coat, and a long wig, to your good old father, who looks at you with his mouth, while you fpout *French* with your *Mon Monfieur.*

Pal. Let me kifs thee again for that, dear rogue.

Mel. And you, I imagine, are my young mafter, whom your mother durft not truft upon falt water, but left you to be your own tutor at fourteen; to be very brifk and *entreprenant;* to endeavour to be debauch'd ere you had learnt the knack on't; to value yourfelf upon an intrigue before you get it, and to make it the height of your ambition to get a player for your miftrefs.

Rho. [*Embracing* Melantha.] Oh dear young bully, thou haft tickled him with a *repartee* i'faith.

Mel. You are one of thofe that applaud our country plays, where drums, and trumpets, and blood and wounds are wit.

Rho. Again, my boy! Let me kifs thee moft abundantly.

Dor. You are an admirer of the dull *French* poetry, which is fo thin, that 'tis the very leaf-gold of wit,

the very wafers and whipp'd cream of fenfe, for which
a man opens his mouth, and gapes to fwallow nothing:
And to be an admirer of fuch profound dulnefs, one
muft be endow'd with a great perfection of impudence
and ignorance.

Pal. Let me embrace thee moft vehemently.

Mel. I'll facrifice my life for *French* poetry. [*Advancing.*

Dor. I'll die upon the fpot for our country wit.

Rho. [*To* Melantha.] Hold, hold, young *Mars*; *Palamede*, draw back your hero.

Pal. 'Tis time; I fhall be drawn in for a fecond elfe,
at the wrong weapon.

Mel. Oh, that I were a man for thy fake!

Dor. You'll be a man as foon as I fhall.

Enter a meffenger to Rhodophil.

Meff. Sir, the King has inftant bufinefs with you. I
faw the guard drawn up by your lieutenant, before
the palace gate, ready to march.

Rho. 'Tis fomewhat fudden; fay that I am coming.
[*Exit Meffenger.*] Now, *Palamede*, what think you of this
fport? This is fome fudden tumult, will you along?

Pal. Yes, yes, I will go; but the devil take me if
ever I was lefs in humour. Why, the pox, could they
not have ftaid their tumult till to-morrow? Then I had
done my bufinefs, and been ready for 'em. Truth is,
I had a little tranfitory crime to have committed firft;
and I am the worft man in the world at repenting, till
a fin be thoroughly done: But what fhall we do with
the two boys?

Rho. Let 'em take a lodging in the houfe, till the
bufinefs be over.

Dor. What, lie with a boy? For my part, I own it,
I cannot endure to lie with a boy.

Pal. The more's my forrow, I cannot accommodate
you with a better bed-fellow.

Mel. Let me die, if I enter into a pair of fheets with
him that hates the *French*. [*Exit.*

Dor. Pifh, take no care for us, but leave us in the
ftreets; I warrant you, as late as it is, I'll find my
lodging as well as any drunken bully of 'em all. [*Exit.*

Rho. *I'll fight in mere revenge, and wreak my passion*
  On all that spoil this hopeful assignation.   [Aside.

Pal. I am sure we fight in a good quarrel.
  Rogues may pretend religion and the laws,
  But a kind mistress is the good old cause. · [Exeunt.

The Scene changes again to the masquerade; Celadon
  looking on at the gaming-table.

Cel. What witchcraft made me put it into fortune's
power to jilt me thus ; not only to lose my money, but,
in all probability, my mistress along with it! Well! I
foresee what it will come to——she'll quarrel with me
upon't, I suppose——so that I have nothing to do but to
set a good face upon the matter, and e'en begin with
her first——Here she comes, faith, and Mrs. *Nimble-
Tongue,* my evil genius, along with her! *Jasper,* come
hither, [*Whispers his Man.*]——that's all.

  Jas. I'll endeavour, Sir.

    Enter Florimel *and* Flavia *unmask'd.*

Flor. So, Sir! I'm as good as my word, you see.
  Cel. I am sorry you came so late, madam, for the
company's broke up, you see. Am I to wait upon you
home, or will you be so kind to take a hard lodging
with me to-night?
  Flor. No, Sir, you shall have the honour, if you
please, to see me to my own lodgings.
  Cel. No more words then, but let's away to prevent
discovery.
  Fla. Dear Sir ! You are in mighty haste to be rid of
the lady, methinks.
  Cel. O fie, madam, but if the lady shou'd want sleep,
you know, 'twould spoil the lustre of her eyes to-morrow, and then ten to one but she loses half a dozen
conquests by it.
  Flor. No, no, Sir, I am a peaceable princess, and
content with my own, I mean your heart and purse:
For the truth is, I have lost my money in masquerade
to-night, and I am come to claim your promise of sup-
plying me.

Cel. Madam, you make me entirely happy in your commands; to-morrow morning my servant shall wait upon you with three hundred pistoles.

Flor. But I left my company with promise to return to play.

Cel. Pshah! Play upon tick, and lose the *Indies*; I'll discharge it all to-morrow.

Flor. No, no, to-night, if you'll oblige me.

Cel. Jasper, go and bring me three hundred pistoles immediately.

Jas. Sir————[*Staring.*]

Cel. Do you expostulate, you rascal ? How he stares ! Why you impudent rogue, you have not been diverting your self with the inside of my strong box, have you ? I'll be hang'd if this villain has not lost all my gold at play : If you have, confess it immediately, sirrah ; and then perhaps I'll pardon you : But if you offer to stand in a lye, you dog, I'll have no mercy on you. Come, did you lose it ?

Jas. Sir, 'tis not for me to dispute with you———— As to the gold, Sir———I———confess———I——...—I————

Cel. O do you so, Sir ? Do you hear him, madam, this impudent rogue confesses he has lost it.

Flor. Ay, as sure as e'er he had it, I dare swear for him : But commend me to you for a kind master, that can let your servant play off three hundred pistoles without the least sign of anger to him.

Fla. 'Tis a sign he has a greater bank in store upon occasion.

Cel. Well, madam, I must confess, I have more by me than I will speak of at this time : But till you have given me satisfaction————

Flor. You satisfaction! what for my being disappointed of your promise ?

Cel. Don't tell me of a promise, madam, my promise was made upon a supposition that your conduct would deserve it; but since I see, madam, how little regard you have to your reputation and your money, and all that, madam————

Flor. What do you mean ?

Cel. Mean ! What, you have done nothing to make

a man jealous, I warrant: Going out a gaming in maſqerade at unreaſonable hours, and loſing your money at play is no fault with you, I ſuppoſe? What do I mean? Have not you been gaming, madam, and extravagantly loſt your money? Your money, madam, death! that loſs above all provokes me.

Fla. I believe you, becauſe ſhe comes to you for more.

Flor. Is this the mighty quarrel then? But ſuppoſe, Sir, I am able to clear myſelf.

Cel. I won't ſuppoſe any ſuch thing, madam, I know it all impoſſible, there's no excuſe in nature can be found for it: I'll ſtop my ears if you but offer it.

Flor. You'll hear me ſure.

Cel. To do this in the beginning of an amour, and to a jealous ſervant as I am: Had I all the wealth of *Peru* after ſuch an extravagance, I would not part with a ſingle *Marevedis* to you.

Flor. To this I anſwer——

Cel. Anſwer nothing at all, madam, for it will but inflame the quarrel between us: I muſt come to myſelf by little and little, and when I am ready for ſatisfaction, if you can think of any that's proper for an injur'd lover to take, I'll then perhaps conſult my honour, whether I ſhall receive it or no.

Flor. Pſhah! Pſhah! this anger's all affected, a mere pretence to ſham me off of the promiſe you made.

Cel. Very fine! ſham you madam!

Flor. Sir, you'll find, I know you at laſt.

Cel. And you'll find, madam, that I know you, and ſo well too, that my poor heart akes for't: I knew by your ſtaying ſo long, you had loſt your money; and therefore I once had it in my mind to go home to bed without ſpeaking to you: But ſince I knew you'd certainly come to borrow more of me, I was reſolv'd to ſtay and——

Flor. And let me have it; that will be kind indeed.

Cel. No, no, madam, to reproach you, to declare my grievances, which are great and many.

Fla. What money he may have about him, I can't tell, but I'm ſure he does not want for impudence.

Cel. And therefore I muſt tell you, madam——

Flor. I'll hear of nothing but the money.

L

Fla. Ay, ſtick to that, madam.

Cel. Do you think me a perſon to be us'd ſo ?

Flor. Look you, Sir, I won't quarrel with you : Where's the money ?

Cel. By your favour, madam, we will quarrel.

Flor. Money, money.

Cel. I am angry, and can hear nothing.

Flor. Money, money, money, money.

Cel. I thank my ſtars, I never was ſo barbarouſly us'd in all my life.

Flor. Then you are reſolv'd to ſtand it out, I ſee.

Cel. Madam, I have ſenſe enough to know when I'm affronted.

Flor. And intend to puſh this quarrel to an extremity ?

Cel. I ſhall venture to carry it up to the provocation, madam.

Flor. Very well, Sir, and becauſe your reſentment ſhan't want a freſh occaſion to ſupport it, know then I have loſt no money to-night, and only pretended that I had, to make a trial of your generoſity, *(toſſes a purſe.)* And now, Sir, I preſume the quarrel lies a little of my ſide, ſo that as ſoon as you pleaſe, Sir, that extraordinary treaſure, your heart, is again at your own diſpoſal.

Cel. O madam! the leaſt I can do in return, is to let go the ſlippery hold I had of your ladyſhip's : And becauſe you ſhan't ſay I keep any thing that belongs to you, madam, take back your picture and your hand-kerchief.

Flor. I have nothing of your's to keep : therefore take back your liberal promiſes, take 'em in imagination.

Cel. Not to be behind hand with you in airs, madam—Here I give you back your locket of diamonds : Take you that in imagination——

Flr. No. Sir, I happen'd to have ſecur'd that in reality, ever ſince your imagination loſt it to the lady *Fatyma·*   [*Shows the Locket.*

Cel. Oh! the Devil, if the lady *Fatyma* be turn'd Chriſtian again, I am routed to all intents and purpoſes.

Flor. By *Alha!* and ſo you are, Sir: By *Mahomet* you are; and to let you ſee I ſcorn to keep any of your heathen-offerings, there, there's your money again;

take it back with your oaths and proteftations, they're never the worfe for wearing, I affure you: Therefore take 'em fpick and fpan, as they are for the ufe of your new *feraglio*.

Fla. Now come away in triumph, madam, the day's your own.

Flor. Let him go firft, I'll ftay and keep the honour of the field.

Cel. I fhall not part with that, madam; I'll not retreat, if you ftay till midnight.

Fla. So, fo; here's like to be more blows, I find: But I'll e'en leave 'em to fight out their weapons by themfelves. [*Afide.*]   [*Exit.*

[Florimel *and* Celadon *walk carelefly by one another, humming a feveral tune*———

Cel. Well, to fee how ridiculous a thing paffion is! How like a fool a man looks, when he has quarrell'd with the woman he would give one of his eyes to be reconcil'd to.

Flor. And a Lover that expects his Miftrefs fhould be reconcil'd to him without his making the firft motion, muft certainly have a ftrong proof of his ignorance.

Cel. Then (as I have often faid) for a woman to lay fnares for a man, and punifh him for being taken——— To have no regard to the frailities of human nature. Well! Nay; for a man to be inclin'd to afk her pardon; and fhe to be fo unmerciful, as not by one fingle look, or word, to encourage his penitence.

Flor. Well, if ever I engage with another fervant, I fancy I fhall have more wit, than to tempt him in a difguife again: For 'tis certainly as direct a folly, as to throw a *Venice-Glafs* to the ground to try if it wou'd not break: And to part with him upon't, is fuperlatively ridiculous.

Cel. Madam, if it were not to pleafe fome people; I don't fee any fuch great neceffity of fome people's parting.

Flor. I proteft, I fancy fome people often do it, only becaufe perhaps they imagine other people have a mind to it.

Cel. And fuppofe a man were directly to afk fom

women's pardon, ten to one they'd have ſtomach enough
to refuſe it.

Flor. A modeſt lover may be refus'd any thing : But
there is a certain gracelefs aſſurance in ſome men, that
ſome rattle-brain'd women are ſtrangely bewitch'd to.

Cel. Come! come! ſince it muſt out then——I do
confefs——that I fancy you think that I have been in
the wrong : Not but at the ſame time you muſt own,
that the worſt you can ſay of me is, that you could not
put yourſelf into any ſhape that I did not like you in.
————In ſhort,

  Tho' moſt of my crime is, I have lov'd you thrice over,
  From whence you this uſe, and advantage diſcover,
  When you're a new miſtreſs, I'm as oft a freſh lover.

                                    [Exeunt.

ACT V.   SCENE I.

The W A L K S.

Enter Palamede, Stratton.   Palamede *with a letter in*
his hand.

Pal. **T**HIS evening, ſay'ſt thou ? Will they be both
            here ?

Stra. Yes, Sir ; both my old maſter, and your miſtreſs's father : The old gentleman rid hard this journey ; they ſay it ſhall be the laſt time they will ſee the
town ; and both of them are ſo pleas'd with this marriage, which they have concluded for you, that I am
afraid they will live ſome years longer to trouble you
with the joy of it.

Pal. But this is ſuch an unreaſonable thing, to impoſe upon me to be marry'd to-morrow ; 'tis hurrying
a man to execution, without giving him time to ſay his
prayers. Go now and provide your maſter's lodgings.

Stra. I go, Sir.   [*Exit.*

Pal. It vexes me to the heart, to leave all my deſigns
with *Doralice* unfiniſh'd to have flown her ſo often to a

mark, and ſtill to be bob'd at retrieve If I had but once enjoy'd her——

Enter Doralice.

Dor. Who's that you are ſo mad to enjoy, *Palamede?*

Pal. You may eaſily imagine that, ſweet *Doralice.*

Dor. More eaſily than you think I can: I met juſt now with a certain man, who came to you with letters from a certain old gentleman, yclep'd your father; whereby I am given to underſtand, that to-morrow you are to take an oath in the church to be grave henceforward, to go ill-dreſs'd and ſlovenly, to get heirs for your eſtate, and to dandle 'em for your diverſion; and in ſhort, that love and courtſhip are to be no more.

Pal. Now have I ſo much ſhame, to be thus apprehended in this manner, that I can neither ſpeak, nor look upon you; I have abundance in me, that I find: But if you have any ſpark of true friendſhip in you, retire a little with me; and beſtow your charity upon a poor dying man. A little comfort from a miſtreſs, before a man is going to give himſelf into marriage, is as good as luſty doſe of ſtrong water to a dying malefactor; it takes away the ſenſe of hanging from him.

Dor. No, good *Palamede*, I muſt not be ſo injurious to your bride: 'Tis ill drawing from the bank to-day, when all your ready money is payable to-morrow.

Pal. A wife is only to have the ripe fruit that falls of itſelf.

Dor. But a wife for the firſt quarter is a miſtreſs.

Pal. But when the ſecond comes.

Dor. When it does come, you are ſo given to variety, that you would make a wife of me in another quarter.

Pal. No, never, except I were marri'd to you: Marry'd people can never oblige one another; for all they do is duty, and conſequently there can be no thanks: But love is more frank and generous, than he is honeſt; he's a liberal giver, but a curſed paymaſter.

Dor. I declare I will have no gallant; but if I wou'd he ſhould never be a marry'd man: A marry'd man is but a miſtreſs's half ſervant; for a lover that comes to me that smells o'th' wife! 'Slife, I wou'd as soon wear her old gown after her, as her husband.

Pal. Am I then to be discarded for ever? Pray do but mark how terrible that word sounds. For ever! Oh *Doralice.*

Dor. Come, come, *Palamede,* we have drawn off already as much of our love as would run clear; after possessing, the rest is but jealousies, and disquiets, and quarrelling and piecing.

Pal. Nay, after one great quarrel, there's never any sound piecing; the love is apt to break in the same place again.

Dor. I declare I would never renew an old love; that's like him, who trims an old coach for ten years together, when he might buy a new one cheaper.

Pal. Well, madam, I am convinc'd that 'tis best for us not to have gone any farther; but gad the strongest reason is, because I can't help it.

Dor. The only way to keep us new to one another, is never to go any further; as they keep grapes, by hanging them upon a line, they must touch nothing if you would preserve 'em fresh.

Pal. But then they wither, and grow dry in the very keeping: However, I shall have a warmth for you, and an eagerness every time I see you; and if I chance to out-live *Melantha*————

Dor. And if I chance to out-live *Rhodophil*————

Pal. Well, I'll cherish my body as well as I can upon that hope. 'Tis true, I would not directly murder the wife of my bosom; but to kill her civilly, by the way of kindness, I'll put as far as another man: I'll begin to-morrow night, and be very wrathful with her, that's resolv'd on.

Dor. Well, *Palamede,* here's my hand, I'll venture to be your second wife, for all your threatnings.

Pal. In the mean time I'll watch you hourly, as I would the ripeness of a melon, and I hope you'll give me leave, now and then, to look on you, and see if you are not ready to be cut yet.

Dor. No, no, that must not be, *Palamede,* for fear the gardener should come and catch you taking up the glass.

Enter Rhodophil.

Rho. [*Aside.*] Billing fo fweetly, now I am confirm'd in my fufpicions: I muft put an end to this, 'e're it go farther. [*To* Doralice.] Cry your mercy, fpoufe, I fear I have interrupted your recreations.

Dor. What recreations ?

Rho. Nay, no excufes, good fpoufe, I faw a fair hand convey'd to lip, and preft, as tho' you had been fqueez-ing foft wax together for an indenture. *Palamede*, you and I muft clear this reckoning; why wou'd you have feduc'd my wife ?

Pal. Why wou'd you have debauch'd my mi'refs ?

Rho. What do you think of that civil couple, that play'd at a game call'd *Hide and feek*, laft evening in the grotto ?

Pal. What do you think of that innocent pair, who made it their pretence to feek for others, but came in-deed to hide themfelves there ?

Rho. All things confider'd, I begin vehemently to fufpect, that the young gentleman I found in your company laft night, was a certain youth of my acquaint-ance.

Pal. And I have an odd imagination, that you never could have fufpected my fmall gallant, if your little villainous *French* man had been a falfe brother.

Rho. Farther arguments are needlefs: Draw off: I fhall fpeak to you now by the way of *Bilbo*.

[*Claps his hand to his fword.*

Pal. And I fhall anfwer you by the way of *Danger-field.*

[*Claps his hand on his.*

Dor. Hold, hold, are not you two a couple of mad fighting fools, to cut one another's throats for nothing ?

Pal. How, for nothing ? he courts the woman I muft marry.

Rho. And he courts you, whom I have marry'd.

Dor. But you can neither of you be jealous of what you love not.

Rho. Faith, I am jealous, and that makes me partly fufpect I love you better than I thought.

Dor. Pifh ! a mere jealoufy of honour.

Rho. Gad, I'm afraid there's something else in't; for *Palamede* has wit; and if he loves you, there's something more in you than I have found; some rich mine for ought I know, that I have not yet discovered.

Pal. 'Slife, what's this? here's an argument for me to love *Melantha*; for he has lov'd her, and he has wit too, and, for ought I know, there may be a mine in her too; but if there be, I'm resolv'd I'll dig for't.

Dor. [*To* Rhodophil.] Then I have found my account in raising your jealousy; O! 'tis the most delicate sharp sauce to a cloy'd stomach; it will give you a new edge, *Rhodophil.*

Rho. And a new point too, *Doralice*, if I cou'd be sure thou art honest.

Dor. If you are wise, believe me for your own sake: Love and religion have but one thing to trust to; that's a sound faith. Consider, if I have play'd false, you can never find it out by any experiment you can make upon me.

Pal. Rhodophil, you know me too well, to imagine I speak for fear; and therefore, in consideration of our past friendship, I will tell you, and bind it by all things holy, that *Doralice* is innocent.

Rho. Friend, I believe you, and vow the same for you *Melantha*; but the devil on't is, How shall we keep 'em to?

Pal. What dost thou think of a blessed community betwixt us four, for the solace of the women, and the relief of the men? Methinks it would be a pleasant kind of life; wife and husband for the standing dish, and mistress and gallant for the desert.

Rho. Then, I think, *Palamede*, we had as good make a firm league, not to invade each other's property.

Pal. Content, I say, from henceforth let all acts of hostility cease betwixt us; and that in the usual form of treaties, as well by sea as by land, and in all fresh waters.

Dor. I will add one proviso, that whosoever breaks the league, either with war abroad, or by neglect at home, both the women shall revenge themselves by the help of the other party.

Rho. That's but reasonable. Come away, *Doralice,* I have a great temptation to be sealing articles.

Pal. Haſt thou ſo? Nay then, [*Claps him on the ſhoulder.*] fall on *Macduff.* And curs'd be he that firſt cries, Hold, enough. [*Exeunt.*

Enter Florimel *in man's habit.*

So! I'gad, I think I am a very pretty fellow! 'Twill be rare now to out-do this mad *Celadon* in all his tricks, and get both his miſtreſſes from him; then I ſhall revenge myſelf upon all three, and ſave my own ſtake into the bargain; for I find I do love the rogue in ſpight of all his infidelities. Yonder they are, and this way they muſt come——If cloaths, noiſe, nonſenſe, and a pert air will carry them, I'll puſh as fair for their favours as the briſkeſt beau of 'em all.

Enter to her Celadon, Olinda, Sabina.

Olin. Never mince the matter!

Sab. You have left your heart with *Florimel*; we know it.

Cel. You know you wrong me; when I am with *Florimel* 'tis ſtill your priſoner, it only draws a longer chain after it.

Flor. Is it e'en ſo! then farewell poor *Florimel*
[*Aſide.*

Cel. But let's leave the difcourſe; 'tis all digreſſion that does not ſpeak of your beauties——

Flor. Now for me in the name of impudence!——
[*Walks with them.*] They are the greateſt beauties, I confeſs, that ever I beheld——

Cel. How now, what's the meaning of this, young fellow?

Flor. And therefore I cannot wonder that this gentleman, who has the honour to be known to you, ſhou'd admire you——ſince I that am a ſtranger——

Cel. And a very impudent one, as I take it, Sir——

Flor. Am ſo extremely ſurpriz'd, that I admire, love, am wounded, and dying in a moment.

Cel. I have ſeen him ſomewhere, but where I know

L 5

not; pr'ythee, my friend, leave us, doft thou think we do not know our way in court?

Flor. I don't pretend to inftruct you in your way, for you fee I do not go before you; but you cannot poffibly deny me the happinefs to wait upon thefe ladies; me, who——

Cel. Thee, who fhall be beaten moft unmercifully, if thou doft follow them.

Flor. You will not draw fo near court, I hope?

Cel. Pox on him an impertinent puppy, I don't know what to do with him: let's walk away fafter, and be rid of him——

Flor. O, take no care for me, Sir, you fhall not lofe me; I'll rather mend my pace, than not wait on you—

Olin. I begin to like this fellow————

Cel. You make bold here in my feraglio, and I fhall find a time to tell you fo, Sir.

Flor. When you find a time to tell me on't, I fhall find a time to anfwer you: but pray what do you find in yourfelf fo extraordinary, that you fhould ferve thefe ladies better than I; let me know what 'tis you value yourfelf upon, and let them judge betwixt us.

Cel. I am fomewhat more a man than you.

Flor. That is, you are fo much older than I: Do you like a man ever the better for his age, ladies?

Sab. Well faid, young gentleman.

Cel. Pifh, thee! a young raw creature, thou haft ne'er been under the barber's hands yet.

Flor. No, nor under the barber-furgeon's yet, as you have been.

Cel. 'Slife, what would'ft thou be at? I am madder than thou art.

Flor. The devil you are: I'll tope with you—I'll fing with you—I'll dance with you—I'll fwagger with you---

Cel. I'll fight with you.

Flor. Out upon fighting: 'tis grown fo common a fafhion, that a modifh man contemns it; a man of garniture and feather is above the difpenfation of the fword: What's your opinion, ladies?

Olin. O, Sir, no young creature can endure a man that's quarrelfome.

Sab. This is the rareft gentleman, I could live and die with him——

Olin. You and I are merry, and juft of an humour, Sir, therefore we two fhould love one another.

Sab. And you and I are juft of an age, Sir; and therefore, methinks, we fhould not hate one another.

Cel. Then I perceive, ladies, I am a caft-away, a reprobate with you : Why faith this is hard luck now, that I fhould be no lefs than one whole hour in getting your affections, and muft now lofe 'em in a quarter of it.

Olin. No matter, let him rail; does the lofs afflict you Sir ?

Cel. No in faith does it not; for if you had not forfaken me, I had you; fo the willows may flourifh, for any branches I fhall rob them of.

Sab. However, we have the advantage to have left you ; not you us.

Cel. That's only a certain nimblenefs in nature you women have to be firft inconftant; but if you had made the more hafte, the wind was veering too upon my weathercock ; the beft on't is, *Florimel* is worth both of you.

Flor. 'Tis like fhe'll accept of their leavings.

Cel. She will accept on't, and fhe fhall accept on't ; I think I know more of her mind than you, Sir.

Enter Meliffa.

Mel. Daughters, there's a poor collation within that waits for you.

Flor. Will you walk, mufty Sir ?

Cel. No, merry Sir, I wo'not ; I have furfeited of that old woman's face already.

Flor. Begin fome frolick then; what will you do for her ?

Cel. Faith, I am no dog, to fhow tricks for her ; I cannot come aloft for an old woman.

Flor. Dare you kifs her ? I never was dar'd by any man—By your leave, old madam—Now, Sir, here's *Florimel's* health to you——   [*Kiffes her.*

L 6

Mel. Away, Sir; a sweet young-man as you are, to abuse the gift of nature so.

Cel. Good mother, do not commend me so; I am flesh and blood, and you do not know what you may pluck upon that reverend person of your's——Come on, follow your leader.

Flor. Stand fair, mother——

Cel. What with your hat on? ——Lie thou there——

Flor. And thou too——

[*He plucks off her hat, and she her peruke, and discovers herself.*

Omnes. Florimel!

Flor. My kind mistresses, how sorry I am, I can do you no further service: I think I had best resign you to *Celadon*, to make amends for me.

Cel. Lord, what a misfortune it was that the gentleman could not hold forth to you.

Olin. We have lost *Celadon* too.

Mel. Come away; this is past enduring.

Exeunt Melissa *and* Olinda.

Sab. Well! if ever I believe a man to be a man for the sake of a peruke and feather again——

Flor. Come, *Celadon*, shall we make accounts even? Lord! what a hanging look was there; indeed if you had been recreant to your mistress, or had forsworn your love, that sinner's face had been but decent; but for the virtuous, the innocent, the constant *Celadon*!

Cel. This is not very heroic in you now, to exult over a man in his misfortunes; but take heed, you have robb'd me of my two mistresses; and I shall grow desperately constant, and all the tempest of my love will fall upon your head, I shall so pay you.

Flor. Who, you pay me? You are a bankrupt, cast beyond all possibility of recovery.

Cel. If I am a bankrupt, I'll be a very honest one; when I cannot pay my debts, at least I'll give you up the possession of my body.

Flor. No, I'll deal better with you; since you are unable to pay, I'll give in your bond.

Cel. Faith, that's so generously said, that the least I can do now, is to pay it off like a man of honour, both principle and interest.

Flor. How do you mean?

Cel. Why since I see nothing but ready love will satisfy you, I'll e'en make up your accounts, and marry you.

Flor. Which is as much as to say, if I'll forgive you the debt, you'll pay me.

Cel. Pshah, pshah, the funds of this constitution are better able to pay than you imagine——Come, come, I'll put you into an handsome pension, make you my wife, that is, sole teller of my exchequer, and then you may pay yourself.

Flor. Well, for assurance——

Cel. Look, you, madam, no airs, for by those breeches——

Flor. Which I, when ever I do marry, am resolved to wear, till all the world calls me *Florimel the wilful.*

Enter Doralice, Rhodophil, Palamede *and* Flavia.

Dor. Florimel.

Flor. Nay, now I shall have no mercy.

Pal. Dear *Celadon,* I give you joy, for I perceive by the lady's breeches you are marry'd.

Flor. So, so, *Flavia* has given them all their lessons, I find. Remember this——   [*Aside to* Flavia.

Fla. Come, come, madam, never mince the matter, for to tell you the truth, I knew your inclinations, and because I was willing to give you a handsome pretence to follow 'em too, I have brought down all your friends upon you, to speak a good word for a poor honest gentleman, that, I know, has not assurance enough to do it himself: And now, Sir, I suppose your quarrel and mine's at an end——   [*To* Celadon.

Cel. I am extremely oblig'd to your good intentions, madam, and if you please to add one more favour to 'em, I shall confess myself your humble servant, as long as I live.

Fla. To my poor power, Sir, you may command me.

Cel. Only that you would be pleas'd, madam, to use your interest with the good company, that they would engage *Florimel* never to be friends with me.

Flor. O, dear Sir, I grant that without your making any interest for't; but pray how come you to be afraid on't?

Cel. Becaufe I am fure, as foon as ever you are, you'll marry me.

Flor. Do you fear it?

Cel. No, 'twill come with a fe r.

Flor. If you think fo, I will not ſtick with you for an oath.

Cel. I require no oath till we come to church, and then, after the prieſt, I hope; for I find it will be my deſtiny to marry thee.

Flor. If ever I fay a word after the black gentleman for thee, *Celadon*——

Cel. Then I hope you'll give me leave to beſtow a faithful heart elfewhere.

Flor. Ay, but if you'll have one, you muſt befpeak it: for I am fure you have none ready made.

Rho. What fay you madam? ſhall he marry *Flavia?*

Flor· No, ſhe'll be too cunning for him.

Dor. What fay you to *Olinda* then? She's tall, and fair, and bonny.

Flor. And foolifh, and apifh, and fickle.

Pal. But *Sabin's*, pretty and loving, and young and innocent.

Flor. And dwarfifh, and childifh, and fond, and flippant; if he marries her fiſter, he will get maypoles; and if he marries her, he will get fairies to dance about them.

Cel. Nay, then the cafe is clear, *Florimel*; if you take 'em all from me, 'tis becaufe you referve me for yourſelf.

Flor. But this marriage is fuch a bug-bear to me; much might be done if we could invent but any way to make it eafy.

Cel. Some foolifh people have made it uneafy by drawing the knot faſter than they need: But we that are wifer, will loofen it a little.

Flor. 'Tis true indeed, there's fome difference between a girdle and a halter.

Cel. As for the firſt year, according to the laudable cuſtom of new marry'd people, we fhall follow one another up into chambers, and down into gardens, and think we fhall never have enough of one another—— So far 'tis pleafant enough, I hope.

Flor. But after that, when we begin to live like hufband and wife, and never come near one another.——what then, Sir?

Cel. Why then our only happinefs muft be to have one mind, and one will, *Florimel.*

Flor. One mind, if you pleafe; but pr'ythee let's have two wills, for I find one will be little enough for me alone. But how if thofe two wills fhould meet and clafh, *Celadon?*

Cel. I warrant thee for that, hufband and wives keep their wills far enough afunder for ever meeting: One thing let's be fuie to agree on, that is, never to be jealous.

Flor. No, but e'en love one another as long as we can, and confefs the truth when we can love no longer.

Cel. When I have been at play, you fhall never afk me what money I have loft.

Flor. When I have been abroad, you fhall never enqu're who treated me.

Cel. Provided always, that whatever liberties we take with other people, we continue very honeft to one another.

Flor. As far as will confift with a pleafant life.

Cel. Laftly, whereas the names of *hufband* and *wife* hold forth nothing, but clafhing and cloying, and dullnefs and faintnefs in their fignification; they fhall be abolifh'd for ever betwixt us.

Flor. And inftead of thofe, we'll be marry'd by the more agreeable names of *miftrefs* and *gallant.*

Cel. None of my privileges to be infring'd by thre, *Florimel*, under the penalty of a month's failing nights.

Flor. None of my privileges to be enfring'd by thre *Celadon*, under the penalty of cuckoldom.

Cel. Well, if it be my fortune to be made a cuckold, I had rather thou fhould'ft make me one, than any one in *Sicily:* And for my comfort, I fhall have thee oftener than any of thy fervants.

Flor. La ye now, is not fuch a marriage as good as wenching, *Celadon?*

Cel. This is very good: but not fo good, *Florimel.*

Omn. A wedding! A wedding!

Pal. So, fo! Here's every body's bufinefs done but mine.

Rho. Here comes a fmall emiffary, *Palamade;* and I faicy, in order to finifh it——

Enter Philotis *haftily.*

Pal. Ha! well my dear, what news?

Phil. O, Sir, I am glad I have found you!

Pal. What's the matter?

Phil. My lady has juft now received a letter from her father, with an abfolute command to difpofe herfelf to marry you to-morrow.

Pal. And fhe takes it to death, I prefume.

Phil. O dear Sir, fhe's under a greater misfortune than the Apprehenfion of being marry'd to fo fine a gentleman.

Pal. O, dear madam—but pray what is it?

Phil. Why, Sir, fhe is in fo unconfolable a concern for her being out of favour with the princefs, that fhe pro-tefts, fhe'll neither, eat, drink, fleep, or marry, till fhe has made her peace with her.

Pal. That's hard.

Phil. Now, Sir, you muft know, upon the extraor-dinary occafions, fhe always practifes what fhe is to do and fay beforehand; and in order to it, fhe is juft com-ing into this part of the walks; where by her own di-rection, Sir, I am to perfonate the princefs, and to re-ceive her with all imaginable coldnefs, while fhe ufes all the efforts of her *French* airs and phrafes to recommend herfelf into my good graces.

Pal. Very good; but what is my part all this while?

Phil. Why, Sir, if you'll defire the good company to retire a little——you fhall bolt out upon her while fhe is in the very agony of her good breeding, and worry her with her own phrafes, till you force her to lend a reafon-able ear to your addreffes.

Pal. Admirable! *Rhodophil.*

Rho. We underftand you——we'll be all ready at the next corner to give you a lift upon occafion.

[*Exeunt all but* Pa'amede *and* Philotis.

Phil. You muft be fure to take no repulfes, and I warrant you do her bufinefs——Here is a lift of her phrafes for the day——ply her home with 'em, right or wrong, upon any occafion: Foil her at her own weapons; for she's like one of the old *Amazons*, she'll never marry, except it be a man who has first conquer'd her.

Pal. Say you so? Faith, I'll lay her on to the best of my assurance then: But you won't forget, I hope, to give me a prompt upon occasion.

Phi. O, dear Sir, if you doubt my memory, put some token upon my finger to refresh it——That diamond would do admirably.

Pal. There 'tis, and I ask your pardon heartily for calling your memory in question.

Phi. Here she comes; to your post.   [Pal. *retires.*

Enter Melantha.

Mel. O! are you there, madam?——Come, are yo^u perfect in the princess?

Phi. Yes, madam, particularly in all the reserv'd airs your ladyship was pleas'd to shew me.

Mel. Very well—move a little that way—so——now you are the princess, and alone; and now is my time to introduce myself, and make my court to you in my new *French* phrases. Stay, let me read my catalogue——*Suite, Figure, chagrin, naviete,* and *let me die,* for the parenthesis of all.

Pal. [*Aside.*] Do, persecute the princess in imagination, and I'll persecute thee as fast in effigy.

Mel. Madam, the princess! let me die, but this is a most horrid spectacle, to see a person who makes so grand a figure in the court, without the *suite* of a princess, and entertaining your *chagrin,* all alone; (*naivete* should have been there, but the disobedient word would not come in)

Phi. You take an unreasonable time, madam, I design'd this hour for solitude.

Pal. [*To* Melantha.] Let me die, madam, if I have not waited here these two long hours, without so much as the suite of a single servant to attend me; entertaining myself with my own *Chagrin,* till I had the honour to see your ladship, who are are a person that makes so considerable a figure in the court.

Mel. Truce, with your *douceurs,* good servant, you see I am addressing the princess; pray do not embarrass me——Embarrass me! what a delicious *French* word do you make me lose upon you too! [*To* Philotis.] Your highness, madam, will please to pardon the *Coup de' etourdy* which I made, in not sooner finding you out to be a princess. But let me die, if this *elaircissement*, which is made this day of your quality, does ravith me; and give me leave to tell you——

Pal. But first give me leave to tell you, madam, that I have so great a tender for your person, and such a *Paunchant* to do you service that——

Mel. What must I still be troubled with your *Sottises?* There's another word lost. that I meant for the princess, (with a mischief to you.) But your highness, madam——

Pal. But your ladyship, madam——
Mel. I say, your highness madam——
Phil. Away impertinent.
Mel. Impertinent! Oh, I am the most unfortunate person this day breathing; that the princess should thus *Rompre en visere,* without occasion; let me die, but I'll follow her to death, till I make my peace.

Pal. [*Holding her.*] And let me die, but I'll follow you to the infernals till you pity me.

Mel. [*Turning towards him angrily.*] Ay, 'tis long of you that this *Malheur* is fall'n upon me; your impertinence has put me out of the good graces of the princess, and all that; which has ruin'd me, and all that; and therefore, let me die, but I'll be reveng'd, and all that.

Pal. Façon, *Façon,* you must, and shall love me, and all that; for my old man is coming up, and all that; and I am *defes peré au dernier,* and will not be disinherited, and all that.

Mel. How durst you interrupt me so *mal a propos,* when you know I was practising my addresses to the princess?

P. l. But why would you address yourself so much a *Contretemps* then?

Mel. Ah, *Mal Peste!*
Pal. and *Phi. Ah j'enrage!*

Mel. *Ad'autres, ad'autres:* He mocks himself of me, he abufes me: *Ah mo unfortunate.*   [*Cries.*

Phi. Indeed you miftake him, madam, he does but accommodate his phrafe to your refin'd language; purfue your point, Sir.——   [*To him.*

Pal. *Ah, qu'il fait beau dans ces boccages:*   [*Singing.*
 Ah, que le ciel donne un bonne jour!
There I was with you with a minuet.

Mel. Let me die now, but this finging is fine, and extremely *French* in him. [*Laughs.*] But then that he fhou'd ufe my own words, as it were in contempt of me, I cannot bear it.   [*Cries.*

Pal. *Ces beaux & Sejours, ces doux ramages.*   [*Singing.*

Mel. *Ces beaux & Sejours, ces doux ramages,*
 Ces beaux Sejous nous invitent a l'amour.
     [*Singing after him.*

Pal. Let me die now but that was fine. Ah, now for three or four brifk *Frenchmen*, to be put into mafking habits, and to fing it on a treatre; how witty it would be! And then to dance helter-fkelter, to a *Chanfon a boire: Toute la terre, toute la terre ef a moy,* What's matter, though it were made, and fung two or three years ago in *Caberets;* how it would attract the admiration, efpecially of every one that's an *Eveillée!*

Mel. Well; I begin to have a a *Tendre* for you; but yet, upon condition, that————when we are marry'd, you——   [*Pal. fings while fhe fpeaks.*

Phi. You muft drown her voice; if fhe makes her *French* conditions, you are a flave for ever.

Mel. Firft, will you engage——that

Pal. Fa, la, la, la, &c.   [*Louder.*

Mel. Will you hear the conditions?

Pal. No, I will hear no conditions! I am refolv'd to win you *en François;* to be very airy with abundance of noife, and no fenfe: *Fa, la, la, la,* &c.

Mel. Hold, hold, I am vanquifh'd with your *Gaieté d'efprit.* I am yours, and will be yours, *fans nulle referve;* and, let me die, if I do not think myfelf the happieft nymph in *Sicily*——My dear *French* Dear, ftay but a minute till I *racomode* myfelf with the princefs; and then I am yours, *Jufqu' a la mort.*   [*Going off.*

Enter Celadon, Florimel, Rhodophil, Doralice, *and* Flavia, *finging.*

Omn. A *Palamede!* A *Palamede!*

Pal. [*Fanning himfelf.*] Poo, I never thought before, wooing was fo laborious an exercife; I'gad, if fhe were worth a million, I deferve her.

Mel. Ah me, was ever nymph under fuch confufion? I fhall have all the *Tendre* of my *Belle Paffion* turn'd into ridicule————I hope, fervant, you did not lay this ambufcade to be witneffes of my *Foiblefs.*

Pal. Not I, upon honour, madam, but 'tis impoffible for us great conquerors to fight without witnefs of our glory.

Dor. Come, come, madam, confider the pains he has taken to deferve you, and don't rob him of the glory of confeffing it————We are all your friends, give him your hand.

Mel. Dear, my dear, don't give this confuffion—I can't do it————he muft take it if he has it.

Pal. Thus I feize it then as my right of conqueft, and now, Madam, I take you prifoner for life.

Mel. Oh barbarous, and plunder me of all!

Pal. All in good time, madam.

Cel. And now, *Palamede*, your bufinefs is done.

Rho. And now, *Doralice*, fince your friend and mine are likely to be bufy for fome few months at leaft, I think we had e'en as good mind our own bufinefs as ftand idle————From this day forward, I'll never dine but at home.

Dor. Why truly, he that's always running to an eating-houfe, will find, at the year's end, ne'er the lefs account in his houfe-keeping. When the meal's ready at home, fomebody muft fit down to it.

And high-fed palates to their coft difcover,
That hufbands leavings often feaft the lover.

      [Exeunt omnes.

        T H E

THE

NON-JUROR.

A

COMEDY.

—————*Pulchra Laverna*
Da mihi fallere; da Juſtum, Sanctumque videri.
Noctem Peccatis, & Fraudibus objice Nubem.

HOR.

To the KING.

S I R,

IN a time, when all communities congratulate your
Majesy on the *Glories* of your reign, which are
continually rifing from the *Profperities* of your people;
be gracioufly pleas'd, *Dread Sir*, to permit the loweft of
your fubjects from the *Theatre*, to take this occafion of
offering their moft humble acknowledgments for your
royal favour and protection.

YOUR comedians SIR, are an unhappy fociety, whom
fome fevere heads think wholly ufelefs, and others dangerous to the young and innocent: This comedy is therefore an attempt to remove that prejudice, and to fhew,
what honeft and laudable ufes may be made of the *Theatre*,
when its performances keep clofe to the true purpofes of
its inftitution : That it may be neceffary to divert the
fullen and difaffected from bufying their brains to difturb
the happinefs of a government, which (for want of proper
amufements) they often enter into wild and feditious
fchemes to reform : And that it may likewife make thofe
very follies the ridicule and diverfion even of thofe that
committed them. Our labours have at leaft this glory to
boaft, that fince plays were firft exibited in *England*,
they were never totally fupprefs'd but by thofe very
people, that turn'd our *Church* and *Conftitution*, into
Irreligion and *Anarchy*.

OF all errors, thofe that are the effect of *Superftition*
make us naturally moft obftinate; it is therefore no
wonder, that the blinded profelytes of our few non-juring
clergy, are fo hard to be recovered by the cleareft evidences of fenfe and reafon. But when a *Principle* is once
made truly *Ridiculous*, it is not in the power of human
nature not to be *afham'd* of it. From which reflection, I
was firft determin'd to attack thofe *lurking* enemies of
our conftitution from the ftage: And though my fuccefs
has far exceeded my expectation, yet I grieve, when I
(perhaps with vanity) imagine it might have had thrice
the good effect on the minds of your MAJESTY's people

were it not under the *Misfortune* of being written by a *Comedian*. I am therefore in some terror, notwithstanding its public applause, to reflect how far your MAJESTY, in your wisdom, may think it proper to with-hold your pardon for the unlicensed boldness of my undertaking. I am sensible it may be justly urg'd against me, that even *Truth* and *Loyalty* might have lost their lustre, by appearing reduc'd to want the defence of so inconsiderable a champion: But as I never believ'd the best play could be supported in an ill cause; so was I assur'd the worst might pass, with favour, in a good one. And though my duty and concern has made me more careful in the conduct of this, than any of my former endeavours; I am convinc'd, that what may have been extraordinary in the success of it, is utterly owing to a happy choice of the subject: And as its meeting no opposition from our publick male-contents, seems in some degree, an argument of the clear and honest truth of those principles it vindicates; so may it of the equal falshood of the rebellious and unchristian tenets it exposes. Nay I have yet a farther hope, that it has even discovered the strength and number of the *Misguided* to be much less, than may have been artfully insinuated; there being no assembly where people are so free, and apt to speak their minds, as in a crowded *Theatre*; of which your MAJESTY may have lately seen an instance, in the insuppressible acclamations that were given on your appearing to honour this play with your royal presence.

But were the disaffected yet as numerous as some few may wish them, What honest *Englishman* can ever think them formidable, that considers his security in the wisdom of your MAJESTY's *Counsels*, and your heroick *Resolution* to execute them? And as every action of your regal power has shewn the nation, that your greatest *Glory* and *Delight* is in being the *Father* of your *People*; so may it convince its enemies, that *they* will always find you KING of your *Subjects*.——But I am wandring into thoughts that awe me into silence; and humbly beg leave to subscribe myself, *May it please your* MAJESTY,

Your MAJESTY's *most dutiful,*
And most obedient, subject and servant.
COLLEY CIBBER.

PROLOGUE.

Written by N. ROWE, Efq;

TO night, ye Wigs and Tories both be safe,
   Nor hope, at one another's cost, to laugh :
We mean to souse old Satan *and the* Pope *;*
They've no relations here, nor friends, we hope.
A Tool of their's supplies the comic stage
With just materials for satyrick rage :
Nor think our colours may too strongly paint
The stiff non-juring separation-saint.
Good breeding ne'er commands us to be civil
To those who give the nation to the devil;
Who at our surest, best foundations strike,
And hate our monarch, and our church alike :
Our church,—which, aw'd with reverential fear,
Scarcely the muse presumes to mention here.
Long may she these her worst of foes defy,
And lift her mitred head triumphant to the sky :
While their's—But satyr silently disdains
To name, what lives not, but in madman's brains.
Like bawds, each lurking pastor seeks the dark,
And fears the Justice's *enquiring clerk.*
In close back rooms his routed flocks he rallies,
And reigns the patriarch of blind lanes and allies.
There safe, he lets his thundring censures fly,
Unchristans, damns us, gives our laws the lie,
And excommunicates three-stories high :
Why, since a land of liberty they hate,
Still will they linger in this free-born state?
Here, ev'ry hour, fresh hateful objects rise,
Peace, and prosperity afflict their eyes :
With anguish, prince and people they survey,
Their just obedience, and his righteous sway.

M

PROLOGUE.

Ship off, ye slaves, and seek some passive land,
Where tyrants after your own hearts command,
To your Transalpine *master's rule resort,*
And fill an empty abdicated court :
Turn your possessions here to ready rhino,
And buy ye lands and lordships at Urbino.

Dramatis Personæ.

M E N.

Sir *John Woodvil,*	Mr. *Mills.*
Colonel *Woodvil,*	Mr. *Booth.*
Mr. *Heartly,*	Mr. *Wilks.*
Doctor *Wolf,*	Mr. *Cibber.*
Charles,	Mr. *Walker*

W O M E N.

Lady *Woodvil,*	Mrs. *Porter.*
Maria,	Mrs. *Oldfield.*

The SCENE, an Anti-chamber of Sir John's House in
L O N D O N.

THE

ACT I. SCENE I.

Sir John Woodvil, *and the Colonel.*

Col. PRAY confider, Sir.

Sir John. So I do, Sir, that I am her father, and will difpofe of her as I pleafe.

Col. I don't difpute your authority, Sir: but as I am your fon too, I think it my duty to be concern'd for your honour: have not you countenanced his addrefles to my fifter? Has not fhe received them? How then is it poffible, that either you or fhe with honour can recede?

Sir John. Why, Sir? Suppofe I was about buying a pad-nag for your fifter, and upon enquiry fhould find him not found: Pray, Sir, would there be any great difhonour in being off o'the bargain?

Col. With Submiffion, Sir, I don't take that to be the cafe. Mr. *Heartly*'s birth and fortune are too well known to you; and I dare fwear he may defy the world to lay a blemifh upon his principles.

Sir John. Why then, Sir, fince I muft be catechiz'd, I muft tell you, I don't like his principles: for I am inform'd he is a time-ferver, one that bafely flatters the government, and has no more religion than you have.

Col. Sir, we don't either of us think it proper to make boaft of our religion; but if you pleafe to enquire, you will find we go to church as orderly as the reft of our neighbours.

Sir John. Ay! to what church?

Col. —St. *James*'s church—the eftablifh'd church.

Sir John. Eftablifh'd church!

Col. Sir——

Sir John. Nay, you need not stare, Sir; and before he values himself upon going to church, I would first have him be sure he is a Christian.

Col. A Christian, Sir!

Sir John. Ay, that's my question, whether he is yet christen'd? I mean by a pastor, that had a divine, un-interrupted, successive right to mark him as a sheep of the true fold?

Col. Is it possible! Are you an *Englishman*, and offer, Sir, a question so uncharitable, not only to him, but the whole nation?

Sir John. Nay, Sir, you may give yourself what airs of amazement you please;—I won't argue with you; you are both of you too harden'd to be converted now; but since you think it your duty, as a son, to be concern'd for my errors, I think it as much mine, as a fa-ther, to be concern'd for yours—I'll only tell you of them, if you think fit to mend them—so—if not—take the consequence.

Col. [*Aside.*] Oh! give me temper, heav'n! this vile non-juring zealot! what poisonous principles has he swell'd him with!—Well, Sir, since you don't think it proper to argue upon this subject, I'll wave it too: but, if I may ask it without offence, are these your only reasons for discountenancing Mr. *Heartly*'s addresses to my sister?

Sir John. These! Are they not flagrant? Would you have me marry my daughter to a Pagan? For so he is, and all of you, 'till you are regularly Christians. In short, son, expect to inherit no estate of mine, unless you resolve to come into the pale of the church, of which I profess myself a member.

Col. I thought I always was, Sir, and hope I am so still, unless you have lately been converted to the *Roman*.

Sir John. No, Sir, I abhor the thoughts on't; and protest against their errors as much as you do.

Col. If so, Sir, where's our difference?

Sir John. Difference! 'twould make you tremble, Sir, to know it! but since 'tis fit you should know it, look there—[*Gives him a book*] read that, and be reform'd.

Col. What's here? [*Reads*]. *The Case of Schism*, &c.

Thank you, Sir, I have feen enough of this in the
Daily Courant, to be forry it's in any hands, but thofe
of the common hangman.

Sir John. Prophanation!

Col. And though I always honour'd your concern for
the church's welfare, I little thought 'twas for a church
that is eftablifh'd no where.

Sir John. O! perverfenefs! But there is no better to
be expected from your courfe of life: this is all the
effects of your modern loyalty, your converfation at
Button's. Will you never leave that foul neft of herefy
and fchifm?

Col. Yes, Sir, when I fee any thing like it there;
and fhould think myfelf oblig'd to retire, where fuch
principles were ftarted——I own I ufe the place, becaufe
I generally meet there inftructive or diverting company.

Sir John. Yes, fine company indeed, *Arians*, party-
poets, players, and Prefbyterians.

Col. That's a very unufual mixture, Sir; but if a man
entertains me innocently, am I oblig'd to enquire into
his profeffion, or principles? Would not it be ridiculous
for a Proteftant that loves mufick, to refufe going to the
Opera, becaufe moft of the performers are Papifts? But,
Sir, this feems foreign to my bufinefs; Mr. *Heartly* intends this morning to pay his refpects to you, in hopes
to obtain your final confent; and defired me to be prefent, as a mediator of articles between you.

Sir John. I am glad to hear it.

Col. That's kind indeed, Sir.

Sir John. May be not, Sir,——for I will not be at
home when he comes.

Col. Nay, pray, Sir, 'twill be but civility, at leaft, to
hear him.

Sir John. And becaufe I won't tell a lie for the matter, I'll go out this moment.

Col. Good Sir.

Sir John. But, becaufe I won't deceive him neither,
tell him, I would not have him lofe his time, in fooling
after your fifter——In fhort, I have another man in
my head for her.　　　　　　　　　　[*Exit Sir* John.

Col. Another man! 'twould be worth one's while now

to know him——Pray heaven this non juring hypocrite
has not got some beggarly traytor in his eye for her——
I muſt rid the houſe of him at any rate, or all the ſettle-
ment I can hope from my father is a caſtle in the air;
nor can indeed his life be ſafe, while ſuch a villain
makes it an act of conſcience to endanger it: if his
eyes are not ſoon open'd againſt him, the crown's more
likely to inherit his eſtate, than I am; and though the
government has been very favourable upon thoſe occa-
ſions, it is but a melancholy buſineſs to petition for
what might have been one's birthright. My ſiſter may
be ruin'd too——Here ſhe comes; if there be another
man in the caſe, ſhe no doubt can let me into the ſecret.

Enter Maria.

Siſter, good morrow——I want to ſpeak with you.

Mar. Nay, but pr'ythee, brother, don't put on that
wiſe politic face then: why you look as if the mino-
rity had like to have carried a queſtion.

Col. Come, come, a truce with your rallery; what
I have to aſk of you is ſerious, and I beg you would be
ſo in your anſwer.

Mar. Well then, provided it is not upon the ſubject
of love, I will be ſo——bnt make haſte too——for I
have not had my tea yet.

Col. Why it is, and is not upon that ſubject.

Mar. O! I love a riddle dearly——come——let's hear it.

Col. Nay, piſh——if you will be ſerious, ſay ſo.

Mar. O Lard! Sir, I beg your pardon——there——
there's my whole form and features totally diſengag'd,
and lifeleſs at your ſervice; now put them in what po-
ſture of attention you think fit.

[*She leans againſt him, with her arms aukwardly falling
    [to her kneeſ.*

Col. Was there ever ſuch a giddy Devil!——pr'ythee
ſtand up. I have been talking with my father, and he
declares poſitively you ſhall not receive any farther ad-
dreſſes from Mr. *Heartly.*

Mar. Are you ſerious?

Col. He ſaid it this minute, and with ſome warmth too.

Mar. I am glad on't with all my heart,

Col. How ! glad !

Mar. To a degree ; do you think a man has any more charms for me for my father's liking him ? No, Sir, if Mr. *Heartly* can make his way to me now, he is oblig'd to me only : besides, now it may have the face of an amour indeed : now one has something to struggle for, there's difficulty, there's danger, there's the dear spirit of contradiction in it too. O I like it mightily.

Col. I am glad this does not make you think the worse of *Heartly*——but, however, a father's consent might have clapt a pair of horses more to your coach perhaps, and the want of that may pinch your fortune.

Mar. Burn fortune; am not I a fine woman ? And have not I above five thousand pounds in my own hands ?

Col. Yes, sister, but with all your charms, you have had it in your hands almost these four years; pray consider that too.

Mar. Pshah ! And have not I had the full swing of my own airs and humours these four years ? But if I'll humour my father, I'll warrant he'll make it three or four thousand more, with some unlick'd lout of a fellow to snub me into the bargain : a comfortable equivalent truly——No, no, let him light his pipe with his consent if he pleases. Wilful against Wife for a wager.

Col. Well said ; nothing goes to your heart I find.

Mar. No, no, Brother ; the suits of my lovers sha'l not be ended, like those at law, by dull council on both sides ; I'll hear nothing but what the plaintiff himself can say to me ; 'twould be a pretty thing indeed to confine my airs to the directions of a solicitor, to look kind, or cruel, only as the jointure propofed, is, or is not, equal to the fortune my father designs me : what do you think I'll have my features put into the *Gazette* to be disposed of, like a parcel of dirty acres, by an old master in chancery to the fairest bidder ? No, if I must have an ill match, I'll have the pleasure of playing my own game at least.

Col. There spoke the spirit of a free-born *English-woman*——Well, I am glad you are not startled at the first part of my news, however ; but farther—pray, sister, has my father ever proposed any other man to you ?

Mar. Any other man ! let me know why you aſk, and I'll tell you.

Col. Why the laſt words he ſaid to me were, That he had another man in his head for you.

Mar. And who is it ? Who is it ? Tell me, dear brother, quickly.

Col. Why you don't ſo much as ſeem ſurpriz'd at it !

Mar. No, but impatient, and that's as well you know.

Col. Why how now, ſiſter ?　　　　　　[*Gravely.*

Mar. Why ſure, brother, you know very little of female happineſs, if you ſuppoſe the ſurpriſe of a new lover ought to ſhock a woman of my, temper—don't you know that I am a *coquette ?*

Col. If you are, you are the firſt that ever was ſincere enough to own her being ſo.

Mar. To a lover I grant you ; but I make no more of you than a ſiſter, I can ſay any thing to you.

Col. I ſhould have been better pleas'd if you had not own'd it to me——it's a hateful character.

Mar. Ay, it's no matter for that, it's violently pleaſant, and there's no law againſt it, that I know of. You had beſt adviſe your friend *Heartly* to bring in a bill to prevent it : all the diſcarded toaſts, prudes, and ſuperannuated virgins would give him their intereſt I dare ſwear : take my word, coquetry has govern'd the world from the beginning, and will do ſo to the end on't.

Col. Heartly's like to have a hopeful time on't with you.

Mar. Well, but don't yon really know who it is my father ſntends me ?

Col. Not I really, but I imagin'd you might, and therefore thought fit to adviſe with you about it.

Mar. Nay, he has not open'd his lips to me yet—— Are you ſure he's gone out ?

Col. You are very impatient to know methinks ? What have you to do to concern yourſelf about any man but *Heartly.?*

Mar. O lud ! o lud ! o lud ! dont be ſo wiſe, pr'ythee brother ;. why if you had an empty houſe to let, would you be diſpleas'd to hear there were two people about it ? Can any woman think herſelf happy, that's oblig'd to marry only with a *Hobſon*'s choice ? No, don't think to

rob me of so innocent a vanity ; for believe me, brother,
there is no fellow upon earth, how disagreeable soever,
but in the long run of his addresses will utter something,
at least, that's worth a poor woman's hearing. Besides,
to be a little serious, *Heartly* has a tincture of jealousy in
his temper, which nothing but a substantial rival can
cure him of.

Col. O your servant, madam, now you talk reason;
I am glad you are concern'd enough for *Heartly*'s faults,
to think them worth your mending————a! ha !

Mar. Concern'd ! why did I say that——look you,
I'll deny it all to him——Well, if ever I am serious with
you again————

Col. Here he comes; be as merry with him as you
please.

Mar. Pshaw !

Enter Heartly. Maria *takes a book from the table and
reads.*

Heart. Dear Colonel, your servant.

Col. I am glad you did not come sooner, for in the
humour my father left me 'twould not have been a proper time to have press'd your affair—I touch'd upon't——
but——I'll tell you more presently ; in the mean time
lose no ground with my sister.

Heart. I shall always think myself oblig'd to your
friendship, let my success be what it will—Madam——
your most obedient—What have you got there pray ?

Mar. [*Repeating*]

" *Her lively looks a sprightly mind disclose,*
" *Quick as her eyes, and as unfix'd as those*————
Hear. Pray, madam, what is it ?
Mar. " *Favours to none, to all she smiles extends*—
Heart. Nay, I will see——   [*Struggling.*
                    Mar. [*Putting him by.*]
" *Oft she rejects*————*but never once offends.*
Col. Have a care, she has dipt into her own character,
and she'll never forgive you, if you don't let her go
through with it.

Heart. I beg your pardon, madam.   [*Gravely.*
Mar. " *Bright as the sun, her eyes the gazers strike,*
" *And like the sun, they shine on all alike*—um—um.

Hear. That's fomething like indeed.

Col. You would fay fo, if you knew all.

Hear. All what? Pray what do you mean?

Col. Have a little patience, I'll tell you immediately.

Hear. [*Afide.*] Confufion! fome coxcomb now has been flattering her, I'll be curft elfe, fhe's fo full of her dear felf upon't,

    Mar. [*Turning to* Heartly.]

 " *If to her fhare fome female errors fall,*

 " *Look on her face——and you'll forget them all.*

Is not that naturel, Mr. *Heartly?*

Hear. For a woman to expect, it is indeed.

Mar. And can you blame her, when 'tis at the fame time a proof of the poor man's paffion, and her power?

Hear. So that you think the greateft compliment a lover can make his miftrefs, is to give up his reafon to her!

Mar. Certainly; for what have your lordly fex to boaft of but your underftanding? And till that's entirely furrendered to her difcretion, while the leaft fentiment holds out againft her, a woman muft be downright vain to think conqueft compleated.

Hear. There we differ, Madam; for in my opinion, nothing but the moft exceffive vanity, could value or defire fuch a conqueft.

Mar. O! d'ye hear him, brother? The creature reafons with me! Nay, has the frontlefs folly to think me in the wrong too! O lud! he'd make a horrid tyrant ——pofitively I won't have him.

Hear. Well, my comfort is, no other man will eafily know whether you'll have him or not.

Mar. [*Affectedly fmiling.*] Am not I a horrid, vain, filly creature, Mr. *Heartly?*

Hear. A little bordering upon the baby, I muft own.

Mar. Laud! how can you love one fo then? But I do'nt think you love me though——do you?

Hear. Yes, faith I do, and fo fhamefully, that I am in hopes you doubt it.

Mar. Poor man! he'd fain bring me to reafon.

       [*Smiling in his face.*

Hear. I would indeed, nor am afhamed to own it—— nay, were it but poffible to make you ferious only when

you fhould be fo, you would be the moft perfect creature
of your fex.

Mar. O lud ! he's civil———

Hear. Come, come, you have good fenfe, ufe me but
with that, and make me what you pleafe.

Mar. Laud ! I don't defire to make any thing of you,
not I.

Hear. Don't look fo cool upon me, by Heaven I can't
bear it.

Mar. Well now you are tolerable.

[*Gently glancing on him.*

Hear. Come then, be generous, and fwear at leaft you'll
never be another's.

Mar. Ah ! laud ! now you have fpoil'd all again; befide, how can I be fure of that before I have feen this
t'other man, my brother fpoke to me of ? [*Reads to herfelf again.*

Hear. What riddles ?   [*To the Col.*

Col. I told you you did not know all : To be ferious, my
ther went out but now, on purpofe to avoid you. In
fhort, he abfolutely retracts his promifes, fays he would
not have you fool away your time after my fifter, and in
plain terms told me, he had another man in his head for
her.

Hear. Another man ! confufion ! who ! what is he ? did
not he name him ?

Col. No, nor has he yet fpoke of him to my fifter.

Hear. This is unaccountable———What can have given
him this fudden turn ?

Col. Some whim our confcientious Doctor has put in
his head I'll lay my life.

Hear. He ! he can't be fuch a villain, he profeffes a
friendfhip for me.

Col. So much the worfe : By the way, I am now upon
the fcent of a fecret, that I hope fhortly will prove him a
rogue to the whole nation.

Hear. You amaze me—But on what pretence, what
ground, what reafon, what intereft can he have to oppofe
me ?—This fhock is infupportable.

[*He ftands fix'd and mute.*

Col. [*Aside to* Maria.] Are you really as unconcern'd now as you feem to be?

Mar. Thou art a ftrange dunce, brother, thou knoweft no more of love, than I do of a regiment———You fhall fee how I'll comfort him———

> [*She goes to* Heartly—*mimicks his pofture and uneafinefs, then looks ferioufly in his face and burfts into a laugh.*

Hear. I don't wonder at your good humour, Madam, when you have fo fubftantial an opportunity to make me uneafy for life.

Mar. O lud! how wife he is? Well! his reproaches have that greatnefs of foul———the confufion they give one is infupportable———*Betty*, is the tea ready?

> *Enter* Betty.

Bet. Yes, Madam.

Mar. Mr. *Heartly* your fervant.			[*Exit.*

Col. So, fo, you have made a fine fpot of work on't indeed.

Hear. Dear *Tom*, you'll pardon me, if I fpeak a little freely, I own the levity of her behaviour, at this time, gives me harder thoughts, than I once believ'd it poffible to have of her.

Col. Indeed, my friend, you miftake her.

Hear. O pardon me, had fhe any real concern for me, the apprehenfions of a man's addreffes, whom yet fhe never faw, muft have alarm'd her to be fomething more than ferious.

Col. Not at all, for (let this man be who he will) I take all this levity, as a proof of her refolution to have nothing to fay to him.

Hear. And pray, Sir, may I not as well fufpect, that this artful delay of her good-nature to me now, is meant as a provifional defence againft my reproaches, in cafe, when fhe has feen this man, fhe fhould think it convenient to prefer him to me?

Col. No, no, fhe's giddy, but not capable of fo ferious a falfhood.

Hear. It's a fign you don't judge her with a lover's eye.

Col. No, but as a ftander by, I often fee more of the game than you do: Don't you know that fhe is naturally

a coquette? And a coquette's play with a ferious lover,
is like a back-game at table, all open at firft; fhe'll
make you twenty blots—and you—fpare none, take them
all up, to be fure, while fhe——gains points upon you :
So that when you eagerly expect to end the game on your
fide, flap—as you were, fhe whips up your man, fhe's
fortified, and you are in a worfe condition, than when
you begun with her—Upon which, you know of courfe,
you curfe your fortune, and fhe laughs at you.

Hear. Faith you judge it rightly——I have always
found it fo.

Col. In fhort you are in hafte to be up, and fhe's refolv'd to make you play out the game at her leifure;
you play for the fair ftake, and fhe for victory.

Hear. But ftill, what could fhe mean by going away fo
abruptly?

Col. You grew too ferious for her.

Hear. Why who could bear fuch trifling?

Col. You fhould have laught at her.

Hear. I can't love at that eafy rate.

Col. No——If you could, the uneafinefs would be
on her fide.

Hear. Do you then really think fhe has any thing in
her heart for me?

Col. Ay, marry, Sir—Ah! if you could but get her to
own that ferioufly now—Lord! how you could love her!

Hear. And fo I could, by Heaven!
　　　　　　　　　　　　[Eagerly embracing him.

Col. Ay, but 'tis not the nature of the creature, you
muft take her upon her own terms; tho' faith I thought
fhe own'd a great deal to you, but now; Did not you
obferve, when you were impatient, with what a confcious
vanity fhe cry'd—Now you are tolerable.

Hear. Nay, the devil can be agreeable when fhe
pleafes.

Col. Well, well, I'll undertake for her; if my father
don't ftand in your way we are well enough, and I
don't queftion, but the alarm he has given us, like his
other political projects will end all in *Fumo.*

Hear. What fays my lady? you don't think fhe's
againft us.

Col. I dare swear she is not, she's of so soft so sweet a disposition, that even provocation can't make her your enemy.

Hear. How came so fine a creature to marry your father in such a vast in-equality of years?

Col. Want of fortune, *Frank.* She was poor and beautiful; he rich and amorous——She made him happy, and he her——

Hear. A lady.

Col. And a jointure——Now she's the only one in the family, that has power with our precise doctor, and I dare engage she'll use it with him, to perfuade my father from any thing that's against your interest; by the way you must know, I have shrew'd suspicions, that this sanctify'd rogue is carnally in love with her.

Hear. O the liquorish rascal!

Col. You shall judge by the symptoms: First, he's jealous of every male thing that comes near her; and under a friendly pretence of guarding my father's honour, has persuaded him to abolish assemblies: Nay, at the last masquerade this conscientious spy (unknown to her) was eternally at her elbow in the habit of a cardinal. At dinner he never fails to sit next her, and will eat nothing but what she helps him to; always takes her side in an argument, and when he bows after grace, constantly ogles her; bids my sister, if she would look lovely, learn to dress by her; and at the tea-table, I have seen the impudent goat most lusciously sip off her leavings. She lost one of her slippers 'tother day, (by the way she has a mighty pretty foot) and what do you think was become of it?

Hear. You puzzle me.

Col. I gad, this love-sick monkey had stole it for a private play thing, and one of the house maids, when she clean'd his study, found it there with one of her old gloves in the middle of it.

Hear. A very proper relique to put him in mind of his devotions to *Venus.*

Col. But mum! here he comes.

Enter Doctor Wolf, *and* Charles.

Doct. Charles, ftep into my ftudy, and bring down half a dozen more of thofe manual devotions that I compos'd for the ufe of our friends in prifon ; and, doft thou hear ? leave this writing there, but bring me the key, and then bid the butler ring to prayers— [*Exit.* Charles.] Mr. *Heartly*, I am your moft faithful fervant, I hope you and the good colonel will ftay and join in the private duties of the family.

Hear. With all my heart, Sir, provided you'll do the duty of a fubject too, and not leave out the prayer for the royal family.

Doct. The good colonel knows, I never do omit it.

Col. Sometimes, doctor; but I don't remember, I ever once heard you name them.

Doct. That's only to fhorten the fervice, left in fo large a family, fome few vain, idle fouls might think it tedious; and we ought as it were, to allure them to what's good, by the gentleft, eafieft means we can.

Hear. How ! how doctor ! are you fure that's your only reafon for leaving their names out ?

Doct. But pray, Sir, why is naming them fo abfolutely neceffary ? when heaven, without it, knows the true intention of our hearts ?——befide, why fhould we, when we fo eafily may avoid it, give the leaft colour of offence to tender confciences ?

Col. Ay, now you begin to open doctor————

Hear. Have a care, Sir, the confcience that equivocates in its devotions, muft have the blackeft colour hell can paint it with.

Col. Well faid ! to him *Heartly*.

Hear. Your confcience, I dare fay, won't be eafily convinc'd, while your fcruples turn to fo good account in a private family.

Doct. What am I to be baited then——but 'twont be always holiday—[*Frowning.*] The time's now yours, but mine may come.

Col. What do you mean, Sir ?

Doct. Sir, I shall not explain myself, but make your best of what I've said. I'm not to be intrap'd by all your servile spies of power————But power perhaps may change its hands, and you 'e're long, as little dare to speak your mind as I do.

Col. [*Taking him by the collar,*] Hark you, Sirrah, dare you menace the government in my hearing?

Hear. Nay, Colonel.. [*Interposing.*

Doct. 'Tis well!

Col. Traytor! but that our laws have chains and gibbets for such villains, I'd this moment crackle all thy bones to splinters. [*Shakes him.*

Doct. Very well; your father, Sir, shall know my treatment.

Hear. Nay, dear colonel, let him go.

Col. I ask your pardon, *Frank*, I am asham'd that such a wretch could move me so.

Hear. Come, compose yourself.

Doct. [*Aside, and recovering himself.*] No! I'll take no notice of it————I know he's warm and weak enough to tell this as his own story to his father————let him ————'tis better so————'twill but confirm Sir *John* in his good opinion of my charity, and serve to ruin him the faster. [*Exit.*

Hear. Was there ever so insolent a rascal?

Col. The dog will one day provoke me to beat his brains out.

Hear. Who could have believ'd such outrageous arrogance could have lurk'd under so lamb-like an outside?

Col. This fellow has the spleen and spirit of ten *Beckets* in him.

Hear. What the devil is he? whence came he? what's his original? Is he really a doctor?

Col. So he pretends, and that he lost his living in *Ireland* upon his refusing the oaths to the goverment. Now I have made the strictest inquiries, and can't find the least evidence, that ever he was in the country. But (as I hinted to you) there is now in prison a poor unhappy rebel, I went to school with, whose pardon I am foliciting, and he affures me, he knew him very well in *Flanders*. and in fuch circumftances, as when it can be ferviceable to me to know them, he faithfully promifes to difcover, but begs till then I will not infift upon it.

Hear. I gad this intelligence may be worth your che-rifhing.

Col. Hah! here's my fifter again.

Enter Maria *haftily*, Do&or Wolf *following.*

Mar. You'll find, Sir, I will not be us'd thus : Nor fhall your credit with my father prote& your infolence to me.

Hear. and *Col.* What's the matter?

Mar. nothing, pray be quiet—I don't want you—ftand out of the way——   [*They retire.*

Col. What has the dog done to her?

Mar. How durft you bolt with fuch authority into my chamber without giving me notice?

Hear. Confufion!

Col. Now, *Frank*, whofe turn is it to keep their temper.   [*Apart.*

Hear. [*Struggling*] 'Tis not mine I'm fure.
Col. Hold—if my father won't refent this, } *Apart*
'tis then time enough for me to do it.

Do&. Compofe your tranfport, madam, I came by your father's defire, who being inform'd, that you were entertaining Mr. *Heartly,* grew impatient, and gave his pofitive command, that you attend him inftantly, or he himfelf, he fays, will fetch you.

Hear. So! now the ftorm is rifing.

Do&. So, for what I have done, madam, I had his authority, and fhall leave him to anfwer you.

Mar. 'Tis falfe, he gave you no authority to infult me ; or if he had, did you fuppofe I would bear it from you? What is it you prefume upon? your func-tion! Does that excempt you from the manners of a gentleman?

Do&. Shall I have any anfwear to your father, lady?
Mar. I'll fend him none by you.

Doȼ. I ſhall inform him ſo——   [*Exit.*

Mar. A ſaucy puppy.

Col. Pr'ythee, ſiſter, what has the fellow done to you?

Hear. I beg you tell us, madam.

Mar. Nay, no great matter————but I was ſitting
careleſly in my dreſſing room——a——a faſtning my
garter with my face juſt towards the door, and this
impudent cur, without the leaſt notice, comes bounce
in upon me——and my deviliſh hoop happening to hitch
in the chair, I was an hour before I could get down my
petticoats.

Hear. The rogue muſt be correȼed.

Col. Yet I gad, I can't help laughing àt the accident!
what a ridiculous figure muſt ſhe make! ha! ha!

Mar. Hah! you're as impudent as he, I think: Well,
but had not I beſt go to my father?

Hear. Now, now, dear *Tom,* ſpeak to her before ſhe
goes, this is the very criſis of my life——

[*Apart to the Col.*

Mar. What does he ſay brother?

Col. Why he wants to have me ſpeak to you, and I
would have him do it himſelf.

Mar. Ay, come, do, *Heartly,* I am in good humour
now.

Hear. O *Maria!*————my heart is burſting————

Mar. Well, well, out with it.

H.ar. Your father, now, I ſee, is bent on parting us
————Nay, what's yet worſe, perhaps, will give you to
another——I cannot ſpeak.——Imagine what I want
from you——

Mar. Well————O lud! one looks ſo ſilly though,
when one's ſerious————O Gad——In ſhort I cannot
get it out.

Col. I warrant you, try again.

Mar. O lud!————well if one muſt be teiz'd then
————why he muſt hope, I think.

Hear. Is't poſſible;————'Thus————

Col. Buz——————[*Stopping his mouth.*] not a ſyllable,
ſhe has done very well, I bar all heroicks; if you preſs

it too far, I'll hold fix to four, fhe's off again in a
moment.

Hear. I am filenc'd.

Mar. Now am I on tiptoe to know what odd fellow my
father has found out for me.

Hear. I'd give fomething to know him.

Mar. He's in a terrible fufs at your being here I find—
I had beft go to him.

Col. By all means.

Mar. O blefs us! here he comes piping hot to fetch
me! Now we are all in a fine pickle.

Enter Sir John *haftily—He takes* Maria *under his arm,
cocks his hat, nods, frowning at* Heartly, *and carries
her off.*

Col. So ——..Well faid doctor! 'tis he, I'm fure has
blown this fire. What horrid hands is this poor family
fallen into? and how the traytor feems to triumph in his
power? How little is my father like himfelf? by nature,
open, juft, and generous, but this vile hypocrite drives
his weak paffions like the wind, and I forefee at laft, will
dafh him on his ruin.

Hear. Nothing but your fpeedily detecting him can
prevent it.

Col. I have a thought, and 'tis the only one that can
expofe him to my father—come, *Frank*, be chearful;
in fome unguarded hour, we yet perhaps, this lurking
thief,

> *Without his holy vizor may furprize,*
> *And lay th' impoftor naked to his eyes.*

[*Exeunt.*

A C T II.

Charles *with a writing in his hand.*

Charles.'TIS fo——I have long fufpected where
his zeal would end, in the making of
his private fortune——But, then to found it on the ruin

of his patron's children, makes me shudde[...]
lany: What defperation may a fon be [...]
barbaroufly difinherited?——Befide his da[...]
Maria too is wrong'd; wrong'd in the moft [...]
For fo extravagant is this fettlement, it leave[...]
fhilling, but on her conditionally marryin[...]
doctor's confent; which feems, by what [...]
intended an an expedient, to oblige her to[...]
doctor himfelf for her hufband: Now 'twe[...]
honeft part to let *Maria* know this fnare, tha[...]
her: This deed's not fign'd, and might be ye[...]
——It fhall be fo——'twere folly not to try—[...]
condition can't be worfe——Who knows h[...]
good nature may think herfelf oblig'd for the[...]
——Muft he ruin, as he has done mine, all f[...]
comes into?

Enter Sir John, *Lady* Woodvil, *and* Maria.

Sir *John.* O, *Charles,* your mafter wants you to tran-
fcribe fome letters.

Charles. Sir, I'll wait on him.

[*Exit.* Charles, *bowing refpectfully to the ladies.*
Mar. A pretty well bred fellow that.

Sir *John.* Ay, ay; but he has better qualities than his
good breeding; he is honeft.

Mar. He's always clean too.

Sir *John.* I wonder, daughter, when thou wilt take
notice of a man's real merit—humph! well bred, and
clean forfooth—Would not one think now, fhe were de-
fcribing a coxcomb?

Mar. But, dear *Papa,* do you make no allowance for
one's tafte?

Sir *John.* Tafte; hah! and one's tafte? That, madam one is to me the moft provoking, impertinent jade
alive; and tafte is the true picture of her fenfelefs,
fickly appetite: When do you hear my wife talk at this
rate; and yet fhe is as young, as your fantaftical ladyfhip.

Lady *Wood. Maria's* of a chearful temper, my dear;
but I know you don't think fhe wants difcretion.

Sir *John,* I fhall try that prefently, and you, fweetheart, fhall judge between us: In fhort, daughter, yous

e is but one continual round of playing
no purpofe: and therefore I am refolv'd to
ink ferioufly, and marry.

Mar. at I fhall do before I marry, Sir, you may
epend on 't.

Sir *Jo.* Um—That I am not fo fure of—but you
may depend upon my having thought ferioufly, and that's
well: For the perfon I intend you is of all the world
the only man can make you truly happy.

Mar. And of all the world, Sir, that's the only man,
Il pofitively marry.

Lad *Wood.* [*Afide to* Mar.] Thou haft rare courage,
Maria; If I had fuch a game to play, I fhould be
righted out of my wits.

Mar. Lord, madam, he'll make nothing on't, depend
pon it.

Sir *John.* Mind what I fay to you——This wonderful
man, I fay——Firft, as to his principles both in church
and ftate, is unqueftionable.

Mar. Sir, I leave all that to you, for I fhould never
afk him a queftion about either of them.

Sir *John.* You need not, I am fully fatisfied of both—
He is is a true, ftanch member of the *Englifh* catholic
church.

Mar. Methinks though, I would not have him a *Roman* catholic, Sir, becaufe you know of double taxes.

Sir *John.* No, he's no *Roman.*

Mar. Very well, Sir——

Sir *John.* Then as to the ftate, he'll fhortly be one of
the moft confiderable men in the kingdom, and that
too in an office for life; which on whatfoever pretence of
mifbehaviour, no civil government can deprive him of.

Mar. That's fine indeed; I was afraid he had been a
clergyman.

Sir *John.* I have not yet faid what his function is——
As for his private life——he's fober.

Mar. O! I fhould hate a fot.

Sir *John.* Chafte.

Mar. A hem.   [*ftifling a laugh.*

Sir *John.* What is't you fneer at, madam——You

want one of your fine gentleman rakes, I fuppofe, that are fnapping at every woman they meet with.

Mar. No, no, Sir, I am very well fatisfied——I——I fhould not care for fuch a fort of man no more than I fhould for one that every woman was ready to fnap at.

Sir *John.* No, you'll be fecure from jealoufy; he has experience, ripenefs of years; he is almoft forty-nine : your fex's vanities will kave no harm for him.

Mar. But all this while, Sir, I dont find that he has any charm for our fex's vanity : How does he look ? Is he tall, well made ? Does he drefs, fing, talk, laugh, and dance well ? Has he a good air, good teeth, fine eyes, fine fair perriwig——Does he keep his chaife, coach, chariot, and berlin, with fix flouncing *Flanders :* Does he wear blue velvet, clear white ftockings, and fubfcribe to the opera ?

Sir *John.* Was there ever fo profligate a creature ! What will this age come to ?

Lady *Wood.* Nay, *Maria,* here I muft be againft you--- Now you are blind indeed, a woman's happinefs has little to do with the pleafure her hufband takes in his own perfon.

Sir *John.* Right.

Lady *Wood.* 'Tis not how he looks, but how he loves, is the point.

Sir *John.* Good again !

Lady *Wood.* And a wife is much more fecure, that has charms for her hufband, than when the hufband has only charms for her.

Sir *John.* Admirable ! Go on, my dear.

Lady *Wood.* Do you think, child, a woman of five and twenty may not be much happier with an honeft man of fifty, than the fineft woman of fifty with a young fellow five and twenty ?

Sir *John.* Mark that.

Mar. Ay, but when two five and twenties come to-gether---Dear *Papa,* you muft allow they have a chance to be fifty times as pleafant and frolickfome.

Sir *John.* Frolickfome ! why you fenfual ideot, what have frolicks to do with folid happinefs ? I am afham'd of you.----Go! you talk worfe than a girl at a boarding-fchool-- Frolickfome! as if marriage were only a li-cence for two people to play the fool according to law? methinks, madam, you have a better example of hap-pinefs before your face—Here's one has ten times your underftanding, and fhe, you find, has made a different choice.

Mar. Lord Sir! how you talk? you don't confider people's temper: I don't fay my lady is not in the right; but then you know, *Papa*, fhe's a prude, and I am a coquette: fhe becomes her character very well, I don't deny it, and I hope you fee every thing I do is as con-fiftent with mine: Your wife folks may lay down what rules they pleafe; but 'tis conftitution that governs us all, and you can no more bring me, Sir, to endure a man of forty-nine, than you can perfuade my lady to dance in a church to the organ.

Sir *John.* Why you wicked wretch, could any thing perfuade you to that?

Mar. Lord, Sir! I won't anfwer for any thing I fhould do when the whim's in my head: You know I always lov'd a little flirtation.

Sir *John.* O horrible! My poor mother has ruin'd her; leaving her a fortune in her own hands, has turn'd her brain: In fhort, your fentiments of life are fhame-ful, and I am refolv'd upon your inftant reformation; therefore, as an earneft of your obedience, I fhall firft infift that you never fee young *Heartly* more; for in one word, the good and pious doctor *Wolf*'s the man that I have decreed your hufband.

Mar. Ho! ho! ho!   *[Laughing aloud.*

Sir *John.* 'Tis very well——this laugh, you think, becomes you, but I fhall fpoil your mirth————no more————give me a ferious anfwer.

Mar. [*Gravely*] I afk your pardon, Sir, I fhould not have fmil'd indeed, could I have fuppos'd it poffible that you were ferious.

Sir *John.* You'll find me fo.

Mar. I am forry for it; but I have an objection to the doctor, Sir, that moft father's think a fubftantial one.

Sir *John*. Name it.

Mar. Why, Sir, you know he is not worth a groat.

Sir *John*. That's more than you know, madam; I am able to give him a better estate than I am afraid you'll deserve.

Mar. How, Sir?

Sir. *John*. I have told you what's my will, and shall leave you to think on't.

Enter Charles.

Charles. [*Aside Sir* John.] Sir, if you are at leisure, the doctor desires a private conference with you, upon business of importance.

Sir *John*. Where is he?

Charles. In his own chamber, Sir, just taking his leave of the Count and another gentleman, that came this morning express from *Avignon:* He has sent you the note you ask'd him for.

Sir *John*. 'Tis well; I'll come to him immediately—— [*Exit* Charles.] Daughter, I'm call'd away, and therefore have only time to tell you, as my last resolution, that if you expect a shilling from me, the doctor is your husband, or I'm no more your father.

[*Exit Sir* John, *and drops the paper.*

Mar. O madam! I am at my wits end, not for the little fortune I may lose in disobeying my father; but it startles me to find what a dangerous influence this fellow has o'er all his actions,

Lady *Wood*. Dear *Maria*, I am now as much alarm'd as you; for though in compliance to your father, I have been always inclin'd to think charitably of this doctor, yet now I am convinc'd 'tis time to be upon our guard—— he's stepping into his estate too!

Mar. Here's my brother, madam, we'll consult with him.

To them the Colonel.

Col. Madam, your most obedient——Well sister, is the secret out? Who is this pretty fellow my father has pickt up for you?

Mar. Ev'n our agreeable doctor.

Col. You are not serious.

Lady *Wood.* He's the very man, I can affure you, Sir.

Col. Confufion! What, would the *Jewifh* cormorant devour the whole family? Your ladyfhip knows he is fecretly in love with you too.

Lady *Wood.* Fy! fy! Colonel.

Col. I ask your pardon, madam, if I fpeak too freely; but I am fure, by what I have feen, your ladyfhip muft fufpect fomething of it.

Lady *Wood.* I am forry any body elfe has feen it; but I muft own his civilities of late have been fomething warmer than I thought became him.

Col. How then are thefe oppofites to be reconcil'd ? can the rafcal have the affurance to think both thefe points are to be carried ?—But he does nothing like other people; he's a contradiction ev'n to his own character: moft of your Non Jurors now are generally people of a free and open difpofition, mighty pretenders to a confcience of honour indeed: But you feldom fee them put on the leaft fhew of *Religion.* But this formal hypocrite always has it at his tongue's end, and there it fticks, for it never gets into his heart, I'll anfwer for him.

Lady *Wood.* Ay, but that's the charm, that firft got him into Sir *John's* heart; who, good man, is himfelf, I am fure, fincere, however now mifguided. 'Twas not fo much his principles of government, as his well-painted piety; his feeming felf-denial, refignation, patience, and humble outfide, that gave him firft fo warm a lodging in his bofom.

Mar. My lady has judg'd it perfectly right.

Col. I am afraid it's too true. There has been his fureft footing! But here we are puzzled again——What fubtle fetch can he have in being really in love with your ladyfhip, and at the fame time making fuch a buftle to marry my fifter ?

Mar. Truly one would not fufpect him to be fo termagant: I fancy the gentleman might have his hands full of one of us.

Col. And yet his zeal pretends to be fo fhock'd at all

Vol. III. N

indecent amours, that in the country he us'd to make the maids lock up the turkey-cocks every *Saturday* night, for fear they fhould gallant the hens on a *Sunday*.

Lady *Wood*, O! ridiculous.

Col. Upon my life, madam, my fifter told me fo.

Mar. I tell you fo! You impudent——

Lady *Wood.* Fy! *Maria*, he only jefts with you.

Mar. How can you be fuch a monfter to be playing the fool here, when you have more reafon to be frighted out of your wits? You don't know, perhaps, that my father declares he'll fettle a fortune upon this fellow too.

Col. What do you mean?

Lady *Wood.* 'Tis too true; 'tis not three minutes fince he faid fo.

Col. Nay, then 'tis time indeed his eyes were open'd; and give me leave to fay, madam, 'tis only in your power to fave not only me, but ev'en my father too from ruin.

Lady *Wood.* I fhall eafily come into any thing of that kind, that's practicable—What is't you propofe?

Col. Why, if this fellow (which I am fure of) is really in love with you, give him a fair opportunity to declare himfelf, and leave me to make my advantage of it.

Lady *Wood.* I apprehend you—I am loth to do a wrong thing——

Mar. Dear madam, it's the only way in the world to expofe him to my father.

Lady *Wood.* I'll think of it ——　　　　　　*[Mufing.*

Col. When you do, madam, I am fure you will come into it.

How now! What paper's this? it's the doctor's hand.

Mar. I believe my father dropt it.

Col. What's here?　　　　　　*[Reads.]*

' Laid out at feveral times for the fecret fervices of
　　　　　　His M——'

	l.	*s.*	*d.*
May the 28th, for fix bafkets of rue and thyme,	oo	18	oo
The 29th, *ditto,* two cart-loads of oaken-boughs,	o2	oo	oo

	l.	*s.*	*d.*
June the 10th, for ten bushels of white roses,	01	10	00
Ditto——Given to the bell-ringers of several parishes,	10	15	00
Ditto — To *Simon Chaunter*, parish-clerk, for his selecting proper staves adapted to the day,	05	07	06
Ditto, — For lemons and arrack sent into *Newgate*,	09	05	00

Col. Well, while they drink it in *Newgate*, much good may it do them.

	l.	*s.*	*d.*
Paid to *Henry Conscience*, Juryman, for his extraordinary trouble in acquitting sir *Preston Rebel* of his indictment,	53	15	00
Allow'd to *Patrick Mac-Rogue*, of the foot-guards, for prevailing with his comrade to desert,	04	06	06
Given as smart-money to *Humphrey Stanch*, cobler, lately whipt for speaking his mind of the government	03	04	06
Paid to *Abel Perkin*, news-writer, for divers seasonable paragraphs,	05	00	00
August the 1st, paid to *John Shoplift* and *Thomas Highway*, for endeavouring to put out the enemies bonfire,	02	03	00
August the 2d, paid the surgeon for searcloth, for their bruises,	01	01	06

Was there ever such a heap of stupid, cold-scented treason! Now, madam, I hope you see the necessity of blowing up this traitor: These are lengths I did not think my father had gone with him : What vile, what low sedition, has he made him stoop to?

Lady *Wood.* I tremble at the precipice he stands on!

Mar. O bless us! I am in a cold sweat; dear brother, leave it where you found it——

Lady *Wood.* By all means; if sir *John* shoud know it's in your hands, it may make him desperate——

Col. You are in the right, madam.

[*He lays down the paper.*

Lady *Wood*. Let's steal into the next room, and observe that no body else takes it up; he'll certainly come back to look for't.

Col. But I must leave you, poor *Heartly* stays for me at *White's*; and he'll sit upon thorns, 'till I bring him an account of his new rival.

Mar. Well, well, get you gone then.   [*Exeunt.*

Enter sir John *in a hurry.*

Sir *John*. Undone! ruin'd! Where could I drop this paper?—Hold—let's see—[*He finds it.*] Ah! here it is. What a blessed 'scape was this? If my hotbrain'd son had found it, I suppose by to-morrow, he would have been begging my estate for the discovery——

Enter Doctor Wolf.

O doctor! all's well : I have found my paper.

Doct. I am sincerely glad of it——It might have ruin'd us.

Sir *John*. Well, sir, what say our last advices from *Avignon?*

Doct. All goes right—The council has approv'd our scheme, and press mightily for dispatch among our friends in *England.*

Sir *John.* But pray, doctor——

Doct. Hold, sir,—now we are alone, give me leave to inform you better.—Not that I am vain of any worldly title; but since it has pleas'd our court to dignify me, our church's right obliges me to take it.

Sir *John.* Pray, sir, explain.

Doct. Our last express has brought me this—[*He shews a writing*] which (far unworthy, as I am) promotes me to the vacant see of *Thetford.*

Sir *John.* Is it possible? My Lord, I joy in your advancement.

Doct. It is indeed a spiritual comfort to find my labours in the cause are not forgotten; though I must own some less conspicuous instance of their favour had better suited me; such high distinctions are invidious; and it

would really grieve me, fir, among my friends, to meet
with envy where I only hope for love; not but I submit
in any way to feve them.

Sir *John.* Ah! good man! this meeknefs will, I hope,
one day be rewarded—but pray, Sir—my Lord!—I beg
your lordfhip's pardon—pray what other news? how do
all our friends? are they in heart, and chearful?

Doct. To a man! never in fuch fanguine hopes—the
court's extremely throng'd—never was there fuch a con-
courfe of warlike exiles: Though they talk, this fharp
feafon, of removing farther into *Italy,* for the benefit of
milder air: Well! the catholicks are the fincereft
friends!

Sir *John.* Nay I muft do them juftice, they are truly
zealous in the caufe, and it has often griev'd my heart
that our church's differences are fo uterly irreconcile-
able.

Doct. O nourifh ftill that charitable thought! there's
fomething truly great and humane in it; and really, if
you examine well the doctrines laid down, by my
learned predeceffor, in his *Cafe of Schifm,* you will find
thofe differences are not fo terribly material, as fome
obftinate fchifmaticks would paint them: Ah! could
we but be brought to temper, a great many feeming
contradictions might be reconcil'd on both fides: But
while the laity will interpret for themfelves, there is
indeed no doing it. Now, could we, Sir, like other
nations, but once reftrain that monftrous licence; ah!
Sir, a union then might foon be practicable.

Sir *John.* Auh! 'twill never do here: The *Englifh* are
a ftubborn headftrong people, and have been fo long in-
dulg'd in the ufe of their own fenfes, that, while they
have eyes in their heads, you will never be able to perfuade them they can't fee, there's no making them give
up their human evidences: and your *Credo, quia impoffi-
bile eft,* is an argument they will always make a jeft of.
No, no, it is not force will do the thing, your prefs'd men
don't always make the beft foldiers. And truly, my
Lord, we feem to be wrong too in another point, to
which I have often imputed the ill fuccefs of our caufe;

and that is, the taking into our party so many loose persons of dissolute and abandon'd morals; fellows whom,
in their daily private course of life, the pillory and gal-
lows seem to groan for.

Doct. 'Tis true indeed, and I have often wish'd 'twere
possible to do without them, but in a multitude all men
won't be all saints; and then again they are really useful;
nay, and in many things, that sober men will not stoop
to——They serve, poor curs, to bark at the government in the open streets, and keep up the wholsome
spirit of clamour in the common people; and, Sir, you
cannot conceive the wonderful use of clamour, 'tis so
teizing to a ministry, it makes them winch and fret, and
grow uneasy in their posts—Ah! many a comfortable
point has been gain'd by clamour! 'tis in the nature of
mankind to yield more to that, than reason----Ev'n
Socrates himself could not resist it; for wise as he was,
yet you see his wife *Xantippe* carried all her points by
clamour. Come, come, clamour is a useful monster,
and we must feed the hungry mouths of it; it being of
the last importance to us, that hope to change the government, to let it have no quiet.

Sir *John.* Well, there is indeed no resisting mere
necessity.

Doct. Besides, if we suffer our spirits to cool here at
home, our friends abroad will send us over nothing but
excuses.

Sir *John.* 'Tis true, but still I am amaz'd, that
France so totally should have left us---*Mardyke,* they
say, will certainly be demolish'd.

Doct. No matter, let them go——we have made a good
exchange, our new ally is yet better, as he is less suspected --But to give them their due, we have no spirits
among us like the women, the ladies have supported
our cause with a surprizing constancy. O! there's no
daunting them, ev'n with ill success! they will starve
their very vanities, their vices, to feed their loyalty:
I am inform'd that my good lady countess of *Night-and-
Day* has never been seen in a new gown, or has once
thrown a die at any of the assemblies, since our last
general contribution.

Sir *John.* O my good lord, if our court abroad but knew what obligations they have to your indefatigable endeavours ———

Doct. Alas! Sir, I can only boaſt an honeſt heart; my power is weak, I only can aſſiſt them with my prayers and zealous wiſhes; or if I had been ſerviceable, have not you, Sir, overpaid me? Your daughter, Sir, the fair *Maria*, is a reward no merit can pretend to.

Sir *John.* Nay, good my lord, this tender gratitude confounds me———O! this inſenſible girl—Pray excuſe me——— [*Weeps.*

Doct. You ſeem concern'd, pray what's amiſs?

Sir *John.* That I ſhould be the father of ſo blind a child. Alas! ſhe ſlights the bleſſing I propos'd, ſhe ſees you not, my lord, with my fond eyes; but lay not, I beſeech you, at my door, the ungrateful ſtubbornneſs of a thoughtleſs girl.

Doct. Nay, good Sir, be not thus concern'd for me, we muſt allow her female modeſty a time, your ſtrict commands perhaps too ſuddenly ſurpriz'd her; maids muſt be ſlowly, gently dealt with; and might I, Sir, preſume to adviſe———

Sir *John.* Any thing, your will ſhall govern me and her.

Doct. Then, Sir, abate of your authority, and let the matter reſt a while: Suppoſe I firſt ſhould beg your good lady, Sir, to be my friend to her: Women will hear from their own ſex, what ſometimes, ev'n from the man they like, would ſtartle them: May I have your permiſſion, Sir, when dinner is remov'd, to enter-tain my lady on this ſubject privately?

Sir *John.* O! by all means, and troth, it is an excel-lent thought, I'll go this inſtant, and prepare her to receive you, and will myſelf contrive your opportunity.

Doct. You are too good to me, Sir———too bountiful.

Sir *John.* Nay, now, my lord, you drive me from you.

Doct. Pray pardon me.

Sir *John.* No more I beg you, good my lord—your ſervant. [*Exit.*

Doct. Ha! ha! What noble harveſts have been reaped

from bigotted credulity, nor ever was a better instance of it. Would it not make one smile; that it should ever enter into the brains of this man (who can in other points distinguish like a man) that a Protestant church can never be secure, till it has a Popish prince to defend it?

Enter Charles.

So *Charles*, hast thou finish'd those letters?

Charles. I have brought them, Sir.

Doct. 'Tis very well, let them be seal'd without a direction, and give them to *Aaron Sham* the Jew, when he calls for them—O! and—here, step yourself this afternoon to Mr. *Defeazance* of *Gray's-Inn*, and give him this thirty pound bill from Sir *Harry Foxhound*; beg him to sit up night and day till the writings are finish'd: For his trial certainly comes on this week; he knows we can't always be sure of a jury, and a moment's delay may make the commissioners lay hold of his estate.

Charles. My lord, I'll take the utmost care.

Doct. Well, *Charles.*　　　　　　　*[Gravely smiling.*

Charles. Sir *John* has told me of the new duty I ought to pay you when in private.

Doct. But take especial heed that it be only in private.

Charles. Your lordship need not caution me——my Lord, I hear another whisper in the family; I'm told you'll shortly be allied to it; sir *John*, they say, has actually consented; I hope, my lord, you'll find the fair *Maria* too as yielding.

Doct. Such a proposal has indeed been started, but it will end in nothing: *Maria* is a giddy wanton thing, not form'd to make a wise man happy; her life's too vain, too sensual to elevate a heart like mine: No, no, I have views more serious.

Charles. O my fluttering joy!　　　　　　　*[Aside.*

Doct. Marriage is a state too turbulent for me.

Charles. But with sir *John's* consent, my lord, her fortune may be considerable.

Doct. Thou know'st, *Charles*, my thoughts of happiness were never form'd on fortune.

Charles. No! I find that by the fettlement.   [*Afide.*

Doct. Or if they were, they would be there impoffible ; *Maria*'s vain diftafte of me, I know,'s as deeply
rooted, as my contempt of her : And can'ft thou think
I'd ftain my character to be a wanton's mockery, to
follow through the wilds of folly fhe would lead me,
to cringe and doat upon a fenfelefs toy, that every feather in a hat can purchafe?

Charles. But mayn't fir *John* take it ill, my Lord, to
have her flighted ?

Doct. No, no, her ridiculous averfion will fecure me
from his-reproaches.

Enter a Servant.

Ser. Sir, my mafter defires to fpeak with you.

Doct. I'll wait on him.—*Charles,* you'll take care of
my directions.

Charles. I'll be fure, Sir.   [*Exit Doctor.*
Kind heaven, I thank thee ! this bar fo unexpectedly
remov'd gives vigour to my heart, and is, I hope, an
omen of its fortune—But I muft lofe no time, the writing may be every moment call'd for——this is her
chamber.

He knocks foftly—and Betty *enters to him.*

Is your lady bufy ?

Bett. I think fhe's only a reading.

Charles. Will you do me the favour to let her know,
if fhe s at leifure, I beg to fpeak with her upon fome
earneft bufinefs ?

Maria entering with a Book.

Mar. Who's that ?

Bett. She's here—Mr. *Charles,* Madam, defires to
fpeak with you.

Mar. O ! your fervant, Mr. *Charles*—Here take this
odious *Homer,* and lay him up again, he tires me.

[*Exit* Betty *with the book.*

How could the blind wretch make fuch a horrid fufs
about a fine woman, for fo many volumes together,
and give us no account of her amours ? You have read
him I fuppofe in the *Greek,* Mr. *Charles.*

Charles. Not lately, madam.

Mar. But do you fo violently admire l i n now ?

N 5

Charles. The criticks fay he has his beauties, madam. But *Ovid* has been always my favourite.

Mar. *Ovid!* O! he's raviſhing——

Charles. And fo art thou, to madneſs.   [*Afide.*

Mar. Lord! how could one do to learn *Greek?* Was you a great while about it?

Charles. It has been half the bufineſs of my life, madam.

Mar. That's cruel now! then you think one can't be miſtreſs of it in a month or two.

Charles. Not eafily, madam.

Mar. They tell me it has the fofteſt tone for love, of any language in the world, I fancy I could foon learn it——I know two words of it already.

Charles. Pray, madam, what are they?

Mar. Stay let me fee——O——ay——*Zoe, kai Pfyche.*

Charles. I hope you know the *Englifh* of 'em, madam.

Mar. O lud! I hope there's no harm in it; I am fure I heard the doctor fay it to my lady——Pray what is it?

Charles. You muſt firſt imagine, madam, a tender lover gazing on his miſtreſs, and then indeed they have a foftneſs in 'em, as thus——*Zoe, kai Pfyche!* my life, my foul!

Mar. O the impudent young rogue! how his eyes fpoke too!   [*Afide.*
What the deuce can he want with me!——

Charles. I have ſtartled her, fhe mufes.

          [*Afide.*
Mar. It always ran in my head this fellow had fome-thing in him above his condition——I'll know prefently.
          [*Afide.*
Well, but your bufineſs with me, Mr. *Charles*, you have fomething of love in your head now, I'll lay my life on't.

Charles. I never yet durſt own it, madam.

Mar. Why, what's the matter?

Charles. My ſtory is too melancholy to entertain a mind fo much at eafe as yours.

Mar. O! I love melancholy ſtories of all things.——

Charles. But mine, madam, can't be told, unlefs I give my life into your power.

Mar. O lud! you have not done any body a mifchief, I hope.

Charles. I never did a private injury; if I have done a public wrong, I'm fure it might in me, at leaft, be called an honeft errcr.

Mar. Pray whom did you ferve before you liv'd with the doctor?

Charles. I was not born to ferve; and had not an unfortunate education ruin'd me, might have now appear'd like what I am by birth, a gentleman.

Mar. I am furpriz'd! Your education, fay you, ruin you? Lord! I am concern'd for you. Pray let me know your ftory; and if any fervices are in my power, I am fure you may command them.

Charles. Such foft compaffion, from fo fair a bofom, o'er-pays the worft that can attend my owning what I am.

Mar. O your fervant——but pray let's hear.

Charles. My father's elder brother, madam, was a gentleman of an ancient family in the north, who, having then no child himfelf, begg'd me from my nurfe's arms, to be adopted as his own, with an affurance too of making me his heir; to which my father (then alas! in the infancy of his fortune) eafily confented. This uncle being himfelf fecretly difaffected to the government, gave me of courfe, in my education, the fame unhappy prejudices, which fince have ended in the ruin of us both.

Mar. Then you were bred a *Roman-catholick.*

Charles. No, madam; but I own, in principles of very little difference, which I imbib'd chiefly from this doctor; he having been five years my governor. As I grew up, my father's merit had rais'd his fortune under the prefent government; and fearing I might be too far fix'd in principles againft it, defired me from my uncle home again: But I, as I then thought myfelf bound in gratitude, excus'd my going in terms of duty to my father; whom fince, alas! I too juftly have provok'd ever to hope a reconciliation. I faw too late my folly, and had no defence againſt his anger, but by artfully confirming him in a belief, that I had periſh'd with my uncle in the late rebellion.

Mar. Bleſs us! what do you mean? you were not actually in it, I hope!

Charles. I can't diſown the guilt—but ſince the royal mercy has been refus'd to none that frankly have confeſs'd with penitence their crime (which from my heart I moſt ſincerely do) in that is all my hope—My youth and education's all th' excuſe I plead; if they deſerve no pity, I am determin'd to throw off my diſguiſe, and bow me to the hand of juſtice.

Mar. Poor creature! Lord! I can't bear it.

[With concern.

Charles. But then, unknown, and friendleſs as I am; to whom, alas! can I apply for ſuccour!   [*Weeps.*

Mar. O Lord! I'll ſerve you, depend upon it: My brother ſhall have no reſt 'till he gets your pardon.

Charles. Your kind compaſſion, madam, has prevented, what, if I durſt, I ſhould have mentioned. I hope too, I ſhall perſonally deſerve his favour; if not, your generous inclination to have ſav'd me, even in my laſt deſpair of life, will give my heart a joy.

Mar. Lord! the poor unfortunate boy loves me too; what ſhall I do with him? But, Mr. *Charles*, pray once more to your ſtory---what was it that really drew you into the rebellion?

Charles. This doctor, madam, who, as he is now your father's, was then my uncle's boſom-counſellor: 'Twas his inſidious tongue that painted it to us as an incumbent duty, on which the welfare of our ſouls depended; he warm'd us too into ſuch a weak belief of vile reports, as infamy ſhould bluſh to mention——we were aſſur'd, that half the churches here in town were lying all in ſacrilegious ruins; which ſince, I found, maliciouſly was meant, even of thoſe that are magnificently riſing from their new foundations!

Mar. But, pray——while you were in arms, how did the doctor diſpoſe of himſelf?

Charles. He!—went with us, madam, none ſo active in the front of reſolution, till danger came to face him;

then indeed a friendly fever feiz'd him, which, on the firft alarm of the king's forces marching towards *Prefton*, gave him a cold pretence to leave the town ; in the defence of which my uncle loft his life, and I my only friend, with all my long-fed hopes of fortune.

Mar. Poor wretch! but how came you to avoid being prifoner ?

Charles. Upon our furrender of the place, I brib'd a townfman to employ me, as his fervant, in a backward working houfe, where, from my youth, and change of habit, I pafs'd without fufpicion till the whole affair was over——But then, alas! whither to turn I knew not: My life grew now no more my care——Perifh, I faw, I muft; whether as a criminal, or a beggar, was my only choice.

Mar. O Lord! tell me quickly how you came hither.

Charles. In this defpair I wander'd up to *London*, where I fcarce knew one mortal, but fome few friends in prifon. What could I do? I ventur'd even thither for my fafety; where 'twas my fortune firft to fee your father, madam, diftributing rel ef to feveral : He knew my uncle well; and being inform'd of my condition, he charitably took me home ; and here has ever fince conceal'd me as a menial fervant to the doctor; the deteftation of whofe vile, difhoneft practices at laft have waked me to a fenfe of all my blinded errors ; of which this writing is his leaft of fordid inftances.

[Gives it to Maria.

Mar. You frighten me ; pray what are the purpofes of it ! 'Tis neither fign'd nor feal'd.

Charles. No, madam, therefore to prevent it by this timely notice, was my bufinefs here with you : Your father gave it the doctor firft to fhew his council, who having fince approv'd it, I underftand this evening 'twill be executed.

Mar. But what is it ?

Charles. It grants to doctor *Wolf* in prefent four hundred pounds *per annum*, of which this very houfe is part; and at your father's death, invefts him in the whole remainder of his freehold eftate. For you indeed there in a charge of four thoufand pounds upon it ; provided you marry with the doctor's confent ; if not, 'tis added to my lady's jointure. But your brother, madam, is without conditions utterly difinherited.

Mar. I am confounded—what will become of us ! my father now I find was ferious—O this infinuating hypo-crite—let me fee—ay—I will go this minute.-Sir, dare you truft this in my hands for an hour only ?

Charles. Any thing to ferve you————My life's already in your hands.

Mar. And I dare fecure it with my own—Hark ! they ring to dinner ; pray, Sir, ftep in, fay I am oblig'd to dine abroad, and whifper one of the footmen to get an hackney coach immediately ; then do you take a proper occafion to flip out after me to Mr. *Double's* chambers in the *Temple,* there I fhall have time to talk farther with you. You'll excufe my hurry——Here *Betty,* my fcarf, and a mask.　　　　　　　　　　　[*Exit* Maria.

Charles. What does my fortune mean me ? She'll there talk farther with me ! Of what ! What will fhe talk of ? O my heart ! methought fhe look'd at parting too, as kindly confcious of fome obligation to me : And then how foft, how amiably tender was her pity of my for-tune ! But O ! I rave ! keep down, my vain afpiring thoughts, and to my loft condition level all my hopes.

Rather content with pity let me live,
Than hope for more than fhe refolves to give. 　　[*Exit.*

———————————————————

A C T III.

Maria, and Betty *taking off her Scarf,* &c.

Mar. HAS any one been to fpeak with me, *Betty ?*
Betty. Only Mr. *Heartly,* madam ; he faid he would call again, and bid his fervant ftay below to give him notice when you came home.

Mar. You don't know what he wanted ?

Bett. No, madam, he feem'd very uneafy at your being abroad,

Mar. Well---go, and lay up thofe things---[*Exit* Betty.
Ten to one, but his wife head now has found out fomething to be jealous of ; if he lets me fee it, I fhall be
fure to make him infinitely eafy---Here he comes.

Enter Heartly.

Hear. Your humble fervant, madam.   } *gravely.*
Mar. Your fervant, Sir.
Hear. You have been abroad, I hear.
Mar. Yes, and now I am come home, you fee.
Hear. You feem to turn upon my words, madam ; is
there any thing particular in them ?
Mar. As much as there is in my being abroad, I
believe.
Hear. Might not I fay you had been abroad, with-
out giving offence ?
Mar. And might not I as well fay, I was come home,
without your being fo grave upon't ?
Hear. Do you know any thing fhould make me grave?
Mar. I know, if you are fo, I am the worft perfon in
the world you could poffibly fhew it to.
Hear. Nay, I don't fuppofe you do any thing, you
won't juftify.
Mar. O! then I find I have done fomething you think
I can't juftify.
Hear. I don't fay that neither; perhaps I am in the
wrong in what I have faid; but I have been fo often
us'd to afk pardon for your being in the wrong, that I
am refolv'd henceforth never to rely on the infolent evidence of my own fenfes.
Mar. You don't know now, perhaps, that I think
this pretty fmart fpeech of yours is very dull; but fince
that's a fault you can't help, I will not take it ill. Come
now, be as fincere on your fide, and tell me ferioufly---
Is not what real bufinefs I had abroad, the very thing you
want to be made eafy in ?
Hear. If I thought you would make me eafy, I would
own it.
Mar. Now we come to the point---To-morrow morning then, I give you my word to let you know it all, till

when there is a neceffity for its being a fecret, and I
infift upon your believing it.

Hear. But pray, madam, what am I to do with my
private imagination in the mean time, that is not in my
power to confine? And fure you won't be offended, if, to
avoid the tortures that may give me, I beg you'll truft me
with the fecret now.

Mar. Don't prefs me; for pofitively I will not.

Hear. Cannot had been a kinder term————Is my difquiet of fo little moment to you?

Mar. Of none; while your difquiet dares not truft
the affurances I have given you; if you expect I fhould
confide in you for life, don't let me fee you dare not take
my word for a day; and if you are wife, you'll think
fo fair a trial of your faith a favour.

Hear. If you intend it fuch————it is a favour, if not
'tis fomething————fo————come let's wave the fubject.

Mar. With all my heart: Have you feen my brother lately?

Hear. Yes, madam, and he tells me, it feems, the
doctor is the man your father has refolv'd upon.

Mar. 'Tis fo; nay, and what will more furprize you,
he leaves me only to the choice of him, or of no fortune.

Hear. And may I, without offence, beg leave to know,
what refolutions, madam, you have taken upon it?

Mar. I have not taken any, I do not know what to do;
what would you advife me to?

Hear. I advife you to? Nay, you are in the right to
make it a queftion.

Mar. He fays he'll fettle all his eftate upon him too.

Hear. O take it, take it, to be fure, it's the fitteft
match in the world, you can't do a wifer thing certainly.

Mar. 'Twill be as wife at leaft, as the ways you take
to prevent it.

Hear. I find, madam, I am not to know what you
intend to do; and I fuppofe I am to be eafy at that too.

Mar. When I intend to marry him, I fhall not care
whether you are eafy, or no.

Hear. If your indifference to me were a proof of
your inclination to him, the gentleman need not defpair.

Mar. Very well, Sir, I'll endeavour to take your advice, I promife you.

Hear. O! that won't coft you much trouble, I dare fay, madam.

Mar. About as much, I fuppofe, as it coft you to give it me.

Hear. Upon my word, madam, I gave it purely to oblige you.

Mar. Then to return your civility, the leaft I can do is to take it.

Hear. Is't poffible? How can you torture me with this indifference?

Mar. Why do you infult me with fuch a bare-fac'd jealoufy?

Hear. Is it a crime to be concern'd for what becomes of you? Has not your father openly declared againft me, in favour of my rival? How is it poffible, at fuch a time, not to have a thoufand fears? What though they all are falfe and groundlefs, are they not ftill the effect of love alarm'd, and anxious to be fatisfied? I have an open artlefs heart, that cannot bear difguifes, but when 'tis griev'd in fpite of me, 'twill fhew it——Pray pardon me—But when I am told you went out in the utmoft hurry with fome writings to a lawyer, and took the doctor's own fervant with you, ev'n in the very hour your father had propos'd him as your hufband! Good heaven! what am I to think? Can I, muft I fuppofe my fenfes fail me? If I have eyes, have ears, and have a heart, muft it be ftill a crime to think I fee, and hear ——Yet by my torments feel I love.

Mar. [*Afide.*] Well, I own it looks ill-natur'd now not to fhew him fome concern——but then this jealoufy—— I muft, and will get the better of.

Hear. Speak, *Maria*, is ftill my jealoufy a-crime?

Mar. If you ftill infift on it, as a proof of love, then I muft tell you, Sir, 'tis of that kind, that only flighted hearts are pleas'd with; when I am fo reduc'd, then I perhaps may bear it.--The fact you charge me with I grant is true, I have been abroad, as you fay: But ftill let appearances look ne'er fo pointing, while there is a

possibility in nature, that what I have done may be innocent, I won't bear a look, that tells me to my face you
dare suspect me : If you have doubts, why don't you satisfy them before you see me ? Can you suppose that I'm
to stand confounded, as a criminal, before you ? How despicable a figure must a woman make, to bear but such
a moment ! Come, come, there's nothing shews so low a
mind, as these grave and insolent jealousies. The man,
that's capable of ever seeing a woman, after he believes
her false, is capable on her submission, and a little
flattery, were she really false, poorly to forgive and
bear it.

Hear. You won't find me, madam, of so low a spirit;
but since I see your tyranny arises from your mean opinion of me, 'tis time to be myself, and disavow your
power: you use it now beyond my bearing ; not only impose on me to disbelieve my senses, but do it with such
an imperious air, as if my honest, manly reason were
your slave, and this poor groveling frame that follows you,
durst shew no signs of life, but what you deign to
give it.

Mar. Oh! you are in the right---go on---suspect me
still, believe the worst you can---'tis all true—I don't jus-
tify myself—Why do you trouble me with your com-
plaints ? If you are master of that manly reason you
have boasted, give me a manly proof it; at once resume your liberty, despise me ; go, go off in triumph now,
and let me see you scorn the woman, whose vile, o'er-
bearing falshood, would insult your senses.

Hear. O heaven ! is this the end of all ? Are then
those tender protestations you have made me (for such I
thought them) when with the softest kind reluctance your
rising blushes gave me something more, than hope ———
What all———O *Maria !* all but come to this ?

Mar. [*Aside.*] O Lud! I am growing silly, if I hear
on, I shall tell him every thing ; 'tis but another
struggle, and I shall conquer it———So, so, you are
not gone, I see.

Hear. Do you then wish me gone, madam?

Mar. Your manly reason will direct you.

Hear. This is too much—my heart can bear no more

O!——what ? am I rooted here ! 'Tis but a pang, and I am free for ever.

Enter Charles, *with two Writings.*

Mar. At laſt I am reliev'd ! Well, Mr. *Charles,* is it done ?

Charles. I did not ſtir from his desk, madam, till it was intirely finiſh'd.

Mar. Where's the original ?

Charles. This is it, madam.

Mar. Very well, that you know you muſt keep, but come, we muſt loſe no time, we will examine this in the next room.   Now I feel for him.   [*Aſide.*
                              [*Exit* Maria *with* Charles.

Hear. O rage ! Rage ! this is not to be borne——ſhe's gone, ſhe's loſt, ſordidly has ſold herſelf to fortune, and I muſt now forget her——Hold, if poſſible, let me cool a moment——Intereſt ! No, that could not tempt her—— She knows I'm maſter of a larger fortune, than there her utmoſt hopes can give her, that on her own condi- tions ſhe may be mine :——But what's this ſecret treaty then within ? what's doing there ? who can reſolve that riddle ?——And yet perhaps, like other riddles, when 'tis explain'd, nothing may ſeem ſo eaſy : But why, again, might ſhe not truſt me too with the ſecret ! That ! that entangles all afreſh, and ſets me on the rack of jea- louſy.

Enter Colonel.

Col. How now, *Frank !* what in a rapture ?

Hear. Pr'ythee, pardon me, I am unfit to talk with you.

Col. What is *Maria* in her airs again ?

Hear. I know not what ſhe is.

Col. Do you know where ſhe is ?

Hear. Retir'd this moment to her chamber, with the doctor's ſervant.

Col. Why, you are not jealous of the doctor, I hope ?

Hear. Perhaps ſhe'll be leſs reſerv'd to you, and tell you wherein I have miſtaken her.

Col. Poor *Frank*, thou art a perfect Sir *Martin* in thy amours; every plot I lay upon my sister's inclination for thee, thou art sure to ruin by thy own unfortunate conduct.

Hear. I own I have too little temper, and too much real passion, for a modish lover.

Col. Come, come, pr'ythee be easy once more, I'll undertake for you, if you'll fetch a cool turn in the *Park* upon *Constitution Hill*, in less than half an hour, I'll come to you.

Hear. Dear *Tom*, thou art a friend indeed! O I have a thousand things——but you shall find me there.

[*Exit* Heartly.

Col. Poor *Frank*! now has he been taking some honest pains to make himself miserable.

Enter Maria *and* Charles.

How now, sister, what have you done to *Heartly?* The poor fellow looks, as if he had kill'd your parrot.

Mar. Pshah! you know him well enough, I have only been setting him a love-lesson, it a little puzzles him to get through it at first, but he'll know it all by to-morrow; you will be sure to be in the way, Mr. *Charles?*

Charles. Madam, you may depend upon me, I have my full instructions.

[*Exit* Charles.

Col. O ho! There's the business then, and it seems *Heartly* was not to be trusted with it; ha! ha! and pr'ythee what is this mighty secret, that's transacting between *Charles* and you?

Mar. That's what he would have known indeed, but you must know, I don't think it proper to let you tell him neither, for all your sly manner of asking.

Col. O! pray take your own time, dear madam, I am not in haste to know, I can assure you, I came about another affair, our design upon the doctor: Now while my father takes his nap after dinner, would be the properest time to put it in execution: Pr'ythee go to my lady, and persuade her to it this moment.

Mar. Why won't you go with me?

Col. No, I'll place myself unknown to her in this passage; for, should I tell her I design to over-hear him, she might be scrupulous.

Mar. That's true——but hold, on second thoughts, you shall know part of this affair between *Charles* and me; nay, I give you leave to tell it *Heartly* too, on some conditions; 'tis true, I did design to have surprized you, but now———my mind's alter'd, that's enough.

Col. Ay, for any mortal's satisfaction——but here comes my lady.

Mar. Away then to your post——but let me see you, when this affair is over.

Col. I'll be with you. [*Exit* Col.

Enter Lady Woodvil.

Mar. Well, madam, has your ladyship consider'd my brother's proposal about the doctor?

Lady *Wood.* I have, child, and am convinc'd it ought not to be delay'd a moment: I have just sent to speak with him here——Sir *John* too presses me to give him a hearing upon your account; but must I play a treacherous part now, and, instead of perfuading you to the doctor, ev'n perfuade the doctor against you?

Mar. Dear madam, don't be so nice; if wives were never to diffemble, what wou'd become of many wilful husbands' happiness?

Lady *Wood.* Nay, that's true too.

Mar. I'd give the world now methinks, to fee this folemn interview: fure there can't be a more ridiculous image than unlawful love peeping his fly head out from under the cloke of fanctity! O! that I were in your ladyship's place, I would lead that dancing blood of his fuch a profane courant—your wife fellows make the rareft fools too; but your ladyship will make a rogue of him, and that will do our bufinefs at prefent.

Lady *Wood.* If he makes himfelf one, 'tis his own fault.

Mar. Dear madam, one moment's truce with the prude, I beg you; don't ftart at his firft declaration, but let him go on till he fhews the very bottom of his ugly heart.

Lady *Wood.* I'll warrant you, I'll give a good account of him——here he comes.

Mar. Then I hope, madam, you will give me leave to be commode, and fteal off.

Lady Wood. Very well. [*Exit* Maria, *and Enter Doctor.*

Doct. I am told, madam, you defign me the happinefs of your commands; I am proud you think me worthy of them in any fort.

Lady Wood. Pleafe to fit, Sir.

Doct. Did not Sir *John* inform you too, that I had defir'd a private conference with your ladyfhip?

Lady Wood. He did, Sir.

Doct. 'Tis then by his permiffion we are thus happily alone.

Lady Wood. True, and 'tis on that account I wanted to advife with you.

Doct. Well, but, dear lady, ah! [*Sighing*] you can't conceive the joyoufnefs I feel, in this fo unexpected interview, ah! ah! I have a thoufand friendly things to fay to you——Ah! ah! and how ftands your precious health? our naughty cold abated yet? I have fcarce clofed my eyes thefe two nights, with my concern for you, and every watchful interval has fent a thoufand fighs and prayers to heaven for your recovery.

Lady Wood. Your charity was too far concern'd for me.

Doct. Ah! don't fay fo, don't fay fo——you merit more than mortal man can do for you.

Lady Wood. Indeed, you over-rate me.

Doct. I fpeak it from my foul! indeed! indeed! indeed! I do.　　　　　　　　　　[*Preffes her hand.*

Lady Wood. O dear, you hurt my hand, Sir.

Doct. Impute it to my zeal, and want of words to exprefs my heart; ah! I would not harm you for the world, no, bright creature, 'tis the whole bufinefs of my foul to——

Lady Wood. But to our affair, Sir.

Doct. Ah! thou heavenly woman!
　　　　　　　　　[*Laying his hand on her knee.*
Lady Wood. Your hand need not be there, Sir.

Doct. Ah! I was admiring the foftnefs of this filk, madam.

Lady Wood. Ay, but I am ticklifh.

Doct. They are indeed come to a prodigious perfection in this manufacture——How wonderful is human art !——Here it difputes the prize with nature——that all this foft, and gaudy luftre, fhould be wrought from the poor labours of a worm !   [*Stroking it.*

Lady *Wood.* But our bufinefs, Sir, is upon another fubject; Sir *John* informs me, that he thinks himfelf under no obligation to Mr. *Heartly,* and therefore refolves to give you *Maria:* Now pray be fincere, and let me know what your real intentions are ?

Doct. Is it poffible! Can you, divine perfection, be ftill a ftranger to my real thoughts! Has no one action of my life inform'd you better? Since I muft plainly fpeak them then, *Maria*'s but a feint, a blind to fcreen my real thoughts from fhrewd fufpicion's eye, and fhield your fpotlefs fame from worldly cenfure. Could you then think 'twas for *Maria*'s fake, your balls, affemblies, and your toilet vifits have been reftrain'd ? Would I have urg'd Sir *John* to make that fence to inclofe a butterfly ? No, foft, and ferious excellence, your virtues only were the object of my care, I could not bear to fee the gay, the young, and the inconftant, daily basking in your dif-fufive beams of beauty, without a fecret grudge, I might fay, envy ev'n of fuch infects happinefs.

Lady *Wood.* Well, Sir, I take all this, as I fuppofe yon intended it, for my good, my fpiritual welfare.

. *Doct.* Indeed I meant you ferious, cordial fervice.

Lady *Wood.* I dare fay you did, you are above the low and momentary views of this world.

Doct. Ah ! I fhould be fo——and yet, alas ! I find this mortal cloathing of my foul is made, like other men's, of fenfual flefh and blood, and has its frailties.

Lady *Wood.* We all have thofe, but yours, I know, are well corrected by your divine and virtuous con-templations.

Doct. And yet our knowledge of eternal beauties, does not reftrain us wholly from the love of all that's mortal——Beauty here, 'tis true, muft die, but while it lives 'twas given us to admire, to wake the fluggifh heart, and charm the fenfible : At the firft fight of you, I felt unufual tranfports in my foul, and trembled at the guilt that might enfue ; but on reflection found my flame receiv'd a fanction from your goodnefs, and might be reconcil'd with virtue; on this I chaced my flandrous fears, let in the harmlefs paffion at my eyes, and gave up all my heart to love.

Col. [*Behind.*] Indeed! fo warm, Sir *Roger!* but I fhall cool your paffion with a witnefs.   [*Exit.*

Lady *Wood.* Thefe gay profeffions, Sir, fhew more the courtier than the zealot; nor could I think a mind fo fortify'd as yours, could have been open to fuch vain temptations.

Doct. What bofom can be proof 'gainft fuch artillery of love? I may refift, call all my prayers, my faftings, tears and penance to my aid, but yet, alas! thefe have not made an angel of me: I am ftill but man; virtue may ftrive, but nature will be uppermoft: permit me then on this fair fhrine to pay my vows, and offer up a heart———

Lady *Wood.* Hold, Sir, you've faid enough to put you in my power; fuppofe I now fhould let my hufband, Sir, your benefactor, know the favour you defign'd him.   [*She rifes.*

Doct. You cannot be fo cruel?

Lady *Wood.* Nor will, on one condition.

Doct. Name it.

Lady *Wood.* That inftantly you renounce all claim and title to *Maria,* and ufe your utmoft intereft with Sir *John* to give her, with her full fortune, to Mr. *Heartly.* If you are wife, confider on't.   [*Sir* John *and Colonel behind.*
        [*The Doctor turning accidentally fees them.*

Doct. Ha! the colonel there! his father with him too! here may have been fome treachery; what's to be done?   [*Afide.*

Col. Now S r, let your eyes convince you.⎫
 Sir John. They do, that yours, Sir, have deceiv'd you; all this I knew of.   ⎬ [*Apart.*
 Col. How, Sir!
 Sir John. Obferve and be convinc'd.   ⎭

Doct. I have it.   [*Mufing.*

Lady *Wood.* [*To the Doctor.*] Methinks this bufinefs needs not, Sir, fo long a paufe;

Doct. Madam, I cannot eafily give up fuch honeft hopes.

Lady *Wood.* Honeft!

Doct. Perhaps my years are thought unequal to my flame, but, Lady, thofe were found no ftrong objection 'twixt Sir *John* and you; and can you blame me then for following fo fure a guide in the fame youthful path to happinefs.

Lady *Wood.* Is this your refolution, then?

Col. Will you let him go on, Sir?

Sir *John.* Yes, Sir, to confound your flander. } *Apart.*

Col. Monftrous!

Doct. Can you fuppofe my heart lefs capable of love, than his? Is it for me to pufh the blefling from me too? For tho' my flame has been of long duration, my confcious want of merit kept it ftill conceal'd, till his good nature brought it to this bleft occafion; and can you then, fo authoriz'd, refufe your friendly pity to my fufferings? One word from you compleats my joy; in you, Madam, is my only hope, my fear, my eafe, my pain, my torment, or my happinefs; *Maria!* O, *Maria!*

Col. Confufion!

Sir *John.* [*Coming forward with the Colonel.*] Now, vile detracter of all virtue, is your outrageous malice yet confounded? Did I not tell you too, he only made an intereft here to gain your fifter?

Col. His devil has out-reach'd me.   [*Afide.*

Sir *John.* Is this your rank detection of his treachery?

Doct. Sir *John,* I did not fee you, Sir, I doubt you are come too foo, I have not yet prevail'd with her,

[*Afide to him.*

Sir *John.* Ah! good man, be not concern'd; your trouble fhall be fhorter for't, I'll force her to compliance.

Lady *Wood.* What have you done—your im-}
patience has ruin'd all.   } *Apart.*

Col. I fee it now too late.   }

Sir John. Now, Sir, will your bafe prejudice of party never be at reft ? Am I to be ftill thought partial, blind, and obftinate to favour fo much injur'd virtue ! if thou art a man not loft to confcience, or to honour, then like a man repair this wrong, confefs the rancour of thy vile fufpicion, and throw thee at his feet for pardon.

Doct. What mean you, Sir ?

Lady *Wood.* [*Afide.*] While he is in this temper, he will not eafily be undeceiv'd——I've yet an after-game to play, till when, 'tis beft to leave him in his error.

[*Exit Lady* Wood.

Sir *John.* What! mute! defencelefs! hardened in thy malice !

Col. I fcorn the imputation, Sir, and with the fame repeated honefty avow (howe'er his cunning may have chang'd appearances) that you are ftill deceiv'd, that all I told you, Sir, was true, thefe eyes, thefe ears were witneffes of his audacious love, without the mention of my fifter's name, directly, plainly, grofly tending to abufe the honour of your bed.

Sir *John.* Audacious monfter! were not your own fenfes evidence againft your frontlefs accufation ? I fee your aim ; wife, children, fervants, all are bent againft him, and think to weary me by groundlefs clamours to difcard him, but all fhall not do, your malice on your own vile heads ; to me it but the more endears him ; either fubmit, and afk his pardon for this wrong——

Doct. Good Sir !

Sir *John.* Or this inftant leave my fight, my houfe, my family for ever.

Doct. What means this rafhnefs, Sir! on my account it muft not be, what would the world report of it ? I grant it poffible he loves me not, but you muft grant it too as poffible he might miftake me ! it muft be fo—He is too much your fon to do his enemy a wilful injury:

If he, I say, ſuppos'd my converſe with your Lady criminal, to accuſe me then, was but the error of his virtue, not his baſeneſs, you ought to love him, thank him for ſuch watchful care : Was it for him to ſee, as he believ'd, your honour in ſo full a danger, and ſtand concernleſs by ? The law of Heaven, of nature, and of filial duty, all oblig'd him to alarm your vengeance, and detect the villainy.

Sir John. O miracle of charity !

Doct. Come, come, ſuch breaches muſt not be, betwixt ſo good a ſon, and father; forget, forgive, embrace him, cheriſh him, and let me bleſs the hour I was the occaſion of ſo ſweet a reconcilement.

Sir John. I cannot bear ſuch goodneſs ! O ſink me not into the earth with ſhame——Hear this, perverſe, and reprobate ! O, couldſt thou wrong ſuch more than mortal virtue !

Col. Wrong him ! the hardened impudence of this painted charity——

Sir John. Peace, monſter——

Col. Is of a blacker, deeper dye, than the great devil himſelf in all his triumphs over innocence ever wore.

Sir John. O graceleſs infidel !

Col. No, Sir, though I would hazard life to ſave you from the ruin he miſleads you to; could die to reconcile my duty to your favour; yet on the terms that villain offers, 'tis merit to refuſe it; I glory in the diſgrace your errors give me——But, Sir, I'll trouble you no more. To-day is his, to-morrow may be mine.

[Exit Col.

Doct. I did not think he had ſo hard a nature.

Sir John. O, my good Lord, your charitable heart diſcovers not the ranker that's in his; but what better can be hop'd for, from a wretch ſo ſwell'd with ſpleen, and rage of party.

O 2

Doct. No, no, Sir, I am the thorn that galls him, 'tis me he hates; he thinks I ſtand before him in your favour; and 'tis not fit indeed I ſhould do ſo; for fallen as he is, he's ſtill your ſon, and I alas! an alien, an intruder here, and ought in con-ſcience to retire, and heal theſe hapleſs breaches in your family.

Sir *John.* What means your Lordſhip?

Doct. But I'll remove this eye-ſore—Here *Charles!*

Enter Charles.

Sir *John.* For goodneſs ſake.

Doct. Bring me that writing I gave you to lay up this morning.

Char. Now fortune favour us.   [*Aſide.*
             [*Exit* Charles.

Sir *John.* Make haſte, good *Charles,* it ſhall be ſign'd this moment.

Doct. Not for the world; 'twas not to that end I ſent for it, but to refuſe your kind intentions; for with your children's curſes, Sir, I dare not, muſt not take it.

Sir *John.* Nay, good my Lord, you carry it now too far; my daughter is not wrong'd by it, but if not ob-ſtinate may ſtill be happy; and for my wicked ſon, ſhall he then heir my lands, to propagate more miſerable ſchiſmaticks? No, let him depend on you, whom he has wrong'd; perhaps in time he may reflect upon his father's juſtice; be reconcil'd to your rewarded virtues, and reform his fatal errors.

Re-enter Charles *with a writing.*

Doct. That would be indeed a bleſſing.

Sir *John.* If heaven ſhould at laſt reclaim him, the power to right him ſtill is yours; in you I know he yet would find a fond forgiving father.

Doct. The imagination of fo bleſt an hour, ſoftens me to a tenderneſs I can't ſupport.

Sir *John.* O the dear, good man! come, come, let's in to execute this deed.

Doct. Will you then force me to accept this truſt? For, call it what you will, with me it ſhall never be more than ſuch.

Sir *John.* Let that depend upon the conduct of my ſon.

Doct. Well, Sir, ſince yet it may prevent his ruin, I conſent.

So ſweet a hope muſt all my fears controul,
I take the truſt, as guardian to his ſoul. [Exeunt.

A C T   IV.

Maria *and* Charles.

Mar. YOU were a witnefs then?

    Charles. I faw it fign'd, feal'd, and deliver'd, Madam.

    Mar. And all pafs'd without the leaft fufpicion?

    Charles. Sir *John* fign'd it with fuch earneftnefs, and the Doctor receiv'd it with fuch a feeming reluctance, that neither had the curiofity to examine a line of it.

    Mar. Well, Mr. *Charles*, whether it fucceeds to our ends, or not, we have ftill the fame obligations to you: You faw with what a friendly warmth my brother heard your ftory, and I don't in the leaft doubt his fuccefs in your affair at court.

    Charles. What I have done, my duty bound me to: But pray, Madam, give me leave, without offence, to afk you one innocent queftion.

    Mar. Freely, Sir.

    Charles. Have you never fufpected then, that in all this affair I have had fome fecret, ftronger motive to it, than barely duty?

    Mar. Yes—but have you been in no apprehenfions I fhould difcover that motive?   [*Gravely.*

    Charles. Pray, pardon me, I fee already, I have gone too far.

    Mar. Not at all, it lofes you no merit with me, nor is it in my nature to ufe any one ill, that loves me, unlefs I lov'd that one again, then indeed, there might be danger—Come, don't look grave, my inclinations to another, fhall not hinder me paying every one, what's due to their merit, I fhall therefore always think myfelf oblig'd to treat your misfortunes and your modefty with the utmoft tendernefs.

Charles. By the dear, foft eafe you have given my heart, I never hop'd for more.

Mar. Then I'll give you a great deal more, and to fhew my particular good opinion of you, I'll do you a favour, Mr. *Charles*, I never did any man fince I was born—I'll be fincere with you.

Charles. Is it then poffible you can have lov'd another, to whom you never were fincere?

Mar. Alas! you are but a novice in the paffion—fincerity is a dangerous virtue, and often furfeits what it ought to nourifh: therefore I take more pains to make the man I love believe I flight him, than (if poffible) I would to convince you of my efteem and friendfhip.

Charles. Be but fincere in that, Madam, and I can't complain.

Mar. Nay, I'll give you a proof of it, I'll fhew you all the good-nature you can defire; you fhall make what love to me you pleafe now; but then I'll tell you the confequence, I fhall certainly be pleas'd with it, and that will flatter you, till I do you a mifchief. Now do you think me fincere?

Charles. I fcarce confider that, but I'm fure you are agreeable.

Mar. Why look you there now! do you confider, that a woman had as lief be thought agreeable, as handfome? And how can you fuppofe, from one of your fenfe, that I am not pleas'd with being told fo?

Charles. Was ever temper fo enchanting?

Mar. Or vanity more venial! I'm pleas'd with you.
[Smiling.

Charles. Diftracting! fure never was defpair adminiftred with a hand fo gentle.

Mar. So! now you have convinc'd me, I have a good underftanding too—why I fhall certainly have the better opinion of your's, for finding it out now.

O 4

Charles. Your good opinion's what I aim at.

Mar. Ay, but the more I give it you, the better you'll think of me ſtill; and then I muſt think the better of you again, and then you the better of me upon that too; and ſo at laſt I ſhall think ſerioufly, and you'll begin to think ill of me. But I hope, Mr. *Charles*, your good ſenſe will prevent all this.

Charles. I ſee my folly now, and bluſh at my preſumption; but yet to cure my weaning heart, and reconcile me to my doom, be yet ſincere and ſatisfy one ſickly longing of my ſoul.

Mar. To my power command me.

Charles. O, tell me then the requiſites I want, and what's the ſecret charm that has preferr'd my rival to your heart.

Mar. Come, then be chearful, and I'll anſwer like a friend. The gentleneſs and modeſty of your temper, would make with mine but an unequal mixture; with you I ſhould be ungovernable, not know myſelf; your compliance would undo me. I am by nature vain, thoughtleſs, wild, and wilful; therefore aſk a higher ſpirit to controul and lead me. For whatever outward airs I give myſelf, I am within convinc'd, a woman makes a very wrong figure in happineſs, that does not think ſuperiority beſt becomes her huſband.—But what's yet more, tho' I confeſs you have qualities uncommon in your ſex, and ſuch as ought to warm a heart to love; yet here you come too late; compaſſion's all within my power: And I know you cannot but have ſeen, I am under obligations, I need not explain to you.

Charles. I am ſatisfied—You treat me with ſo kind and gentle a concern, that I muſt ſubmit to it.

Mar. [*Apart.*] Well! when all's done, he's a pretty fellow; and the firſt ſure, that ever heard reaſon againſt himſelf with ſo good an underſtanding.

Enter a Servant with a letter to Charles.

Serv. Sir, the *Colonel* ordered me to give this into your own hands.

Mar. From my brother ?——Where is he ?

Serv. I left him, Madam, at the *Secretary*'s *Office* with one Sir *Charles Trueman*, and Mr. *Heartly*.

[*Exit* Serv.

Charles. Ha! my father! O, Heaven! 'tis his hand too: Now I tremble!

Mar. Come, Sir, take heart; I dare fay there's good new's in't, and I fhould be glad to hear it——But no ceremony; pray read to yourfelf firft.

Charles. Since you command me, Madam.

[*Reads to himfelf.*

Mar. [*Apart.*] Lord! how one may live, and learn! I could not have believ'd, that modefty, in a young fellow could have been fo amiable a virtue: And though, I own, there is I know not what of dear delight in indulging one's vanity with them; yet, upon ferious reflection, we muft confefs, that truth and fincerity have a thoufand charms beyond it. And I now find more pleafure in my felf-denying endeavours to make this poor creature eafy, than ever I took in humbling the airs and affurance of a man of quality—I believe I had as good confefs all this to *Heartly*, and ev'n make up the buftle with him too—But then he will fo teaze one for inftances of real inclination—O Gad—I can't bear the thought on't—And yet we muft come together too —Well! nature knows the way to be fure, and fo I'll ev'n truft to her for't——Blefs me! what's the matter? you feem'd concern'd, Sir.

[*To* Charles, *wiping his tears.*

Charles. I am indeed, but 'tis with joy! O, Madam! my father's reconcil'd to me: This letter is from him.

Mar. Pray let's hear.

Charles. [*Reading.*]

Dear *Charles,*

This day by Colonel Woodvil, *I receiv'd the joyful news of your being yet alive, and well: Tho' that's but half my comfort. He has affur'd me too, you have renounc'd thofe*

principles, *that made me think your death my happiness.
The services you have intended his family, and may do the
government, in your just detection of a traytor that would
ruin both, have been so well receiv'd at court, and so generously represented there by the* Colonel *and* Mr. Heartly,
*that they have obtain'd an order for your pardon; which I
now stay the passing of, before I throw my arms about you,
that I may leave no doubt or fear behind to interrupt the
fullness of my joy. I am inform'd, that in revealing yourself to a certain fair Lady, you have let fall some words,
that shew you have an innocent, tho' hopeless passion for her.
Your youth excuses what is past; but how consider how far
you owe your life to Mr.* Heartly: *I therefore charge you,
on my blessing, to give up every idle thought of love, that may
interrupt his happiness, or abate the merit of what you've
done to deserve the pardon of your sovereign, or of your af-
fectionate forgiving father,*

Charles Truman.

Mar. I am overjoy'd at your good fortune.

Charles. You, Madam, are the source of all—but I
am now unfit to thank you.   [*Weeps.*

Mar. You owe me nothing, Sir; success was all I
hoped for.

Charles. Pray excuse me—It would be rudeness to
trouble you with the tender thoughts this must give a
heart oblig'd like mine.

[*Exit* Charles.

Mar. Poor creature! how full his honest heart is!
What early vicissitudes of fortune has he run through!
Well! this was handsomely done of *Hearsly,* considering
what he had felt upon his account, to be so concern'd
for his pardon.

Enter Lady Woodvil.

Lady *Wood.* Dear *Maria,* what will become of us?
the tyranny of this subtle priest is insupportable: He
has so fortified himself in Sir *John's* opinion by this last
misconduct of your brother, that I begin to lose my usual
power with him.

Mar. Pray explain, Madam.

Lady *Wood.* In fpight of all I could urge, he is this minute bringing the Doctor to make his addreffes to you.

Mar. I am glad on't; for the beaft muft come like a bear to the ftake, I'm fure: He knows I fhall I bait him.

Lady *Wood.* No, no, he preffes it, to keep Sir *John* ftill blind to his wicked defign upon me—Therefore I came to give you notice, that you might be prepar'd to receive him.

Mar. I am oblig'd to your Ladyfhip: Our meeting will be a tender fcene no doubt.

Lady *Wood.* You have heard, I fuppofe, what an extravagant fettlement your father has fign'd too.

Mar. Yes, Madam; but I am glad your Ladyfhip's like to be a gainer by it, however: For when I marry, it will be without the Doctor's confent, depend upon't.

Lady *Wood.* No, child, I did not come into Sir *John*'s family with a defign to injure it, or make any of it my enemy: Whenever that four thoufand pound falls into my hands, you'll find it as firmly yours, as if it had been given you, without that odious condition.

Mar. Madam, I think myfelf as much oblig'd by this kind intention, as the performance: But if your Ladyfhip could yet find a way to prove this hypocrite a private villain to my father, I am not without hopes the public will foon have enough againft him, to give a turn to the fettlement.

Lady *Wood.* But fuppofe that fails, what will become of your poor brother?

Mar. But, dear Madam, I cannot fuppofe this fellow muft not be hang'd at laft; and then, you know, the fame honeft hand that ties him up, releafes the fettlement.

Lady *Wood.* Not abfolutely, neither; for this very houfe is given him in prefent, which, tho' that were to be the end of him, would then be forfeited.

Mar. Why, then my brother muſt even petition the government. There have been precedents of the ſame favour, Madam. If not he muſt pay for his blundering, and lay his next plot deeper, I think.

Lady *Wood.* I am glad you are ſo chearful upon it, however ; it looks as if you had ſomething *in petto* to depend upon. But here comes the Doctor.

Enter Sir John *with the* Doctor.

Sir *John.* Daughter, ſince you have the happineſs to be thought amiable in the eye of this good man, I expect you give him an inſtant opportunity to improve it into an amity for life.

Mar. I hope, Sir, I ſhall give him no occaſion to alter his opinion of me.

Sir *John.* Why, that's well ſaid ; come, ſweet-heart, we'll uſe no ceremony.

> [*Exit Sir* John, *with Lady* Woodvil, Maria *and the* Doctor *ſtand ſome time mute, in formal civilities, and a conſcious contempt of each other.*]

Mar. Pleaſe to ſit, Sir.——What can the ugly cur ſay to me? He ſeems a little puzzled. This puts me in mind of the tender interview between Lady *Charlotte,* and Lord *Hardy* in the Funeral.   [*Aſide.*

Doct. Look you, fair Lady, not to make many words, I am convinc'd, notwithſtanding your good father's favour, I am not the perſon you deſire to be alone with, upon this occaſion.

Mar. Your modeſty—is pleas'd to be in the right, Sir.

Doct. Humh ! if I don't flatter myſelf, you have always had a very ill opinion of me.

Mar. A worſe, Sir, of no mortal breathing.

Doct. Humh ! and it is likely, it may be immoveable.

Mar. No rock ſo firm.

Doct. Humh ! from theſe premiſes then, I may reaſonably conclude——you hate me heartily.

Mar. Moſt ſincerely, Sir.   -

Doct. Well! there is, however, ſome merit in ſpeaking truth; therefore to be as juſt on my ſide, I ought in conſcience to let you know, that I have as cordial a contempt for you too.

Mar. O! fy! you flatter me.   [*Affecting a bluſh.*

Doct. Indeed I don't; you wrong your own imperfections to think ſo.

Mar. Theſe words from any tongue but yours, might ſhock me; but coming from the only man I hate———— they charm me.

Doct. Admirable! there ſeems good ſenſe in this: Have you never obſerv'd, Madam, that ſometimes the greateſt diſcords raiſe the moſt agreeable harmony?

Mar. Yes. But what do you infer from thence?

Doct. That while we ſtill preſerve this temper in our hate, a mutual benefit may riſe from it.

Mar. O! never fear me, Sir; I ſhall not fly out; being convinc'd, that nothing gives ſo ſharp a point to one's averſion, as good breeding; as on the contrary, ill manners often hide a ſecret inclination.

Doct. Moſt accurately diſtinguiſh'd————Well, Madam, is there no project you can think of now, to turn this mutual averſion, as I ſaid, into a mutual benefit?

Mar. None that I know of, unleſs we were to marry for our mutual mortification.

Doct. What would you give then, to avoid marrying me?

Mar. My life, with joy, if death alone could ſhun you.

Doct. When you marry any other perſon——my conſent is neceſſary.

Mar. So I hear indeed————But pray, *Doctor*, tell me, how could your modeſty receive ſo inſolent a power, without putting my poor father out of countenance with your bluſhes?

Doct. You over-rate my prudence: I ſought it not, but he would crowd it in among other obligations:

He is good-natur'd, and I could not shock him by a
refusal. Would you have had me plainly told him, what
a despicable opinion I had of his daughter?

Mar. Or rather, what a favourable one you had of
his wife, Sir?

Doct. Humh! you seem to lose your temper.

Mar. Why do you suppose, the whole family does
not see it, except my father?

Doct. If you will keep your temper, I have something
to propose to you.

Mar. Your reproof is just; but I only rais'd my voice,
to let you know, I know you.

Doct. You might have spar'd your pains, it being
of no consequence to my proposal, what you think
of me.

Mar. Not unlikely. Come, Sir, I am ready to receive it.

Doct. In one word then—I take it for granted, that
you would marry Mr. *Heartly*——Am I right?

Mar. Once in your life, you are.

Doct. Nay, no compliments; let us be plain—Would
you marry him?

Mar. You are mighty nice, methinks——Well—
I would.

Doct. Then I won't consent to it—Now, if you have
any proposal to make me—so—if not our amour's at an
end; and we part as civil enemies, as if we had been married this twelvemonth——Think of it.

Mar. [*Aside.*] O the mercenary villain, he wants
to have a fellow feeling, I find—What shall I do
with him——bite him——pretend to comply, and
make my advantage of it——Well, Sir, I understand
every thing but the sum—if we agree upon that, it's
a bargain.

Doct. Half.

Mar. What, two thousand pounds for your consent
only?

Doct. Why, is not two thousand pound worth two
thousand pound? Don't you actually get so much by

it? Is not the half better than nothing? Come, come,
fay, I have us'd you like a friend.

Mar. Nay, think it's the only civil thing you have
done fince you came into the family.

Doct. Do you then make your advantage of it.

Mar. Why, as you fay, *Doctor,* 'tis better than
nothing.' But how is my father to be brought into
this!

Doct. Leave that to my management.

Mar. What fecurity though do you expect for this
money?

Doct. When I deliver my confent in writing, *Heartly*
fhall lay it me down in *Bank* bills.

Mar. Well! on one provifo, I'll undertake that too.

Doct. Name it.

Mar. Upon your immediately owning to my father,
that you are willing to give up your interest to Mr.
Heartly.

Doct. Humh! ftay——I agree to it——you fhall
have proof of it this evening——But in the mean time,
let me warn you too: Don't expect, after I have
hinted what you defire to your father, to make your
advantages now by betraying me to him. You know
my power there; if you do, I can eafily give it a
counter-turn: So difcover what you pleafe, I fhall only
pity you.

Mar. O! I fhall not ftand in my own light; I
know your power, and your confcience too well, dear
Doctor.

Doct. Nay, I dare depend upon your being true to
your own interest. Here comes your father, I will break
it to him immediately. You'll prepare Mr. *Heartly* in
the mean time.

Mar. Without fail.

Doct. I am fatisfied.

Enter Sir John.

Sir *John.* Well, Sir, is my daughter prudent? Has
fhe at laft, a true and virtuous fenfe of happinefs?

Doct. She underſtands me better than I hop'd, Sir.

Mar. Well ſaid equivocation.   [*Aſide.*

Doct. If you pleaſe, Sir *John*, we'll take a turn in the garden, I have ſomething there to offer to you.

Sir *John.* With all my heart, Sir——*Maria*———— There's a toy for thee——Now thou art again my daughter. [*Gives her a ring.*] Come, Sir, I wait on you.

[*Exeunt* Sir *John* and *Doctor.*

Mar. What this fellow's original was, I know not; but by his conſcience and cunning, he would make an admirable Jeſuit—Here comes my brother, and I hope with a good account of him————Well, brother, what ſucceſs?

Enter Colonel.

Col. All that my honeſt heart could wiſh for——Subſtantial affidavits! that will puzzle him to anſwer; I have planted a meſſenger at the next door, who has a warrant in his pocket, when I give the word, to take him.

Mar. Why ſhould not you do it immediately—he's now in the garden with my father.

Col. No; our ſeizing him now for treaſon, I am afraid won't convince my father of his villainy: My deſign is not only to get my father out of his hands, but to drive the pernicious principles he has inſtill'd, out of my father too.

Mar. That I doubt will be difficult.

Col. Not at all; if we can firſt prove him a private villain to him. My father's honeſty will ſoon reflect, and may receive as ſudden a turn as his credulity.

Mar. That's true again; and I hope I am furniſh'd with a new occaſion to begin the alarm to him.

Col. Pray what is't?

Mar. Not to trouble you with particulars; but in ſhort, I have agree'd with the *Doctor*, that *Heartly* ſhall give him two thouſand pounds for his conſent; without which, you know, by my father's late settlement, *Heartly* and I can never come together.

Col. And does the monster really insist upon't ?

Mar. Not only that, but ev'n defies me to make an advantage of the difcovery.

Col. One would think the villain fufpects his footing in the family is but fhort-liv'd, he's in fuch hafte to have his penny-worths out on't. But pr'ythee, fifter, what fecret's this, that you have yet behind in thofe writings that *Charles* brought to you ?

Mar. O ! that's what I can't yet tell you.

Col. Why, pray ?

Mar. Becaufe, when you have done all you can, I am refolv'd to referve fome merit againft him to myfelf.

Col. But why do you fuppofe I would not affift in it ?

Mar. You can't, it's now too late.

Col. Pfhah ! this is rafh and ridiculous.

Mar. Ay, may be fo ; I fuppofe *Heartly* will be of that opinion too : But if he is, you had better advife him to keep it to himfelf.

Col. You will have your obftinate way, I find.

Mar. It can't be worfe than yours, I'm fure; remember how you came off in your laft project; I know you meant well, but you are difinherited for all that.

Col. That's no furprize to me; but I am afham'd however.

Mar. By the way, what have you done with *Heartly ?* why is he not here ?

Col. He has been here, but you muft excufe him ; he was oblig'd to call in hafte for *Charles,* whom he took home with him in his own coach, where his father waited to receive him.

Mar. The poor boy by this time then has feen him. Sure their meeting muft have been a moving fight; I would give the world methinks for a true ac-count of it.

Col. You'll have it from *Heartly* by and by ; 'tis at his houfe they meet : The father, Sir *Charles*

Trueman, happened to be *Heartly*'s intimate acquaintance.

Mar. Well! I own *Heartly* has gained upon me
by this.

Col. I am glad to hear that at leaft. But I muft let
my Lady know what progrefs we have made in the
Doctor's bufinefs, and beg her affiftance to finifh him.

[Exit Col.

Enter a Servant.

Serv. Madam, Mr. *Heartly*.
Mar. Defire him to walk in.

Enter Heartly.

Hear. To find you thus alone, Madam, was an happinefs I did not expect from the temper of our laft
parting.

Mar. I fhould have been as well pleas'd now to have
been thank'd, as reproach'd for my good nature; but
you will be in the right, I find.

Hear. Indeed you take me wrong; I literally meant,
that I was afraid you would not fo foon think I had deferv'd this favour.

Mar. Well, then, one of us has been in the wrong
at leaft.

Hear. 'Twas I, I own it—More is not in my power;
all the amends that have been, I have made you: My
very joy of feeing you, has waited, 'till what you had at
heart unafk'd, was perfected; my own pardon was
poftpon'd, 'till I had fecur'd one ev'n for a rival's life,
whom you fo juftly had compaffionated.

Mar. Pooh? but why would you fay *unafk'd* now?
Don't you confider your doing it fo, is half the merit of
the action?—Lord! you have no art; you fhould have
left me to have taken notice of that; only imagine now,
how kind, and handfome an acknowledgment you have
robb'd me of!

Hear. And yet how artfully you have paid it! With
what a wanton, charming eafe you play upon my tendernefs!

Mar. Well, but was not you filly now?

Hear [*Gazing on her.*] Come—You fhall not be ferious—You can't be more agreeable.

Mar. O! but I am ferious.

Hear. Then I'll be fo——Do you forgive me all?

Mar. What. [*Looking on her fan, as not hearing him.*

Hear. Are we friends, *Maria*?

Mar. O Lord! but you have told me nothing of poor *Charles*; pray how did his father receive him?

Hear. Muft you needs know that, before you anfwer me?

Mar. Lord! you are never well till you have talk'd one out of countenance.

Hear. Come, I won't be too particular, you fhall anfwer nothing—Give me but your hand only.

Mar. Pfhah! I won't pull off my glove, not I.

Hear. I'll take it as it is then.

Mar. Lord! there, there, eat it, eat it.

[*Putting it aukwardly to him.*

Hear. And fo I could, by heav'n.

[*Kiffes it eagerly, and pulls off her glove.*

Mar. O my glove! my glove! my glove!—Pooh! you are in a perfect ftorm! Lord! if you make fuch a rout with one's hand only, what would you do if you had one's heart?

Hear. That's impoffible to tell—but you were afking me of *Charles*, Madam.

Mar. O! ay, that's true—Well, now you are good again——Come, tell me all that affair, and then you fhall fee——how I will like you. [*Wantonly.*

Hear. O! that I could thus play with inclination!

Mar. Pfhah! but you don't tell me now.

Hear. There is not much to tell—Where two fuch tender paffions meet, words had but faintly fpoke them. The fon conducted to the door, with fudden fear ftopt fhort, and burfting into fighs, o'er-charg'd with fhame, and joy, had almoft fainted in my arms; the father, touch'd with his concern, mov'd forward with a kindly fmile to meet him. At this he took new life, and fpringing from his hold, fell proftrate at his feet; where mute, and trembling, for awhile he lay : At length with streaming eyes, and faultering tongue, he begged his blessing, and his pardon. The tender father caught him in his arms, and dropping his fond head upon his cheek, kifs'd him, and figh'd out, *Heaven protect thee !* then gave into his hand the royal pardon ; and turning back his face to dry his manly eyes, he cried, *Deferve this royal mercy,* Charles, *and I am still thy father.* The grateful youth, raifing his heart-fwollen voice, replied, *May Heaven preferve the royal life that gave it !* But here, their paffions grew too ftrong for farther fpeech : Silent embraces, alternate fighs, and mingling tears, were all their language now. The moving fcene became too tender for my eyes, and call'd methought, for privacy ; there unperceived I left them, to recover into breathing fenfe, and utterable joy.

Mar. Well ! of all the inmoft tranfports of the foul, there's none that dance into the heart, like friendly re-concilements.

Hear. Thofe tranfports might be ours, *Maria,* would you but try your power to pardon.

Mar. Which of thofe two now do you think was happieft at that meeting ?

Hear. O ! the father, doubtlefs : Great fouls feel a kind of honeft glory in forgiving, that far exceeds the tranfport of receiving pardon.

Mar. Now I think to bend the ftubborn mind to afk it, is an equal conqueft ; and the joy fuperior to receive, where the heart wifhes to be under obligations.

Hear. Put me into the happy boy's condition, and I may then, perhaps, refolve you better.

Mar. You fhall pofitively bring him into acquaintance.

Hear. Upon my word I will.

Mar. And fhew him to all the women of tafte ; and I'll have you call him my pretty fellow too.

Hear. I will indeed : But hear me——

Mar. I'm pofitive if he had white ftockings he would cut down all the danglers at court in a fortnight !

Hear. O ! no doubt on't ; but——

Mar. You can't conceive how prettily he makes love now.

Hear. Not fo well, as you make your defence, *Maria.*

Mar. O Lord! I had forgot————he's to teach me *Greek* too.

Hear. O, the trifling tyrant! How long, *Maria*, do you think you can find out new evafions for what I fay unto you?

Mar. Lord, you are horrid filly! But fince 'tis love that makes you fuch a dunce——poor *Heartly*,——I forgive you.

Enter Colonel *unfeen.*

Hear. That's kind, however——But to compleat my joy, be kinder yet——and——

Mar. O! I can't, I can't——Lord! did you never ride a horfe-match?

Hear. Was ever fo wild a queftion?

Mar. Becaufe if you have, it runs in my head, you certainly gallop'd a mile beyond the winning-poft to make fure on't.

Hear. Now I underftand you: But fince you will have me touch every thing fo very tenderly, *Maria*, How fhall I find proper words to afk you the lover's laft necef-fary queftion?

Mar. O! there's a thoufand points to be adjufted, before that's anfwer'd.

Col. [*Coming unexpeBedly between them.*] Name them this moment then, for pofitively this is the laft time of afking.

Mar. Pfhah! Who fent for you?

Col. I only came to teach you to fpeak plain *Englifh,* my dear.

Mar. Lord! mind your own bufinefs, can't you?

Col. So I will; for I will make you do more of yours in two minutes, than you would have done without me in a twelvemonth. Why, how now! What! do you think the man's to dangle after your ridiculous airs for ever?

Mar. This is mighty pretty.

Col. You'll fay fo on *Thurfday* fevennight, (for let affairs take what turn they will in the family) that's pofitively your wedding-day—Nay, you fhan't ftir.

Mar. Was ever fuch affurance?

Hear. Upon my life, madam, I am out of countenance: I don't know how to behave myfelf to him.

Mar. No, no, let him go on, only————This is beyond whatever was known, fure!

Hear. Admirable! I hope it will come to fomething.
[Afide.

Col. Ha! ha! If I were to leave you to yourfelves now, what a couple of pretty out-of-countenance figures you would make; humming and hawing upon the vulgar points of jointure, and pin-money————Come, come! I know what's proper o'both fides, you fhall leave it to me.

Hear. I had rather *Maria* would name her own terms to me.

Col. Have you a mind to any thing particular?
[To Maria.

Mar. Why fure! What! Do you think I'm only to be fill'd out here as you pleafe, and fweetned, and fupp'd up like a difh of *Bohea*.

Col. Why, pray madam, when your tea's ready, what have you to do but to drink it? But you, I fuppofe, expect a lover's heart, like your lamp, fhould be always flaming at your elbow, and when it's ready to go out, you indolently fupply it with the fpirit of contradiction.

Mar. And fo you fuppofe, that your affurance has made an end of this matter?

Col. Not till you have given him your hand upon it.

Mar. That then would compleat it?

Col. Perfectly.

Mar. Why then take it, *Heartily.*
[Giving her hand to Heartly.

Hear. O foft furprize! Extatick joy.

Mar. Now I prefume you are in high triumph, Sir.
[*To the* Col.

Col. No, fifter, now you are confiftent with that good fenfe I always thought you miftrefs of.

Mar. I'm afraid Mr. *Heartly,* we are both obliged to him.

Hear. If you think fo, *Maria,* my heart————
Is under double obligations laid.   [*Embracing him.*

Col. —If it cements our friendfhip, I am overpaid.

[*Exeunt.*

A C T V. S C E N E I.

Heartly *and* Maria.

Mar. WELL, now, *Heartly*, now you have nothing to do but to look forward, and, if poffible, to forget what I have been to you: Though 'tis a horrid reftraint you lay upon our fex: You firft make it the bufinefs of your lives to blow up our vanity, and then prepofteroufly expect we fhould be prudent and humble: That is, you invite us to a feaft, where 'tis criminal to tafte, or have an appetite; you put a fword into a child's hand, and then are angry if it does mifchief.

Hear. You give up too much, *Maria*; I never treated you fo: What might have been flattery to moft women, was but honeft truth to you.

Mar. Why look you there now! Is not that enough to turn any poor woman into a changeling?

Hear. No, becaufe 'tis true; charge me with a falfhood and I fubmit.

Mar. Nay then, did you not once tell me, that all my airs and follies were merely put on in compliance to the world, and that good fenfe was only natural to me; that ev'n my affectation (I have not forgot your words) carried more fincerity, than the ferious vows of other women.

Hear. By all my happinefs I think fo ftill.

Mar. What, ferioufly?

Hear. Upon my foul I do.

Mar. Lord! that's delightful! Do you really love me then, *Heartly?* Do tell, for now I begin to believe every thing you fay to me. But don't neither—I am vain ftill —'Twas my vanity that made me afk you.

Hear. Now I don't take it fo.

Mar. There was some in't I am sure, tho' it begins to dwindle, I can tell you.

Hear. No matter, I love you as you are, I would not have you lose your pleasantry, *Maria.*

Mar. Well, do, let me be silly sometimes.

Hear. O! I can play with you, for that matter.

Mar. Pshah! you'll laugh at me.

Hear. Not while you are good in essentials.

Mar. Indeed I'll be very good.

Hear. O fy! that will be the way to make me so.

Mar. Lord! What signifies sense, where there is so much pleasure in folly?

Hear. No perfect passion ever was without it; the pleasure would subside were we always to be wise in it.

Mar. For my part I think so: But will you really stand to the agreement tho', that I have made with the doctor?

Hear. Why not? You shall not break your word upon my account, though he might be a villain you gave it to.

Mar. Well, I take it as a compliment; not but I have some hopes of getting over it, and justly too; but don't let me tell you now. I love to surprize——Tho' you shall know all if you desire it.

Hear. No, *Maria*, I don't want the secret; I am satisfied in your inclination to trust me.

Mar. Well then, I'll keep the secret, only to shew you, that you upon occasion may trust me with one.

Hear. After that, *Maria*, it would be wronging you to ask it: But pray, madam, has the doctor yet given you any proof of his having declined his interest to your father?

Mar. Yes, he told me just now, he had brought him to pause upon it, and does not question in two days to compleat it; but desires in the mean time you will be ready and punctual with the *præmium.*

Hear. Suppose I should talk with Sir *John* myself;

'tis true he has flighted me of late, but however, I ought at leaft to afk his confent, though I have but little hopes of it.

Mar. By all means, do fo——— Here he comes——— This may open another fcene of action too, that we are preparing for.

Enter Sir John, *and Lady* Woodvil, *who walks apart with* Maria.

Sir *John.* Mr. *Heartly,* I am glad I have met with you here.

Hear. I have endeavoured twice to day, Sir, to pay my refpects to you.

Sir *John.* Sir, I'll be plain with you—I went out to avoid you ; but where the welfare of a child is concern'd, you muft not take it ill, if we don't ftand upon cere-mony.——However, fince I have reafon now to be more in temper, than perhaps I was, at that time, I fhould be glad to talk with you.

Hear. I take it as a favour, Sir.

Sir *John.* Sir,—Doctor *Wolf* informs me, that he is well affured you were born the year before the revolu-tion: Now, Sir, I fhould be glad to be well fatisfied in that point ; a greater confequence depending oh it, per-haps, than you imagine.

Hear. Sir, I have been always told that was my age ; but for your farther fatisfaction I appeal to the regifter.

Sir *John.* Sir, I dare believe you, and am glad to hear it.

Hear. But pray, Sir, may I beg leave to afk, why you are fo concerned to know this ?

Sir *John.* Becaufe, Sir, if this be true, I am fatisfied you may be a *regular chriftian* ; the doubt of which, may have, perhaps, done you fcme differvice in my private opinion.

Hear. Sir, if that can reconcile me to it, I fhall be thankful for the benefit, without confidering why I that way came to deferve it.

Sir John. That argument might hold us now too long——— But, Sir,———— here's the case——— your principles and mine have the misfortune to differ.: Yours being (as I take it) entirely on the revolution side.

Hear. If I am not misinformed, Sir, you yourself commanded a regiment in defence of it.

Sir John. I did so, and thought it juft.——'Twould be fruitlefs, perhaps, to offer you the reafons, that fince have altered my opinion : But now, Sir, even fuppofing that I err in principle, you muft ftill allow, that confcience is the rule that every honeft man ought to' walk by.

Hear. 'Tis granted, Sir.

Sir John. Then give me leave to tell you, Sir, that giving you my daughter, would be to act againft that confcience I pretend to, and confequently the fame ties oblige me to beftow her, where the fame principles with mine, I think deferve her——— Now, Sir, confult your own honour, and tell me, how you can ftill purfue my daughter, without doing violence to mine ?

Hear. But, Sir, to fhorten this difpute, fuppofe the doctor (whom I prefume you defign her for) actually confents to give me up his intereft ; might not that foften your objections to me ?

Sir John. But why do you fuppofe, Sir, he would give up his intereft ?

Hear. I only judge from what your daughter tells me, Sir.

Sir John. My daughter !

Hear. I appeal to her.

Mar. And I appeal ev'n to yourfelf, Sir——— Has not the doctor juft now in the garden fpoke in favour of Mr. *Heartly* to you ? Nay, pray, Sir, be plain, becaufe more depends on that, than you can eafily imagine, I believe.

Sir John. What fenfelefs infinuation have you got in your head now?

Mar. Be so kind, Sir, first to answer me, that I may be better able to inform you.

Sir *John.* Well, I own he has declined his interest in favour of Mr. *Heartly:* But I must tell you, madam, he did it in so modest, so friendly, so good-natur'd, so conscientious a manner, that I now think myself more than ever bound in honour to espouse him.

Mar. But now, Sir, (only for argument's sake) suppose I could prove, that all this seeming virtue was utterly artificial; that his regard to Mr. *Heartly* was neither founded upon modesty, friendship, good-nature, nor conscience; or in short, that he has basely betrayed and sold the trust you made him; like a villain barter'd, bargain'd to give me to Mr. *Heartly* for half the four thousand pound you have valued his consent at. I say, suppose this were the case, where would be his virtue then, Sir?

Sir *John.* And I say 'tis impious to suppose it.

Hear. Under favour, Sir, how is it possible your daughter could know the doctor had spoke to you upon this head, if he himself had not told her so, in consequence of his agreement?

Sir *John.* Sir, I don't admit your consequence: Her knowing it from him is no proof, that he might not still resign her from a principle of modesty or good-nature.

Mar. Then, Sir, from what principle must you suppose that I accuse him?

Sir *John.* From an obstinate prejudice to all that's good and virtuous.

Mar. That's too hard, Sir. What blot has stain'd my life, that you can think so of me? But, Sir, the worst your opinion can provoke me to, is to marry Mr. *Heartly,* without either his consent or yours.

Sir *John.* What, do you brave me, madam?

Mar. [*In Tears.*] No, Sir, but I scorn a lye, and will so far vindicate my integrity, as to insist on your believing me, if not, as a child whom you abandon, I have a right to throw myself into other arms for protection.

Heart. O *Maria!* How thy spirit charms me!

[*Apart to her.*

Sir John. I am confounded! those tears cannot be counterfeit; nor can this be true.

Lady Wood. Indeed, my dear; I fear it is; it would be cruel to her concern to think it wholly false; can you suppose she'd urge so gross an accusation only to expose herself to the justice of your resentment?

Sir John. What are you against him too? then he has no friend but me; and I cannot, at so short a warning; give him up to infamy, and baseness.

Lady Wood. Good Sir, be composed, and ask your heart one farther question.

Sir John. What would you say to me?

Lady Wood. In all our mutual course of happiness; have I ever yet deceived you with a falshood?

Sir John. Never, I grant it; nor has my honest heart yet wronged thy goodness with a jealous thought of it.

Lady Wood. Would you then believe me, should I accuse him too, even of crimes, that virtue blushes but to mention?

Sir John. To what extravagance would you drive me?

Lady Wood. I would before have undeceived you, when his late artifice turned the honest duty of your son, into his own reproach and ruin: But knowing then your temper was inaccessible, I durst not offer it. But now, in better hope of being believed, I here avow the truth of all he was accused of then.

Sir John. Will you distract me? my senses could not be deceiv'd.

Lady Wood. Indeed they were, he saw you listning, and at the instant turn'd his impious bare-fac'd love to me, into equivocal intercessions pretending to *Maria.*

Sir John. You startle me.

Lady Wood. Could you otherwise suppose, your son would have brought you to be witness of his own weak malice in accusing him?

P 3

Sir John. I'm all astonishment!

Lady *Wood.* Come, Sir, suspend your wonder, respite your belief ev'n of this, till grosser evidence convinces you: Suppose I here, before your face, should let you see his villainy, make him repeat his odious love to me, at once throw off his mask, and shew the barefac'd traitor.

Sir John. Is it possible? Make me but witness of that fact, and I shall soon accuse myself, and own my folly equal to his baseness: But pardon me, as I in such a case would not believe, ev'n him accusing you, so am I bound in equal charity to think, you yet may be deceiv'd, in what you charge on him.

Lady *Wood.* 'Tis just—let it be so—we'll yet suppose him innocent, till you yourself pronounce him guilty; and since I have staked my faith upon the truth of what I urge, 'tis fit we bring him to immediate trial. But then, Sir, I must beg you to descend ev'n to the poor shifts we are reduced to.

Sir John. All, to any thing to ease me of my doubts, propose them.

Lady *Wood.* They that would set toils for beasts of prey, must lurk in humble caves to watch their haunts.

Sir John. Place me where you please.

Lady *Wood.* Under this table is your only stand, the carpet will conceal you.

Sir John. Be it so, I'll take my post, what more?

Lady *Wood.* Mr. *Heartly,* shall we beg your leave, and you *Maria,* take the least suspected way to send the *Doctor* to me immediately.

Mar. I have a thought will do it, madam,——come, Sir.

[Exit Mar. and Hear.

Lady *Wood.* Here, Sir, take this cushion, you will be easier. [*Sir* John *goes under the table.*] Now, Sir, you must consider how desperate a disease I have undertaken to cure, therefore you must not winch nor stir too soon, at any freedom you observe me take with him; be sure, lie clofe and ftill, and when the proof is full, appear at your difcretion.

Sir *John*. Fear not, I'll be patient.

Lady *Wood*. Hufh! he comes.

Enter Doctor *with a Book.*

Doct. Your woman told me, madam, you were here alone, and defired to fpeak with me.

Lady *Wood*. I did, Sir, but that we may be fure we are alone, pray fhut the outward door, and fee that paf-fage too be clear, another furprize might ruin us———is all fafe?

Doct. I have taken care, madam.

Lady *Wood*. I am afraid I interrupt your meditations.

Doct. Say rather you improve them: You, madam, were the fubject of my folitary thoughts, I take in all the little aids I can to guard my frailty, and truly I have receiv'd great confolation from an unfortunate ex-ample here before me.

Lady *Wood*. Pray of what kind, Sir?

Doct. I had juft dipt into poor *Eloifa's* paffion for *Abelard:* It is indeed a piteous conflict! How ter-rible! How penitent a fenfe fhe fhews of guilty plea-fures paft, and fruitlefs pains to fhut them from her memory.

Lady *Wood*. I have read her ftory, Sir.

Doct. Is it not pitiful?

Lady *Wood*. A heart of ftone might feel for her.

Doct. O! think then, what I endure for you, fuch are my pains, but fuch is my fincerity, tho' I fear my being reduc'd to feign a paffion for *Maria*, in my late fur-prize, has done difhonour to the vows I then preferr'd to you.

Lady *Wood*. 'Twas on that point, I wanted now to talk with you, not knowing then, how far you might miftake my filence: Now had I clos'd with the Colonel in accufing you, it would have been plain I was your enemy; as had I join'd in your defence againft him, it

had been as grofsly evident I was his; but fince I
have ufes for his friendfhip, and, as I faw your credit
with Sir *John* needed no fupport, I hope you'll think
betwixt the two extremes I have acted but a prudent
part.

Doct. Let me prefume to hope then, what I did, you
judge was felf-defence, and pure neceffity.

Lady *Wood.* 'Twas wonderful! Surprizing to perfection! The wit of it—but I won't tell you, what effect it
had upon me.

Doct. Why, madam? let me befeech you.

Lady *Wood.* No, 'twas nothing====befide===what need
you afk me?

Doct. Why do you thus decoy my foolifh heart, and
feed it with fuch *Hybla* drops of flattery? You cannot
fure think kindly of me.

Lady *Wood.* O well feign'd fear! You too, I
find can flatter in your turn: You know how well
the fubtle force of modefty prevails. O Men! Men!
Men!

Doct. 'Twere arrogance to think I have deferv'd this
goodnefs: But treat me as you pleafe, I'll be at leaft
fincere to you, and frankly own, I ftill fufpect, that all
this foftning favour is but artifice.

Lady *Wood.* Well! well! I'd have you think fo.

Doct. What tranfport would it give, to be affured I
wrong you! but O! I fear this fhadow of compliance is
only meant to lure me from *Maria*, and then as fond
Ixion's were of old, to fill my arms with air.

- Lady *Wood.* Methinks this doubt of me, feems rather
founded on your fecond thoughts of not refigning her;
'tis fhe, I find is your fubftantial happinefs.

Doct. O that you could but fear I thought fo! how
eafy 'twere to prove my coldnefs, or my love.

Lady *Wood.* O, Sir, you have convinc'd me now of
both.

Doct. Can all this pretty anger then be real? take
heed, fair creature, it flatters more than kindnefs.

Lady *Wood.* I can affure you, Sir, I fhould have fpared you this trouble, had I known how deeply you were engaged to her.

Doct. Nay then I muft believe you: But indeed you wrong me, to prove my innocence, 'tis not an hour fince I prefs'd Sir *John* to give *Maria* to young *Heartly.*

Lady *Wood.* O! all artifice! you knew that modeft refignation, would make Sir *John* but warmer in your intereft.

Doct. Since you will rip the fecret from my heart ———know then, I actually have fold her, like a bawble, to her childifh lover, for two thoufand times her value.

Lady *Wood.* Are you ferious?

Doct. As this is true, or falfe, may I in you be bleft, or miferable.

Lady *Wood.* But how can you fuppofe Sir *John* will ever hear of it.

Doct. Alas! poor man! he knows not his own weaknefs, he's moulded into any fhape, if you but gently ftroke his humour: I dare depend on his confent—— befide, I intend to-morrow to perfuade him 'tis for the intereft of our *Caufe*; it fhould be fo, and then I have him fure.

Lady *Wood.* Fy! how is that poffible? he can't be fo implicitly credulous. You don't take him fure for a *Roman* Catholic.

Doct. Um———not abfolutely———But, poor foul! he little thinks how near he is one. 'Tis true, name to him but *Rome*, or popery, he ftartles, as at a monfter: But gild its groffeft doctrines with the ftile of *Englifh Catholick*, he fwallows down the poifon like a cordial.

Lady *Wood.* Nay, if he's fo far within your power, it cannot fail, He muft confent: Well, Sir, now I give you leave to guefs the reafon, why I too, at our laft meeting, fo warmly preft you to refign *Maria*.

Doct. Is it poffible? was I then fo early your concern?

Lady *Wood.* You cannot blame me sure, for having there oppos'd your happiness.

Doct. I dye upon the tranfport.　　[*Taking her hand.*

Lady *Wood.* Be fure you are fecret now: Your leaft imprudence makes thefe, like fairy favours, vanifh in a moment.

Doct. How can you form fo vain a fear?

Lady *Wood.* Call it not vain, for let our converfe end in what it may, you ftill fhall find, my fame is dear to me as life.

Doct. Where can it find fo fure a guard? the grave aufterity of my life will ftrike fufpicion dumb, and yours may mock the malice of detraction: I am no giddy, loofe-liv'd courtier, whofe falfe profeffions end only in his boaft of favours: No, fair fpotlefs miracle, the myfteries of love are only fit for hearts reclufe, and elevate as mine: My happinefs, like yours, depending on my fecrecy.

Lady *Wood.* 'Tis you muft anfwer for this folly.

Doct. I take it whole upon myfelf, the guilt be only mine, but be our tranfports mutual —— come, lovely creature, let us withdraw to privacy, where murmuring love fhall hufh thy fears, and lofe them in the burning joy.

[*Sir* John *ftepping foftly behind him feizes him by the throat.*

Sir *John.* Traytor!

Doct. Ah! [*Aftonifh'd.*]

Sir *John.* Is this thy fanctity! this thy doctrine! thefe thy meditations! If ftung with my abufes I now fhould ftab thee to the heart, what devil durft murmur 'twere not an act of juftice? But fince thy vile hypocrify unmafk'd, muft make mankind abhor thee, be thy own fhame thy living punifhment.

Doct. Do! Triumph, Sir———your artifice has well fucceeded——I fee your ends! you needed not fo deep a plot to part with me.　　　　　　　　[*Trembling.*

Sir *John.* Supprefs thy weak evafions——Ungrateful wretch! Have I for this redeem'd thee from the jaws of gaping poverty, fed, cloath'd, lov'd, preferr'd thee to my bosom, to my family, and fortune? Wife, children, friends, servants, all that were not friends to thee, accounted as my enemies; nay, more, to crown my faith in thee, I have relied on thy integrity ev'n for my future happiness: And how hast thou, in one short day, requited me? Taking the advantage of my blinded passion, thou hast turn'd the duty of my son to his undoing; sordidly hast sold the trust I made thee of my daughter, attempted, like a felonious traytor, to seduce my wife, and hast, I fear, with poisonous doctrines too infnar'd my soul.

Lady *Wood.* Now Heav'n be prais'd his heart seems conscious of his error. [*Aside.*

Sir *John.* But why do I reproach thee? had I not been the weakest of mankind, thou never could'st have proved so great a villain——whether Heaven intends all this to punish, or to save me, yet I know not; my senses stagger at the view, and my reflexion's lost in wild astonishment. [*He stands musing.*

Doct. This snare was worthy of you, madam; 'tis you have made this villain of me.
[*Apart to Lady* Wood.

Lady *Wood.* You would have made me worse, but I have only shewn him what you were before.

Doct. I thank you.

Lady *Wood.* Thank your own ingratitude and wickedness; but I must now pursue my victory. [*Exit Lady* W.

Doct. [*Apart.*] No it ends not here. He was not brought to listen to this proof alone! There's something deeper yet designed against me—I must be speedy—suppose I talk with *Charles,* alarm him with our common danger, point out his ruin as our only means of safety, and like the panther in the toil provok'd, turn short with vengeance on my hunters.

Sir *John.* What! still within my sight! of all my follies, which is it tells thee, that I now shall keep my temper.

Doct. [*Turning boldly to him.*] Whom do you menace, me, Sir? Reflect upon your own condition first, and where you are.

Sir John. What would the villain drive at! I pr'ythee leave me, I cannot look on thee! thy over-bearing insolence confounds me: But since thy wickedness has turn'd my eyes upon myself, and to thy crimes detected, I hope to owe my future innocence, as the sore wound the viper gives, the viper best can cure: For that one good may Heaven like me forgive thee: But seek thy biding in some other place———out of my house this instant, Hence! be gone! and see my shameful face no more.

Doct. Nay, then, 'tis time to be myself, and let you know, that I am master here, turn you out, Sir, this house is mine! and now, Sir, at your peril dare to insult me.

Sir John. O! Heav'n! 'tis true, thou hast disarm'd my justice, and turn'd its sword into my own weak bosom———I had forgot my folly, 'tis fit it should be so, and Heav'n is just, at once to let me see my crime, and punishment—O my poor injur'd son!—Whether shall I fly to hide me from the world?

Enter Lady Woodvil.

Lady *Wood.* Whither are you going, Sir?

Sir John. I know not———but here it seems I am a trespasser—the master of this house has warn'd me hence, and since the right is now in him, 'tis just I should resign it.

Lady *Wood.* You shall not stir: He dares not act with such abandon'd insolence, No, Sir, possession still is yours, if he pretends a right, let him by open course of law maintain it.

Doct. Are these the shifts you are reduced to? no, madam, I shall not wait so slow a vengeance, you'll find I have a shorter way to rout you.—Here! *Charles!*

[*Exit* Doctor.

Sir John. Nay, then there is an end of all———I have provok'd a serpent———my life, I see, must pay the forfeit of my folly!

Lady *Wood.* Come, Sir, take heart! your life, in spite of him, is free; and I hope your actions too: However, tell me freely, have you rashly done any thing, for which the law must question you?

Sir *John.* I think, not strictly; 'tis true I have lately trusted him with sums of money, which he pretended, if accounted for, might endanger both of us.

Lady *Wood.* O! the subtle villain! those sums are innocent, I dare answer for them: But is there nothing more?

Sir *John.* Not that I can call to mind more criminal.

Lady *Wood.* Pray tell the worst, that we may arm against him.

Sir *John.* Sometimes with my own hand, I have relieved the wants of wretched prisoners to the state.

Lady *Wood.* We have no laws that frown on acts of charity, if that were criminal, the Government itself is guilty.

Sir *John.* How far our private converse may effect me ——That I know not. If *Charles* betrays me not, I think his malice cannot reach me.

Lady *Wood.* Then Sir, be easy, for he has lost his influence there: *Charles* has long since perceived his villainy, and grew from thence a secret convert to the cause of truth and loyalty; of which he has given such meritorious proof, that Mr. *Heartly*, and your son, this very day, Sir, have obtained his pardon.

Sir *John.* You tell me wonders! Pardon'd! and a convert say you! how strongly are our hearts perfuaded by example! what darkness have I wander'd in! How amiable is such royal mercy! yet with what hardned malice has that slave traduced it?

Enter Maria *hastily.*

Mar. O Sir! I am frighted out of my senses! for Heaven's sake be gone! Fly, this moment, this wicked fellow has designs upon your life.

Lady *Wood.* How!

Sir John. What doft thou mean ? explain.

Mar. As I was paffing by the hall, I heard him earneft in difcourfe with *Charles*, aud upon their naming
you, I ftopt awhile to liften, where I heard the *Doctor*
urge to him, that you were falfe at heart, that from
your late frivolous pretence to break with him, he was
convinc'd your malice now would ftop at nothing to undo
him, that *Charles* himfelf was equally in danger, and
that to fave your own life, you certainly defign'd to facrifice theirs to the Government, which there was no
poffibility of preventing, but by their immediate joining
in a charge of treafon againft you.

Lady Wood. O the villain ! 'tis well we are fecure in
Charles.

Sir John. If we are not, why be it as it may—I will
not ftir—I'll ftand upon my innocence, or if that's betray'd, will throw me on the mercy of that royal breaft,
whofe virtues my credulity has injur'd.

Lady Wood. and *Mar.* Ah !

         [*A piftol is heard from within.*

Sir John. What means that piftol ?

Lady Wood. Don't ftir, I beg you, Sir.

Mar. What terrors has this monfter brought into our
family ?

Lady Wood. What will it end in ?

Sir John. How wretched has my folly made me ?

Lady Wood. How now ! what's the matter ?

Enter Betty.

Bet. O, dear madam ! I fhall faint away, there's murder doing.

Sir John. Who ! where, what is it !

Bet. The *Doctor*, Sir, and Mr. *Charles*, were at high
words juft now in the hall, and upon a fudden there was
a piftol fir'd between them : Oh ! I am afraid poor Mr.
Charles is kill'd.

Sir John. How !

Bet. Oh ! here he comes himfelf, Sir, he will tell you
more.

Enter Heartly, Charles, *and the* Doctor *held by*
Servants.

Hear. Here bring in this ruffian, this is villainy beyond
example.

Sir John. What means this outrage?

Lady *Wood.* I tremble.

Charles. Don't be alarm'd, madam, there's no mifchief done ; what was intended, the *Doctor* here can beft
inform you.

Doct. [*To Heartly.*] You, Sir, fhall anfwer for this infult? What am I held for? who's here that dares affume
a right to queftion me?

Hear. Keep your temper, Sir, we'll releafe you prefently, but Sir *John* muft firft know the bottom of his
obligations to you.

Sir John. Mr. *Heartly,* I am afhamed to look on
you.

Doct. What, Sir! fhall my own fervant abufe me,
brave me, lift his hand againft me, and I not dare to
punifh him.

Hear. Your fervant, Sir! we know him better.

Doct. Then, Sir, I demand my liberty, that the Government too may know him.

Charles. Yes, and let it too be known, you firft feduc'd me to rebel, and now would have me expiate my
offence with perjury.

Doct. How, Sir?

Charles. Yes, perjury! for fuch it muft have been,
fhould I have charg'd, as you'd have had me, this gentleman with treafon : What facts have I been privy to,
that reach that name? The worft I know of him, is,
that all the factious falfhoods you have raifed againft the
beft of princes, he, blinded with your hypocrify, believed.

Doct. 'Tis well, Sir, you are protected now.

Charles. This, Sir, in fhort has been our caufe of
quarrel : The *Doctor* finding I received with coldnefs his
vile defigns againft your life, began to offer menaces on

mine, if I comply'd not; at which I smiling, told him, the disappointments of his love had made him desperate: This stung him into rage, and fastning at my throat, he answer'd, villain! you'll be humbler, when you groan in chains for this: Here indeed all temper left me, when disengaging from his hold, with one home blow I fell'd him reeling to the pavement; at this grown desperate, he ran with fury to some pistols that hung above the chimney, to revenge him, I in the instant as he reached one, seized upon his wrist, and as we grappled, Sir, the pistol firing to the cieling, alarm'd the family, when Mr. *Heartly*, and your servants, rusht in to part us.

Sir *John*. Insatiate villain! O my shame!

Doct. Well, Sir, now you have heard this mighty charge! what have you more against me?

Hear. More, Sir, I hope is needless, but if Sir *John* is yet unsatisfied————

Sir *John*. O! I have seen too much! every new instance of his wickedness but adds afresh to my confusion.

Lady *Wood.* Now, Sir, is your time. ⎫
Hear. I go this minute, madam. ⎬ *Apart.*

Doct. I value not your whisper'd menaces, for know, to your confusion, my vengeance is not yet defeated: You'll find, Sir, that to rebel, or to conceal a rebel are in the eye of law both equal acts of treason: That fact I'm sure is evident against you: There! there stands in proof the stripling-traitor you have shelter'd! this, Sir, your whole family can charge you with; and swear it home they shall, or load their souls with perjury; but then to dash your few remaining days with bitterness of misery, remember I, Sir, whom mortally you hate, succeed the instant heir to your possessions: Now farewel, and let disgrace and beggary be your childrens portion.

As he is going out, the Colonel *stops him.*

Col. Hold, Sir, not so fast, you cannot pass.

Doct. Who, Sir, ſhall dare to ſtop me?

Col. Within there! March!

Enter a Meſſenger *with a File of Muſquetéers.*

Meſſ. Is your name *Wolf,* Sir?

Doct. What if it be, Sir?

Meſſ. Then, Sir, I have a Warrant againſt you for high treaſon.

Doct. Me, Sir? [*Startled.*]

Meſſ. Do you know one *Colonel Perth,* Sir?

Doct. Ha! then I am betray'd, indeed.

Hear. This *Perth,* it ſeems, Sir, has manag'd his correſpondence at *Avignon,* from whence he came laſt night expreſs, but the Government having immediate notice of his arrival, he was this morning ſeiz'd, and examin'd before the Council, where, among other facts, he has confeſt he knew the *Doctor* actually in arms at the firſt rebellious riſing in *Northumberland,* which has been ſince by other witneſſes confirm'd.

Col. And, Sir, to convince you, that ev'n the doctrine he has broach'd could never flow from the pure fountain of our eſtabliſhed faith: Here are affidavits in my hand that prove him under his diſguiſe a lurking emiſſary of *Rome,* that he is actually a prieſt in *Popiſh* orders, and has ſeveral times been ſeen, as ſuch, to officiate public maſs in the church of *Noſtre Dame,* at *Antwerp.*

Mar. Hear. and Lady *Wood.* How!

Sir John. I ſtart with horror, ev'n at the danger I am freed from.

Col. And now, Sir, had not your inſatiate villanies to this family forced me to this cloſe enquiry into your private life, perhaps you might have paſs'd unqueſtion'd, among the rout of enemies, whom our Government deſpiſes.

Doct. Well, Sir! now then you know your worſt of me: But know, what you call criminal, may

yet before your triumph is secure, not only find its
pardon, but reward: I yet may live, Sir, to retort
your insult, at least the days that are allotted me, will
want for no supports of life, while this conveyance calls
me master.

Sir John. There! there indeed he stings me to the
heart! for that rash act, reproach and endless shame will
haunt me.

Mar. No, Sir—be comforted! for ev'n there too his
abandoned hope must leave him.

Sir John. Why dost thou torture me! did I not sign
that deed!

Mar. Yes, Sir, but in that deed you'll find, my brother, not that traitor, is your heir: For know the fatal
deed, which you intended, Sir, to sign, is here ev'n yet
unseal'd and innocent.

Omnes. Ha!   [*The* Doctor *hastily opens the deed to
examine it, and all the company seem'd
surpriz'd.*

Sir John. What means she?

Mar. I mean, Sir, that this deed, by accident falling
into this gentleman's hands, his generous concern for
our family discover'd it to me; when I, reduc'd to this
extremity, instantly procur'd that other to be drawn exactly like it, which in your impatience, Sir, to execute,
pass'd unsuspected for the original; their only difference
is, that, wherever here you read the *Doctor's* name,
there you'll find my brother's only, throughout, and
wholly, Sir, in every article investing him in all that
right and title, which you intended for your mortal
enemy.

Doct. Distraction! outwitted by a brainless girl.
                        [*Throws down the writing in rage.*
*All the servants having attended to the discovery, break
out into huzzas of joy, &c. while Sir* John, *the* Colonel, Charles, *and* Maria *severally embrace:*
Heartly, *and Lady* Woodvil *silently join in their con-
gratulations.*

Doct. I cannot bear their irkſome joy—come, Sir, lead me where you pleaſe—a dungeon would relieve me now.

Col. Secure your priſoner.

Ser. Huzza! a traitor! a traitor!

　　　[*Exeunt* Meſſ. Soldiers, Doctor, *and* Servants.

Mar. Now *Heartly,* I hope I have made atonement for your jealouſy.

Hear. You have baniſht it for ever: This was beyond yourſelf ſurprizing.

Col. Siſter————

Mar. Come, no ſet ſpeeches, If I deſerve your thanks, return them in a friendſhip here.

　　　　　　　　[*Pointing to* Charles.

Col. The buſineſs of my life ſhall be to merit it.

Charles. And mine to ſpeak my ſenſe of obligations.

Sir John. O my child! for this deliverance, I only can reward thee here.

　　　　　　　　[*Gives* Maria *to* Heartly.

For thee, my ſon, whoſe filial virtues I have injur'd; this honeſt deed in every article ſhall be ratified: I ſee your eyes are all upon me, expecting from that vile traitor's practices, ſome voluntary inſtance of my heart's converſion: I muſt be blind indeed, were I not now convinc'd he muſt in all things have alike deceiv'd me, as the dial that miſ-tels one hour, of conſequence is falſe through the whole round of day. Let it ſuffice, I ſee my errors with a conſcious ſhame; but hope, when I am juſtly weigh'd, you'll find thoſe errors roſe but from a ductile heart, not diſinclin'd to truth, but fatally miſled by falſe appearances.

Col. Whoever knows your private life, muſt think you, Sir, in this ſincere.

Hear. And now, Sir, ſince I am ſure, it will no more offend you, give me leave to obſerve, that of all the arts our enemies make uſe on to embroil us, none ſeem ſo audaciouſly prepoſterous, as their inſiſting, that a na-

tions beſt ſecurity is the word of a prince, whoſe religion
indulges him to give it; and at the ſame time obliges
him to break it: and though perhaps in leſſer points our
politic diſputes won't ſuddenly be ended; methinks
there's one principle, that all parties might eaſily come
into, that no change of Government can give us a bleſſing equal to our liberty.

> *Grant us but this and then of courſe you'll own,*
> *To guard that freedom,* GEORGE *muſt fill the throne.*

EPILOGUE.

Spoken by Mrs. OLDFIELD.

HOW wild, how frantic is the vain essay,
That builds on modern politics a play !
Methinks to write at all, is bold enough,
But in a play to stand a faction buff !
Not Rome's *old stage presum'd, (or fame's a fibber,*
And moderns to attempt it.! well said Cibber !
Was't not enough the critics might pursue him !
But must he rouse a party to undo him !
These blows I told him on his play would fall,
But he unmov'd, cry'd—Blood ! we'll stand it all,
When Priests *turn Traitors where's the mighty matter ?*
Since when has treason been exempt from Satire ?
And should from Guilt a factious clamour rise,
Such spite must speak them England's *enemies,*
But if Old England's *friends allow 'tis right,*
W'are sure their power can chace the Jacobite,
And put their malice, like their troops, to flight.
As for the critics, those, he owns may tease him,
Because he never took such pains to please them,
In time, place, action, rules by which old wits
Made plays, as—dames do puddings, by receipts :
But hopes again ev'n rebels cannot say,
Tho' vanquisht, they're insulted in his play :
Nay more————to set their cause in fairest light,
H'has made a man of sense———a Jacobite !
(Tho' by our bard's good leave, to take it right,
His sense was shewn, when turn'd from Jacobite)
Thus to the Fair that may be wrong inclin'd,
He hopes to Charles's *passion will be kind,*
And own, at worst, on their reflecting pillow,
The rebel, after all's, a pretty fellow !

EPILOGUE.

But why, you'll say, was I made Heartly's wife?
Confider, Fair-ones, Heartly fav'd his life :
So that you fee, the boy han't quite mifcarried,
Befide————
Are all thofe Dears fo happy you have married?
How often in that ftate has love feen elves
So cramm'd with comfort they could hang themfelves?
The worft you can againft his fatire plead,
Is that my Lord of Thetford's hang'd indeed.
If that feems hard, why grant him your reprieve,
And by an act of grace, let this NON-JUROR live.

End of the THIRD VOLUME.

www.ingramcontent.com/pod-product-compliance
Lightning Source LLC
Chambersburg PA
CBHW021729110726
47902CB00005B/1401